World Engines
Creator

Stephen Baxter

GOLLANCZ

LONDON

First published in Great Britain in 2020 by Gollancz
an imprint of The Orion Publishing Group Ltd
Carmelite House, 50 Victoria Embankment
London EC4Y 0DZ

An Hachette UK Company

1 3 5 7 9 10 8 6 4 2

A CIP catalogue record for this book is
available from the British Library.

ISBN (Hardback) 978 1 473 22322 6
ISBN (Export Trade Paperback) 978 1 473 22323 3
ISBN (eBook) 978 1 473 22325 7

Typeset by Input Data Services Ltd, Somerset

Printed and bound in Great Britain by Clays Ltd, Elcograf S.p.A.

To Tony and Jacqui Jones
and
Guy and Elizabeth Soulsby

My name is Greggson Deirdra.

Aged seventeen, I left home. I left Earth. I promised my mother I would come back.

I guess I was seeking a kind of revenge. Revenge for the looming destruction of my world.

What I found, though, is magnificent. Magnificent and terrible . . .

ONE

On Her Descent to the
Second Persephone

Note: Section headings are taken from *The Second Testament of Greggson Deirdra*, compiled by Cdr Nicola Mott, RAF retd., New Paris, Demeter, AD 2031.

Listen now.

This is how it is, how it was, how it came to be.

Listen now. Just listen.

It began in the afterglow of the Big Bang, that brief age when stars still burned.

Humans arose on an Earth. Deirdra, Emma, Malenfant, perhaps it was your Earth.

Who spread over their world.

Who spread in waves across the universe, sprawling and brawling and breeding and dying and evolving.

Who, finally, realised they were alone.

Who took me with them.

My name is Michael.

1

'You tell them, kid . . .'

He had been dreaming of . . .

Of Michael. Not his lost son Michael. Another Michael, somehow important . . .

It faded.

He coughed, coming fully awake.

And saw a roof above him.

That was his first impression. A slanting, rough surface, brown, seen in some flickering light – a candle? Canvas, maybe. No – leather. He could smell it, a kind of mixture of stockyard and new shoes.

'Damn big sheets, though, if it is leather. Can't see any stitching. What kind of animal . . .'

'You'll find out.'

'Did I say that out loud?'

A shadowed face like a moon, hanging over him. 'Yes, you did say it out loud, Malenfant. Though you've been mumbling a lot. Irina has been spending a great deal of time talking to you, as you drifted in and out.'

'Irina? Who?'

'Umm – do you know who *you* are?'

'Hell, yes.' He had a coughing spasm. 'Though my voice is

evidently a croak. My name is Reid Malenfant. *Still* is. And you are—' An instant's hesitation, as if his brain was slowly rebooting. 'Bartholomew.'

A grin on that face.

'Where are we, Tin Man? In some kind of circus tent?' He turned his head cautiously, and he didn't feel like he was spinning around or about to pass out again so *that* was a good sign. He saw that the tent was actually a kind of tepee, supported by one big central upright, what looked like a trimmed tree trunk. But a *big* trunk, a regular pillar, the stumps of crudely hacked-away branches showing, the whole fairly rammed into the ground. He had an immediate impression of immense strength, crudely applied, in the building of this place.

'And, no stitching. In that big tent up there. The leather. Not that I can see.'

'Stop repeating yourself.'

'I'm not. Stop diagnosing.'

'I'm not. So you think you can sit up this time?'

'This time? . . . Never mind.'

He took a breath, got his arms under his body, clenched his stomach muscles, and pushed upwards. He felt Bartholomew's arm around his shoulders. Solid, strong, steady – too steady, clearly artificial – but hugely reassuring just the same. Not that he was going to admit that.

Raised up, he looked around some more.

A dirt floor, loosely covered with leather throws. That big central pole. Yeah, candles, he was right about that, big fat stubs of wax burning on flat stones. What looked like pallets, beds – heaps of leather and straw roughly the size and shape of beds anyhow. Bits of clothing, coloured blue, orange, slate grey, dumped everywhere, that stood out against the mud colours of the rest of this structure. And a few pieces of modern

4

equipment – 'modern' meaning deriving from the time epoch he and Bartholomew and Greggson Deirdra had come from, the twenty-fifth century, and the slightly clunkier, halfway-to-steampunk gear that came from the early twenty-first-century British expedition they had stumbled across at Phobos (or, he reminded himself, a *version* of Phobos).

Nobody in here right now, save for Malenfant and Bartholomew.

Malenfant found that he was wearing nothing but grimy underwear.

He lifted his own scrawny wrist, to see a bangle hanging there, a bronze bracelet. This was a very advanced product of the tech of the twenty-fifth century that, by reading from and writing to his cerebral cortex, performed various useful miracles, seamless translation being one of them.

He was wearing nothing but underwear and the bangle.

'Where is everybody else?'

Bartholomew hesitated. 'You do remember—'

'The crash. We lost Niki . . . Nicola Mott. And Bob Nash. Yeah, I remember. I remember it all. I think.' He pursed his lips. 'And I remember going through it all with Irina. Irina Viktorenkova. Who I presume was here already, when we fell out of the sky. She fished us out. I talked about it all with her.'

'That you did. I was there, too.'

'Eavesdropping as usual.'

'As to where everybody is – hate to tell you, Malenfant, the other survivors are all a little further along the road to recovery than you. Nobody badly injured in the crash, aside from our two fatalities. They *are* all younger than you.'

'And fitter. I get it.'

'I mean, centuries younger according to the calendar, thanks to the time you spent in a coldsleep pod on the Moon – but biologically so too.'

'Yeah, yeah.' He pushed Bartholomew's arm away and swung his legs away from the bed. 'Well, I need to see them even so.'

'I bet that's not the very first thing you need.'

As his body's systems slowly reconnected to his brain, he had to agree. 'So where's the head in this M.A.S.H.?'

'Not far away. A hole in the ground, essentially, but hygienic enough. Irina has been getting that stuff right as far as I can see. Here.'

From the ground beside the pallet Bartholomew produced a metre-long stick, evidently a cut-down branch, with a roughly shaped end. Again Malenfant had the impression of great strength crudely applied to make this thing.

Still, its function was obvious, and he recoiled. 'You expect me to walk with a stick?'

'Malenfant, you are a very old man. You have been through one hell of a gruelling experience. And, let me remind you, you are on Persephone. A different Persephone.'

'Persephone II, we said we'd call it.'

'Whatever. But just as in the comet-cloud version we visited before, this is a super Earth. Nearly one-third higher gravity, remember? So take the stick, and be damn grateful I don't just carry you in my arms like an infant. Also you need a drink of water before—'

'Ah, give me the damn stick.'

So Bartholomew walked him into a kind of side-structure to the big tent, evidently the privy, a place you could get to without going out in the rain. (If there was ever rain here.) Just a hole in the ground with a couple of planks set over it. But the stench was surprisingly mild; it seemed that layers of some kind of moist earth had been thrown down over the detritus.

When he was done, Bartholomew helped him take a brisk shower under a bucket of lukewarm water, and then dress in a reasonably clean coverall – NASA blue, but a product of twenty-fifth-century matter printers. Apparently undamaged, but Malenfant knew such garments were, to a degree, self-repairing.

Then Bartholomew led him through a tangle of tie ropes, thick strands of what looked like tree bark – bark that had been *chewed* to make it pliable, it appeared – held down by fat stakes driven into a ground of what looked like flood-plain clay.

And out into the open. At last Malenfant got a look at the world he was stranded on. His first conscious look from the ground, anyhow.

'You're doing a lot better than the first time you woke, Malenfant. Do you remember? Irina was very patient. You were half-conscious. Some of what you babbled was . . . strange. She sat with you for hours, as you talked and talked . . .'

Slowly, Malenfant started to remember. *Can you hear me?* She'd asked that, over and over . . .

2

Can you hear me?

Hear, yes. I can't see.

Try to be calm. It's over now.

Over? . . .

Do you know who you are?

Are we at Persephone? Or whatever the hell we ought to call this big green version of that rock ball . . . Persephone II, not like the frozen rock ball we found off in the outer Solar System in that different strand, that different reality . . . all those continents and oceans and . . . I remember . . . the British ship, the *Harmonia* . . . no, we were in the lander, we'd had to rebuild it, the *Charon II*, we called it. And, yes, this . . . different Solar System we are in. A different reality strand, plucked out of the manifold of all possible realities.

And here, a strand where Saturn has no rings.

Saturn?

Yeah . . . Amid all the strangeness, a radio-silent Earth and so forth, that was what struck Deirdra most when we found it through the telescopes. Turns out she always had a thing about Saturn. Here, no rings, *and* a funny-looking extra moon . . . But we came here first, to Persephone. Because it looked even more Earthlike than Earth, the version hereabouts anyhow. A big fat green ball where Mars ought to be. We're going down, down to Persephone, we're going to land. But . . .

Let's go back. First things first. Do you know who you are?

I . . . Yes.

Your name?

My name. I—

Lie back. Don't try to open your eyes.

I'm fine. And I know my damn name. I'm Reid Malenfant. You know me. The guy who crashed the space shuttle. And now I crashed again, I guess.

Listen to me, Reid Malenfant.

Just Malenfant.

Listen. Your Russian is very good. But I am afraid that I do not in fact know you. I never heard your name before you came here. I know nothing of this 'space shuttle'. Apparently not the craft in which you landed—

What do you mean, my Russian is good? I don't know a damn word of Russian. Save for a few cuss words I picked up from Vladimir Viktorenko when we picked him up from his wrecked ship on Phobos.

Hello.

Hello? You still there?

I am still here.

You dropped out for a moment there. I was worried . . . You shut up when I mentioned Vlad. Vladimir Pavlovich Viktorenko . . . Do you know *his* name?

In a sense. Possibly.

What does that mean?

My own name is Viktorenkova. Irina Viktorenkova. That is my marriage name. And I have a son. A son called Vladimir. Vladimir Pavlovich Viktorenko. He is not here. I am far from home.

I . . . ah. OK. I'm guessing now that isn't a coincidence at all.

One thing we have learned about the manifold is that, even if it is some kind of infinite multiverse, the – Roads – it is comprised of, that's a British term, group together in bundles. Alternate histories sprouting from some common origin, a point of divergence. America gets to the Moon first, or Russia does. Or, much deeper divergences. Planet Mars exists, or it doesn't. But these bundles, these similar Roads, can interact in more subtle ways. There are – resonances. Nicola Mott, who flew down in the *Charon* with me – I flew with her before, or a version of her, in a different reality, a different Road, a different spacecraft.

Manifold. Resonance. Roads. Bundles.

Yes?

We know of your 'manifold'. We too tentatively explore it. But we have a different vocabulary. We call it 'moving in the higher dimensions'. Your Russian is very clear, Malenfant. Even concerning such abstract concepts.

Ah. OK. Actually I know no Russian at all. Can you see my right arm? Do I have a bangle on my wrist? Like a copper bracelet?

I . . . Yes. You have it.

That's how we're communicating. Through a smart technology, from a time centuries after my own era – from the twenty-fifth century.

The twenty-fifth century. To me – this is the year 1992.

Never mind. I'm taking it too fast as ever. You do get used to it. Believe me. Ask Bartholomew. Maybe he has a bangle to spare for you. Sure would help, I guess.

Actually he, Bartholomew, is not here. He is tending to the others.

The others.

Shit.

I need to know about my crew.

You just woke up. You have been through a crash, a serious medical trauma. I don't think you can expect—

Tell me, damn it.

Very well. But, let's take it in order.

Tell me what you remember.

3

I remember . . .

Eight of us came through the Phobos passageways to this new system. Eight, including Bartholomew.

Except we found Phobos orbiting *Venus*, not Mars. I remember how the Sun blinded us. It was so unexpected; we didn't anticipate emerging so deep in the Solar System.

But we looked around the System. Earth was radio-silent. It didn't even *look* like Earth. But Persephone – well, we could see its oceans glint, with the naked eye, across astronomical units.

We weren't where we expected to be, you see.

Where was that?

Or when, maybe. We had been trying to get back to the dawn of the Solar System. Crazy as that sounds. We wanted to figure out *why* we find ourselves tumbling across a manifold of possible realities, where histories are different – even the planets are different, wildly so. Different timelines, connected by – portals. Well, the British had found passages, what they called *chimneys*, in that tangle of spacetime anomalies you can reach through Phobos, chimneys that they thought extended, not just across the manifold, but to the deep past.

You see, they thought they had seen anomalous sunlight, coming through the chimneys. Too dim, and with a subtly different spectral mix . . . They thought it was the light of a much *younger* Sun. Sunlight of the past. So we figured we could – well, study that deep past. Even visit it. Find out about who might have been meddling, back there. To create those deep divergences in the present.

So we dived back into Phobos, moon of Mars. But maybe we lost our way. Where we came out, the Sun looked – modern. And even Phobos wasn't Phobos any more. Or anyhow not in the same place.

Yes. The portal-moon. But we call it Anteros. It is indeed one of the two moons of Venus, where I came from. As it is here.

Two moons, yeah, I remember now, we saw it when we came through . . . Here, Venus has two moons.

So instead of a young Solar System, we emerged into . . . this. Different. What looked like the present day to us – our present, that is – but with the planets all wrong. A different Venus, Mercury – a different Earth. A silent Earth, no radio we could detect. And, instead of Mars – *this*. What looked like the Persephone we had schlepped out to the edge of the Solar System to find, but *here*, not out in the cold, but here, where Mars was supposed to be . . . The same, but different. Like James Bond in the movies, with a new face every ten years. We actually called this world Persephone II, like a sequel in some franchise. Ha!

I know little of this James Bond.

Forget it. Pop culture, my Achilles heel.

However, we have evidently spent more time here than you have . . .

Who's 'we'?

We can come to that. As to the date, though, we have made estimates based on the positions of the stars, and indeed of the outer planets. Jupiter onwards . . . These, save for Pluto, appear to follow much the same orbits as, umm, as where we came from.

Yeah. We noticed that. If all these different parallel realities result in some kind of perturbation of the formation of the Solar System, which is what it *looks* like – well, maybe it takes one hell of a big perturbation to deflect Jupiter significantly. Like a cannonball sitting on a pool table; you aren't going to deflect *that* baby, no matter how skilfully you strike the cue ball.

Our best estimate is that the date, in this version of the Solar System, is AD 2020. We cannot be more precise.

That's pretty impressive . . . But you said it isn't 2020 where you came from?

No. 1992, by the western Christian calendar.

Slips in time as well as differences in the unfolding history. We did observe this before.

Before?

Long story. On our way here we . . . Damn it. *We*. My people. I keep losing focus. I was piloting that damn ship, the *Charon* lander, me and Nicola Mott . . .

Tell me, then. Take your time. Start again.

You said there were eight of you.

Yeah. So eight of us came through Phobos to this place, in the *Harmonia*. Big interplanetary exploration ship.

Once we were clear of Phobos, or Anteros, we had that big debate on where to go. Persephone or Earth or even ringless Saturn. That extra moon of Saturn, you know, we found it glows with a light that isn't – natural. Like reflected sunlight, but not quite. As if from a different Sun – or a younger Sun, Josh Morris said, in one of those flashes of intuitive brilliance he can have . . . And that turned out to be the lure that drew us through the portal to this place, remember. That young sunlight, leaking out of that ice moon.

But in the end, we were attracted by Persephone, this fat, rich, sunlit version of the Persephone we visited before. And when we got here we could see a lot, even from orbit. Life, what looked like forest, grasslands. Herds of animals, some of them huge on those big sprawling continents.

And threads of smoke, the mark of fires that looked – well, human-made. Maybe. We saw two fairly significant, fairly persistent occurrences. And both of them on this big continent we call Caina, north of the equator. We saw your own camp fires here at this southern shore, the mouth of a big river, right? And the other, what even might be some kind of technical development, off on a big volcanic plateau in the middle of the continent. We also saw what looked like a gas burner, a flare. Our orbit wasn't favourable—

We call the plateau itself the Shield. We have no name for this continent. Your Caina.

We had to come down and see – also replenishing our stores would have been a good idea – and find out who was already here. So we plotted our landing site. Look, we chose what looked like the less developed of the two human-type settlements.

You were cautious. Understandable. It is a strange world to you; you had no idea who we were, what we were doing.

Besides, we needed an equatorial landing place. We also wanted to check out whether there was any sign of the Towers we had seen on that other Persephone, out in the comet cloud.

Towers?

Strung around the equator . . . Never mind. If they were here, you would know about them. Our plan was to land on Iscariot – the continent like an equatorial belt – due south of here, across the strait from the river delta, your camp. Then we would cross the water when we were secure.

15

But even before we could leave orbit we had to rebuild our lander, which we lost in that other reality, at that other Persephone. And we had lost two of our crew in the process, two Brits. But *Harmonia* is designed for long-duration flight without resupply or refitting, and she has this main hold that is like a museum of spare parts, and we raided that, and we cannibalised the mother ship a little, and we got the *Charon II* built.

We decided to take seven of our eight crew down. We thought it was going to be a while before we figured out this new world, even with a lot of us working at it . . .

Lighthill stayed in orbit. Wing Commander Geoff Lighthill. Cambridge man, as he reminds you several times a day . . . Ha! Good officer, and overall commander of the ship. He stayed up there, working comms, maintaining the *Harmonia*, and running an astronomical survey.

And the rest of us – the *Charon* seven, including myself and Bartholomew. Emma, Deirdra, and the Brits: Nicola, Josh Morris, Bob Nash. Strictly speaking I was co-pilot to Nicola Mott – and, as I may have said, in the year 2019, in another version of history, it had been two versions of *us* who had tried to bring the space shuttle booster stage *Constitution* down from orbit to Cape Canaveral. Tried and failed, and that descent killed that version of Nicola. And now—

Nicola. The second Nicola. She did not survive the descent to Persephone.

I know. I know. I stayed aware myself long enough to see that . . . Damn it, she was right beside me. *Again*. Those damn manifold resonances.

Be calm.

She died at my side, *twice*. How the hell am I supposed to stay calm about that?

The others, though. Let me think it through. You have to imagine them in the lander, sitting behind us two pilots, racked up on fold-out couches. They kept quiet during the landing, as they were supposed to. Trained to, in fact, the British crew anyhow. There was Deirdra, and Emma II—

You actually call her Emma II?

Just tell me if they're OK.

Five of you survived. Including Bartholomew. All save Nicola, and one other. The others are unharmed – so I would say. Bartholomew describes minor medical conditions—

Who else? Who did we lose?

Bob Nash.

Damn it. *Damn* it. Lighthill called him 'Oxford'. Pipe-smoker. And the British crew's engineer – we will miss him. I guess we're stranded down here, until we get the *Charon* fixed up to take us back to orbit and the *Harmonia*, and he would have led that effort.

But the rest survived. Greggson Deirdra—

Met her as a teenager. She was right there when I was defrosted, in a drowned London. She's from the twenty-fifth century, and one of the strongest human beings I have ever encountered, young as she is. Another long story. And the young scientist – Josh Morris?

He is safe. Traumatised, says Bartholomew, but—

He's a right to be. Young guy, awkward. His twentieth, twenty-first-century science grounding is out of date, but his mind would shine in any epoch, and he will be a hell of an asset in the days to come. But we will have to look after him.

Hello?

Are you still there?

I am making notes.

Ha! Not a bad idea. When I was a kid my father used to try

to drum good habits into me. Making notes was one of them, when I was doing my amateur astronomy and stuff . . .

Tell me about your father.

I'm remembering more of it. The descent, in the *Charon*. We were doing fine . . . Then, something in the sky ahead of us . . . A damn huge obstruction, bright blue, a — a circle, turned out to be, we saw it first as an oval, nearly edge on.

Malenfant.

Phobos blue. Yeah, like the wheels we saw in the place we called the Sculpture Garden, inside Phobos. Manifold technology.

Malenfant.

World Engineer technology. Yeah. And we were just flying at the damn thing, it came out of nowhere—

Malenfant—

We couldn't turn fast enough in that bucket, it was little more than a glider—

Stay calm.

Calm. Yeah.

Tell me about your father.

4

Bartholomew helped him outside.

They were in some kind of river valley. Well, hell, there was the river, maybe half a kilometre away, a grey, fast-flowing stream. But the floor of this valley was broad, contained by shallow sandstone walls to either side – he made out thick strata, banded layers in the brown-crimson rock – and beyond that, visible in the misty air, more walls, much more distant, rising up. As if the river had cut through some immense pre-existing canyon. The light was diffuse, scattered by a low cloud layer. In fact, he saw now, the cloud seemed to dip down below the level of the remote canyon walls, blurring them to invisibility.

He turned to look downstream, and saw the Sun, hanging high in the sky over this long, complex valley. Almost overhead – but it looked dimmer, smaller, for this wasn't Earth. This version of Persephone, Earthlike as it seemed to be, was at the position of Mars, not Earth, so a good fifty per cent or more further from the Sun.

There was a wind, not that strong, but uneven, unsettling. The higher clouds were moving fast.

'Weather feels kind of blustery. What time of year is it – spring, the fall? It has that unstable feel.'

'Actually we're close to midsummer just here,' Bartholomew said. 'It's not that seasonal – so I'm told. Not much of an axial tilt. But it's a big world, with big, energetic weather systems.'

'And not comfortable, I'm guessing.'

Bartholomew shrugged. 'It's not built for humans. Or rather, humans didn't evolve here. Your problem. You're the tropical ape. I'm a waterproof mech with a built-in hundred-year power pack.'

'Show-off.'

Malenfant glanced around at the small settlement, on the valley floor. The big tent he had come out of was the dominant structure, he saw. But there were smaller tents, maybe used for storage, carefully lashed down – evidently you had to expect high winds here. Super Earth, Malenfant. Super weather.

And now he saw what he was looking for. People.

A small knot, too far away to distinguish, some in blue or grey coveralls, and some not, a couple of them dressed in what looked like leather, or crudely made cloth . . . Some sat beside a couple of frames on the ground, like home-made stretchers, with bundles wrapped in cloth heaped on top. Smoke from a small fire snaked into the air, dispersing quickly, like the thicker smoke that came from the fire in the big tepee.

And a couple of other bundles, lying on the ground. Longer. Isolated. Body length.

He took one limping step that way before Bartholomew took his arm.

Malenfant pulled away. 'That's where I need to be. With my people.'

Bartholomew glanced at him with a look Malenfant might have read as pity, if he hadn't known that there was nothing inside the medic's waterproof exterior but a kind of animated rule set. So Bartholomew claimed, at least.

'First of all,' Bartholomew said gently, 'they aren't *your* anything. Second of all, they've been functioning perfectly well – OK, maybe not so well, but well enough – without you so far. And what they don't need is you blundering in half awake and with zero briefing. For instance, do you even know where you are?'

'Persephone. Yeah, but where on Persephone?' He thought back. Half-remembered reconstructing it all with Irina, his muse during his recovery. 'OK. We intended to land on the northern coast of Iscariot, south of the strait between Iscariot and Caina. But in fact we fell into the sea to the south of Caina . . .'

He tried to visualise it. He glanced around again, at the river valley, the canyon's steep sandstone walls, the glimpse of a canyon structure beyond, all under that lid of turbulent cloud. 'If I remember, much of Caina is pretty high altitude. It was so even on that other, lifeless Persephone out in the dark. *That* was a big granite dome. But here, a lot of sandstone . . . The river.' Malenfant was still thinking slowly. 'Which must be flowing towards the coast, right? So' – he pointed down the valley – '*that* way must be south. How far are we from the coast?'

'Further than you might think, Malenfant.'

'Right. We aren't so far from the equator, given how high the Sun is . . . I guess the local time is around midday? The middle of a twenty-five-hour day.'

'Well done.'

He whirled around, pivoting on his stick. Would have fallen if Bartholomew hadn't grabbed him around the waist, more or less discreetly.

Greggson Deirdra was approaching, with Emma Stoney.

The hell with it. He threw away the stick, and ran to them.

5

My father. Right.

So I was born in 1960, Christian calendar.

I came from a family of flyers. My father flew in the Korean War, my grandfather in the Second World War. Umm . . . I think Stalin called it your 'Great Patriotic War'.

Who?

Here we go again. Stick to the point, Malenfant. So I grew up with a head full of flying – and of space. I was nine years old when Apollo 11 landed – first to the Moon – and I cried my eyes out when it was revealed that Armstrong died at the moment of touchdown.

Hello?

You've gone quiet on me again.

You are speaking of American space programmes? The first American to walk on the Moon was, if I remember correctly, John Glenn, as a guest aboard the Vernadsky *in . . . Never mind. You were telling me of your life. You were nine, ten years old when this Armstrong landed on the Moon?*

Yeah. Perfect age, right? After that I had a head full of space. My father always encouraged me.

OK. So after the triumph and the tragedy of Apollo, we – America – started on a more sustainable space strategy. We

22

had the space shuttle, a two-stage Earth-to-orbit transport, two fully reusable aircraft mated at launch. We had space stations in the Skylabs, and later Space Station Freedom. And we built on Apollo-Saturn, the technology that had taken us to the Moon, to venture further. The first humans to land on Mars were American, who landed there in 1986. So there were plenty of opportunities to get into space.

Meanwhile Emma and I had grown up together – kind of, she was ten years younger. We had drifted apart, got back together . . . We married in 1992. She was twenty-two. But by then—

You were flying in space?

Actually, no. I had applied to NASA, that is our space agency, and failed to make the cut, at first. This was the 1980s. So I decided to take time out to build up my flying skills, and joined the USAF. Our air force.

But Emma, meanwhile, had ambitions of her own. She was picking a smarter stratagem. Phobos had been big in the news since the late eighties, when Carl Sagan pushed for NASA to send a specialised probe there – and of course the Phobos anomalies had already been a mystery for decades. So Emma had picked up on that . . .

Phobos, moon of Mars. Anteros, moon of Venus.

Right. I think it *is* Anteros. And Phobos, at the same time. Not some kind of copy. The same thing. One thing we learned about the manifold is that you can have an object *in two places at once* . . . It's not reality as we know it. Some quantum thing, probably.

But as for Phobos, actually the first anomalies – visible from Earth – were first pointed out by a Russian astronomer. Guy named Shklovsky . . .

The main problem was what they called the secular

deceleration of Phobos. The moon's orbit was apparently decaying, like the first Skylab – umm, like a space station orbiting too low, and skimming Earth's atmosphere. The drag brings it down, eventually. Now, Phobos was a pretty hefty chunk of rock, and shouldn't have been decaying so quickly. It was Shklovsky who suggested that the moon might be *hollow*. Anyhow, that's why agitation was growing to send a dedicated, properly equipped crewed mission there – as opposed to having the Mangala Station crew take a detour from the surface of Mars.

To us, Phobos's anomalies are the key to everything. Well, as you know. Even if we had no idea what we were walking into, at first.

Tell me about Emma, and Phobos, then.

OK. Look, Emma had always had her own ambitions to fly into space. She blamed me for infecting her with the bug, when I was a teenager with my head full of stars and planets and astronauts, and she was just a little kid. But she grew up smarter than I ever was. And, as I said, she figured out a smarter way into space.

NASA is – was – was, *somewhere* – in the 1970s and '80s anyhow, a place with a real patriarchal kind of flavour. The first astronauts had been test pilots, and military, so you had that hyper-masculine, super-competitive spirit. Oh, there were women all through the organisation, on the technical side, in management, even in flight roles. But Emma could see it would be a push to compete with the male pilots who overstocked the place.

But, she could also see, she didn't need to do that. She just focused on getting on that Phobos mission. She was never going to be the top pick of the pilots, and she wasn't so interested in the engineering – so from her early college days she set out to become the best Phobos specialist there could be.

Well, it worked. In her late twenties, by which time we had had a kid – Michael – she started trying the NASA recruitment rounds, got in on her second attempt as a mission specialist candidate, and within a year she was *teaching* the rest of NASA, more or less, about how to explore Phobos.

And did you follow her?

No. Not then, anyhow. Kept failing the draft – though I wondered later if Emma getting in there first damaged my application.

Would they not accept married couples?

Not that . . . Maybe it affected me. The attitude I showed. Truth was, I was *jealous*, of my younger, smarter wife getting there ahead of me. Does that make sense? Even though I loved her more than life itself. And even though I suspected, deep down, that I was doing harm to our son, Michael. And boy, did I pay for that in the year 2469, when . . . never mind. Another story.

So I stayed in the military. I flew military missions, in fact – stratotanker flights over Iraq. My long-term justification was that it was good experience for flying a shuttle booster, which is another big flying fuel tank, basically.

A war in Iraq? No, ignore that; I doubt if the answer would mean very much. Meanwhile, Emma and Phobos . . .

So she got a place on the Phobos mission. Cobbled together with Ares-Saturn tech – that is, the system we had used to reach Mars and set up Mangala Station. She and her crew left Earth in the 2004–5 launch window.

Hmm. More than a decade in my own future.

But – she never got there. The craft went silent during a final approach to Phobos. Best guess is that a nuclear-propulsion stage – they were always semi-experimental, temperamental

25

bastards – failed on them during the final burns.

My sympathies. To you and your son.

Thank you. The years after that – well, it all seems a blur now.

By then I was involved in a private space start-up called Bootstrap, Inc. Involved me in even more travelling than the military tours, looking back. Michael and I started growing apart, from that moment, probably the moment we lost her. I never saw it at the time. Shit, I couldn't see anything at all.

And then I applied to NASA again, and this time got accepted.

Really? You chose this moment, of maximum grief for yourself and your young son, to disappear into the space programme?

It doesn't sound so good when you put it like that. And that's pretty much the point Emma made later, when I first got her back. Or a kind of . . . a twenty-fifth-century avatar of her . . . Maybe I'll get to that.

So I made it through this time. As I expected, with my USAF experience I now fit the profile for a shuttle booster pilot, and I grabbed the job with both hands. I was never going to reach space itself, formally speaking – we broke away from the orbiter before we reached that altitude – but I would get to fly one of the most extraordinary aircraft that had yet been built.

And that was pretty much my life, for the last decade or so before – well, before it effectively ended. Michael was growing up. He did get a lot of support from Emma's family, from mother Blanche, sister Joan . . . Got to college. Started making noises about a career in the coal industry. And then—

Your life effectively ended. In your own laconic words.

Well, so it did.

STS-719. Flew in 2019. I was mission commander, my pilot was Nicola Mott. Look, I won't go through the technical detail. In short, a minor flaw in the craft escalated. The orbiter got away safely, but we lost control of the booster. Nicola was killed during an attempted ejection. I couldn't save the ship. I ditched in the ocean. There were no casualties or infrastructure damage on land. I barely escaped alive.

It sounds – heroic. And, yes, a precursor of your experience here on Persephone.

We did the best we could, that's all. And then the doctors did the best they could for me.

Ah. They could not restore you to health. So—

So they put me in the freezer.

6

Deirdra and Emma both wore the British jumpsuits, cut to fit and patched, that they had worn aboard the *Harmonia*.

Deirdra, a native of the twenty-fifth century, who was now – he stumbled over the count in his head – now twenty-three years old, or thereabouts, having spent six years flying across the Solar System, or a version of it, with Malenfant. She had grown tall, strong, dark, grave, quiet. Hugely charismatic, Malenfant thought, and a hell of a rock to have around.

And Emma, early forties now, from roughly Malenfant's own epoch but delivered into his presence from a different timeline altogether.

But when he dropped his cane and staggered forward, she wouldn't let him hold her, not at first. She stood back, looked him in the eye.

'You do remember who I am, don't you? Which *one* I am? Not the Emma you married. Not the mother of Michael.' Her voice caught at that.

He grinned. 'You're Emma. The Emma who got stranded on Phobos with a crazy Russian, and had to call for help.'

'And you *came*—'

'You're Emma. You all are.'

He reached out, and grabbed her at last, enfolded her in a hug that she returned with interest. They just fit together, he had time to reflect. Two halves of the same person, sundered, now joined again. The same person in all the realities.

And in a heartbeat, Deirdra, who for better or worse had followed Malenfant so far from home, came forward and joined in, wrapping her arms around the pair of them.

Malenfant was dimly aware of Bartholomew picking up the walking cane, standing back. The robot medic was capable of empathy, or anyhow mimicking it. Good programming.

He stopped thinking.

After a time Deirdra drew back, subtly. 'Come on. You need to talk to Josh.' She turned, walked off; they followed.

'Poor old Josh,' Malenfant murmured. 'Alone down here, last of his crew, save Lighthill, and even he's out of touch.'

'Deirdra is doing a hell of a job with him. Well, you'd expect that.'

'Yeah. But how is she herself?'

Emma frowned. 'It's complicated. She's bound up with the people around her. Well, she always is. And especially Josh, who clearly needs her. She can be very . . . tender. Understanding. But sometimes I think there's a nagging impatience in there.'

'Umm. Well, we didn't come to this system to meet stranded Russians and whatnot. We came chasing the World Engineers—'

'And that seems a long way off right now. She'll endure, I think. But there's more to life than goals, Malenfant. She's alone too, after all. Of her time period, I mean. She does have Bartholomew, and she seems to spend a lot of time with him. Shadows him as he does his rounds.'

'Better him than no twenty-fifth-century companion at all.'

'True. I doubt that the Russians see any of this,' she said. 'They see a complex, caring person. They all like her, I think. She's good with the little kid too.'

29

'Maybe she's missing her mom,' Malenfant said.

She looked up at him. 'And that, Malenfant, may be one of the smartest things you ever said.' She linked her arm in his. 'Come on. Let's go see Josh.'

7

So, Malenfant, after your crash, they froze you.

Not quite. Cryogenic medicine was in its infancy then – experimental even. I was lodged first in a covert USAF facility, and then in a hospital in London – England – where they were pioneers in the technique. And, in the course of time, stored as a long-term sleeper, I was moved to a kind of hibernaculum on the Moon.

While, back on Earth, the world went to hell.

All of which lies in my own future. Or a possible future—

Climate collapse. Rising sea levels. Massive refugee flows. War. Look, if you want the details of all this, ask Greggson Deirdra, my companion. Although to her it was all history.

However. By the year 2469, when I was finally woken up, they had gone through all this and come out the other side. And the world was – changed. Recovered, I guess, but changed.

You don't sound terribly comfortable about that. Or engaged.

Hell, I was the man out of time, Irina. I was a product of the magnificent but flawed culture that, in the end, had been unable to fix its own brakes before hurtling off the cliff. And I showed that, I think, every time I opened my mouth.

Look – ask Deirdra. I can only give you hasty impressions. For a start they had pulled back from human spaceflight centuries before. They had turned their biggest efforts to the Earth, I guess. For example, greening the Sahara to draw down excess carbon dioxide. I saw that, from space and the ground. Population was drastically down. Construction, industry in general – everything was at a slow pace. They made cars, for instance, designed to last for centuries without replacement.

Oh, and nobody worked for a living. Everything essential – food, clothing, heating, data – came for free. You worked at whatever you wanted, whyever you wanted to do it. Or not.

This does not seem so strange to me.

It doesn't?

What you describe sounds not dissimilar to the social solution of my own homeland, of Russia. Americans customarily sneer at us for our monarchy, under Tsar Alexander IV, for our centralised command economy. But the monarchy is constitutional, like our close allies the British. And we have sought ways to integrate the technical innovations of the American free-market system into our economy without the social abuses and economic fragility of unfettered capitalism. Which is how Russia weathered the depression crises of the 1930s better than the western powers. And why, in my time, ours is the second-largest economy, after Germany.

Really? I need to understand this better. You still have a Tsar? And no Stalin?

I never heard of Stalin. But I am a cosmonaut, not a historian.

Well, as alternate histories go that's – different. But Deirdra's future evidently works – even if she herself is an outlier.

An outlier? In what way?

Well, because she became – no, on some instinctive level she always *had* been – disturbed by what troubled me about her world, when I arrived in it.

But that wasn't the specific reason they woke me. In the

year 2469, I mean. Out of nowhere, they received a message from Emma Stoney, at Phobos, asking for help – and my help in particular. Fragmented, short, in what was by then archaic language . . .

Archaic. The language of the year 2005. I consult my notes. I can see how you, a man born in 1960, ended up in the year 2469.

I slept through most of it.

But Emma, who called from Phobos, had had no such . . . preservation.

No. I suspect she thought it was still 2005 or '06, until proven otherwise.

The Phobos anomalies had brought you together.

Hmph. Kind of. That's what the anomalies *do*. But even before I went out there to retrieve her, in an antique craft along with Deirdra and Bartholomew, I already knew this wasn't *my* Emma at all . . . Like I said. For a time we even referred to her as Emma II. Still do, sometimes.

She was a refugee from elsewhere in the manifold. A different Road from you, and Deirdra. Emma II.

Exactly. But Phobos drew us together.

And later, through the Phobos anomalies, we met other, umm, refugees. The British – Lighthill, Morris and the rest – with a different version of Nicola Mott. By *their* body clocks it's now around AD 2011, I think.

More of your cross-manifold resonances.

Seems like it, doesn't it? And listen. I should tell you this. *My* Emma went to Phobos on an all-American mission. But the Emma you have met here – Emma II, who I found at Phobos – well, for her it was different. For her, America retreated from crewed space travel, pretty much, after the Moon landings. We never went to Mars, for instance. The Soviets pushed ahead, though—

The Soviets? I know that word as a rather archaic political term.

Umm. Where I came from, and Emma II, the Soviet Union was a Communist state. Kind of a Russian empire, I guess. Totalitarian. In fact it was the global template for totalitarianism.

Hello.

Hello? You dropped out again. Are you still there?

I apologise. I am simply . . . astonished by your words. Or appalled. You speak of Stalin, I suppose. I will be fascinated to discuss this in more depth.

Anyhow the Soviets, in Emma's reality, had gone ahead with a limited space programme of their own. So, in a spirit of strained cooperation, I think, the US and USSR – Soviet Russia – mounted a joint mission to Phobos. Combined technologies, and so forth. Meanwhile Emma II had followed a similar career path to *my* Emma, and was prime candidate for a Phobos mission, whoever was mounting it.

So they made it to Phobos. And she descended to that little moon with a Russian companion.

Not Vladimir . . .

Not in this thread, Irina. I'm sorry.

And so, then, it was this Emma who called for you from Phobos. Or a version of you.

And that call got me revived in the year 2469. And *that* drew Deirdra to me, when I woke.

But there was, you said, another factor. For Deirdra. Another motive.

Yeah. Another factor.

One other small thing.

The end of the world. Or Deirdra's world, anyhow.

She told me something of this. Of Shiva.

*

Yes. A rogue planet, a giant, thrown out of the Solar System by random perturbations back when the System was young, and the gas giants were migrating back and forth, towards the Sun and away from it . . .

A rogue planet that would become the Destroyer, after a fall back into the inner Solar System, an impact with Neptune. Smash Venus entirely. Drag Earth into an orbit away from the habitable zone. Oh, and we'll lose the Moon.

Earth will survive. Humanity will not. Not on Earth.

Not on Earth, no. And, look, that was why we went chasing Persephone – before.

I don't understand.

Well, in my, Deirdra's timeline, in the year 2469, we know Shiva is out there somewhere, beyond Neptune, on its way to its date with destiny. But, we discover, *Persephone is out there too.* Not sitting here, where Mars should be.

Ah. More of these random deflections, at the birth of the Solar System?

That's it, yeah . . . but not quite. To push Persephone out into the cold, on that potentially rich and fecund world, somebody – we called them the World Engineers – had mounted rockets.

Rockets?

Huge fusion-powered thrusters, mounted around the equator – along the spine of the equatorial continent we call Iscariot, in fact. They used the world's oceans, and possibly giant-planet volatiles, as fuel. And the rockets just kept firing. We figured it may have taken a million years to push Persephone out to a thousand AU – that is, a thousand times as far from the Sun as the Earth. Out into the inner edge of the comet cloud.

Why? What was the purpose?

Hell, we don't know. We wondered if it was part of some

35

wider scheme. A way to adjust the larger-scale migration processes going on in the inner System, maybe.

Ah. A small nudge—

Relatively small. To deliver much larger outcomes. The birth of the Solar System was chaotic. Masses the size of small planets rushing everywhere, colliding, even huge gas giants unstable in their orbits. And that can be manipulated, precisely because it was chaotic.

So maybe the push given to Persephone was designed to eject Shiva from the inner System. In just such a manner as to cause the eventual disruption, when it returned from its long orbit.

Maybe. We don't *know*. Not yet.

You called these meddlers 'World Engineers'.

That might be too polite.

Ha! That is a very Russian joke. Bleak, yet appropriate. And the people of this year 2469. Do they accept their looming fate? Or do they fight back?

Well, that's the thing. Yeah, they *accept* it. It took me a while to figure that out, but they do. *We* wouldn't have. And I'm proud to say that at least one person from that bewildered culture thought of doing something about it, eventually.

You mean Greggson Deirdra.

And *that* is where Persephone came in. Persephone I.

You will have to explain.

So we chased Persephone I out of the System . . . I say *we*.

We had gone to Phobos, and encountered the British, who had wandered across from another timeline entirely. And they were already on their way out to Persephone, and Shiva beyond . . . Their own mission plan actually had been based on the alignments of the planets in Deirdra's reality strand, at that epoch.

Persephone happened to be, by chance we think, *almost lined up with the approach of Shiva to the Sun*. So the British planned on using Persephone as a refuelling stop, and then going on further out to Shiva. A science expedition, essentially, or possibly colonial. That's the British for you.

But perhaps all this could be an opportunity for Deirdra's people too. *That* was what Deirdra intuited very early on, I think.

So, following a hunch, we travelled in the British ship. And at Persephone we found – well, *this* world, the same basic geology and stuff, but lifeless, with the air frozen out, the oceans sealed under ice – towering mountains, because erosion had had no chance to work. Persephone, out in the dark. And what we did – we tried to fire up those ancient rockets one more time, to push the damn world a little further over—

Ah. So that Shiva might collide with Persephone on the way in.

Another small deflection delivering huge outcomes. Our modelling was terrible; we couldn't be sure it would work. But if we *could* divert Shiva from its path to Neptune . . . It was worth a try.

It was magnificent.

Yeah. But it didn't work.

And we were out of options.

And so—

And so we decided to find out what this is all about. *Why* our Solar System is such a patchwork of meddling.

Ah. You decided to find the World Engineers. And confront them?

Well, that was the goal. So we went back to Phobos, the freeway intersection of the manifold. The British have become quite adept at navigating their way through there.

Yes. And you told me you believed you had found routes, not just across the timelines, but to the deep past. The origin of it all, perhaps.

But it went wrong. We don't know how. We ended up here instead. A version of 2020 where everything looks . . . different. Persephone, even Earth.

Maybe we should have gone on. Back into Phobos, in search of the time chimneys. We didn't. We came here. To Persephone, to explore. We piled into the lander, all seven of us.

And you crashed.

And we crashed.

8

On their way to find Josh Morris, they walked past that pair of wrapped-up bundles, laid out neatly on the ground, side by side.

Bodies, obviously. Nicola Mott, Bob Nash.

Malenfant tried not to stare. He saw there were flowers scattered over them, what to him looked like poppies, magnolias. Emma might know better, he thought absently. And he tried not to get hung up on what animal those furs had come from. Not really the point, Malenfant.

He felt nothing inside. Hollow.

He tried to focus on Josh, who came walking out to meet him.

Joshua Philip Morris was thirty-one years old, Malenfant knew. Now, as he stood over the bundles on the ground, wearing a fur wrap over a battered RASF-issue jumpsuit, Josh looked much younger than that. He always had seemed younger than his years, Malenfant reflected now, right back to when they had first met, a gawky, wide-eyed science boffin full of theories about life on an ice moon of a different Persephone.

And now, this. Now he'd had to process the two deaths they had suffered during the botched landing – of Nicola

Mott, in this reality an astronaut and decent flyer for the Royal Air and Space Force, and Bob Nash, an elegant public-school-and-Oxford engineer who had once worked on nuclear weapons for a Britain that had come out of Hitler's war strengthened, not weakened . . . They had been Morris's colleagues, and, more than that, a link to home, to his own lost timeline. And with his commander Geoff Lighthill stranded in orbit, Joshua was effectively alone, the only representative of his culture on this world. Much as Malenfant was of his own.

Deirdra whispered in Malenfant's ear, 'He's been here all day. He'd be here all night, around the whole twenty-five-hour clock, if we let him. Maybe you can talk to him.'

He glanced at her. 'Why me?'

She smiled. 'Go be Malenfant.' She touched his arm and hung back.

So Malenfant, leaning on his cane, approached Josh Morris alone.

'Hey, Josh.'

Morris glanced at him, hesitant. Malenfant saw now that his John Lennon spectacles had been damaged. The lenses were intact, but the bridge had been broken, and fixed, Malenfant saw, by bits of wire, and what looked like some kind of gum, or pitch. Malenfant would have sworn he saw tooth marks in the gum.

Morris said faintly, 'I'm glad to see you're up and about, sir.'

'After all this time – call me Malenfant.'

'The others were less badly hurt than you. Emma and Deirdra. I was less badly hurt than *them*. My worst accident was to my glasses, and that was thanks to me stepping on them when we were dragged out onto the shore. That was it for me. Just my glasses. Huh.'

Malenfant absorbed that. 'So how's Commander Lighthill? No contact since we lost the lander, I guess.'

'We have no radio. It's all back in the lander. We don't know how he is.'

'He'll be doing his duty, Josh. As you would expect. I think I know him well enough for that.' Malenfant chose his words carefully. 'Look, Josh, this isn't the first time I've lived through a crash. Not even the second time. And I can tell you—'

'I'm upset. I'm having bad dreams. *I broke my glasses.* Bob Nash and Nicola Mott are *dead*. Don't tell me it's just blind chance, sir, I know that. If I'd sat in Bob's seat instead of my own—'

'I know, I know. And I'd be a liar if I tried to tell you that you won't be going over this the rest of your life. Over it and over it. If only I'd done this or that. But in the end, you said it. Blind chance. Dumb luck. What we need to do now is make their deaths worthwhile. To do our jobs here, on the ground . . .'

Malenfant knew he wasn't getting through to this boy-man, this lost kid.

For some reason Malenfant thought of his own son, Michael, who he had never been able to comfort either, even over the death of his mother – a different Emma Stoney. That was even before Malenfant had disappeared into a coldsleep tube for the rest of Michael's *life*. He glanced at Emma, who was sitting on more junk some distance away with Deirdra, talking softly. What would Emma say, if he asked her advice? Or Deirdra, even.

Tell him what you think he needs to hear, Malenfant.

'Say, Josh. Listen to me now. As if I was wiser, as well as older.'

Josh looked at him, owlish behind the glasses, his expression empty.

'Geoff Lighthill is in charge. Nothing's going to change that. But while he's out of touch we have to make our own decisions, and do the best we can.

'I'm going to make you two promises. And if I don't keep them you can kick my butt from here to, hell, wherever butts go to die in this version of the Solar System.

'First. You're going to get to do what you came here for, Josh. I mean, all of us too – but you are the prime science guy now. We're going to follow whatever trail we need, onwards from here, whatever mysteries we come up against, until we figure out this world, this version of Persephone. And answer the questions posed when we were trying to push that other Persephone into the path of Shiva, to save a world. Who are the World Engineers? Why are they screwing with reality? With *us*?'

'Yes.' For the first time Josh's demeanour changed; he seemed to sit a little straighter, look a little further. 'That's why we came here. Although we don't yet know even what questions to frame. Some of this world makes sense, however.'

He was thinking now, not obsessing. Malenfant tried to encourage that. 'Such as?'

Josh shrugged. 'Nothing that isn't fairly obvious. This is a big planet. So it has big-planet features – but different from the frozen, airless version of itself that we saw out in the comet cloud. The Caina we saw before was frost-cracked granite. Here, the granite is covered by deep sandstone beds. There must have been a deep ocean over this part of the continent, long ago. The sandstone is the relic of even older granite uplands, mountains, eroded and washed down into the sea. And after that sea receded, or the land rose – well, there would have been another episode of more ferocious erosion.' He glanced at the sky. 'And then there's the low cloud.'

'What of it?'

'Higher gravity means a steeper density gradient in the atmosphere . . . I mean, the air thins out quicker with altitude, because the gravity compresses the planet's layer of air that much more. So you get lower cloud layers. There are probably uplands permanently above the cloud layers. Flying creatures would be favoured here, by the way.'

'Big ones, you mean? You would think the heavier gravity—'

'The thicker air trumps that. More oxygen as fuel, thicker air to push against. And then there are the flowers.'

Malenfant was getting confused. 'The flowers?' He stared at the flowers scattered over the bodies. 'Like poppies? Magnolias?'

'Yes. Which are among the earliest flowers in the fossil record, when the whole episode of co-evolution with the insects began. Primitive. And primitive flowers from Earth. You know, a planet like this isn't just a sort of big Earth. It ought to be *more* habitable than Earth itself. It will stay habitable longer, for one thing – all that inner heat. The faster erosion delivers more shorelines, shallower oceans – all of that is good for life. If Earth spawned life, so should this Persephone. Its *own* suite of life forms. And yet, what we see . . .'

'Scraps. Of what looks like primitive Earth life.'

'Not all of it primitive.'

'What do you mean?'

Josh cast around, and walked over to an untidy mound of gear. These were the bundles Malenfant had noticed before, some wrapped in modern materials, evidently from the *Charon*, others in what looked like leather. And they were heaped on those big heavy frames, evidently meant for transport, built of pairs of thick poles and sheets of thick leather.

Josh pointed at the frames. 'See those? The travois? *That* is how we were brought in from the coast, the crash. Those of us unable to walk, anyhow. They don't use draught animals here. They just piled everybody up on the two travois, under Irina's direction, and then the two of them hauled it all back here.'

'The two of them? Who?'

'Bartholomew was one. Your mechanical medic.'

'Fair enough. He is far stronger than you would think he needs to be . . . And the other?'

Josh pointed again, into the distance this time, to two figures walking down the upper river valley. Both looked squat, strong, hulking. Neither looked like Irina.

'You'll see. Anyhow some of what goes on here makes sense, at least. Other stuff makes less sense. To me, at any rate.'

'Such as?'

'Such as, the blue circle that clipped us as we came down in the *Charon*.'

Malenfant tried to remain impassive. 'Just tell me. It's OK.'

'I . . . you were fighting to save the lander. You and Nicola. I tried to look out of the window . . . I remember Bob telling me to sit still, to sit back, but I thought I ought at least to try to observe. Anyhow I saw the blue wheel – I couldn't swear to it, but it looked like the same engineering, the same *shade* of blue, that peculiar electric blue, as we saw inside Phobos.'

'The same engineering, then. I think we suspected that.'

'That would be my guess too. And I saw – stuff – coming through the hoop, the wheel in the sky. Coming out of nowhere – you know.'

'The way we just disappeared *into* nowhere through a different set of hoops. What stuff?'

'I thought I saw . . . people. Falling into the sky. Or out of it . . . falling out of the hoop, and then just dropping down, towards the ground. I couldn't see them all the way down – I mean, the crashing lander was hardly a stable observation platform, and there was a layer of cloud in the way.'

'People. Did they – I don't know, I saw nothing of this – did they use parachutes to land safely? Or aerofoils? Something like jet packs maybe—'

Josh shook his head. 'Nothing like that. Of course not. Without equipment. Just falling.'

Malenfant frowned, thinking about that. 'Were they clothed, even?'

'Good question. I wasn't sure. I wasn't sure if they were human at all, if I'm truthful. Some looked more like apes, like gorillas. And some like chimpanzees, but stretched out.' He smiled tightly. 'I'm supposed to be a biologist, among other specialisms. But it was always microbiology with me because it was just bugs, bacteria, that everybody expected to find on the other planets of the Solar System. I don't know much more about animals than I picked up at visits to the zoo. Anyhow Irina, Madame Viktorenkova, might be able to help with that.'

'Why do you say that? Just because she's been here longer than us?'

He looked nonplussed. 'No. Because of Ham . . . You haven't seen Ham yet?' He glanced over at the approaching couple. 'It's better if you meet him yourself. I think. Malenfant – before they get here. You said two promises. One is, we'll figure out the world. What's the second?'

Malenfant nodded grimly. 'That before we do one more damn

thing, we give Nicola and Bob the funeral they deserve.' He covered Morris's hand with his.

And yet the talk had thrust him back into the horror of the landing.

That damn blue hoop.

9

Just tell me how it was.

So once we had made a decision where to land, we were constrained by the engineering.

You've seen the *Charon* lander, or what's left of it. Even rebuilt as it was, it's like everything I've seen of the engineering from that particular Brit-dominated timeline. A mixture of advanced propulsion and pretty basic everything else – and the Brits got a start with their propulsion tech, of course, by acquiring German rocket engineers after the fall of the Third Reich. Which means nothing to you. Never mind, for now.

So everything is big and kind of over-powered, but it does the job. For instance we just landed on that airless Persephone by standing on our rockets and coming straight down. But, landing here, on *your* Persephone, we had a towering atmosphere to penetrate first. So *Charon* flew down like a stubby spaceplane, with a heat shield, a kind of blunt detachable mask over half of the upper body, and wings, and parachutes. I think the design reference was the capability of a descent into Venus. You can imagine the landing sequence . . .

I saw much of it, once you had entered the atmosphere. You created quite a streak in the sky.

So we are sitting up, all seven, with the machinery of the

lander humming and whirring around us – I'll swear some of it *is* clockwork – and, with the heat shield under us, we are hitting the upper atmosphere, we're in a kind of shimmering tunnel of light as we ionise the air, lavenders and greens around a core of yellow-orange plasma. Nicola and I are calling out numbers to each other, checking range, elevation, attitude, external temperature and other parameters. And the G-forces are pushing lengthways down our spines. We're still sitting up.

But as soon as the light starts to fade, *clatter, slam,* the heat shield detaches with a rattle of explosive bolts, and flies away. And now the capsule tips up, nose high, tail first, with those big rocket engine bells pointing downwards. It's quite a jolt for us, we are swung through more than ninety degrees in a fraction of a second, and suddenly we are lying on our backs. Through the small windows before me now all I can see is a deep blue sky, wow, the sky of Persephone – and then Nicola nudges me, and points up, and I see a much sweeter sight, which is like three flower blossoms. The drogue chutes deploying above us, preparing to drag our main chute out of the compartment at the apex of our truncated cone of a ship.

We are five miles high.

Which is when it starts to go wrong. I think. Because I saw, or thought I saw . . .

Yes?

Electric blue. An arc of it, like a monochrome rainbow. And I recognised it.

From Phobos.

Yeah. The blue wheels in the guts of Phobos, in what we called the Sculpture Garden, and deeper in that little moon's complicated core . . . Portals that span a multiverse.

Look, I paid no more attention. Because suddenly Nicola and I were coping with a catastrophe.

It was that damn wheel. We fell right past it – there was a wind blowing *into* it, like there was a pressure differential one side to the other – what I *think* happened is we got dragged across by that sucking wind, and the edge, that blue blade, clipped our drogue chutes. We, the lander, were far beneath the wheel, because our strings were good and long. But we couldn't afford to lose those damn drogues.

Because without them your main chutes could not deploy properly.

That's exactly it. They didn't deploy right. I could *see* that. So we started falling too fast – and, worse, spinning, under those raggedy, lopsided chutes.

We still had the landing rockets, and we had always planned to use those in the closing stages, just a squirt as we approached the ground. But we couldn't stand on them all the way down, like Armstrong landing on the Moon.

And the spinning got worse. I think some of the others blacked out; if not, they just gritted their teeth and stayed quiet. While Nicola and I did what we could. I was trying to use the attitude controls to cut the spin, while Nicola pulsed those big engines to slow us down, firing even as she worked out in her head what impulses we needed, *and* tried to take into account the fuel depletion, which was in the end a lot higher than we had anticipated.

All while lying on our backs, by the way.

You came down in the water.

Yeah. In the strait between the north coast of Iscariot and the south coast of Caina. That was Nicola's doing, I knew nothing about it at the time. She could see we were coming down too hard. In the last stages she deflected us over the water, where the landing would be softer, if problematic in other ways. I remember her calling out. I guess it was the last thing she ever said. *'Brace for impact!'*

49

I knew enough to flop in my couch, tuck my arms in, not to stiffen up. At least we were coming down on our backs . . .

Do you remember hitting the water? And afterwards?
Not well.
I guess we ducked down into the sea. And then got pushed back up again, back to the surface, we shot up so hard it felt like another launch.
Sunlight through the windows, as the water streamed off.
People screaming below me. My crewmates, my friends. Even then I tried to count the voices, at least, to guess how many had come through it.
And the cabin wall had pushed in to my right, where Nicola had been sitting. We had come down harder on that side, and the wall was bent, crumpled. It was like Nicola had been swallowed. Couch and all. I thought I could smell blood.
That was all in the first few seconds, I guess.
Then we started to fill with water, from the base of the cabin. People screamed and struggled some more. I felt like I couldn't move. It was happening too fast. And then—
Yes?
And then the access hatch was popped, just above my head. I saw daylight. I could smell the sea. I thought I could see that damn blue wheel, hanging in the sky. And something blocked my view. Yeah, I remember. A face, big and round and hairy. It kind of took a second to click into focus. It was this guy, with a big broad brow, flat nose, jaws on an industrial scale.
Ham.
Ham?
My closest companion here, on this planet. I live away from my fellow Russians, you know. Differences of opinion. But I'm not alone; Ham is here. There will be time for all this.

Your landing – your crash. I saw it from the shore. We had both run that way as we watched you descend.

Ham reacted very quickly. Even as you fell he came out with flotation bags, as I call them, just antelope skins tied up and sealed and inflated. He uses them for fishing. What else do you remember?

He reached down into the cabin. Reached down with this huge scarred hand. I didn't know if he wanted to shake my hand or rip my face off. He grabbed my uniform collar, and I could guess what was coming. I pushed off my helmet and opened my restraints, just as he hauled me out by the scruff. And my head slammed against the hatch on the way out, and . . .

And I woke up here.

I think perhaps that's enough for now.

You need to thank this character Ham for me. The first responder. The hull must have been blistering hot still, and there would have been venting from the fuel tanks. He took a risk. But he got us out. Even the bodies, of Bob, Nicola.

He brought you back here too, on the travois, with the others. And the bodies. He and Bartholomew, hauling the bodies and the wounded. You'll be able to thank him yourself. He's around. But there's something I should tell you. It may – comfort you.

Comfort?

Blue wheels in the sky. We have seen them. They are rare here, but they do visit. We measure them, photograph them. They exist, objectively. And—

Yes?

And it was a blue wheel that snared us too, our craft – the Elektrod, *mightier than yours – as we, some ten years ago, descended to land on this place.*

Malenfant?

I'm thinking. Sorry. OK. Thanks for telling me that.

51

So there was probably nothing you could have done to avoid the crash. It was no accident; you were brought down purposefully.

As we were.

Yes. If these things are as rare as you say. A hell of a coincidence for them to show up just right to snare both our ships. Wow. Then — I guess I hold a grudge.

Yes. You should rest soon, however. But there's one thing I must ask.

What?

You spoke of a Russian you encountered—

Vladimir Pavlovich Viktorenko. The man with your name.

Tell me about him.

Yeah. He had come to Phobos, with his companion cosmonaut. And our timelines crossed.

Do you know when he was born?

If I recall what Emma said about his age — 1975, I think. I do remember she said he had a famous father. Son of a man who flew on a spacecraft called Voskhod 3. Before Vladimir was born.

There was no such spacecraft, in my reality. But, yes, an elder Vladimir Viktorenko flew into space – with me, his wife, at his side. And yes, that was before Vladimir Pavlovich, my son Vladimir, was born. Tell me – did he live a good life?

In the brief time we had, Emma knew him better. She —

Tell me.

His Russia was – unhappy, I think. In his timeline there was a great deal of conflict with the West. We met him in 2028, by his personal calendar. In that year a war erupted – an atomic war, that devastated Russia. He saw it from Mars, from Phobos. Listened on the radio links.

I . . . see. What became of him? He did not travel with you?

He chose to go home. He wanted to find the family of his companion, who was called Misha Glaskov, to tell them how he died at Phobos.

I only knew him a little. He had a good sense of humour.

Do you really think he was your son, in a different reality? I think that in all the realities he would have made you proud.

You are a kind man, Malenfant.

You should sleep now.

While I remember my son, lost in the manifold.

10

It took three days after Malenfant's awkward wakening before the funerals were done. Three days before pits had been dug deep enough, mostly by Ham – deep enough, Irina promised, that the bodies would not be disturbed by the scavengers of this landscape.

They held a short and simple ceremony on that third day, as the Sun began to set over the huge landscape of Persephone.

At first there was an awkward silence. So, in the absence of Lighthill, Malenfant said some words of remembrance: a couple of lines about Nicola and Bob, personal, blunt and simple, the way astronauts spoke of each other, when sober anyhow. Or so he hoped would be the same for the British.

Then Josh Morris, the sole surviving Brit on Persephone, stepped up, evidently fulfilling a duty. He seemed barely articulate. With Deirdra holding his hand, he mumbled half-remembered prayers from his Anglican upbringing – promises of everlasting peace for his colleagues, interred for ever in this alien ground.

Deirdra stood with him, a pillar of strength and calm. She didn't say a word through the service – she seemed habitually quiet these days – but to Malenfant she was by far the most impressive presence. And her relationship with Josh seemed to have gone far deeper than his helpless crush.

Irina had helped set up all this, but kept her peace. She was dark of complexion, her black hair speckled with grey, crudely cut and pulled back from her face. Malenfant guessed she was late forties.

And when all the words had been spoken, as they prepared to withdraw from the graves, Irina's enigmatic companion, Ham, stepped forward.

Abruptly, over the graves, Malenfant met his gaze.

Oddly, this was the first time Malenfant had seen Ham, in daylight, close to. After all Malenfant had been unconscious when Ham and Irina had pulled him from the wreck of the *Charon* and dragged him across the dirt in their crude travois to this place – and he'd stayed unconscious for days afterwards. Even after Malenfant had started to function again, to get out of the tepee-like shelter, he had seen little of Ham: glimpses, generally remote as the man went about some chore or other. Including digging these graves, with some help from Emma, Deirdra.

It was clear that Ham did not live in this little settlement, of which Irina had been the only permanent inhabitant before the *Charon* survivors had been brought back. He came here every day; he built up the fires that were never allowed to die out completely. He even prepared food, hunks of meat cooked on the fire, parcels of vegetables and fruit wrapped in animal skin. But at night he went off to some shelter of his own, Malenfant guessed, maybe with more of his own kind.

His kind. What did that mean?

Ham was short in stature, well under six feet. He was massively built, but with not an ounce of fat that Malenfant could make out on a body like a wrestler's. He habitually wore a kind of fur jacket, what looked like trousers covered in skin pouches, all crammed with stuff. Even shoes of some kind of tough leather, thick with what looked like teeth-marks. Maybe that showed how the material had been worked. His face, framed by a red-blond mane of hair and a scrappy beard that he cut with stone flakes, was a human face. A thick, cavernous nose, heavy brows, a pretty massive jaw.

But the eyes—

Those eyes were fully human too. Deep blue. But, Malenfant saw now, there was some combination of the features, something in that gaze, that set Ham apart – that would have made him stand out even if he had been dressed in a city suit. A directness in that stare, a calculation.

Not like some hood planning to take his wallet and phone. A predator's gaze, Malenfant mused. Like looking into the eyes of a lion. Eyes like death windows. And he, Malenfant, was, just for that instant, prey. Nothing more. Malenfant suppressed a shudder.

But, after that moment of contact, Ham turned away. And he walked up to the graves, his gait heavy but graceful enough, dug out a handful of flowers from one of the small pouches attached to his trousers, and scattered petals on the two earth mounds, muttering words too low for Malenfant to make out.

As the group broke up, Malenfant drifted over to Emma.

'So who do you think that guy is? Or what? It's pretty clear he didn't arrive here with the Russians. That stocky build—'

'Could be an adaptation to the higher gravity, here on Persephone. Nice thick bones, big muscles.' She added slowly, 'Or maybe he was pre-adapted. And that's why he's survived here, him and his people. Wherever they are. Because, of all the human types that might have found their way here, however that happened – through the blue portals, I guess – his kind fits best.'

'Found their way here?'

She kicked at a tuft of grass. 'Look around, Malenfant. Look at the critters we've seen here. Look at the flowers on the graves.'

'I've seen nothing much but the inside of that tepee.'

'OK. Well, I'm no expert. I'm like Josh; I was trained to look for bugs on Phobos, remember. But I did soak up some biology.

'Look, this place is Earthlike. But it's not Earth. Yet the life forms seem identical to those we knew on Earth. Shit, we can eat the meat. We *know* that our kind of life evolved on Earth. The record that survives of evolution on Earth, *our* Earth anyhow, the fossils, the genetics, is too convincing. So—'

'So all the life we see must have been *brought* here.' He shook his head. 'I feel like I'm still waking up. We know the Engineers have systems that transfer human travellers, at least, from one Road to another. People in spacecraft, coming through Phobos to another world.'

'Or through Anteros,' Emma murmured. 'As Irina would have it.'

'So maybe, you think, there is some wider mechanism going on here, a wider transfer. Of animals too.'

'Of flowers and trees and grass. From Earth, or versions of Earth, to – here.'

He nodded grimly. 'And people? Or versions of people?'

'Looks like it,' she said. 'Don't you think? And maybe we even saw this – mechanism – in action.'

'You're thinking of the crash. The blue wheel in the air.

We all glimpsed that. People falling out, Josh told me he saw. Kilometres high maybe. None of them could have survived.'

She nodded. 'So maybe the mechanisms that – populate – this place ain't too reliable.'

'Yeah. And, shoving planets around. Do you think these Engineers are kind of ramshackle? I wouldn't let them fix my roof, let alone build me a world.'

She laughed. 'Make sure you tell them that when you meet them, Malenfant.'

'Dropping people out of the sky, though.' Malenfant closed his eyes. He imagined falling, falling. Even the most primitive kind of human would surely have been utterly terrified in those terrible moments – no, minutes, a fall like that would last that long.

He opened his eyes, and glanced over at Ham. 'So you think *he* is – what, a different human? A Neanderthal, maybe?'

'It seems possible, doesn't it? Surely he's a hominin.'

'A what?'

'Hominins. The group of primates that includes modern humans, extinct humans like the Neanderthals, and ancestors like the australopithecines.'

'Like Lucy?'

'Right. I've seen stockier bodies in the gym, pumping-iron addicts. It's not the body shape so much. He can even swim, you know. Since he evidently hauled us all out of the lander and brought us back to shore. A Neanderthal, though?' She shrugged. 'In our time the archaeologists were starting to sequence DNA from fossils, and beginning to figure out that the human family tree is actually one hell of a mess. We always looked for patterns. Simple origin stories, species and subspecies neatly splitting. In fact you had whole populations migrating back and forth, different kinds of humans interbreeding . . . I doubt if any neat label like "Neanderthal" is going to fit exactly. So, he is who he is. Irina doesn't call him a Neanderthal. She just calls him Ham – the name he seems to accept. And, a little lazily, she calls his people Hams, too.'

'The eyes.'

'Yes,' she said. 'It's what's inside that counts, isn't it?'

He watched Ham now as he walked, or shambled, away from the grave, and approached Irina. They spoke softly, in what sounded like short, curt sentences.

'I've tried listening without the bangle,' Emma said. 'That's some kind of pidgin Russian, I'm sure. Or a Ham-Russian creole?'

'What do you think keeps him here? He must be some kind of exception, even among his own kind. Otherwise they'd all be here, right?'

'I can make a guess. The Neanderthals were less inventive tool-makers than we are, the archaeologists thought. But that's not to say they couldn't have made use of technology more advanced than they could have manufactured for themselves.'

He snorted. 'So he's King Louie now?'

'OK, smartass.' She pointed at Ham. 'Look at what he's wearing. The trousers. All those pouches.'

'Pockets,' Malenfant said, wondering. 'Irina Viktorenkova crossed the world lines and won the heart of a Neanderthal, by giving him pockets?'

'Evidently the greatest legacy of *H. Sap*. Well worth all the trouble of evolving these giant forebrains.'

He looked back at the graves once more, then turned away. 'Anyhow, now that's over with, we got work to do.'

She smiled. 'Enough of the mourning and the existential wonder, eh, Malenfant? So what's first?'

'What do you think? We need to get back in touch with Geoff Lighthill, in the *Harmonia*. And to do that we need an old-fashioned radio. Because these bangles of Bartholomew's, miracles as they are, are short-range only. And to do *that* we need to get back to the wreck of our lander.

'We need to take a walk.'

11

It took seven long Persephone days before Bartholomew gave his grudging consent to an expedition south to the coastal site where the lander had come down – a walk back, which, Irina estimated, might take them three or four more days. Much as it had taken for Irina and Ham to bring them all here in the first place.

They made their preparations, discussing tactics. It was agreed that Ham, Bartholomew, and a rotating team drawn from the rest would drag the travois behind them, laden with gear, but relatively lightly. They carried food, for instance, but no water in this riverine landscape, only empty containers – and, at Bartholomew's insistence, purifier pills from their emergency supplies. It was clear that if things went badly wrong, patients could be loaded up on the travois and taken back to Irina's camp, just as they had before. Malenfant himself had had to be carried from the sea that way, the first time, more or less unconscious.

Malenfant knew Bartholomew had a point when he objected to Malenfant's participation. He found just the packing exhausting as the days wore away – heady, slightly breathless days of heavy gravity and thick air – twenty-five-hour days which were, as an added bonus, just overlong enough to give him a mounting feeling of jetlag.

And of course it got worse once they started the trek itself. Even when you weren't dragging a travois behind you, the ground on its own was tough enough. On this high-gravity world the river they tracked was an unpredictable beast which evidently changed its course frequently, and the landscape around the central channel was difficult, with braids, gravel beds, mud flats, and places where the banks were undercut and prone to collapse. This was a dark world too, Malenfant was finding. Breaks in the low cloud were rare, and that and the diminished sunlight made for a murky, almost twilit panorama. *Depressing for a tropical ape like you, Malenfant.*

But they endured. Malenfant told himself he had been on worse survival-training exercises with the USAF and NASA. That had been decades earlier by his body clock, but the principles still stood, and the techniques for enduring. You dropped your head, shut your mouth, took your diarrhoea pills, and got through it. In fact at the end of the first day Malenfant found he had done better than Josh, at least, who had a fine mind trapped in a frail, underprepared body.

And on the second day, Malenfant started to notice his surroundings.

As they neared the coast and the altitude dropped, the air grew thicker still, murkier, a little heavier to breathe. And the landscape changed too, from a parched grassland higher up to a greener, more varied country, with thicker grass interrupted by pockets of trees, and the underlying red-sandstone bedrock better concealed by thick, rich-looking soil. The trees might have been pine, or some might have been oak, and some specimens Malenfant couldn't recognise at all. The trees seemed generally squat and broad and low, and Malenfant guessed that made sense. Didn't trees have to lift sap up from their roots to their topmost leaves? So, in a higher gravity – and with less direct sunlight too, so less photosynthetic energy, he supposed – you grew short and fat, not tall and elegantly slender.

In this landscape, Malenfant suspected, the newcomers all felt better. More at home. But as the party, relaxing, spread out a little, Malenfant tried to stay wary – tried to remind himself, without unduly alarming the others, that where there was a clump of trees there was room to conceal predators. They had seen plenty of animal life from orbit – meat on the hoof, herbivores, presumably, in great herds – and there were sure to be hunters down here, even if they hadn't met any yet, and even if Irina had not said anything about such dangers.

He felt he needed to learn more, and fast.

So when he took his turn with Irina on a travois – well aware that she was probably putting in a lot more of the work than he was – he tried to make conversation, with a woman who seemed barely less taciturn than her Neanderthal-ish companion. It didn't help that she clearly didn't like the bangle, or any of the manifold-delivered high tech her visitors had arrived with, and he sympathised with that.

He essayed, 'Your pal Ham seems happy enough.'

She frowned. 'Happy?'

'I don't know anything about his – people. Hell, I haven't seen any aside from him. He seems content enough to wander far from home.'

She shrugged. 'He is human. Not as you or I, but human. And humans rove far from home, don't they? As you and I have proved.'

'True enough. So where is his home?'

She pointed a thumb over her shoulder. 'North of my own camp. His clan home.'

'Clan?'

'Ham's people do lead quite isolated lives. In extended

families, with little contact with other groups.'

He thought that through. 'I guess it's not unknown for humans. The pioneers, the opening up of the West – you would have had a lot of isolation then. But that's not seen as particularly healthy, psychologically. Is it? Or viable economically. So you start opening up trading contacts, settlements become villages become cities . . .'

'Ham's way is not as ours. There are cooperative hunts, I believe. Especially on the seasonal trails of the migratory animals. Or at the coast. And when there are reasons for larger groups to gather, that's the opportunity for the young to move from group to group.'

'To keep the gene pool mixed up?'

'But much of their life is solitary.'

'Hm. Like your own,' he dared to say. 'We did survey from orbit. You know we spotted the big development some way to the north of here, in the interior, the upland. What you call the Shield, right?'

'Hardly a *big development*. Merely our own crash site. Where we, my comrades, survive.'

'Umm.' Was that a new bit of information? That these Russians had *crashed*, that they could be stranded here too? And then, had there been some dispute among the Russians? A conflict serious enough to drive Irina into self-exile?

'And you came out so far as this with Ham's people?'

She sighed, and gave the travois pole a particularly sharp tug. 'You need not probe me. We are humans, of Earth, together in this place. I will tell you all you need to know in due course. If not all you would wish to know.'

Later, then.

Now he became aware that Josh Morris had broken from the ragged line, and was making for the river, where clots of some kind of weed floated in knots near the bank, green and dense and sickly-looking. Malenfant knew that Josh, his attention snagged by some scientific puzzle, could be lost to the group for long minutes – hours, even.

Well, why not?

Malenfant slowed to a halt. 'Take a break.'

The line broke up.

Irina and Ham, after taking a glance around, presumably in case of looming threats, dropped their travois poles and sat easily on the ground. The *Charon* travellers, visibly less cautious to Malenfant's irritation, just gathered around the travois where their water bottles were stacked, barely looking over their shoulders.

And Josh Morris, alone, crouching on his haunches by the river, hardly seemed aware of his surroundings at all.

Deirdra caught Malenfant's eye. *Lighthill's not here. Go see to him, Malenfant.*

Malenfant approached slowly, wary of startling an evidently nervous young man.

And as he neared the bank, the far side of the river, off to the east, opened up in Malenfant's gaze. He could make out more of those squat Persephone trees on the far bank, huddled as if for mutual protection.

And against the shadows of the trees, Malenfant saw—

'*Look* at this.'

His attention snapped back to Josh, who was gazing at bits of mud and weed. He was using a cup, probably his drinking cup, Malenfant thought with chagrin, to scoop up bits of the green mat that clung to the river bank. His patched-up glasses were smeared with native green.

Malenfant, with one eye still on the far bank, bent down to

see. 'Wow. I never saw green glop quite like it.'

'I know you're teasing me.'

Now those forms on the far bank came out from the trees into brighter light. 'Josh.'

'I would need my equipment to be sure, my lab on the *Harmonia* – I have some kit on the lander – but I believe this is very old. A very old form indeed.'

And more pale forms, tall, slimmer, wandered in a loose herd towards that same clump of trees.

'Josh, I think—'

'I suspect this is a young stromatolite, or the beginning of one, a bacterial community – a very old form, and a kind of pioneering ecosystem.' He grinned. 'A city of bugs, if you like, Malenfant.'

'A city of bugs? Josh—'

'Exotic life! I am a biologist, Malenfant, you know that. It was I who characterised the life forms we discovered on Melinoe, moon of Persephone, in – well, in your and Deirdra's reality. But that doesn't compare to *this*. What a find! And furthermore—'

Malenfant got hold of Josh's skull with one big hand and, gently enough, turned his head to face across the river.

Where dwarf horses were scampering around the feet of giant camels.

'You were saying about exotic life?'

66

12

The two of them stood up, and stared.

The others gathered around: Emma, Deirdra, Irina. Deirdra carried binoculars, retrieved from the *Charon* lander. Even Bartholomew came to see, and Malenfant had time to notice that the artificial flesh on the medic's hands was starting to look unnatural, polished by the friction with the travois poles.

Time to notice that, in between his continuing study of the exotica on the far side of the river.

'Browsers,' Josh said now. 'The camels, I mean. I think, anyhow. Underdeveloped humps, so used to moist conditions. Tells us something about the climate here, then.'

'What about those horses?' That was Deirdra. 'They're so tiny. Are they young – foals?'

'Doubt it,' Josh said. 'And not even dwarf forms. If I recall correctly, the earliest horses were forest browsers, and small to boot. They grew bigger when they adapted to the open grasslands. I wish I could get hold of one.'

'Me first,' Emma said, grinning. 'How cute can you get?'

Josh was too absorbed to rise to this. 'I'd like to take a look at its feet. I'm prepared to bet it will have soft feet – not hooved; still adapted to the softer forest floor. And I—'

The roar, even from the far side of the river, made them all jump. It was a deep, tearing sound that seemed to Malenfant to fill the landscape. As if it was something geological, not biological.

And the lion, when it appeared, was a gold-yellow blur.

It was in among the horses and camels before they were aware of it, it seemed. The prey animals scattered, bleating and whinnying, and there was a moment of confusion, chaos, as the beasts tumbled over each other to escape.

When the scatter was done, there was the lion, with one small horse limp in its jaws, a splash of red at its throat. A tiny life ended in an instant; Malenfant felt a pang of sympathy.

Yet even as he watched this, he noticed odd details about the lion – if a lion it was. No mane, but if he recalled correctly only the males of African lions had manes. A female, then? Its brown fur had an oddly mottled texture. Its limbs looked flexible, with long, grasping talons on the feet. And it had a thick tail. Not like the rope-like lion tails Malenfant remembered from boyhood zoo trips, this was heavy, muscled, and coated with striped fur, almost a fifth limb. It might have been pregnant, with a bump suspended from its belly.

A lion but not a lion. Malenfant squinted to see more, inwardly cursing his elderly eyes. But the animal stayed still only for a heartbeat. Then, the prey in its jaws, it reared up – it seemed to use its tail for balance, making a tripod with its two hind legs – and leapt into the lowest branches of one tree, and then scrambled higher, working its way up the trunk.

'That's no lion,' he said. 'Or is it? The way it climbs, grasping onto the trunk like that.'

Emma said quietly, 'I saw a koala once. Up close. In a zoo. Baby on its back. Cutest thing you ever saw. *That* climbed that way.'

'So what the hell kind of lion is that? And don't lions take their prey back to their young to feed?'

'No need,' Josh said in a small voice. 'It brought its young with it . . . Ah. *Look* at that.'

It took Malenfant a while to see it. The lion, clinging to its tree, was contentedly feeding – and a small kitten-face poked out of a pouch in the lion's belly, and pulled at loose scraps of meat from its mother's mouth.

'It's a marsupial,' Emma said, wondering.

'A marsupial lion,' Josh said. 'I think. So from Australia, on Earth. I told you that microbiology is my bag, not the big stuff with teeth and muscles, but still . . . Same kind of niche as the African lion, but different in the details. That muscly tail helps with the balance. And, yes, it has those hefty forelimbs that help it climb, though it's not so good at chasing down prey. More an ambush hunter, a scavenger. But you can see it's effective enough at getting its victim.'

He sounded oddly upset to Malenfant.

Malenfant put a hand on his shoulder. 'Hey. Don't take it personal. Nature red in tooth and claw – that's life, and death.'

But Josh shook him away. 'That's not why I'm upset, you fool.'

Malenfant was shocked rather than offended.

Deirdra approached calmly. 'So why then, Josh?'

'Because it makes no sense. That scene we saw over there. Camels and horses, and a marsupial lion? Oh, they are rough contemporaries, from what I remember. Pleistocene fauna, from the age before the ice, before human expansion drove them all, or most, to extinction. But the camels and horses – well, they crossed the land bridges into Asia, but they came from North America.'

Malenfant saw it. 'Ah. And the marsupial lion – Australia.'

'Of course! So how can they be together?'

Emma was trying to think it through. 'We're guessing there is some kind of – sampling – going on. By the blue portals? But mixed up. What about other animals? Or might the same be true of the plants, even? Trees, flowers, or at least their seeds brought here. Collisions of creatures from different epochs, and even different geographical zones, mixed together.'

Different kinds of humans too, Malenfant thought to himself.

'Why, though?' Josh asked now. 'What's the point?'

He sounded miserable and deflated, even irritated, Malenfant thought. Offended, even, by the very *untidiness* of this cosmic circus. As opposed to being appalled to be in the presence of a power that was capable of dragging whole species across the timelines, to another planet entirely. Malenfant supposed that everybody had their trigger point.

Deirdra rubbed Josh's back. 'I guess that's what we're here to find out. It will be dark soon; we should think about making camp. A little further down the river maybe.'

Malenfant was impressed by her easy assumption of command. And he glanced over at the lion, which was now shredding what was left of its prey, with red-stained teeth and claws. 'Yeah. A little further.'

The last day was almost an anticlimax, with just a few hours' more walk. The river, having drained a good chunk of the continent, had now spread out into an impressive delta, and they had to skirt laterally to stay on reasonably firm ground.

But as they neared the coast, they came upon the tracks made by the travois in the first evacuation from the crashed lander – neat furrows in the softer soil, an unmistakable guide.

And there was the lander, at last. Stranded on a beach, just above high tide, evidently washed up. Malenfant made a cursory inspection as they approached.

The lander lay on its side. One support leg had snapped entirely, and another was bent and stuck in the sand. A crumpling of the lower compartment led him to fear that the delicate fusion engine, that had once easily lifted this ship from the surface of a clone of this big planet, was unlikely to be repairable.

'The pressure hull looks intact, though,' he murmured to Emma.

'So what? That bird is surely never going to fly again.'

'Just looking for positives. Come on, let's get inside; Joshua is longing to speak to heaven.'

'If the radio works. I never saw much of the electrics of these RASF ships; I hope they weren't relying on valves . . .'

Once inside the lightless cabin, it took Josh, with Emma's help, a few minutes to hook up the main radio transmitter to backup battery power and an antenna embedded in the hull. And only a few minutes more to contact Lighthill, in orbit, who, in *Harmonia*, was fortuitously above the horizon.

Once contact formalities were done, Lighthill got quickly to the point.

'About bloody time!'

Joshua burst into tears.

13

Charon *to* Harmonia. *Persephone to orbit. You awake yet, Lighthill?*

I – damn it, is this thing on? Bob Nash, wherever you are now, and it's a better place than this I am sure, your former commander misses you badly. *Harmonia* to the ground. That you, I suppose, Malenfant?

Who else?

What the bloody hell's the time? One's sense of the clock does tend to drift somewhat, when one is alone, and crawling through these wretched two-hour orbits. Sun set, Sun rise . . .

Local mid-morning, Wing Commander. The day after our arrival here at the Southern Caina Riviera.

So, twenty-four hours since our first contact. Riviera, eh. Ha! I almost envy you. Actually, I do envy you. Lonely business, up here alone. Not sure indeed if you chaps were dead or alive, as I mentioned to Morris – how is he, by the way?

Your one remaining crew? He's as well as we can make him. Bartholomew is taking care of his medical needs. In Emma and Deirdra you have two very empathetic companions. Far more so than me, for sure.

Ha! Or me. But don't underestimate yourself, Malenfant. Looks up to you. He's a young chap but with an innately good judgement of character, I think. But still, yes, he isn't among his own. Ah . . . How is he with Deirdra?

Fine. What are you getting at?

Oh, I'm sure you know as well as I do. I always had the impression that during our long flight he developed something of a crush on her. Even though she, and he, spent most of our six years of deep-space travelling in coldsleep. A crush that did not appear to be reciprocated, as far as I could tell.

Me neither. But what do we know? She's very kind to him, Lighthill. Supportive.

Would expect nothing less. She's become a very impressive human being. Even I have watched her grow enough to see that. And of course, Josh is a young buck, and there's not much choice of a subject for him to have a crush on, is there? Well, we'll have to let them work that out for themselves.

By the way it was good of you to allow him to make the first call up to *Harmonia* yesterday. Even if he has struggled with such things as contact protocols all the way back to his cadet days. It did him good, I'm sure, and me come to that.

Certainly a relief to hear from you at all.

Seconded, old chap. Seconded. Yes! Well, your crash site is very visible. The wreckage washed up on the shore. I had followed you down visually, of course. I suppose we are lucky it did wash up at all; everything might have been lost.

I saw the blue hoop, by the way, which brought you down. The fingerprints of your World Engineers, it seems, Malenfant. What bad luck that was – or sheer malevolence. And I was able to see movement, trails, what were evidently small camp fires. *Somebody* was alive down there, at the crash site, I could see as much. So I knew some of you had survived, at least.

Though I did not know who had lived and who died until poor Morris finally spoke to me yesterday. I had no solid news of any of you for three weeks, nearly. Three weeks! Why, that's half a summer vac, and the days felt just as long as those of my boyhood.

But I did learn a great deal in the interim. Never one to waste time. I have attempted a telescopic survey of the planet, and more widely of the rather silent Solar System we find ourselves in. And of the stars, by the way. I always was a bit of a whizz when it came to star-sighting. Why, once, back at school – this was Linbury prep – Billy 'Slippers' Tennent and I rigged up our own sextants with broom-handle lengths and bits of card and so forth, and sneaked out one starry night onto the roof of the gym—

You've spent way too much time on your own, haven't you, Lighthill?

. . . Where was I?

Ah yes, adrift and alone.

Malenfant, from up here Persephone, *this* Persephone, seems a rugged world, but an evidently habitable one. It is full of life, and so far as I could tell of a familiar sort. As you saw for yourself from up here before the landing. Trees, and grass, and animals, great herds, that browse and graze on the trees and the grass, and other animals that browse on *them*, in what looks from up here very like what you might find on Earth. Life, then.

Just as we're seeing down here in close-up, Lighthill. Though there are interesting differences in detail. Josh will tell you about that.

I've seen the odd campfire. Glimmers in the dark. But, Malenfant, in terms of signs of civilisation, there's nothing to compare with that fairly large community – township, engineering camp, whatever – off in the middle of the continent. Caina, a good way to the north of you. From what you've told me—

That's Irina's Russians. The crew she came down with. She's told us very little of them.

Definitely technological, however. And that could be *very* significant. Morris gabbled out a quick report on the status of the lander, yesterday. From what he says it ain't going to be serviceable any time soon.

You're saying that if we want to get off the planet again, we may need to work with the Russians to do it.

Quite so, I'm afraid. But that's all for the future, I imagine.

I am confident that my amateur astronomy from up here in orbit has established one thing – that we are in roughly the right place and time. By which I mean that the sky I see out there, judging from the slow drift of the stars, tells me that we are somewhere in the twenty-first century. I'm trying to get a better fix using the orbits of the outer planets, which make for a slow clock; Neptune's year is over a hundred and sixty Earth years, for instance.

Our host here, Irina Viktorenkova, has made similar computations. She sets the date at 2020. AD, that is.

Well, that ties up with my numbers. Always gratifying to get a gold star on one's homework, what?

Like old Billy 'Slippers' Tennent?

Yes, yes, all right, Malenfant. Riffling through my notes, here . . . Am I the only bod in the world who can't read his own handwriting?

I can make out nothing of the outer System, I mean beyond Neptune. The comet cloud and so forth. Equipment not good enough. I couldn't even find Pluto. But all of the big outer worlds are where I would have expected them to be, Malenfant, Jupiter to Neptune. Which gives me confidence, you see, that what lies *beyond* them has not been significantly deflected.

We discussed that. It's comforting to know that the Engineers

75

have their limits. They can push around an Earth or even a Persephone, but evidently not a Jupiter.

Very well. One exception, though, as previously discussed. Saturn here has no rings, not that I've been able to spot . . . And it does have that strange, too-hot little moon. We must go take a look at that at some point.

As to the inner worlds, it's a different story.

Take Mercury. The closest to the Sun, of course. I have some imagery. Photographs of surface features, and so on. A little blurred. If necessary we could rig something up to send down facsimiles—

I can wait for that. Just tell me.

Some things are unchanged, Malenfant. Mercury here is where it should be, and a solitary world – no moons. Closest to the Sun. But *this* Mercury is bigger than ours.

It's bigger?

In fact it is about the size of Mars – I mean, *our* Mars, which doesn't seem to exist here. Actually this Mercury's mass is a little greater than Mars. No idea what to make of this, not yet.

Consider the next – Venus. Well, we saw something of that when we found ourselves emerging from a manifold portal at a moon, not of Mars, but of our sister planet. I am suspicious of this Venus too, however. If Mercury is too large, it seems to me Venus is too *cool*. I need to take another look. But in the meantime I found—

A second moon. Of Venus.

Damn it. How did you know?

I cheated. Irina told me.

Oh, very well. I did determine these odd little bodies' orbital parameters. The outer is some sixty Venusian radii out and orbits in twenty-seven days – not unlike Earth's Moon. The inner, much smaller – the one we came out of – is only a couple of radii out and orbits in less than five hours. More like Phobos than Luna. I had thought of naming them—

Eros and Anteros. Irina got there first.

Hmm. Greek gods, companions of Aphrodite? An Oxford man would be irritated at jumbling up the Greek and Latin. But I'm a Cambridge man, and I forgive her.

Tell you something odd about these Venusian moons, though – I checked a few references. And I found that there *had* been – in my timeline anyhow – partial, scattered observations of moons of Venus. This was all after Galileo, who as you know was the first to spot Jupiter's moons. I think there was something of a planetary-moon craze in the next decades. Well, about half a century on, Cassini – who we remember for observing structure in the rings of Saturn, and so on – *thought* he saw a Venusian moon. Matched the parameters of Anteros, as we know it now. Glimpsed it again a decade or so later . . . Sightings never confirmed. Then in the eighteenth century a Frenchman called Montaigne spotted a second moon about sixty Venusian radii out—

He saw Eros, then.

Got the period wrong, though. But the observations were never followed up. And never confirmed once we had decent modern telescopes, and indeed sent probes to Venus. But it makes you wonder—

There are Venusian moons in some parts of the manifold. And maybe the manifold is . . .

Leaky? Offering us partial glimpses of what may lie elsewhere, in other universes than your own? That way lies madness, Malenfant, I fear. How could one ever rule out any observation, no matter how wild?

Maybe we are sane. It's just the universe that's crazy.

That's some diagnosis. And so we come to Earth.

Well, Malenfant, it sits in the right orbit, more or less. But it looks like – a cannonball. A grey mass of cloud, a little like Venus, actually, but with a hint of Jupiter: the clouds have persistent bands, white against grey, with here and there an ugly black knot that is, I surmise, a storm.

Oh, and no Moon! Which has many implications, of course.

Isn't the Moon supposed to have been formed by some giant primordial impact?

That's the theory. Not here. Evidently the impacting object was turned away – or maybe it was never lined up for collision in the first place. I need to take a closer look.

And so we reach Persephone. Which, as you know, is sitting right where Mars should be. And a life-sustaining world.

I know. It's sustaining me right now.

Even though Persephone sits *outside* the habitable zone. Do you know the concept, Malenfant? If a planet is potentially life-bearing, with liquid water on the surface – well, it needs to be just the right distance from the Sun. Or at least in a place where a carbon dioxide greenhouse can moderate the temperature. Too close in and you get a runaway, where all the carbon dioxide bakes out of the rocks – a Venus. But too far out you reach a limit where it gets so cold that the carbon dioxide freezes in the night. That causes high reflective clouds, which *deflect* away the heat, you see. Your world sinks into an ice age, from which it can never recover. That happened to Mars, at least. Our Mars. But—

But Persephone is not Mars. Persephone shouldn't even be here.

You say that, Malenfant. I'm not so sure. Consider the progression of the rocky worlds, as they formed – as they congealed out of the protoplanetary cloud, a big disc of dust and ice around the young Sun. Mercury is closest to the Sun, so it draws in a certain percentage of the local cloud, all the dust and ice at that orbit. Venus forms a little further out, so the belt of dust which spawned *it* was that much wider, that much more massive. So Venus is heavier than Mercury.

I see where you're going. And Earth formed further out still—

And Earth is more massive than Venus. Far enough out and you get ice and stuff dominating, and Jupiter forms. But between Earth and Jupiter, there's surely room for one more rocky world—

Which should have been more massive than Earth.

But not in our Solar System. *We* got poor, shrivelled Mars, so small it just froze. You see, I think, *we* should have a Persephone. At most Mars might have been a moon. This system may be a more complete picture of how the Solar System *should* have formed. But even so there has been meddling – some, at least, of the great impacts that finally sculpted the planets deflected, such as the big whack that created the Moon . . . All of which has clear implications.

What implications?

One has to get into the right way of thinking—

Of treating planetary formation as a crime scene?

Something like that. Enough. Speak soon.

Lighthill out.

14

The thirtieth day after his revival from that long recuperative unconsciousness – and a few days after the return from the coast – felt like a milestone to Malenfant.

He got out of his pallet early that morning. Stood straight up, as if defying the heavy gravity that clutched at his aged bones. As every morning, he was rewarded with a brief spell of dizziness, of disorientation.

It passed. Always did.

He ate some cold meat for breakfast.

Walked down the river to wash, took a leak, downstream of the camp, away from the stink of the privy.

He was back at the camp before it was properly light, before the rest had stirred, not yet ready for the day. The camp that had been Irina's – well, hers and Ham's – and was now crowded out with five unexpected guests.

He walked past the multiple hearths, the big central hut. And piles of gear, some of it evidently inherited from the Russian expedition Irina had been part of, some of it, of leather, wood and stone, obviously Ham's gear, and some an odd hybrid. Such as a thick caveman-type spear, really a slim tree trunk stripped of branches, with a sharpened kitchen knife for a blade – stainless steel, fixed by the pitch-like gum they seemed to use everywhere.

He saw Bartholomew, bent over, studying the vegetation. Maybe looking for some kind of medicinal plant.

Malenfant had been walking around amid this stuff for days, dully. Now curiosity sparked. This was a hell of a place when you looked at it.

Deirdra, sitting by the hearth, saw him moving. She got up and walked with him, wordless, at her ease. On a cold, somewhat dull day, she was wearing a kind of throw over her jumpsuit. Like a long blanket, it was the hide of some animal, scraped on one side and with the fur still attached on the other. She just stuck her head through a hole cut in the centre of the hide, let it drape down around her, and tied it off with a belt of leather rope. Comfortable, and it kept you warm, though it was a little heavy, Malenfant had found, when he'd tried a larger version. It also stank of whoever had worn it last – and, he suspected, of the animal it came from.

It suited her, kind of. It made her look like she fitted in here, he thought. But it clashed with the bronze colour of her high-tech bangle, the only overt relic of her own world, her time, the twenty-fifth century. He noticed she touched this frequently, a new habit. Rubbing it. All she had from her own century, moment to moment, he supposed.

She smiled at him.

She did a lot of smiling here, even laughing. While Malenfant mostly groused, and spoke to Lighthill by the lander's ripped-out radio, and pored over sketch maps and such with Emma and Josh. Thinking, planning, exploring options. Fretting. Deirdra did what she always did. Lived in the moment. Dealt with what was in front of her. You had to hand it to her; you would hardly call it command, or a leadership style. But – he had seen this before – she had a knack of opening doors, and hearts.

Now she linked her arm in his as they walked. 'You're quiet this morning. Quieter than usual anyhow.'

'Less grumpy than usual, Emma would say.'

She waved a hand. 'What's different about this morning? Not a bad day.'

'You sure? Thirty-five days.'

'Hmm?'

'Since we landed. Or, crashed. More than a month. Maybe I'm waking up at last. Starting to think ahead.' He glanced up at the sky, the Sun just visible as a pale, shrunken disc through the customary layer of cloud. 'This is a big world, and I suspect it does big weather – and, just here, even though we aren't so far from the equator, we are heading into the fall. I don't want to be stuck down here under whatever kind of misery you get in winter on a giant world.'

'Well, you're not thinking like you're on Persephone, then. And you're not thinking like Ham.'

He frowned. 'The first part of that, I don't follow. Sure I know I'm on Persephone. Every day I wake up and *see* it.'

'But you haven't let the truth sink in. So we've been here a month.' She shrugged. 'So what? A year on Persephone lasts over eight hundred days. Two and a bit Earth years. So a month doesn't carry the weight it does back home, Malenfant. A month is like – two weeks. Winter is coming, yes, and I don't know what it will be like – Irina doesn't talk about it, but she's evidently survived before. Malenfant, this is a big world but a slow one. You have time to figure stuff out. *We* have time.'

'OK,' he said. 'I'm not entirely convinced. But what about Ham? He's helped us a hell of a lot, when he surely didn't need to. Just as he helped out Irina before we even showed up. But we aren't his people. We aren't even his *kind* of people. There must be a limit to his generosity. What will his priorities be when the winter does come? We shouldn't count on him.'

She shrugged. 'Sure. But we've yet to find that limit. I think Irina has yet to find it. And besides, it's not that he's doing this out of some kindness, some abstract quality. It's more— I think it's a kind of trade. Irina gives him stuff he can't get elsewhere, in return for his help, one way or another.'

He thought about that. 'The kitchen knife on his spear.'

'That kind of thing, yes. More that we don't know about yet.'

'What do *we* have that we can give him? He dragged us all from the crash at the coast, and back again. Hell, is he going to come to us some day with a bill?'

She looked at him. 'I don't think it works that way with his people. And they *are* people, Malenfant. Irina told me she called them "Hams" after a son of Noah, in the Bible. It's more obvious when you see them at home. You should see it for yourself. They just – work together. Help each other, and strangers when they show up. In the expectation, the unspoken expectation, that you will be helped out in turn. Everybody wins, and nobody cheats.'

He tried not to scoff. 'Come on. People always cheat. And I think I remember stories about monkeys cheating. Or chimps? Giving out fake alarm cries, to scare everybody else off while the cheat gets the nuts, or whatever.'

Now Bartholomew strolled over, wearing his own scarred coverall. 'I overheard that – sorry. Look, Malenfant, you do need to go see them. You are projecting humanity onto these people – I mean, your kind of humanity. Things are different for them, the Hams. Irina seems to find the culture comforting, actually. She says it is very Russian – or like old Russian traditions anyhow, the life in isolated country villages. Self-reliance, mutual aid.'

'OK. So how come Irina got so close to Ham in the first place?'

Deirdra shrugged. 'There's a lot we don't know. That we haven't the right to know yet, probably. You should come and see for yourself. Look, I'm going over this morning. To Ham's home base. I said I'd take over more of Irina's soup. Wait here.'

She hurried over to Irina's tent, emerged with what looked like a stainless steel saucepan.

'Go with her,' Bartholomew pressed.

Malenfant frowned. 'I am kind of busy.'

Bartholomew sighed. 'With what? Spending your waking hours on the radio to Lighthill?'

'Well, we're working on a strategy. Planning our next steps.'

'Emma's been over there. To the Hams. Also me.'

'*You*? Why?'

Bartholomew sighed, convincingly enough. 'Well, because I can treat the locals as well as I can treat you, Malenfant. And to keep Deirdra safe.'

'Right. Your prime directive. A bodyguard? You don't think we can trust these Hams?'

'I'm being over-cautious. That's my rule set. We told you. Ham's people seem remarkably honest. They rarely cheat. Humans *always* do.'

Malenfant raised an eyebrow. 'And what about AIs?'

'Ah,' Bartholomew said solemnly. 'When *we* cheat, it's called game theory. You ready to go?'

15

Ham's camp was a few kilometres north of Irina's base. That, Malenfant supposed, was as close as Ham's people wanted to be.

So Malenfant, Deirdra and Bartholomew – Emma too, in the end – walked, following the river as it wound through its gravel bed.

The walk soon started to feel easier to Malenfant. Even the pack on his back, with medical essentials and spare clothing for a possible couple of days' stay away, didn't feel like the concrete block with straps that it had at first. His carcass was recovering, even adapting to the rigours of this heavy new world – and remarkably quickly given all said carcass had been through, he thought wryly.

They reached an area of higher ground, a kind of sandstone bluff. Here a tributary of the river, itself a healthy flow as the water responded to the higher gravity, had incised a valley of its own. They walked steadily up this narrow side valley, keeping away from the river bed itself; the bed's big, eroded stones made for uncomfortable footing.

'So,' Emma said after a while. 'How's your geology these days, Malenfant?'

'Never was as good as yours, in any timeline. It got you a ride to Phobos, after all.'

'Well, there's plenty of geology here.' She pointed at the sandstone bluff – at bands, strata, in the rust-red rock. 'Classic deposition formation. All this was under the sea, once. All this sandstone was laid down in the water, until the land was uplifted, and the ocean drained away. Lots of erosion on this high-gravity world; lots of neat sedimentary strata. And lots of uplift too.'

'I spoke to Josh about all this. Shouldn't you get fossils in sedimentary rocks?'

'On Earth you do. It's all compressed sea bed. Here – well, I haven't had time to look at this stuff through a microscope. Nor indeed do I *have* a microscope. So I don't know what's going on below the visible. But you can see there are no big bones sticking out of there . . . There have to be the remains of life, if not old enough to be fossils, on this planet, in these rocks. But I don't know how old, how deep they might go. Or,' she said more severely, 'if they might make any kind of stratigraphic sense.'

'You mean, evidence of evolution. One set of animals and plants giving way to another.'

She sighed. 'That's the Flintstones version, Malenfant, but – yes. You ought to see an orderly sequence if life *evolved* here. Even if it was punctuated by big catastrophes, like the dinosaur-killer impact on Earth.'

Deirdra nodded. 'Whereas, if life forms are just dumped here by the blue wheels?'

Emma bent to trace strata with one finger. 'If the deposition of life here is disorderly, essentially random, then there might be no coherent fossil record here at all.' She shook her head, frowning. 'Which is somehow – offensive to me. I think Josh hates this too. This isn't how a world is supposed to be. All this *meddling*.'

Deirdra was distracted now. Standing straight and looking further up the valley. Looking at a figure she saw there, Malenfant noticed, dark and squat.

Emma was still focused on the geology. 'Meanwhile, the rocks themselves never lie. There's been a lot of drama in this landscape. There must have been ice here once. An ice age, I mean. After the sandstone beds formed, and were uplifted. All this gravel is what you get when rock is broken up by the ice sheets, carried around, mixed up, then dumped when the ice finally melts . . .'

Malenfant murmured, 'Emma.'

'And the river now finds itself winding through a valley much too big for it . . .'

'*Emma*. We got company.'

She looked up at last, stood. And joined Malenfant and Deirdra in looking at their visitor.

Their visitor was a child, evidently, and female, but otherwise a miniature edition of Ham, Malenfant realised. Dressed in a cut-down version of the skin wrap Deirdra was sporting, tied with that chewed-looking rope. Bare feet, though.

She seemed to stand more erect than Ham did.

Her face was rounder, softer in contour, but she had Ham's big nose, his heavy brows. That facial architecture, almost like a Klingon in classic *Star Trek*, Malenfant thought vaguely, seemed more striking on her than on Ham himself. Her hair was a reddish blond – apparently cut short, if crudely.

Her eyes, wide open, were blue. Her expression had the openness, that odd mix of caution and fascination, that very small children could show when confronted by a stranger. Yet she was tall – tall as a ten-year-old back in Houston, maybe. She didn't quite make sense, Malenfant thought. She seemed that bit closer to the human, his kind of human. And yet not.

Staring at the visitors, she pushed a finger into one cavernous nostril.

Deirdra waved at her. The kid waved back, cautiously.

'We call her Strawberry,' Emma said. 'We met her before.'

'For the hair?' Malenfant asked. 'Strawberry blond? OK, but what does she call herself? What do *her* folk call her?'

'Not as simple as that, Malenfant. Their language – their true language, not the pidgin Ham will sometimes speak to Irina – is as much gestural as verbal.'

'Yes,' Deirdra said. 'Mostly they just point. And when they gossip, everybody knows who they are talking about.'

Emma said, 'The group is very small, and static, Malenfant. They don't really need names. You'll see.'

Malenfant felt like taking the initiative. With a fixed smile he walked towards the girl. 'Hi. You don't know me yet . . .'

She held her ground, her eyes widening further.

'Take it easy, Malenfant,' Emma cautioned him. 'She's younger than she looks.'

'Really? She looks – what, nine, ten?'

'Only about four. I think. They grow faster. So, easily scared. Or easily angered, and you don't want to see *that* just now.'

Malenfant smiled wider and spread his hands. 'Call me Malenfant. Everybody does.'

She just looked back at him, held the pose for a couple of seconds. Then she burst out laughing, and folded her arms and rocked them before her.

Then she turned, evidently excited rather than scared, and ran off northwards.

Malenfant felt peculiarly embarrassed. 'What the hell was that?'

Deirdra laughed herself, and copied the rock-the-baby mime.

'She thinks you're an infant, Malenfant. A big, lanky, bald, wrinkled—'

'OK, OK.'

'Kid!'

'Don't take it personally,' Emma said, grinning herself. 'We all get it, that reaction. You'll see. Although they don't usually burst out laughing.'

Malenfant suppressed his irritation. 'Well, if a four-year-old has wandered out this far, I take it we're close to the home base. Let's get this done.'

He stalked off, not waiting to see if the rest followed.

Ham's camp – village, family home, whatever – was neater than Malenfant had expected.

It was set under a south-facing stretch of stratified cliff. A large sheet of leather – the sort of leather Irina had used in her tepee, it looked like – shadowed some kind of inlet, or cave even, behind. The ground before this cover, a bed of pebbles, bore scars that looked like old hearths, but was free of debris as far as he could see.

The kid, Strawberry, was waiting for them. Upright as she was and relatively slim, still she was chunky, muscly, with biceps prominent on her bare arms. She really was an odd mix, Malenfant thought, looking at her more closely now, a mix of four-year-old, ten-year-old, and all-in wrestler.

She laughed at Malenfant again. Then she turned and ran into the shadow of the leather sheet.

The walking party slowed to a halt, and with some relief dumped their packs on the ground outside the shelter. Emma opened hers, and took a swig of water, purified by a pill, from a stainless steel British-made flask.

Irina emerged from the shelter. 'So,' she said.

'So?'

'This is Ham's lodge.'

Lodge. He stowed away the word.

'Malenfant, you are the only newcomer to this place today. Your first impressions?'

Think of it as another survival training exercise, Malenfant. You've been dumped in the middle of nowhere. What can you figure out? He glanced around again. 'I'd like to know where they got that leather. The size of that sheet. What kind of beast—'

'You'll find out.'

'Smart location. Close to running water, but high enough to escape all but the worst floods, I would think. The lodge itself is in some kind of – hollow? That I can't see behind that sheet. Facing south, so it will get the light, even so close to the equator as we are – and there's shelter from the prevailing winds, I'd guess. Good location. Is it on a game trail?'

'The game tends to follow the water courses. So, yes. Anything else?'

He tried to think laterally. What *wasn't* here, on this bare bit of ground? 'No heaps of bones, no rotting carcasses. No mess. They're tidy, then.'

'Not that. Not exactly. They are not tidy, not for its own sake. It is just that they use *everything*. Every scrap of an animal, for instance: bone, marrow, skin, flesh, sinew. Even stomach contents – and the stomach bag itself. But they are hygienic, in a way. They know to piss and void their bowels in the river, downstream, so it is taken away. Unless they need to keep the urine, for example for treating leather. Of course they have no understanding of the mechanisms of disease. But they have common sense and folk medicine.'

Malenfant looked at her now, trying to read between the

lines. Here was this person, stranded on an alien world, who had chosen to live apart from her companions – the Russians, up on the high ground – in favour of these Neanderthal lookalikes.

'Did your companions mistreat these people? Or others like them?'

She held his gaze. She did not reply.

'Some day you must tell us your story. The rest of it.'

'When you are ready.'

'When you trust me, you mean.'

She actually smiled. 'Is there a difference? Come now.' She turned and led the way towards the lodge.

Malenfant followed, with the others. He saw that their watery shadows were short before them. 'Must be getting on to midday already. So what will these folks be doing right now?'

Emma grinned. 'Having brunch. Every day is a Saturday here, Malenfant. You'll see.'

Irina, Emma, Deirdra, Bartholomew, went in ahead of Malenfant. He had no excuse to hang around.

He pushed his way past the leather tarp.

He found himself in a dim place, behind the screen, despite the ruddy glow of a hearth where a banked-down fire burned low. He saw people as shadows, shapes, with glimpses of clothing of leather and fur, and splashes of skin glistening with sweat.

But he did smell something. Something *sharp*. Not sweat – a kind of adrenaline, maybe. It made the hairs on the back of his neck stand up, and he had to suppress an immediate instinct to bolt. *You're not a prey animal, Malenfant. Show some dignity here.*

And besides, his companions were making their way forward, apparently at ease. Splitting up, greeting people. Irina went in deep with Emma in tow, heading towards what looked like a couple of women at the rear of the cave. They spoke as they went, with short bursts of speech, hand gestures, smiles.

Deirdra went over to Strawberry, the kid, and another female, a good bit older – the leather clothes were loose and did not conceal breasts and genitalia particularly well. The three of them squatted down by the fire, and started working on lumps of what looked like some kind of black gum. Deirdra worked the stuff in her hands, while the others chewed lumps in big, powerful jaws. Neither Deirdra nor Strawberry were particularly effective at whatever it was they were doing with the 'gum' – but the older female worked briskly, chomping on the gum and pulling it with her hands.

Bartholomew, though, hung back with Malenfant. The locals seemed to ignore the medic entirely – perhaps sensing something of the truth of him, the layer of artifice. Maybe he *smelled* wrong, to those big cavernous nostrils. But Bartholomew, not a person but evidently not a threat, was just ignored.

Standing there, Malenfant tried to count them. Five adults, it looked like in the gloom, plus Strawberry and her adolescent companion, and a few more kids tumbling in the shadows. Everybody seemed relaxed. But all the adults had their eyes on Malenfant. All of them.

'Just stay calm,' Bartholomew murmured to him. 'Hold your hands by your sides; show they are empty.'

'Shit. I feel like I'm in a cage of wolves.'

'I suspect that's not a bad analogy,' Emma said drily, walking back to him.

'What are they doing with that gum stuff?'

'You mean the pitch? It's made from birch bark. You roll it up in sheets, and bury it under the ashes of a cooling hearth. When it is heated you get a kind of sticky mess that you can work into—'

'Glue?'

'Correct.'

'Which is how Ham sticks his stone blades to the wooden shafts of his spears.'

Irina came back to him now, speaking quietly, calmly. 'This is what they do in the mornings, Malenfant. They eat what's left from yesterday's meal. They do their chores. They work on tools – or raw materials like the pitch, or stone blades to sharpen. They have sex.'

That took Malenfant by surprise. 'Hadn't noticed that.'

'Not this morning. They are all too aware of you, Malenfant. I should take you to Nicholas.'

'Nicholas?'

'My name for the boss of the bachelors, the men. The old fellow at the back there. Named for our famous and long-lived ruler of the Russian empire, you see.'

Indistinct in the shadows. With his two companions, Ham and that other, younger adult male.

'And I *have* to meet him?'

'Before they kill you, yes,' she said mildly. 'Don't worry. I have a gift for you to present.'

Malenfant's heart was hammering. 'OK. OK. I trust you. And the females—'

'Only two adults here at present. The older woman I call Alexandra. The wife of Nicholas. She is perhaps forty years old.'

But looked a lot older, from what Malenfant could see in the shadows. Kind of bent, slow, greying. More children scrambled around at her feet. Three, four kids? He had no idea how old *they* might be, given his poor guessing with Strawberry.

'Here is the gift you will present.' Out of sight, Irina tucked a bangle into Malenfant's hand. 'Nicholas has been coveting these bits of jewellery since you arrived – since, presumably, Ham described them to him.'

Malenfant looked sharply at Bartholomew.

The android shrugged. 'It's not activated. We have plenty of spares.'

'Very well . . .'

Irina nudged him. 'Look him in the eye. Nicholas. Not as a challenger, but an equal. No more than that. And *don't run*, whatever happens.'

Dreading the answer, Malenfant asked, 'Why not?'

'You are a puppy dog approaching a pack of wolves, Malenfant. These people are not – domesticated. As you are.'

'Domesticated? Me? That's ridiculous.'

'Of course it is. But if you run, they'll tear you to pieces.'

He crossed with her to the back of the hollow, to where the males were huddled under the rocky surface of this overhang. Walking into their stares was like walking into a bank of laser beams.

'So,' Irina said. 'You must understand that Nicholas is not the dominant figure in this society. Not a patriarch. He dominates the males, yes.'

'Alexandra, then?'

'Indeed. The women dominate – the women and their young children *live* here. The men come and go, if over a period of years. They seek other groups of males, who will hunt and migrate, before scattering and joining other groups. The females will move too, but in a more orderly fashion. Keeping the family together. When a settlement is flooded out, for instance. I suspect some move seasonally, following the flora and fauna, the herds.

'With the men it is more instinctive. The subordinates simply seek to get away, as once Viking younger brothers sailed to Britain and Russia. In this case, it is time for Ham to leave. His rivalry with his brother over a relationship with Lola, the younger female, is coming to a head. But Nicholas sides with the brother.'

'Why? Why one, not the other?'

'I can tell you were an only child, Malenfant.'

He dared to glance at her. Had the dour Russian made a joke?

'And, you see,' she went on, 'it is Ham's instinct to roam that has presumably guided him to me. He needs to be somewhere else – why not with me, and my curious projects, for now at least? Also he does seem to have a peculiar fascination with pterosaurs.'

'*Pterosaurs?*'

'You'll see. You are close to Nicholas now.'

Well, Malenfant knew that.

With a kind of grunt, Nicholas got up, leaning heavily on Ham – and Malenfant saw, for the first time, that the older man was missing a foot. His leg ended in a crude stump, that looked as if it had been bound up with some kind of rope, and burned black.

'Don't react to that,' Irina murmured. 'Don't make him think you are challenging him.'

'Point taken.'

'I have seen other amputees. Others with grave injuries, deformities, disease. They have a practical medicine for traumatic wounds, as you can see. They dip it in the fire, seal it with tar. Nearly there . . . Hand him your gift. You are here as an equal, not a supplicant, not a challenger.'

'I'm thinking cold but dignified.'

She sighed. 'That will have to do.'

So Malenfant faced Nicholas.

The face was extraordinary, that wide nose, the heavy brows – the whole head thrust forward from a stooping gait, which itself seemed a remarkably aggressive posture. And the eyes that stared into his own – it was an intensity of challenge that Malenfant had never met before, he sensed, even in the worst bear-pit alpha-male gatherings in the air force or NASA. Not even Ham had been like this.

A wolf versus a puppy dog. She got that right, Malenfant.

But when Malenfant held out his gift, the old man took the bangle. He fingered it, suspended it on one finger. Then he turned his back without a word, without a gesture, a contemptuous movement that alone would have started a fight in any redneck bar.

Even the younger males turned away, more curious about the bangle than Malenfant.

Malenfant, however, was still alive.

'You did well,' Irina said.

But now Malenfant saw that Ham and the other young male were . . . laughing. Glancing over their shoulder at Malenfant, laughing again. Then the second male pointed at Strawberry, and imitated the rocking motions she had made.

Emma walked up. 'I think I get this,' she murmured. 'They've picked a name for you.'

'Why don't I like the sound of that?'

'Look, Malenfant, sooner named than dead. Also, oddly enough, it reflects what Irina's been saying to you.'

'What?'

'Domestication, Malenfant. That's the difference between us and these guys. Like wolves before puppy dogs. We humans have domesticated *ourselves* – I think the theory is we evolved this way so that we could cooperate better in large groups, even on a global scale. And look how well *that* turned out.'

'OK, OK.'

'But domestication comes with certain characteristics. In the human case, less sexual dimorphism – males have a slimmer, more female form – and the retention of adolescent features. Look at the kids, Malenfant. A rounder head, a smaller face, a less prominent brow ridge. *We look more like their kids than the adults.* But you especially – I think it's the bald head—'

'What's my name?'

'Can't you guess? Big Baby.'

16

Obeying some ingrained instinct, Malenfant kept track of the days and nights they spent at the Ham camp. Just notches in the trunk of a tree. Two, three, four long Persephone days.

And as the evening drew in on the seventh day, the *Charon* crew settled down in the shelter of the lodge in a manner that was becoming routine.

Ham's extended family split up during their daily tasks, but would spend as much time together as they could, even during the daylight hours – working, jabbering, gesturing, helping each other finish the chores, fiddling with each other's hair and clothing, tending minor wounds. Sometimes obviously just gossiping, with cupped hands over mouths and pointing fingers. And every night, once the cloudy daylight faded and the glow of the always-lit hearth grew bright, they would gather in the shelter until sleep overtook them, one by one.

On Irina's blunt but firm advice, the *Charon* crew had quickly learned not to be too loud, not too pushy, not to get in the way, not to interfere where it wasn't wanted. But it seemed overwhelmingly important that the crew should act like part of the family, as much as possible.

You got used to it, Malenfant thought. So now he sat quietly with Bartholomew, just watching.

Emma, with Irina, was sitting with Alexandra and Lola, the matriarch and the one other adult woman. They were working leather, evidently cleaned of fur already: pulling at sheets of it, using their teeth to hold it, scraping with stone blades and stretching it some more to make it supple. Emma was doing her best to keep up, but using her crossed legs to trap the leather, not her mouth. The women didn't seem to mind. Once Alexandra seemed to make some joke, and Lola opened her mouth to laugh out loud. Malenfant saw how her front teeth were worn to stubs, despite her youth, presumably by their habitual use in tasks like this. The teeth oddly made her look much older.

It was curiously soothing to watch the three of them work.

Deirdra was playing with Strawberry and the other kids. They were painting on the wall behind them. They all had hollow straws, and they sucked up some reddish fluid from a scooped-pit shell on the floor between them, and blew the stuff out over the wall surface. Mostly they just made an unholy mess, but sometimes they managed to make silhouettes by holding up their small hands before the wall surface. Five-finger reverse shadows, Malenfant saw. Deirdra tried it, but made an even worse mess than the others, to much hilarity.

Malenfant found himself keeping an eye on Deirdra. On the surface she seemed as sociable as ever. But there were times when she receded, almost, into the background. She was driven, he knew that – none of the *Charon* crew would even be here without that, probably – and sometimes she became distant, as if looking beyond the walls of rock and leather that surrounded her. Or looking deep inside herself. Other times, he had noticed, she would touch that bangle on her wrist, even stroke it, eyes closed. Malenfant wondered if she was accessing stuff from the bangle – memories, family recordings. She had lost her father long before she had left her mother behind, he recalled. She was torn, he thought. She had to deal with the people around her; she had this overriding goal that was surely too big for most human heads – and she was entirely isolated from her culture, even more so than Josh, say, who at least had Lighthill. And she was probably missing her mother.

No wonder she was quiet, at times.

Meanwhile the latest nightly farting contest between Ham, Nicholas and Seth – the third adult male, tentatively named by Irina – got going. The three of them would rest against the rock wall, spread their legs, trumping with visible effort and laughing uproariously. Close your eyes and those three might be just guys loosening up in some bar in Houston, Malenfant thought. Not Neanderthals at all.

Neanderthals? Whatever they were, these guys were highly competent in their environment. Just wired differently, that was all. And he wondered now how much humanity, his own variant, had lost when all these other types went extinct. Would they have screwed up the planet so much if they had had these examples of other ways of living, of being human, in front of their noses instead of buried in museum dioramas?

'I love the way they laugh,' Malenfant said to Bartholomew. 'That big booming. Even the kids.'

'Yes. And I hate to be pedantic, but I think their anatomy helps with that. Big chests, big ribcages – bigger lung capacities.'

'Bigger than what?'

'Than the classic Neanderthal type. What I know of it – what was stored in my background reference data set in the year 2469, anyhow. There was a variant – a cousin subspecies, maybe, or just a slightly differently evolved subgroup – called the Denisovans.'

'Never heard of them.'

'Lived mostly in central Asia. And *they* seem to have had a greater lung capacity, maybe because they had adapted to altitude. On the Tibetan plateau, perhaps. Thinner air, bigger lungs.'

Malenfant thought that over. 'There is higher altitude at the heart of *this* continent, we know that. So you think maybe these guys are from that part of the world?'

Bartholomew shrugged. 'It's possible.'

'OK. But here we are almost at sea level. Rather than up on the high ground . . . Oh. That's where the Russians are now.' He glanced over at Irina, sitting quietly, watching Emma and the women work. 'So maybe that's not a coincidence.'

'Lots of questions, Malenfant.'

'And few answers. As ever. Well, I guess we'll figure it out.'

Irina got to her feet, gathered a leather wrap around her, and drifted over to them. 'You might want to get some sleep. Busy day tomorrow.'

Malenfant frowned. 'Doing what?'

She glanced over at the males, where the farting contest was winding down. 'Weren't you listening to the conversation? They're going hunting, since the weather looks fine. And you're invited.'

'Oh, shit,' said Bartholomew.

17

So, the next day, off they went, further up the river valley. Ham and Lola led the way, with Strawberry tagging along behind, evidently as a learning exercise, Malenfant suspected.

Bartholomew stumped resentfully along behind them, his veto of this trip having been ignored by Malenfant, Deirdra and Emma.

A short way up from the camp site, the forest closed in, the banks crowding the river. The cloudy Persephone daylight was occluded even more, and Malenfant started to feel as if he was entering some kind of dark green tunnel.

But the Hams moved through the forest with remarkable grace and silence, given their bulk, and given the adults both carried two short spears on their backs, supported by loops of chewed-leather rope. They seemed to tread only on beds of moss and such, avoiding bark or dry leaves, anything that would make a sound. And, as they walked along, they grabbed handfuls of moss and mud and what looked like dry animal dung, and rubbed it absently into their hair and feet and ponchos, evidently to mask their own scents.

By comparison Malenfant felt like a drunken elephant as he crashed his way through the low branches. Emma, and especially Deirdra, did a better job than he did.

Bartholomew, despite his bulk, was the quietest of all, which would have driven Malenfant nuts if he'd let himself think about it.

Things got more interesting when the Hams drew suddenly to a stop.

They lifted their heads, surveyed the forest with eyes narrowed. And they smelled something too; Malenfant could see huge nostrils flaring, imagined the forest scents carried on gusts of dank air into those roomy nasal cavities.

Malenfant could smell nothing different, detected no sights, no sounds.

Lola took one step to the right, into the blank dark green of the forest. She turned, put one big hand on Deirdra's shoulder.

The invitation was obvious.

Emma whispered, 'Do we let Deirdra follow her?'

Malenfant hesitated.

'Yes,' Deirdra hissed. 'This is what we came for.'

'No,' Bartholomew said, just as softly.

'It is an honour,' Irina put in. 'To be asked to participate in this crucial part of the hunt.'

Malenfant was well aware he had no kind of guardian duty over Deirdra. But nevertheless – *damn it, she is young enough to be my granddaughter*.

'I won't ask if it's safe,' he hissed at Irina.

'Of course it's not safe. But if the odds of survival were not favourable, these people would not attempt the hunt.'

'She's right,' Deirdra said, with a touch of impatience. 'It's no more dangerous for me than for Lola. Damn it, I'm going to do it.'

Malenfant had to suppress a grin. 'Did you use that twentieth-century cuss word, or has the bangle translated one of your own? Never mind. Go. Do it. Just come back safe.'

So Deirdra followed Lola into the gloom. She glanced around with a final grin, then in moments she was out of sight.

Emma said to Malenfant, 'You couldn't have stopped her. It would have been wrong to try.'

'I know. So now what?'

Irina began to slip her pack, leather, home-made, off her back. 'Now we wait. But we get off the trail.' She pushed her way deeper into shadow.

Malenfant glanced around at impenetrable forest. 'What trail? OK. Never mind.'

They came to a place where the ground was pretty much covered by the fat roots of a tall tree, some kind of oak maybe, Malenfant thought. Following the lead of Irina, they backed up against the trunk, for protection from some angles at least. Bartholomew took small flasks of water from his pockets and handed them to Malenfant and Emma.

And Ham handed Malenfant and Emma a spear each.

Malenfant had tried out with these things. The specimen he lifted now was short, stubby, thick – he couldn't wrap one hand around the full girth – and it was heavy, more like a sawn-off tree branch. The blade, shaped from basalt of some kind, was heavy too; he could feel its weight now as he hefted the spear, experimentally.

He'd tried throwing such a spear, and could barely hurl it four yards. Irina, with a kind of amused exasperation, had had to explain that the spear wasn't for throwing, but thrusting. Thrusting, at close quarters.

There was no spear for Bartholomew, Malenfant noted. Evidently the Hams still saw Bartholomew as belonging to some different category of being, apparently harmless – but, perhaps, not quite to be trusted.

Emma tried to hand her spear back. 'I've never even practised with one of these things. I doubt if I will be able to do much damage.'

Irina laid a hand on her arm. 'No. Keep it. If only as a defence. You will see.'

'See what?' Malenfant asked, feeling increasingly uneasy. 'I feel like the bait in a trap.'

Irina leaned forward. She was a round bundle in her coat of dung-smeared leather. She had her own spear, lighter, evidently custom-made. 'You must keep your jabber to a minimum—'

That was when Lola and Deirdra came crashing back from the deeper forest.

Malenfant, Emma, Irina all jumped to their feet, grasping their weapons.

In that first confused glance, Malenfant saw that Lola was carrying what looked like a boulder, maybe a half-metre across, its surface shining, speckled. Her grin wide, she just dumped her load on the ground, at the foot of the oak. Malenfant thought he heard a crunch, as if something had broken.

'What the hell's that?'

Deirdra, panting hard, looked exhilarated and terrified all at once. 'What does it look like? It's an egg.'

'An *egg*?'

A big, soft, heavy footstep.

For one heartbeat, they froze.

Then the low branches up to three, maybe four metres, just disintegrated into shreds that spun into the air, making them all duck, turn away.

Ham gave a one-word shout that may or may not have needed translation by the bangles.

'*Run!*'

Just as *it* exploded from the forest cover. It was as if a

monstrous vehicle, a tank – a tank adorned with muscle and talons and *feathers* – was coming for them.

They ran.

In hasty glances over his shoulder, Malenfant couldn't make out the whole creature. Just glimpses of feathers and claws. Feathers that looked like weapons in themselves, long, razor-sharp, coloured black, white, a drab grey. Yes, of course, he thought even in that moment, of course your feathers would be drab, you were hunting in the uncertain light and shade of a dense forest, you wouldn't want bright, colourful plumage, you weren't attracting mates . . .

And, looming almost above him now, a beak like an industrial-strength grinder. An eye the size of a dinner plate. Then the stench hit him: of dung, of blood, of *feathers*, a sharp, burning smell. It wasn't like a creature at all; it was a nightmare, disjointed, incoherent, made flesh.

Daring to glance back, he saw Ham and Lola stop dead and turn to face the predator.

Malenfant ducked out of the way, out of the bird's line of attack, and looked back again.

As the Hams braced the butts of their spears against their muscular bellies, the blades pointing at the onrushing bird.

They were both breathing hard. Standing their ground.

There was a collision like a car wreck, as bird-monster hit Neanderthal stone blades.

Malenfant heard a roar, of anger and agony. Saw a fountain of blood.

More howls and roars from Ham and Lola. He saw they were pushing back now, plunging, twisting with the spears. Throwing themselves at a flightless bird as big, surely, as a tyrannosaur.

Irina was right beside Malenfant, her face blood-smeared, grinning hugely. 'And *that* is how Neanderthals hunt! Come on – keep moving!'

It took Malenfant days to recover.

18

A week after the party had limped back home from the Ham camp and the Great Turkey Hunt, Lighthill decided he had done enough astronomical and planetary surveying for now, and called a conference on next steps.

They talked around noon of a bright day. Five of them – Malenfant, Josh, Deirdra, Emma and Irina – gathered on the straw-scattered floor, sitting in a circle around the scavenged radio, like supplicants before some idol, Malenfant thought. Josh fiddled with the tuning, as well as with the connections to a spindly fold-out antenna outside, and to a power supply consisting of a bulky battery recharged by a fold-out solar-cell blanket.

Bartholomew, as was his habit, sat back a little, in the shadows.

There was nobody else around – no Hams. Josh, always fearful for the electronics of the radio – all those big, fragile glass valves – insisted on keeping the gear stashed at the back of the cavern, out of sight, out of reach of the sometimes clumsy inhabitants, the sometimes curious children.

'. . . to ground station. *Harmonia* to *Charon* crew. Are you receiving, Josh?'

Josh Morris grinned widely. 'Loud and clear, Commander.

Umm, *Harmonia*, this is *Charon II*. Good signal strength . . .'

Not long after restoring contact with the crew of the *Charon II*, Geoff Lighthill had moved the mother ship *Harmonia* to a higher orbit. Seven Persephone radii out from the centre of the planet – some fifty thousand kilometres above the ground – *Harmonia* was now in a synchronous orbit, like some of Earth's earliest telecommunications satellites, orbiting the planet once every twenty-five hours – once a Persephone day, a stationary moon. And the ship hovered over a point on the equatorial continent Iscariot, due south of the position of Malenfant and the rest of the crew with Ham and his people on Caina. From up here, Lighthill could stay in constant contact with Joshua and the stranded crew through the lander's salvaged radio.

But the high orbit induced a signal delay of a third of a second or so between message and response. Malenfant oddly found the subtle, almost subliminal delay almost comforting, an element of technology he was used to. On a world where you got your lunch by wrestling a giant flightless carnivorous bird into submission, he would take any comfort he could get.

'Is everybody there? Malenfant?'

Malenfant called, 'We fallen angels can hear you clearly, Lighthill. How is it up there?'

'Lonely,' Lighthill said firmly. 'All systems fine, though I'm fed up making my own tea in the morning. I even miss that stew you served up when it was your name on the breakfast rota, Morris.'

Josh grinned. 'Wish I could say I'd been practising, Wing Commander. But Neanderthals generally don't drink tea. If these people are Neanderthals.'

'Well, whatever they are, I have a feeling you are going to need their help if we are ever going to get you off this planet.'

Emma leaned forward. 'Help with what, exactly, Geoff?'

109

'A walk of six hundred miles. And probably some heavy engineering at the end of it . . .'

Malenfant frowned. 'Six hundred miles?'

Deirdra seemed to grasp it straight away. 'A thousand kilometres. Due north of here, right? To the Russian camp.'

'Correct. Thought six hundred sounded a little less scary a number than a thousand. Suit yourself. Now. Geography lesson. You might want to take notes.'

'So. You are aware of the overall layout of the planet.'

'Oceans and continents,' Malenfant said.

'Well done, that man. You came down on a continent in the northern hemisphere: Caina. Near the southern coast. Well, you know that much. The continent is around two thousand miles wide – similar in scale to North America, back on Earth. But it is rather lost on a bigger planet; Persephone has a circumference of some thirty thousand miles.

'But it is the southern half of the continent, the half nearest you, that concerns us now. For that part of the landmass is dominated by a single massive geological feature—'

'We called it the Shield,' Irina said in her low, smoothly translated voice.

'Apt name. I'm looking down on it now. A big shield volcano – what, four hundred miles across?'

'Or six hundred kilometres,' Irina said drily.

'Like Hawaii on Earth. Or Olympus Mons on Mars. *Our* Mars. What you get when there's a vertical current in the planet's liquid-rock mantle, under the crust.'

'As Russian geologists knew,' Irina said flatly.

'And so did we,' Emma said. 'On Earth, the movement of the continental and ocean plates kept the crust drifting over the fountain from the mantle. So at Hawaii you didn't get a single huge volcanic mountain, but a series of them, a chain, a straight line. Whereas at Olympus Mons there was no tectonic movement to speak of, and it just sits there. For millions, even billions of years. It's as if the crust develops an enormous blister. And *that* is a shield volcano.'

'Correct,' Lighthill called down. 'Well, the Shield is more Olympus than Hawaii, for whatever reason. Take a braver man than me to speculate on the details of plate tectonics on a giant world like Persephone. Anyhow we have that one monstrous extrusion – monstrous in volume, if not in height. The width of the uplifted region is similar to Olympus – around four hundred miles. Says here that Olympus Mons is around thirteen miles high. The highest point on the Shield on Persephone is a bit less than four miles – or anyhow that's the height of the summits of the mountains at the rim of the central caldera plain. Which is a kind of big crater full of volcanic vents—'

'And was where we landed,' Irina cut in, speaking over his time-delayed words. 'We Russians. When we fell.'

Malenfant thought that over. *Shit. Then that plateau in the sky is where we will need to get to.*

Lighthill said, 'About the Russians. We should discuss this. The landing was not purposeful, then. The Russians', I mean.'

'No,' Irina said. 'We had intended an atmospheric scout, at high altitude. But the blue wheel attacked us. We crashed on the plateau. But we would have chosen to come down on high ground, to reduce the thickness of atmosphere we would need to pass through to escape again. We clung to hope, you see.'

'And that's where most of them seem to have stayed,' Lighthill said. 'The survivors. As I can see clearly from orbit, what they are building up there is a regular township. Or a sprawling technical facility anyhow. I can see solar-cell plants, what look like greenhouses – even a kind of well-head, I think, with a burn-off gas plume—'

'Can't get off,' Irina said glumly.

Emma turned, frowning. 'What's that?'

'Can't get off this planet. Gravity too high. Futile exercise. Soon figured that out. We, we stranded Russians, should have accepted it. Should have abandoned godhood and climbed down from Mount Olympus. All of us, as I did. Instead . . .' And she waved a hand, evasively, Malenfant thought.

'Well,' Lighthill said, 'it's to be hoped that you are wrong, Irina. And somehow we can after all indeed adapt the Russians' technology for the purpose. Because otherwise, given the wreck of the *Charon II*, you are *all* stranded down there – for good.'

That hung in the air. After all, Malenfant thought uneasily, these Russians were spacegoers too. If they thought it was impossible to get off the planet, who was he to contradict them?

But we have to try, he thought.

They were silent for a moment, save for ionospheric hiss and crackle from the radio.

And Deirdra was focused, intent. 'We have to do this.' She looked around. 'So where do we start?'

'Well, we must get to the Russian camp,' Josh Morris said gloomily. 'Obviously. But to get there, a thousand-kilometre hike, you said, Wing Commander?' He ticked off the points. 'On foot. In higher gravity. Across wild terrain all the way—'

'Yes, yes, Morris, no need to be quite so negative from the off. And, very well, let's stick to the kilometres if you insist – you traitor! But yes, that is the journey you must endure – strange that I can span it in a single glance from up here.'

'Bully for you,' Malenfant said sourly.

'A thousand kilometres from the goal. I assume you will

follow the valley of your river – it's not exactly straight, but it does cross a coastal plain that is, umm, some four hundred kilometres deep at your location. Draining, you see, the higher ground beyond. After that it's pretty much rising ground all the way, I'm afraid. To the cliffs at the rim of the Shield, and the mountains around the caldera. A steady upward slope for hundreds of kilometres. Well, you probably won't even notice the ground isn't level, most of the time.'

Malenfant snorted. 'Easy for you to say.'

Emma was thinking hard. 'And how high are the rim mountains? You said the summits—'

'About six kilometres above the mean,' Irina replied. 'There are passes.'

Malenfant studied Emma uneasily. 'What's on your mind? Six kilometres isn't too high, is it? I mean, Everest is around eight kilometres, I think, and people have made it to the summit without carrying oxygen up.'

'Yes,' Emma said bleakly. 'On Earth. The air density gradient is different here, Malenfant.'

'Ah.'

'I'm not following,' Deirdra said with a frown.

Emma looked at her. 'Air density drops off as you rise up from the surface of a planet – such as Earth. Yes? The stuff lower down is compressed by the weight of the layers above. Now suppose you turned up Earth's gravity by twenty-five per cent. What happens to the air?'

Deirdra frowned. 'It gets pulled down harder. Right? All those layers would compress.'

'Exactly. Atmospheres have scale heights, Deirdra. If we have to climb a wall six kilometres high, it is going to feel like Everest would on Earth. Also the gravity well we are climbing out of . . .'

'I know a way through,' Irina said. 'Or rather, Ham and his people do. Through the cliffs. We came that way. When we descended from this Olympus together. Like mortals fleeing the gods.'

Malenfant nodded. 'So it's achievable.'

'So you say,' Emma said. She shook her head. 'Maybe. If we can even get that far – you're looking at a thousand-kilometre trek, even without the altitude. And, we've been skirting around this. *All we have down here are the travois*. The sleds that Ham and his people, use, Geoff.'

'Right,' Lighthill said. 'And so you must drag your stuff along the ground?'

'That's pretty much it,' Malenfant said. 'Tough break.'

Irina glared at him. '"Tough break", you say. Let us make it explicit. You expect Ham and his people to do this for you.'

Malenfant was acutely embarrassed. 'Well – to help us.'

'Help?'

Emma looked faintly irritated. 'Are you accusing us of exploiting these creatures, Irina? What about you? Didn't you use them as porters, or draught animals, when you came down from the Shield and out here in the first place?'

'That was different,' Irina said. '*I was saving their lives*. They understood that.'

There was a brief, shocked silence.

Malenfant asked, feeling bewildered, 'So that's why Ham has stayed with you? Saving them from what?'

Irina stood up. 'I will consult. This will be their decision, Ham and his people. But I will do my best to make them understand.'

Malenfant frowned. 'So do you think they will buy it? Sorry, that's a coarse way of putting it . . .'

But, to his surprise, she seemed positive. She nodded her head. Even half-smiled. 'Perhaps. They remember, you know.

In some ways better than we do. They pay back debts. And they do owe us a debt, even if all I did was help them survive the wrongs we inflicted ourselves. And I know that Ham misses his pterosaurs.'

Pterosaurs. That word again.

'So,' Malenfant said briskly, and with some relief. 'Are we done? Do we have a plan?'

Lighthill, through the radio link, audibly snorted. 'No, Malenfant, you do not have a plan. You have the bare bones of a strategy which, with much thought and preparation, may someday evolve *into* a plan.'

'Then let's get started.'

And Deirdra, cautiously, took Irina's hand again. 'I think we should talk.'

19

Like I said. I thought we should talk. Soon.

I agree, Deirdra.

I see myself through your eyes. To you I am a wild person. Yes? Who has chosen to live here, in the village of the Hams, with these still wilder folk. The life here. This is what you see, when you see me.

But this is not me. This is how I survive – how I choose to survive, to live. But it is not *me*.

Tell me, then.

I was a cosmonaut.

And a biologist. Indeed, a biologist first.

Ultimately I specialised in life-support systems for spacecraft. It was intense, interdisciplinary work, a mix of biology, mechanical engineering, and – well – plumbing. *That* is my true environment. That is how you must imagine me. Not like *this*.

I've travelled with Malenfant and his companions for some years now. Pilots and engineers, space travellers, of the same era as yourself. Roughly. Even space plumbers.

Umm. But of different 'Roads', in your terms.

I always knew I could not travel in space for ever. I dreaded old age – I am forty-seven years old now. I never imagined it would end in *this*. When I would find a need to walk away from my colleagues, and the wreck of our craft. And I never imagined I would be sundered from my family in such an irrevocable way.

Look — I sympathise. I came away from my family, it was a deliberate choice . . . I thought finding Malenfant was a chance I couldn't pass up. I didn't know where it would lead . . . It may be possible to take you home—

Ha! Let's see how we get on with our trek to the Shield first, shall we?

But still there are consolations. The way I live here is not so unlike, I think, the way my grandmothers lived, not so long ago. I miss the smell of rockets, the tang of kerosene — but perhaps some deeper part of me has always missed the tang of wood smoke.

Your grandmothers? Tell me about them.

The first the family has reliable information about was my great-grandmother. Another Irina, so I was told, but that may have been a lie for children. She was born in 1860 — she was born a serf — but lived as a serf for only one year, for the Tsar abolished serfdom before her first birthday.

That was after the disaster of the Crimean War. Wars do seem to be a trigger for change in my country. But in the heart of the countryside the nation itself, Russia, can seem as remote an entity as the clouds, its wars like distant thunder.

In the Kaluga region our life was sustained by the *mir*, the community of the village, the area, the local people. Through trade, support, loans of tools and draught animals, mutual help. The *zemstvos*, the local councils — the lowest administrative layer of the national government established after serfdom — were better than nothing, but, in the hands of the gentry, often corrupt, mostly useless. So you looked after yourself, and your neighbours.

Still, things became much better for the peasants. We became literate; there were new roads, rail, access to towns.

We raised up our eyes from the soil.

My grandmother, Irina's daughter, was born in 1891, an ill-starred year of famine and plague.

And yet, oddly, a dream of flying, of spaceflight, was already part of my family's story by then. A dream, I suppose, that would, a century later, bring me here.

That does seem odd.

It came through Irina's older children. A few years before my grandmother was born, an itinerant teacher had worked in the area. His name was Konstantin Tsiolkovsky. He was a kindly man – so the family remembered later when he became famous – if not a terribly good teacher, not of elementary mathematics and such for the smallest children. But they all loved him for his patience and enthusiasm.

And for the stories he would tell of the future age, when mankind would stand astride the stars, as the Tsar stood astride all of Russia, from Europe to the Pacific!

He told all this to the children of serfs, remember, in a remote agricultural province. And he said he had worked it all out, it was all in his notebooks and in his head, the mathematics of how it might be done. While outside the schoolhouse, horses laboured to drag ploughs across the dirt!

Konstantin went back to Moscow. He became a librarian, and worked with Fedorov himself, father of Cosmism. And much later, of course – in the 1930s, I think – the Tsar himself honoured him. This was when the foundations of the Rocketry Institute in Moscow were laid. I was not yet born, but my family listened on the radio. Our Konstantin, with Tsar Alexei himself! It is no wonder that his legend remained strong in our family – strong enough to influence my own life choices.

You are silent.

I'm sorry. I'm listening to my bangle.

Your translator?

Yes. It's more than that. Each bangle stores a – well, a kind of encyclopaedia. Including details of history, or anyhow history as it was known in the Road Malenfant and I come from. In our records, Tsiolkovsky was honoured in the 1930s, but on behalf of the Soviet Union. By Stalin.

Who? Ah. Malenfant mentioned that name.

Malenfant bet me that you don't know what he would mean by a jonbar hinge.

Given the context, I think I can guess. A hinge, a branch point? A fork in history's path. And this is how the manifold you speak of is populated. Branching histories, like a crowded tree canopy.

So it seems. Don't ask me to explain it all. Least of all the mathematics.

Tsiolkovsky would have understood. In both our worlds.

We have found that the best way to handle this is just to talk. The manifold is about humanity, not mathematics. The more we talk, the more we understand each other. Go on. Please. Tell me more of your family's story.

All this is long before I myself was born, of course . . .

I never heard of the Soviet Union, before Malenfant.

I do remember my mother saying that her family, an uncle or two, dabbled with politics at the beginning of the twentieth century. An unstable time, as you know – well, perhaps you don't. One uncle joined a Socialist Revolutionary Party around 1900, 1901. In 1904 we went to war with Japan, in the east – a disastrous, costly adventure, and another war that seemed to point out the faults of the state, the poor judgement of Tsar Nicholas.

There was an uprising, I think, in the cities at least, that led to the founding of the Duma. A kind of parliament. My own family could follow the national news by this time. And my own family understood by then how backward Russia had become, under the Tsar – well, it was not all his fault. While Britain and Germany, and France, even America, had embraced industrial revolutions and social development, we had only just abandoned serfdom!

Now we had the Duma, a channel for discontent. Better than revolt. Still, progress was uncertain, and marked by violence, even assassination. Reforms were often abandoned.

War came again in 1914, as you know. I presume you know.

We had at least a version of it. Germany against Britain, France, and Russia – America became involved.

I was born in 1945. By the time I came to study my own history – oh, around 1960 – I think this war was understood as a collision of crumbling empires, of the Austrian, Russian, Ottoman. Perhaps some version of that war was inevitable in any timeline. I doubt if anybody on this world is competent to judge.

I think you're right about that.

But the war changed everything – as wars so often do. By 1917 things were desperate. There was even an epidemic, of influenza. Perhaps the soldiers brought it back from the battlefields. There was an uprising in the cities. My parents were in Moscow; my grandmother told me it started over a shortage of bread. It was a messy business – made more lethal by disenchanted soldiers, many of them peasants, now armed and educated. Tsar Nicholas was forced to abdicate. The Duma and its related organisations took over the conduct of the war – we sought peace, though not at any cost.

Then in October—

The final revolution?

What? No, no. The news came that the Tsar, in exile at the Black Sea, had died of the influenza plague. Deposed as he was – foolish as he had been at times – his mundane death, of a kind shared with so many of his citizens, seemed to change minds. The monarchy was restored, amid pledges of it becoming a constitutional monarchy on the British model. Alexei Nikolayevich, the Tsar's eldest son, was only thirteen years old and a haemophiliac at that. He would die young. And until he was grown, his uncle, Grand Duke Mikhail Alexandrovich, would serve as regent. These events became legends told to schoolchildren. In the Duma—

My bangle is prompting me. What about Lenin?

Who?

Umm, Vladimir Ilyich Ulyanov. Political agitator. 'Lenin' was some kind of alias. He led a revolution that October, 1917, that toppled the democratic institutions in Russia. From then on his legacy was a one-party state, under the Communists. Called the Soviet Union. I'm scanning through what the bangle can show me about it. Lasted for decades – until the 1990s, when—

Lenin? Never heard of him. A one-party state? I don't understand. Under the Tsar?

No. The Tsar – and Alexei, and his brother Mikhail, all the family – were assassinated in 1918.

But that is – obscene. Alexei, his sisters – they were children! It could not have happened that way. We were not animals.

I think we've found the jonbar hinge, Irina. Maybe it is to do with Lenin. His revolution in October was small-scale in terms of the number of people involved, but what followed – the establishment of the Soviet Union – changed the world. And nearly ended it, given how close the Soviets and the Americans came to global nuclear warfare in the decades that followed.

All because of this Lenin?

This is what I'm getting from the bangle. I can check it out with the others later . . . Lenin was the leader, the firebrand. He had been exiled, arrested, but always returned, escaped, was released . . . Maybe the authorities got to him in your reality, but not ours. And, if no Lenin – presumably no Stalin, who you hadn't heard of either.

If you are right . . . How astonishing. I have no way of judging whether one history is better than another. So many lives distorted. So many lives wiped away, I suppose, so many lives created that might never have been! Who can say? Did this Soviet Union achieve nothing worthy?

It was a brutal totalitarianism, apparently. Millions were displaced, died. But it did in the end dissolve itself peacefully, and you can't argue against that.

As opposed to having to be overthrown by force.

Yes. And, yes, it achieved some greatness. It played the most significant part in the war against Hitler, for one thing. And paid the highest price in lives. I can't believe the numbers the bangle is whispering into my head. I'm not a historian, Irina, and I never knew this. When I left home I was just a kid, really . . . Millions and millions dead, in that war.

And, achievements in space: Russia launched the first Earth-orbiting satellite. First human in space.

But at the price of millions of lives? And besides, *we*, I suspect – the Russians of my Road – have come further. Perhaps *we* listened more closely to Tsiolkovsky and Fedorov than this Lenin.

Perhaps. So, umm, then what?

So then we wait for my own auspicious birth in 1945.

*

I can only recount to you what I remember from stories muttered among my mother's generation. I do know we had a couple of decades of comparative peace, once the Kaiser's war was done, and before Hitler's invasion. And it was a time of growth, I think. Politics settled down. Lots of voting, my mother said, plebiscites and referendums and elections.

And in the country, even in the Kaluga region, there was much investment. The profits from the farms were not extracted for such follies as foreign wars, but were ploughed back into rail, roads, heavy machinery. Tractors everywhere, my mother said! And I believe the discovery of oil fields in Siberia helped with the balance of foreign trade; suddenly we became a significant exporter.

The bangle is telling me about a Depression of the 1930s. Following some kind of stock market crash. Maybe the computer systems of the time couldn't keep up with — oh, they had no computers. No AI at all. No wonder it became unstable, then.

I remember smug school lessons about that. And one of my great-aunts had been a representative at the Duma. We were humble folk from Kaluga, and one of us sat in the Duma! My family were very proud of her, and her contributions – and thereby I must have soaked up a great deal of history. Having only just emerged from under an absolute monarchy, perhaps we had a regrettable instinct for authority, for centralisation of command. But when instability came we, more soundly based, our investment structure more heavily policed, were able to weather the storm. And we had plentiful raw materials, a healthy internal market – lots of farmers wanting to buy lots of tractors!

My great-aunt, the Duma representative, was invited to attend the funeral of Tsar Alexei. He died aged thirty. His

123

son succeeded him, Alexander IV, then aged just four; Prince Mikhail served again as Regent. My aunt is quite visible in the newsreels of the time . . .

You mentioned Hitler's war.

Well – I know Hitler came to power on the back of a ruinous settlement after the previous war. As populists will do. He may have sought a global war, in fact.

It is known that, as he planned an invasion of Belgium, France and perhaps Britain in the west, he sought a non-aggression pact with Russia in the east. The Duma rejected this shabby arrangement.

Hitler had his war. He was stopped at the English Channel in the west; in the east he was pushed back from Poland by Russian and other forces. His gains looked spectacular for a time, but he was easily toppled, his armies defeated.

Malenfant has talked of this war. His grandfather fought in it, I think. He will want to know, what about America?

What of it? It was a European war. It had nothing to do with America. Although America did join, as a junior partner, the new World Congress established in 1947—

Junior partner? I'll tell Malenfant that!

My mother says I watched the opening of the Congress on a newsreel – lots of glittering royalty, including Prince Mikhail and our seventeen-year-old Tsar. I was only two years old. I do remember when Tsar Alexander married Princess Margaret of Britain – a distant cousin, but that's the royals for you. I was twelve years old by then.

But I never wanted to be a princess, you know, marrying a boy-king! For by then our nuclear rockets were already flying to orbit, old schoolmaster Konstantin's dreams were starting to come true, and *that* was where I wanted to be. It started with those old family dreams, I think. Through Tsiolkovsky

I read of the other Cosmists. Fedorov, who boldly claimed mankind's destiny is to populate space. Vernadsky, who spoke of whole planets being quickened by the activity of intelligence.

These were the dreamers, but there were practical realisations too. In particular we had nuclear energy. As I grew up, atomic power plants sprouted across Russia and beyond – growing like mushrooms, I remember my father saying as he watched the news. And, most exciting for me, experiments were made in nuclear propulsion. A closed town called Arzamas-16, in remote Russia, where the first atomic piles had been developed, now became a centre of the new technologies.

The first nuclear-thermal rocket, not much more than a portable fission pile driven into the air by superheated steam, was launched as a test around 1950. By 1955 the first crewed experiments were being flown.

So, in 1964, the first person to land on the Moon was a Russian – Leonov, as everybody knows. And the fourth was Vladimir Pavlovich Viktorenko.

Your husband?

And indeed my son's name, who you somehow encountered in a different reality, a different world . . . Yes, Vladimir would become my husband. He was thirty-five years old when he landed on the Moon – ten years older than me – a test pilot, in the days when it was thought that piloting skills were more important in spaceflight than engineering expertise.

Tell me how you met.

I could say that destiny drew us together. I was fascinated by space – I was determined to be a cosmonaut. I had maths, an engineering intuition, and practical skills. I grew up fixing tractors during summer vacations back on the family farms in Kaluga.

But as for flying, I don't have the physique, the fast reflexes – even the keen vision.

Malenfant asks, or the right gender?

Hmph. You must remember that my country, backward in 1920, had become the world's greatest industrial and economic power within fifty years. And we did not achieve that by ignoring the possible contribution of half the population. The provisional government granted universal suffrage as one of its first acts, in 1919. Before many of the other advanced nations. My gender was irrelevant.

So, anticipating that space would welcome engineers, I became the best engineer I could. My speciality, in the end, was life support and other ancillary systems – as I told you. I studied at the Vernadsky Institute in Moscow, but was soon winning grants jointly awarded by the armed forces and the space agency.

By the age of thirty I was in the space agency, and had been transferred to Akademgorodok, a city of science, engineering and experimentation in Siberia. I soon met my husband, then a senior cosmonaut.

What a place to work! We live in modern flats, in tower blocks, but we are surrounded by nature: woods of pine and birch, and in the summer the meadow grass is thigh-high. A wonderful place to raise a child. Our son was born in Akademgorodok.

As to my own career – I had undertaken several spaceflights, mostly restricted to Earth orbit, before and after the birth of my son. As a life-support specialist, I was engaged in long-duration missions. Little Vladimir was, however, just six when I was assigned to the Anteros mission – the very first to that enigmatic moon.

There had been anomalous radiation signatures which . . . Well. We have discussed this. I admit I was conflicted about taking a journey so long and so far away from my son. But his father would stay with him while I was gone.

We departed Earth in October 1981. Reached Mars in March of 1982.

So I fell into the manifold, as you call it. We emerged in this place – a different Solar System! We knew nothing of your manifold, not then; we had been transported elsewhere, as if by magic, a flying carpet.

And so you made for Persephone?

It is a large planet. Even as seen from afar it evidently had an oxygen-nitrogen atmosphere, liquid water . . . It evidently bore life. We could survive there indefinitely, we thought, exploring, while seeking a way to return to our own, umm, Road.

So we crossed the Solar System, from within the orbit of Earth to far beyond.

We attempted a landing on Persephone. You understand that our craft is designed for a direct ascent and descent: we launch vertically on our rocket plume; we land vertically, standing on the plume. We were soon in difficulties. Some combination of the thicker air and higher gravity of Persephone, and unsuspected flaws in the systems revealed only under the stress of landing—

And then the blue hoops attacked you.

Indeed.

You crashed. Some of you survived.

Not all. But, yes, I survived, and others.

Once we had stabilised our situation – once we had dug the graves – we set about inspecting our circumstances, and planning how to get off the planet, back to orbit – back out of the double trap in which we had now immersed ourselves. At the bottom of a deep gravity well, and in the wrong reality

127

altogether. All we wanted to do was to get off Persephone – and to do that we needed to find reserves of fissionable ore. I imagined we would continue with that work, or we would die trying.

But then Persephone itself intervened. Or rather, our dealings with its inhabitants became complicated.

Complicated. And you ended up here, far from your crewmates.

It is ten years now, since our landing on this world. Ten years.

Do you regret it?

The outcome, yes, of course. The motive, no. We came here to explore. We accepted the risks, unknown as they were.

Understood. I sympathise. And – Cosmism. How to be at home in the universe . . .

Yes?

I kind of think that's what I've been looking for all my life. Without knowing how to pose the question, even. And even if that question dragged me away from my mother.

And I, from my son. We will talk more.

Oh, one thing. Malenfant is here now. He has something to say about your history, after the jonbar hinge. Your history as a model of how our Russia might have been, if not for Lenin?

What's that?

'What a pity.'

TWO

On Her Trek to New Akademgorodok

20

It took only a few days for Ham's folk to tear down their home, a home where they had lived for years, Malenfant guessed, ever since they had walked here with Irina. Indeed Irina herself seemed vague on precise dates. But maybe that was a feature of her life with Ham, Malenfant speculated. It had rubbed off on her. *They* had no clocks or calendars, save, he supposed, the cycle of day and night, and Persephone's grand seasons. Hams didn't count the days; why should Irina?

Only a few days of preparation, then, and much of that was spent pulling together new travois, and repairing those they already had: ground sleds that would now have to be dragged, Malenfant reminded himself, all of a thousand kilometres to the heart of a shield volcano. The work was done quickly, with those fine-edged stone blades wielded by strong hands, cutting and slashing at leather, and slicing into the trunks of young saplings and stripping them of branches with brisk efficiency. It was evident these Hams had a limited tool set, but what they had was effective, robust, was used skilfully – and was quick and easy to make and repair, in practised hands, anyhow. The five adults took evident care to include the older children, especially Strawberry, in the process. Learning on the job.

Malenfant and the other humans tried to help, but proved

capable of screwing up even the simplest of tasks, and basically were shooed away, more or less gently.

Malenfant wondered whether, if he had come here a century back, or a thousand years, he would have found a bunch of people just like this, making, repairing and using much the same tool set.

Irina told Malenfant she had seen the Hams make and use more specialist tools when the occasion demanded. 'Once, there was a flood of the river,' she said. 'Alexandra and Nicholas showed the rest how to fashion spears with hooked barbs made from horns, to nab fish stranded in shallow flood water. Tools I never saw before, or since. They didn't keep them when the flood was done; they dumped them, broke them up for useful parts . . .'

'So the old folk remember the flood, or the drought or the stampede or whatever, that happened when they were kids, and what kind of tools were useful then. If so, a reason to cherish the oldsters. Even if they get wounded, like old Nicholas there.'

'A reason beyond simple humanity, you mean,' she said with a trace of reproof. 'Well, yes. Whereas in our societies there is so much innovation that old folk can be overwhelmed by change, lost in an unfamiliar present. My great-grandmother, born in 1860 in the shadow of serfdom, would have been baffled had she lived to have seen the space-age Moscow of 1960.'

'Kind of an obvious moral, isn't there? Our way, the *H. sapiens* way, isn't necessarily the best way.'

She snorted. 'Oh, you think so? And do you think that is the point of all this? This . . . this super Earth in a lifeless Solar System, stuffed with samples of lost life from the *real* Earth. To show us what we missed? This is clearly a comparative exercise.

But I doubt very much it is for our benefit.'

He frowned. 'Whose, then?'

'It would be useful to find out,' she said drily.

Four days after the decision to move had been made, the camp was broken down, the travois and backpacks loaded up with their bits of stuff.

And, to a hooting cry from old Nicholas, they set off.

21

For that first day (the first of *a hundred*, Malenfant reminded himself with dismay), as they dragged themselves north up the river valley, they just concentrated on the logistics. There were four travois. A Ham adult was capable of dragging one on their own, with some human help. Ham, Seth, Lola – incredibly, even the elderly Alexandra – all took a turn. Bartholomew, too, tireless and excessively strong, could take the place of a Ham.

And that was the basic pattern, for much of the time they moved.

The rest helped, one way or another. Nicholas mostly hobbled along using a suitably shaped tree branch as a crutch. Sometimes he would play-act at dragging one of the travois himself, only to fall on his butt, to the hooting laughter of the children. He did help if a travois got stuck, or had to be lifted over some boulder or other obstruction.

At times the children helped too, though they weren't much practical use. Still, the adults were patient, and seemed not to fret about the delays as the children pulled, stumbled, climbed laughing onto the cargo of the travois, and learned.

The humans took their turn, or tried to. These travois, robustly built and heavily laden, were designed for a Ham's physique rather than a human's, and so were too much for one human to pull alone. Still, of the *Charon* party, Malenfant observed that Emma and Deirdra, after learning the ropes for an hour or so each, became pretty efficient, though they tired quickly – but not so quickly as he felt he did himself, in the heavy gravity, in air that was oppressive rather than too warm, but in which he quickly sweated up.

Josh Morris, meanwhile, was the classic clumsy academic, mostly got in the way, but gamely helped where he could.

That first morning, it seemed a long time before the Sun had passed its noon height, and old Nicholas, squinting at the sky, with a barked command, called a halt for the day. Ham's people began to break down the loads, preparatory, maybe, to making camp for the night.

Malenfant dropped the pole he had been dragging with a gratitude he tried to conceal, and sought out Irina.

She walked with him to the river bank, bent to scoop up water in a leather flask. She didn't drink immediately. Malenfant knew that she had come to this world equipped with some kind of water-purification technology, as the British had, in their case tablets to drop into the supply. She had long run out, but made sure she drank only boiled water.

'So,' he said. 'Was that ten klicks? Didn't feel like it.'

She shrugged. 'Just about. I didn't count my steps but I have made such treks before, remember. It felt about right. And your colleague in the sky can give us precise locations.'

'It's pretty early to stop.' He felt impatient. He was heavily aware of the weight of journey that still lay ahead of them – one day down, ninety-nine more days to come. 'Maybe we could make more distance while we're in the swing of it.'

She pursed her lips. 'I remind you, I have done this before. It is easy to burn yourself out in the first day or two. You have to manage your resources. You will see the wisdom of it. And besides, it has been a test for the travois too – it is often the first few days when faults show up.'

Squatting by the water, they glanced back at the impromptu camp that was quickly self-assembling. One travois had already been emptied, to reveal its blunt fork shape. And indeed Ham was turning the travois over, with Lola's help, testing the surfaces and tugging at rope knots. The travois was really just two poles, cut-down tree trunks, joined in a V-shape. The person hauling it, or persons, stood at the join of the fork, and dragged the two poles, splayed, behind them, scraping over the ground.

Malenfant watched. 'I've been *calling* these things travois . . . I know the Native Americans used such things before the Europeans showed up. And I think the early fur trappers used them too.'

'Other parts of the world found similar solutions. Quick and easy to make, and actually often a better solution than wheeled vehicles on rough ground.' She shrugged. 'Otherwise, I would have shown them how to make wheels.'

He hesitated. 'You didn't teach these characters to make travois, then?'

'Certainly not.' She thought back. 'I don't, in fact, think I have *taught* them anything. I did lead them away from the Shield, from a situation they could not comprehend.' As with similar such enigmatic remarks in the past, she would say no more. 'But, no, I don't think I have donated any *Homo sapiens* innovations.'

Malenfant grinned, and pointed to the rough trousers Ham wore, as he always did. 'You gave them pockets.'

She had to laugh. 'Very well. Pockets. But aside from that . . .'

'I guess they already had fire. Stone-tipped spears. Now travois. Inventions we still use. But they are evidently all older than humanity itself.'

'Does that make you feel humble, Malenfant?'

'Probably would if I let it. Come on, I think there's a bunch of people of various species over there getting thirstier. And I can see Nicholas has nearly got the fire going.'

Hams were good at building and starting fires. Nicholas had built a tiny heap of kindling, scraps carefully carried here, in the hollow of a log. He had a sharpened stick that he caught between his hands, rubbing them back and forth to make the stick spin. His movements were strong and fast, a blur. Within minutes, no more, a curl of smoke was rising towards his smiling face.

When Malenfant woke next morning, he found Bartholomew hovering over his pallet. The light was dim, under a tent improvised with a leather sheet hastily hung between a couple of low trees.

And when Malenfant tried to move, he understood why Bartholomew was here.

'Shit.'

'Yes?'

'Every joint aches. Every damn muscle. Ow, my *feet*.'

'Seem to recall you wanted to go on yesterday, after Irina decided we should quit.'

'Yeah, yeah.'

'Does anything feel broken?'

'No—'

'Good. I'll go and find a worthy cause to treat. As your contemporaries would have said, have a nice day.' He stood lithely, turned and walked away.

So Malenfant began the second day.

It wasn't so bad when he started moving, and had some breakfast inside him. Then he grudgingly allowed Emma to lead him, Deirdra and Josh through some yoga moves. They all tended to their more vulnerable parts, notably hands, feet and crotches, places that got rubbed, before getting to work and helping the Hams to load up the travois once again. And then they walked.

As soon as they had begun, Malenfant thought, or maybe his body reminded him, it was as if yesterday had never stopped. It was the same physical effort, the same kind of landscape, the sparsely wooded hinterland of the river valley. The same actors in the same show. Even the weather felt much the same, a kind of heavy, low-cloud oppressiveness that on Earth might have presaged a storm, but here was pretty much the norm.

But as they walked the river slowly changed. Overall it had to be flowing faster the further up its course they walked, but it depended on the landscape, the broader primordial valley through which the river flowed, here pushing vigorously through narrows, and elsewhere, in more open country, curving into wide meanders or pools.

And it was where the river flowed more gently that the animals came to congregate.

They kept their distance from the human party, naturally enough. Deirdra held up her bangle to capture images, and Josh made scribbled notes on his pads.

Malenfant generally made out only enigmatic, shadowy shapes. Still, as he plodded along, it was quite a thrill to see a bunch of some kind of elephant types, the adults dipping their long trunks into the water, calves trotting between the legs of their parents as if pushing through a forest.

'You're staring,' Emma murmured at one point as he trailed a little behind the group. 'Never had you down as a wildlife fan.'

'Spent too much time locked up inside some huge machine or other. I know this isn't our world. Those aren't elephants.

Any more than those critters' – and he pointed to a herd of big, skittish, lolloping beasts on the far bank – 'are kangaroos. And that roar' – a distant, thunder-like rumble – 'isn't a lion. This isn't my kind of landscape at all. But—'

'But it feels like it, doesn't it? I don't know what we are going to find in the rest of this world. If it's all random sampling there's no way of predicting. But just here – according to Josh, these are the kind of critters that populated the world when humans evolved. A Pleistocene fauna.'

'We killed them all off.'

'Well, yes. But that took some time. We *evolved* alongside these critters. And that's why you feel at home, on some deep level. Even if you don't understand it.'

'Yeah. I feel at home.' He kissed her brow.

She smiled but pulled back. 'Please, Malenfant. Not in front of the Neanderthals—'

There was a high-pitched squeal. Malenfant heard an adult, he thought it was Lola, yelling angrily.

They turned.

One of the smaller children, whose name he had never learned – if she had one yet – was evidently entranced by the roo types, those big, clumsy, toy-like critters on the far side of the water. '*Funny! Funny!*' Repeating the human word – and from her accent it sounded like it had been picked up from Deirdra – she stumbled forward, carelessly, into the water.

Lola, calling, ran after her, as did Deirdra. And then Bartholomew.

And Malenfant, further away, could only watch the disaster unfold.

The river bed just here was carpeted with boulders – basalt, maybe – big, black, smooth and slippery, even when they weren't draped in moss and weed. The kid, staring at the animals across the river, not watching her footing at all, only took a couple of steps before her bare right foot slipped and got caught between two boulders. And as she lifted her left foot for the next step, she fell forward, over her right leg.

Malenfant could *hear* the snap. Neanderthal bones were tough, but not that tough. The little girl screamed in pain.

Bartholomew was first to reach her, moving in a mechanical blur, beating even Lola – who might, Malenfant realised now, be the kid's mother.

The others dropped their loads, the travois. While the other adults rushed over to help, with Emma and Deirdra following as best they could, old Nicholas grimly began dismantling the load of one of the travois. It was evident they were going no further today.

Malenfant looked back. He saw that the roos, that alluring vision on the far side of the river, had vanished. Then he went over to help Nicholas unload the travois.

And still the kid called, through tears and cries of pain. *'Funny! Ah-h! Funny!'*

As the rest made camp, Bartholomew tended to the child, with Deirdra as a makeshift nurse, reassuringly smiling.

Bartholomew quickly administered anaesthetics, diagnosed a clean break to the shin, and, with the girl unconscious, briskly set the bone. He made splints from wooden slats and bound up the leg with rope. Ham and the others let him work. They seemed just to accept it, as they might the wind or the rain, or the sprouting of some edible mushroom. If the world provided what they needed, they took without question.

With the girl falling asleep in the arms of Alexandra, Bartholomew drew Malenfant and Irina aside. 'I'm not belittling the care these people show to each other. Why – old Nicholas over there is an amputee. But the longer I can tend to her the better chance she will have of a clean, pain-free, seamless recovery.'

'I wouldn't bank on that,' Irina murmured. 'It's not their way, to transport the injured far.'

That was enigmatic. But Malenfant learned what she meant on day five of the trek.

22

They came to a place where the river crowded through low cliffs of layered sandstone, with a lot of shadowed places, overhangs and folds and undercut shelters, not unlike the place Ham's people had made their home.

They drew to a stop, out in the open, by the river. Everyone seemed wary, the humans out of some gut instinct, Malenfant thought – good place for an ambush, his hind brain was telling him – and the Neanderthals, he suspected, because *they already knew something was here.*

But the only sound was the subdued murmur of the flowing water – and, from somewhere, what sounded like the cry of a bird.

Irina nodded. 'This is the place.'

She and Ham walked forward, he with his arms spread wide and his hands open, empty, and she waving and calling out – words Malenfant's bangle translated as 'Hello! We're back! Anybody home?'

This went on for thirty long seconds.

Then, at last, a small figure came running out of the shade of an overhang. '*Rina! Rina!*'

It was a Ham child, a little boy, not much older than broken-leg girl. He bore an old wound too, a crimson stripe across a bare belly that looked like a healed burn. His giant nose glistened with snot, but even that managed to look cute.

Irina held out her arms, but Malenfant saw her brace; she knew what was coming. The boy leapt at her, a boulder of muscle and fur and snot, and sent her staggering back when he hit.

Now, one by one, more folk came out of the rock overhangs, adults, children. They quickly mingled with the newcomers, breaking up into groups of two or three for gabbled conversations.

Emma stood with Malenfant. She pointed. 'Look at that. They have a leather sheet over most of that overhang, just like Ham's camp, but they've sprinkled it with sand, or crushed rock I guess. Hardly perfect camouflage but it fits in – distracts the eye.'

Malenfant hadn't even noticed. 'Looks like a prop from *Blazing Saddles*. They seem wary. The silence as we approached, the camouflage.'

'You're just not used to them, not yet.' That was Irina, who came walking over to them, trailed by the little boy. 'This is a tougher landscape than nearer the coast, where we were. Bigger predators roaming. And other kinds of people too.'

Malenfant frowned. 'You mean, aside from us and Ham's folk?'

Irina said, 'Also they have an instinct to be wary of their own kind. On first contact anyhow. They live in small bands, remember – I've seen few much bigger than Ham's in numbers. And when other folk do show up, especially in numbers like this, it's unusual, and they are cautious. Maybe because of what might have driven such an emigration, rather than the people themselves.'

Malenfant thought further. 'So we got here, what, five days' walk out of the old camp? Might have been four if not for the leg-break. Close enough for some kind of social contact to be possible, but not so close that hunting ranges, say, are going to overlap.'

Irina nodded. 'Now you're getting it. They spread out, not too far, but far enough.'

'And yet,' Malenfant pressed, 'they seem to recognise *you*.'

She hesitated before replying. 'Well,' she said at last, 'I am part of the reason these people are here in the first place. In this valley . . . I led them here, you see. All the Hams who would follow me out.'

Emma asked, 'Out? Out of where?'

But Malenfant thought he saw it. 'Out of the Shield. Away from your colleagues' camp, where you crashed?'

Reluctantly, she nodded. 'Essentially. I had spotted this valley, leading south to the equatorial sea, on our own imaging from space. I think I always had it tucked in the back of my mind as an escape route from the Shield if we ever needed one. I never imagined I would use it to take the Hams away. They came in a crowd, at first. They were uncomfortable with that, as was I. So, as soon as we were off the central massif and had reached the deepening valley, groups started to split off.'

'And they made camps like these?'

'Right. Just used the local resources, and dug in. I think the first were probably too close to the massif, but I couldn't persuade them, let alone coerce them. I had done all I could. This group will take in Leaf, now. With her broken leg.'

Emma asked, 'Why would they take her?'

Irina looked at her as if she were the alien subspecies. 'Because that's what these people do. If they can. Maybe a couple of our group, the adults, will stay too. Even if not, the locals will help the kid. But conversely, a couple of the residents here will follow us. This is how they live. Splitting off, looking to find partners outside the home band.'

Malenfant thought that through. 'And this will continue to happen all the way to the Shield? This fissioning and fusing?'

'I expect so. Ham will stay with us, though.'

Emma frowned. 'Why do you say that?'

'Because he was the first I persuaded to come with me. I think he sees further than his fellows. He will follow this through to the end.'

But, Malenfant realised, he himself, right now, had no idea what that end would be.

23

The next day worked out much as Irina had predicted. Most of Ham's group stayed with him and Irina; one new young woman joined, in exchange for the young male Seth.

After the short rest, and with fresher legs, they actually made faster progress, or so Malenfant judged. He began to hope that they would still make their destination, the heart of the Shield, in something like the hundred days he had budgeted in his head.

On the ninth day, and then the fourteenth, they encountered more groups of Neanderthals, one in another sandstone overhang, and the other in the heart of a forest clump. They were reclusive, suspicious.

And their shelters also had the ubiquitous leather sheets to keep out the rain.

'It's the way you might use parachute silk during a survival training exercise,' Malenfant murmured to Emma on the fourteenth day. 'What the hell is that stuff?'

'Patience,' she murmured. 'I suspect all will be revealed.'

Maybe she would be proved right in the end.

But in the short term things got only more mysterious.

On the sixteenth day – the river now getting narrower and faster-flowing – they saw another group, off in the distance.

Bulky like Ham's folk, these were crouched on the open ground, near a tributary of the river, around some kind of kill. They were butchering the meat with what looked like big stone blades. When they glanced around, Malenfant saw blood smeared around their mouths, adults and children alike.

Ham's people hung back, watching warily. Then, still wary, they started to move on.

'So,' Malenfant said to Irina. 'More of your folk? We ain't going over for a night of socialising?'

'I thought your eyes were sharp, Malenfant the pilot,' she said softly. 'Take a closer look.'

In the kit they had the binoculars they had retrieved from the wrecked *Charon*; now Irina handed these to Malenfant.

They looked like Ham's folk. The robust bodies, the big, thrust-forward heads with those ferocious eye ridges. But—

'No clothes,' Malenfant said now. 'No tools, save for those big stone blades.' He tried to think what else was missing. 'Fire. They haven't built a fire.'

'I call them robusts,' Irina said. 'I don't know the human family tree well enough to go beyond that.'

'More primitive than Ham's folk,' Deirdra said. Her young eyes, Malenfant noted wryly, seemed sharp enough to see what was going on without the binoculars.

'They look it,' Irina murmured. 'But I have grown wary of words like "primitive". Ham and his people have a very sophisticated way of life which, I am pretty sure, lasted on Earth a great deal longer than the sojourn of *Homo sapiens* to date. They can make things *I* could not. Who, then, is the primitive? But these people – yes. No fire, no clothing. Perhaps they are an ancestral sort to the Hams, and, perhaps, our kind.'

'But that needn't mean they come from some earlier time,' Josh said. 'In terms of the sampling that seems to have populated this world, I mean. Older kinds of humans lingered on, didn't they, side by side? Until *we*—'

'Until we evolved,' Emma said, 'and almost every animal larger than us went extinct. Including our own cousins.'

Irina said now, 'We have encountered this kind before. Once, I saw them mate. A male from Ham's group, a female from the robusts.'

'Wow,' Malenfant said. 'I bet that was – vigorous. Dinner and a movie first?'

Deirdra didn't seem amused. 'Was there a baby? I guess you wouldn't know . . .'

Irina said, 'I have seen other such couplings, and some of them did produce offspring. Isn't it the definition of a species that its members must be able to breed with each other? Well, then, the "human species" is a wider category than I for one ever imagined.'

But her manner was odd as she said this. She was hiding something, Malenfant thought. Mystery within mystery. But he had long learned there was no point pressing her.

Ham's folk were already moving on. Quietly, Malenfant stowed away the binoculars, and they followed.

That was the sixteenth day. It was on the twenty-second, by Malenfant's count, that they saw the bodies.

By now the ground was slowly rising, and becoming more barren.

And on the bare ground the corpses were like dumped shop-window dummies, Malenfant thought. Animals circled. Birds wheeled. Or at any rate, what looked like birds.

They approached cautiously. Ham shouted, and the scavengers backed off or flew away. But Malenfant was aware that they didn't go far, and he was encircled by jealous eyes.

Corpses. Broken bodies. Given what was left after some time – hours, days? – of attention from the scavengers, it took a while for Malenfant and the others to piece together what they were seeing. At first these looked like some breed of chimpanzee, ape-like bodies with brownish fur, the tallest only a metre and a half if stretched out, Malenfant thought. The young were a lot smaller. The tiniest of all must have been a suckling baby. A choice morsel almost ripped to pieces.

Josh Morris, a handkerchief over his mouth to keep out the stench and the flies, proved more analytical than usual. 'Chimp-like heads,' he said. 'Small brains, comparatively. But, look at the hips, the legs . . .'

Where they were even partially intact Malenfant could see the bodies had been slim, the legs straight, though the arms looked too long. And the hands and feet were similar – feet with toes like fingers – as if the feet could be used to grasp as well as support a standing posture.

'Bipeds,' Deirdra murmured. 'Ape-like. But bipeds.'

'Not entirely,' Josh said. 'The grasping feet, the long arms – well, they could probably climb trees. And the hairy bodies . . . Early hominins, then. Earlier than Ham and his kind, or the robusts, clearly.' He glanced around. 'There is no forest nearby, certainly not the dense tropical forest that would have suited these creatures. Presumably this is a sampling gone wrong.'

'I'll say,' Emma said. 'They must have come out of the blue portals baffled. Jumped by predators as soon as they landed.'

'Oh, no,' Bartholomew said grimly. 'I don't think it was like that at all. *That* wasn't what killed them. The scavengers found their corpses, already dead. If you want my own diagnosis, these bodies show every indication of a fall, from height. *That* was what killed them. The pattern of bone breaks, the ruptured internal organs, the burst stomachs—'

'OK, OK.' Malenfant looked at Emma, Deirdra. 'We saw this. Or something like it. A blue wheel high in the sky. What looked like bodies, raining out of it. Into mid-air. It was what screwed up our landing—'

'No, *they* screwed up,' Deirdra said angrily. 'The Engineers. Whoever. And this was the result. We move on. But we do not forget. These people deserve that much.'

Malenfant looked at her. Disturbed at a glimpse of a hardening core inside her, young as she still was. She was changing, he thought. Or emerging.

He just nodded.

After a respectful, silent pause, they moved on.

The land still rose steadily, and life grew sparser – not that that made it any safer for the travellers, Malenfant became aware, as the pace of both prey and predator species was that much faster in the open.

Around day thirty, for two whole days they were tracked by what looked like a big, muscular leopard.

Otherwise, every few days they encountered another Ham band. And, as before, people came and went, swapping one band for another. But every band they encountered remembered Irina, and how she had brought them here.

And on the fortieth day, some four hundred kilometres north of their starting point, they reached what looked like the source of their river, a small spring north of all the tributaries that fed it further downstream.

From here, the land became noticeably steeper.

24

As they ascended it got hotter, drier, the vegetation sparser, although, following Irina and the Hams, they still tracked sluggish, silt-laden rivers, heading steadily upstream. Just now the Hams seemed determined to walk parallel to the river, but not too close to the water itself – maybe fifty metres out.

And there seemed to be a persistent wind in your face as you walked, as if the air was rolling past you down the slope. As, perhaps, it was, Malenfant thought: a *katabatic wind*, and his bangle quietly confirmed that random memory. A drainage wind, as air spilled down from a higher altitude. For sure there was plenty of higher ground ahead for that wind to come from, and there was the planet's heavy gravity to help drag it down.

He tried to ignore it, as he tried to ignore much of his physical experiences just now.

On the fifth day in this terrain, he found his thoughts wandering.

That wasn't unusual. He thought over a lot of stuff during the long hours of just walking, or travois-dragging. Some of it was his usual general anxiety concerning those around him, in this latest perilous venture; he couldn't seem to put aside a duty of care. And some of it was the usual cosmic angst – a kind of general astonishment he still felt at being alive and functioning so far removed from his home world, even his home time zone – astonishment at all he had done and seen, at being transported to this place, a different Solar System, for God's sake.

'You're muttering again, Malenfant.' Deirdra walked beside him in the traces, with Bartholomew on her other side. She spoke in gasps as she hauled.

'I am?'

'It's not an uncommon habit, Bartholomew says. For you, anyhow. For older people in general.'

Malenfant glared across at Bartholomew, who did not react.

'Memory almost full, eh?'

'Hmm?'

'My brain's like an early cellphone. You would get that message when their chips started to get clogged up.'

'A fascinating snippet from the dead past. What was it you were specifically thinking about?'

The meaning of life and death.

'Hell, I don't know. What were *you* thinking about? . . . Come on. Tell me. I do think you're too quiet sometimes as well. Too shut in.'

'You sound like my mother.'

'So you're thinking about her, right?'

She shrugged. 'Not really. Well, maybe. I'm thinking about the solstice house-builds, if you want to know.'

He had seen some of this, during his time in the England of AD 2469. 'Right. When you and your neighbours get together to put up a house for the new engaged couple, or whatnot.'

'Yeah. I've been doing that since I was a little kid. As young as Strawberry, maybe. My dad used to take me over . . . I suppose I miss—'

'The rhythms of your old life.'

'Yeah. My mother and I did become very close after Dad died. I miss the sound of her voice.' She looked at him uncertainly. 'Does that make sense?'

'Oh, yes. I missed family the whole time I was away on one mission or another, military, in space. Even if Emma never believed it, quite. The sound of my father's voice. And my son's. Michael.'

'But you flew in space anyhow. Just as—'

'Just as you have been drawn away. Even further than I went. Off into the manifold. But you'll go back, one day.'

'Will I? You never did, Malenfant. And I . . . I don't quite trust myself. My future self. No, it's not that. It's like I have a magnet inside me, a magnet inside a paper doll.'

He knew damn well she had long-term goals. Her ultimate purpose was in fact to figure out why her Earth, in her home timeline, was doomed to destruction a few thousand years after she was born. And that was after she had tried, using Malenfant and others on the way, to *save* her world. Tried and failed. You couldn't get a much longer-range vision than that.

But he hated to see her beat herself up like this.

'Don't think like that. You'll go home some day.'

'That's just it, Malenfant. I'm not sure I ever will. Because' – and she rubbed her bangle absently, her relic of home – 'whenever it's a choice between going back and going *on*, further out, I always choose *out*. I always have so far. I think I always will. This pull inside me, the magnet inside the doll . . . Are you listening, Malenfant?'

'Yes. Of course. Sorry. But I'm also wondering why we are stopping.'

The rest of the troop was indeed slowing to a halt, the bearers still clasping the frames of their travois, looking around anxiously at the river, the bare landscape. Old Nicholas too, rheumy eyes squinting, those big nostrils flaring as he sniffed the air.

And then Malenfant heard the sound.

Deep, throaty rumbles. Not roars. Just an announcement of a presence, coming from the landscape to his left, the river to his right.

He peered that way. Animals, distant, like clouds in the dusty air.

The regular humans, Josh, Emma, Deirdra, Malenfant – even Irina – seemed to huddle closer together, as if by some instinct. Malenfant stood tall, trying not to let his own nervousness show.

He made out details. A herd, crossing the riverine plain. He saw low-slung bodies, solid, muscular, set on stout, widespread legs. Truly massive heads, he thought, heads that almost looked too big for the bodies, with big jaws that gaped and closed. Evidently some way off, the beasts were working their way through a clump of trees, a rarity on this dry slope. And Malenfant saw how, despite the low-slung bodies, those heads could rise up, those big jaws could reach at low-hanging branches and pull them down. He even saw one beast rear up on hind legs, its low body twisting back to reach higher.

He heard more low rumbles, like distant artillery fire. The huge voices of the beasts.

Deirdra seemed to be back to her usual mixture of sensible caution and wonder. 'I'm guessing that however big I think those animals are—'

'They're bigger,' Irina said flatly. 'And faster too.'

'Faster?'

'They will take vegetation, but they are basically carnivores. Hunters. Clumsy, but hunters.'

Josh Morris, notebook in hand, was looking at the animals through their one set of binoculars. 'Question is, *what* are they? They are like lizards. Like huge – salamanders. Amphibians for sure, the way they stay close to the river.' He lowered the binoculars and frowned. 'Up to now we've seen a lot of exotic life forms. Down on the lower plains, towards the coast. Including exotic kinds of humans, of course. But it was all – familiar. Human-era stuff. Elephants and lions . . . Even if they are now extinct, on Earth. *This* is different.'

Josh glanced at his notes, made a few marks.

Malenfant knew Josh used the bangles for communication; even, cautiously, for information, from the encyclopaedia-like database in its memory. But he always wrote out his own notes: in a tiny, crabby hand, to use up as little space as possible in his few precious notebooks salvaged from the *Charon* crash, and in pencil so he could erase stuff too. Malenfant had the feeling that if he ever made it back home with these journals, Josh Morris's work on this version of Persephone could be as celebrated as Lewis and Clark's accounts – or, to take a British example, the data Darwin brought back from the *Beagle*.

Malenfant asked, 'So you know what those big . . . salamander beasts . . . are?'

'I think so. Given I never specialised in palaeontology, you know. And given that all palaeontology relies on trace relics, preserved by chance, so you can only ever *guess* at what living things actually looked like—'

'This isn't a seminar, Josh.' *This is survival*, he didn't add. 'Go ahead, leap to a few hasty conclusions.'

'OK.' He put down his notes with a sigh. 'Look. The creatures we encountered at first – including the Hams, actually, the types of people. And the vegetation. I think they came from the age we call the Pleistocene. Meaning, from the last couple of million years. Which is why they looked familiar to us.'

Malenfant thought that over. 'Relatively familiar. But the salamanders come from some other epoch,' he guessed. 'Older. Right? How old? You said two million years for the Pleistocene. What now, ten, twenty—'

'Try more than two *hundred* million.' He looked miserable as he said it.

'Shit,' Malenfant murmured. 'Shit! That's astounding. What a discovery. Hey, why the long face about it?'

'Because it's outrageous. Yet the evidence is here, all around us. Two hundred million years ago, or more – that was the Triassic age, as the geologists call it. There was one massive continent on Earth. Like a huge Australia, dry and weathered at the centre, not much in the way of nutrients. Not a great time for life. But there *was* life, in the temperate latitudes. Your big salamander beasts were from early in the period, relatively. Carnivorous amphibians. So it's as if you have two geological eras, widely separated in time, jammed up against each other. It's more as if the sampling that we've seen—'

'The blue wheels. People dropping out of the sky.'

'It really is as if it is being done at random – from different points in Earth's history. And the results are just being dumped here, all mixed up. Maybe it's like the games we played as kids at school. Could an antelope with a machine gun beat a giant meat-eating frog? Could King Kong beat Superman?'

And Malenfant was reminded how recent was the jonbar

hinge that separated his own reality from that of Josh, the spacefaring Brit. More recent than Superman, then. Not to mention King Kong.

Josh went on, 'Maybe that's all it is, to the World Engineers. A kind of game. No, an arena. Where one kind of creature from Earth's past, or even one ecology type, is tested against another.'

Malenfant thought that through. 'Well, that sounds crazy. But it's exactly what it looks like, Josh. And until we get a better idea, let's run with it as a working hypothesis . . . We still have to figure out *why*, though.'

He heard distant voices call.

'Sounds like our friends are moving on. I wonder what the eggs of big carnivorous frogs taste like.'

Josh shuddered. 'Sir, I sincerely hope I never find out.'

They walked on.

After ten more days of steady climbing, they reached what felt like a distinctly different landscape.

The weather seemed more temperate here, cooler, moister, the air a little less thick. Josh mused that perhaps with altitude the conditions were becoming a little more Earthlike, and a little more hospitable to life that had come from Earth – though there was nothing to be done about the force of gravity, which remained at its twenty-five per cent excess.

There was more profuse vegetation here: clumps of conifers and ferns and cycads, and a few splashes of colour that were flowering plants: magnolias, poppies. But there was no grass.

And there was animal life here, evidently. On these great broad uplands, much of it open despite the forest clumps, great herds could be dimly glimpsed, far distant. There were birds, too, closer by. Big, ungainly creatures with fluffy feathers, that would thrust out of a clump of trees if disturbed and fly raggedly away, squawking and honking their protest.

It was on the twentieth day after the salamanders that they came upon the last of the Ham camps – the last of the settlements made by the Hams who Irina had brought out of the caldera zone, she told them.

'Or rather, the first group to split off when we came down this way,' Irina murmured as they approached this group.

Malenfant saw what he was coming to recognise as the typical architecture of such a camp: a well-chosen rock bluff, shelters created with sheets of leather. But it looked to him as if some of this had been abandoned, the group shrunk down from some maximum.

'It was early,' she went on. 'Only six days after coming off the flank of the Shield itself. But there were some among them who were sickly . . . It was thought best not to risk those lives by going further. Their families, and some others, stayed with them. In the end, because of those special conditions, it was a large settlement for a Ham camp.'

These individuals seemed more cautious than other groups they had encountered, Still, Ham and his people were made welcome here, as were the humans, grudgingly.

There was the usual couple of days and nights of hunting, kit-mending and, in the night, some noisy Ham humping.

When they left, though, it was noticeable that none of Ham's group split off to stay behind, and none of the sedentary group came with Ham. Malenfant had noticed nothing like negotiation, nor any obvious disputes. It simply didn't happen this time.

As far as Malenfant was concerned, all this just deepened the mystery of whatever it was that had driven Irina to leave the caldera camp of her fellows, and had driven so many of the Hams to follow her.

And now, Irina said, they were only a few days' walk from the Shield itself.

They left in the morning.

25

Soon, with the increasing altitude, the vegetation, the animal life – even the air – seemed to be thinning out. And as they climbed steadily rising ground, Malenfant saw what looked like a range of worn cliffs, their bases still invisible, still over the horizon. This was the edge of the Shield itself, he knew. The local Olympus Mons.

They came to what Irina said was the last big forest clump, which pressed close to the latest river, or rather stream, they were following. It seemed wider than Irina or Ham remembered: a barrier, right in front of them.

They paused to debate their options, humans and Hams separately, with Irina as a go-between. To pass all the way around the forest clump was a detour, it meant backing up before they even began – and they would be out in the open more than they would have preferred. On the other hand, any path by the water would be tough for the travois to cross – and, trapped by the river, they would be suckers in the face of any attack.

The travois difficulty trumped the rest. They backed up and circled west then north, passing just outside the thinning ranks of trees. Malenfant gloomily figured it had cost them a day to that point.

Which was when the dinosaurs came crashing out of the forest.

It was a flock, heading west, making for the open plain. The travellers had to shrink back, fast, to let them pass.

Malenfant saw them in glimpses, masses of muscular flesh hurtling past in a burst of scattered greenery. *Duckbills.* They were duckbills, a *Jurassic Park* label Malenfant had to dig out of his memory, but quickly confirmed by Josh's pattern-matching with his bangle.

Fast as the duckbills ran, such a flock – or herd? – took a perceptible time to cross their path, and Malenfant and the rest could only wait. Each one a hefty quadruped with a strange extended face, and a big colourful crest over its skull. A bill that, Josh muttered, it was thought to have evolved to strain vegetation from the water. The males had more vivid colours than the females, but as they ran they all gave off a surprisingly loud honking, sounds created in the cavernous hollows of their skulls.

Malenfant dreaded meeting whatever was chasing these fleeing duckbills.

He glanced around at his group, making sure they kept together and kept back. Ham and his people had their thrusting-spears at the ready, he saw. Which was some reassurance.

But not much, when the predators finally emerged.

The young came out first.

Few smaller than the size of an adult human, they were nightmares of teeth and claws, and scaly skin from which livid green feathers protruded in tufts. A blur of movement, they snarled and snapped as they burst from the forest cover, hissing after the prey, taking sideswipe nips at each other as they crowded, and glaring at the human party as they passed.

Under Irina's stern command Malenfant and the rest stayed dead still. 'These are just the young,' Irina murmured. 'The chicks. But, believe me – I once saw one take down an adult Ham. Dead in a heartbeat, throat ripped out, and the belly opened up for the feeding, probably even before the exposed heart had stopped beating. Probably. Just one chick. So – keep – still . . .'

These are just the young.

Now the parent came smashing its way through the forest thicket. Malenfant cowered back.

Over ten metres tall, surely. Startling green skin covered in scales and tufty, oddly comical feathers. Eyes the size of grapefruit – a ruby grapefruit cut in two, Malenfant thought, for they were a vivid red. Small but useful-looking grasping hands. And oddly slow-moving, surely because of the mass of its main, astonishing feature, a truly huge head, more like the claw of a mechanical excavator than anything biological.

It barely seemed to notice the humans, even the bristling spears of the Hams, as it lumbered by.

The ground shook, as if an eighteen-wheeler was passing.

When it had safely gone, Malenfant felt the tension seep palpably out of the group.

They started to pick up the travois and their other gear.

Josh, particularly, seemed shocked, trembling.

Deirdra went to him, and Malenfant followed. Deirdra rubbed Josh's back. 'Hey,' she said gently. 'Hey. It's gone now.'

Josh seemed to be struggling for self-control. Malenfant felt he admired him hugely.

Josh said at length, 'China.'

Malenfant shook his head. 'China? What the hell *was* that

thing?' But he suspected he knew the answer already. *Jurassic Park*, again.

Joshua, reading his bangle, muttered a confirmation. *T. rex* – or a similar species as near as damn it.

Josh said the beast was an effective ambush hunter on its own – and what made it more lethal yet was the way it evidently hunted in family packs, with its own young, the chicks, faster than the parent, vicious, relentless, flushing out and disabling the prey. It was a pattern of predation that had been all but invisible to the archaeologists, Josh said, though some had made smart guesses.

'And China?'

'The tyrannosaur evolved in China, and then crossed land bridges to America, where it made its main range . . . A successful species, then . . . But more muddle! All the life here. *Dinosaurs*, now. An entirely different epoch from the salamanders. Or the Neanderthals. All of it! All these forms of life just jammed together, across space and time. All jumbled up, like this is one tremendous snow-globe. It's such a muddle . . . Oh, God!'

Abruptly, he burst into tears.

Malenfant stood by silently. Deirdra patiently rubbed Josh's back, over and over.

And Emma, wordless, went to break the *Charon* radio out of its pack, so Josh could talk to Lighthill for a while.

26

They passed more milestones.

Now they were about seven hundred kilometres north of Irina's camp at the river mouth, after around seventy days' walking. Overall they had kept more or less to that target of ten klicks per day.

Malenfant tried not to count the days.

Maybe that was because Josh Morris evidently was keeping a count in his notebooks. And Malenfant thought Irina was counting too, in her head, as she led this little expedition, on a journey she had made at least once before. A count of the days, as a rough means of keeping track.

But at the other extreme were the Hams, who, quite evidently, didn't count at all, because they didn't need to. It seemed to Malenfant that at any moment, if you were a Ham, you knew who was with you, everybody important in the world was within touching distance – you always knew *where* you were. Right here. It was as if every day was as perfect as it could be, with future and past dimming in comparison. A rolling optimum, Malenfant supposed.

He found he envied them, when his own head, during the too long, too silent hours of walking, filled up with plans and schemes, what-ifs and regrets.

He found himself oddly envying Emma too. Or at least admiring her.

Obviously Emma was more like he was – from the same cultural background, albeit not from identical time streams and from different variants of their fractured relationships. She was used to planning long term, both her own life and such magnificent achievements as missions to Phobos. But she didn't seem to obsess about it the whole time. Didn't fret about what might befall them on Day Ninety-Some of this endless trek, as Malenfant did. Day to day, she seemed to live in the moment too. She did more than her share of the hauling. She talked a lot to Josh, about his life, his dreams, about his observations of the world unfolding around them. She spoke to Irina, evidently trying to puzzle out the very different culture the Russian had come from. Deirdra too seemed fascinated by this 'Cosmism', which Malenfant, himself from an astronautics background, had barely heard of.

And Emma spoke to the Hams, or anyhow shared their strange, fractured, in-your-face, moment-by-moment talks. Conversation with a Ham was more like a pooling of streams of consciousness, Malenfant had concluded. It was all about the now. He'd have said it was like talking to small children, except that it wasn't, and that was a deeply patronising observation. Emma evidently got it, though.

In short, Malenfant thought she was perhaps the most balanced, most sane human being he had ever met, and he envied her that quality. Even as he loved her for it.

Meanwhile, in the external world, they approached that wall of low cliffs. A wall that surrounded a shield volcano six hundred kilometres across.

It took a day to get through the cliffs. Irina and Ham knew passes. There was little real climbing, to everyone's relief. But the passes were twisty, narrow, rubble-strewn. It was a tough day, before they broke through the top of the cliff line, and made it up onto a plateau.

Irina announced that they were on the Shield proper, at last.

And then a steady slope, that got steeper yet, as they walked on, and on.

27

In the dim daylight, under a stubborn layer of low cloud, the grass cover was thin or non-existent, the trees lone, scattered. The tree types were a jumble too, it seemed to Malenfant. Some looked deciduous, even up here, some more like conifers. Horsetails and ferns, which Josh said were very ancient forms, in evolutionary terms. And there were remarkable trees that Josh called lycopsids, maybe thirty metres tall and a metre wide, lacking side branches, and a crown of blade-like leaves at the top.

More antiques from a jumble of epochs, to offend Josh anew.

As for animal life, Malenfant figured that the lack of cover of any kind over much of this tilted plain must make it unattractive for the usual game of predator and prey – though he did spot a few birds in the trees, and things that *looked* like birds but were surely too big and bony . . .

They walked on, slowly climbing higher and higher. The trees got more sparse, and meanwhile that cloud, mostly unbroken, got lower and lower.

Until they ascended into a kind of fog, grey and cold. Irina and Ham led them over more or less bare rock, evidently following some kind of direction-finding instinct as much as any landmarks Malenfant could see.

The camp they made that night was chilly, and Malenfant woke to find himself coughing in the pervasive mist.

About noon on the next day – the sixth on the Shield proper – they broke out of the cloud, into brighter light. The Sun hung, shrunken but still brilliant, in a sky that was pale blue, and scattered with higher cloud layers. The slope stretched ahead of Malenfant just as before, studded with isolated trees, or occasional forest clumps.

'But,' Malenfant said aloud, his spirit lifting, 'that prospect looks a hell of a lot more cheerful in the sunshine than it did before.'

Josh showed him his altimeter, a simple device scavenged from the wreck of the *Charon*, and adjusted with hand markings for Persephone's un-Earthly conditions. 'We're around four hundred metres high, Malenfant. Not that high in the bigger scheme of things, but—'

'But high enough. We're above one cloud deck, already.'

'All of which will be lower than on Earth, of course.' He blinked around, smiling. 'We hardly had any days as clear as this, did we? Not down at sea level. Amazing what a difference a bit of sunshine makes.'

'I totally agree,' Bartholomew said. He produced two tiny vials of cream, and handed them to Malenfant and Josh. 'Put this on.'

Malenfant automatically took his tube. 'Sun block,' he said. 'You're kidding. Bartholomew, we're barely in this system's habitable zone.'

'And the air is treacherously thin. Put it on. Twenty-fifth-century tech, Malenfant. Should protect you for, oh, weeks.'

'You've a gift for spoiling the moment, Tin Man.'

'I'll take that as a compliment.' Bartholomew walked off with tubes of the stuff for Irina, Emma, Deirdra.

Josh was squinting into the distance, eyes shielded from the Sun with a hand bruised and callused by weeks of hauling.

Malenfant came to stand by him again. 'What is it? What do you see?'

'Not sure.' He fumbled in his pack, producing their one set of binoculars.

Malenfant just shielded his own eyes and looked . . .

He saw it now.

At first he could only make out a shadow, sweeping over the rocky ground. Long, bare, clean, angular. Whatever was casting the shadow, in the air, was low, skimming only metres maybe above the bare rock. Surely too big for any bird. Some kind of plane, a glider? Something to do with the Russians? But Irina wasn't reacting as if that were it.

Now he made out wings. Long, fragile-looking, reduced to fine black lines when seen edge on. Wings that dwarfed a compact central body. And he saw a head on a long neck, with a sharp beak, it seemed, and what looked like bony protuberances at the back – a forked shape, some kind of keel? All this in silhouette; he could make out no colour.

Before he had got a full grasp of it, it had turned away, and receded into the distance, further up the slope.

'Damn it,' he said.

Irina stood with him. 'Just a visitor,' she murmured. 'Come for a first look. There will be more.'

'That wasn't a bird, was it?'

'No, Malenfant. It wasn't a bird. Come on. The day's walking is not done yet.'

When Malenfant looked back, the cloud deck from which they had emerged was like a sea, stretching to the horizon and covering the ground of this super Earth.

He turned away and walked on, up the slope, into the light.

*

The next significant transition came around six days later.

Again they seemed to have climbed into a bank of fog, and, after a night camping in what felt like cold grey dampness, they scrambled up and out into a still clearer sky, a deep high blue laced by still higher banks of cloud. The morning Sun hung low over the flank of the giant volcano.

The ground seemed still more barren, with no trees in sight, save for one straggly clump.

And behind them, clouds bobbing on a smooth, flat, invisible layer of air, all the way to a distant horizon. All hugging the same altitude. Like scoops of foam on a huge bowl of coffee, Malenfant thought.

As he peered around, Emma joined him.

He said, 'I guess we crashed up through another cloud layer.'

'I think so. We're nearly a kilometre high now. We really are crawling out of this big old world, one step at a time. Malenfant, back in the trees down there—'

'Yeah, I noticed that last clump too. I guess we passed through the final treeline. Just like climbing in Colorado. Even that sun looks fine, doesn't it? If a little odd, so much smaller.'

'Shit, Malenfant, do I have to punch you? You were always the world's worst listener, in any universe. And observer. You're looking at the *clouds*? Damn it, look at that tree clump.'

He turned to look again. A few of the Hams – he picked out Ham himself, Lola, little Strawberry, others who had joined them on the journey whose names he had never learned – were sprinting down the shallow slope towards that last cluster of trees.

Shadows swept over the fleeing Hams.

Malenfant looked up, squinting against the sunlight. This time he recognised the shapes immediately, the basic design:

those long wings, the extended heads with their long beaks, and gaunt crowns of bone and skin, almost like immense aerials. *Jurassic Park* imagery, again. Just as he had glimpsed a few days ago, save now there were many of them, and so much closer.

'Not birds,' he said softly.

Josh Morris stumbled over to them. 'No. Not birds. Pterosaurs,' he gasped.

Malenfant grinned.

'I hoped we would get a decent display,' Irina said, joining them. 'More than just the glimpses last night. Remarkable creatures, aren't they? We never hunted them, of course – if you don't believe me, try it some time – but we scavenged. The Hams and I. That's how we got the wing leather. Those big sheets that so fascinated you, Malenfant? *That's* the secret.

'And up in our camp – I mean the Russian camp – we dissected specimens. Just from curiosity. The Hams scavenge carcasses that wash downriver. That happens sometimes. The creature in flight is like a tremendous adjustable kite. Their body plans are essentially as ours, remarkably enough, four limbs and a spine, but – distorted.' She held up her hand with forefinger extended. 'The main wing strut is *one finger*, grossly lengthened.'

Deirdra asked, 'What are they doing up here?'

'Why, it's obvious. Hunting the creatures of those scraps of forest. I suppose they could hunt anywhere, but if I could fly unaided, *I* would choose to live up here, under that sky, in all this light! Would you not?'

'Hey,' Deirdra said now, focusing the RASF binoculars. 'I can see a pack of them on the ground. Walking. They look like . . . I don't know. Is it a flock?'

'Call it whatever you like,' Irina said. 'They aren't birds. For one thing they have teeth – some of them. In one specimen we caught I counted a *thousand* teeth . . .'

All Malenfant could see were smudgy shadows in front of the block of forest.

Bartholomew approached now and murmured in his ear. 'You're longing to rip those glasses out of Deirdra's hands, aren't you, Malenfant?'

'Leave me alone.'

Deirdra heard all this. She dragged it out for a couple more seconds, then handed the glasses to Malenfant.

And suddenly, through the glasses, he could see pterosaurs walking. Four, five, six of them.

On the ground they looked like dinosaurs, big four-legged, long-necked beasts with scaly, feathery skin – not proper feathers, he thought, they were some kind of tufts, but very colourful. The slim body and the long neck reminded him of giraffes. But they had a feature no giraffe ever shared, a kind of thin sheet of skin, stiffened by bone, that was folded up from the base of each of the forefeet.

'That's the wings,' he breathed. 'A giraffe with wings.'

'Folded wings,' Irina said. 'To them it's just as if they closed that big wing-strut finger back against the palm of the hand. There are a lot more rookeries inside the caldera than outside, of course.'

'Rookeries? *Eggs?* They lay eggs?'

'Of course. But as I said they aren't birds. The chicks are independent immediately they hatch, and just flap off. Astonishing sight. Take five years or so to reach maturity, if they survive.'

'The walking group. The one in the lead looks a little bigger than the rest. More colourful with those stubby feathers too.'

'They seem to gather in groups of females, with one male. Females spend a lot of time guarding their nests. The feathers seem to be for warmth and display, not flight—'

'Holy shit, they're taking off.'

It was a blur of motion in his enhanced vision, a complicated dance of running, shoving off from the ground with the back legs, pushing with the forelimbs, unfolding those huge wings and dragging at the air.

'I thought pterosaurs could only take off by jumping off cliffs.'

'No,' Josh said patiently. 'Evidently the archaeologists of our day could only *imagine* such huge beasts flying by jumping off cliffs. Nature is more ingenious. I mean, how could that jumping behaviour ever evolve?'

'Hey,' Deirdra said, sounding puzzled. 'What's Ham doing? It looks like he's setting a fire . . . Look, at the edge of the tree clump.'

Malenfant, using the glasses, peered. Ham had his back turned. But he had seen Ham make fires; it could take him only seconds to start a blaze with the friction generated by sticks rubbed in those powerful, callused hands. Malenfant wasn't surprised to see, almost immediately, a curl of smoke, rising above Ham's head from a splash of fame.

And *then* he saw the pterosaurs.

Flying from all over the sky, a fantasia of gliders.

Swarming towards the sudden blaze.

They had seemed to come from all over, out of the tree clumps, from the wider landscape. Malenfant hadn't consciously logged so many in the air, on the ground. They all seemed to share the same basic design, the wings of finger bones and membranes. But they came in all sizes and colours, some differing, he supposed, much as a robin differed from a bald eagle, even if it did share its body plan. Some must be older or younger, there could be differentiation of females versus males . . .

As more and more joined the impromptu flock, he lost count, lost the ability to discriminate. It was a crowd of pterosaurs, the vast majority hanging in the air, waiting for an opening to dive, he guessed.

And they were all heading for the blaze Ham had started. Flying *at* it.

Now Ham's purpose became obvious, as creatures came streaming out of the tree cover – mostly quadruped, some upright bipeds running tyrannosaur-style. Dozens in a glance, Malenfant thought, and he would never have guessed that such an isolated forest belt, so far up this world-scale mountain, would host so much life.

Or had hosted. With huge flappings, the pterosaur flocks descended on the prey, and Malenfant saw running and squirming, and the bright red splash of blood.

'A thousand teeth per head,' Malenfant murmured to himself.

Then one more huge pterosaur burst out of the smoking canopy. *Huge.* Its spread wings seemed to blacken the sky. Its wingspan might have been ten metres, the size of a small plane. Its head alone, with its tremendous beak, must have been three metres long.

And Malenfant could scale all this quite precisely because he had a comparison: a Ham, sitting on the pterosaur's neck, hanging on to tufty feathers with one huge hand, waving a stabbing-spear with the other. It was Lola. And she was yelling in triumph, too far away for Malenfant to hear.

Josh seemed astounded. 'Well,' he said. 'Well. If the whole purpose of this cage of a world is to see how life forms from different Earth epochs can interact, compete, even cooperate – I think *that* proves the point.'

'And I,' Deirdra said, 'would *love* to ride up there with her.'

Irina smiled, almost like a parent, Malenfant thought, a parent who had given her children a successful treat.

28

After leaving the pterosaur country, it was going to take, Irina estimated, another twenty days for the party to complete the climb to the mountainous rim of the caldera, and a few more days to the Russian camp itself.

But it was at the treeline that the last of their Ham escorts turned and went back – all save Ham himself. It was a simplified group that continued on.

The scenery too became still more elemental. They ascended through another cloud layer after eight more days. After that there was only the bare, all but lifeless ground under their feet, the flawless blue of the daytime sky with that very diminished Sun above, and a sea of cloud below them.

At last they reached the Rim Mountains, as Irina called them. The perimeter of the caldera itself. Himalayan peaks, assembled by the huge geological forces of a super Earth in a tidy circle more than two hundred kilometres in circumference – a circle that embraced the cauldron of a planetary-scale volcano.

Irina brought them without error or hesitation to a pass through the mountains to the interior. Malenfant peered into the shadowed cleft, eager to know what lay beyond, eager to make the next step in this extraordinary adventure. But mostly eager to get this journey over with.

They walked deep into the pass.

It was a valley, in fact, shallow, dry and cold, lying between looming peaks that were streaked with the dirty ice of old glaciers. Peaks which, Malenfant realised with relief, he would not have to scale.

At last they came to a crude cairn, just a heap of stones. Evidently this was a way well travelled.

'This is as high as we go,' Irina said. 'About two kilometres above the mean, four kilometres below the summits. Downhill from here. Mostly.'

'Then we take a break.' Malenfant's own voice sounded like a gasp in his ears.

The others took the cue, Emma, Deirdra, Josh, dropping their travois, flopping down on the rocky ground where they stood. Malenfant followed suit. The ground was rock, with a thin scraping of dust and rubble, presumably frost-shattered. Lifeless at first glance.

Ham climbed a little higher, until he came to a ledge maybe five metres above the floor of the pass, apparently a familiar spot. Here he sat squat, his huge legs drawn up to his barrel chest, and he glared north, the direction they were travelling, and south, the direction they had come from. It was unusual for him to settle so far away from the others.

Meanwhile Irina and Bartholomew stayed on their feet. Irina, apparently tireless, looked over the travois, checking bindings and covering and knots, while hauling out water sacks and throwing them around the group.

And Bartholomew made his own subtle inspection, passing from one exhausted individual to another. He had developed a way of gently resting his hand on the crown of his potential patient's head. That brief physical contact, together with the data fed to him continually by the bangles, was, Malenfant knew, all he needed to monitor their health. Once, Emma murmured to Malenfant that watching Bartholomew make his rounds reminded her of a Catholic priest delivering a blessing. Well, if so, Malenfant thought, maybe that wasn't a bad thing.

Josh looked utterly spent, as he always did. Oddly, he seemed to have shed little of the excess weight he had carried from when Malenfant first met him. He had looked unfit back then, and looked unfit now. But right now Josh, bootless and sockless, as he massaged his feet, was getting a hug and murmured support from Emma.

Emma herself had a look of determination under her near-exhaustion, and that was a signal of inner strength that Malenfant knew very well from *his* Emma. Irina meanwhile was a force of nature – driving them on, leading through the example of her own strength and competence – implacable.

And Deirdra was . . . Well, Deirdra was Deirdra, as tired, grimy, worn down as the rest, sitting quietly with Josh, and yet with a look of abstraction about her. As if none of this mattered compared to pursuing her latest goal, whatever it was. A magnet inside a paper doll, she'd said. Well, that magnet inside her was hard, Malenfant saw, hard and implacable – hard, yet beautiful too, surely, like the intricate structure of a diamond. Or a Phobos crystal. A flawless structure that just endured.

Maybe so. But Malenfant knew that she could still sometimes let up a little. And it was obvious that Josh was still drawn to her – more every day, it seemed to Malenfant. Maybe she could give him a little more attention.

Nobody was speaking, as they sipped water or ate a bit of smoked meat or tended to their worn-down bodies, or just rested.

Certainly there was no mood of triumph at having attained this highest point of the trek, if Irina was right, and Malenfant had every reason to believe her. Downhill from here, then, and one last push across what looked like level ground to the Russian camp. But still there were thirty or forty kilometres to go, according to Lighthill's orbital scouting – several more days of the relentless routine of the trek.

Nobody spoke.

Until Emma sat up, distracted, looking over Malenfant's shoulder.

He twisted to see.

Ham had stood up. His hands empty, his feet bare, wrapped in his own rough clothes of pterosaur skin and knotted rope, he looked out from this highest point to the south, the way they had come, and then back at the group.

With a sigh, Irina clambered to her feet, and walked up the incline to Ham. She had a slight limp, Malenfant saw, that seemed to wear off as she took a few steps. Maybe they all walked like that, he mused.

And, standing before Ham, wrapped in her own mix of antique Russian clothes and pterosaur-skin cloak and leggings, Irina once again looked more Ham than human.

They spoke now, a rapid exchange of sharp syllables and crisp hand gestures.

Deirdra joined Malenfant and Emma. 'I'm not sure what they're saying,' she said. 'But—'

Malenfant said, 'He's going back, isn't he? Rather than follow us down into the caldera. But why turn back here? And do you think she's trying to persuade him to change his mind?'

'Doesn't look like it, does it?'

'So what are they talking about?'

Emma smiled sadly. 'They're friends. Companions. I guess they're saying goodbye.'

The talk went on for a few more minutes, before a moment of silence. A last look, between human and Ham.

Then Ham strode boldly away, down the slope, heading south.

Irina came back to Malenfant and Emma. Deirdra, Josh, Bartholomew drifted over too. The remaining group gathering.

Josh pushed dusty spectacles up the bridge of his nose. 'So he's gone.'

'Always the plan,' Irina said. 'He was never going to come with us much further than this, into the caldera.'

'Why not?'

Irina did not reply.

Malenfant said, 'I suspect we'll find out in the end.'

Josh seemed perturbed, Malenfant thought, like a child abandoned by a wayward adult. 'So,' he said, 'what do we do now?'

Bartholomew put in, 'Well, we've lost our strongest bearer. We should dump whatever we can, whatever we don't need for these last few days. And I suggest we break down one of these travois and redistribute the load. Now's not the time for pride. Now that we've lost Ham, I can probably handle a travois myself for most of the terrain. I can load up with a backpack too. It's obvious I can carry more than I have been.'

Josh forced a grin. 'Can you take a passenger? Ever heard of a fireman's lift?'

Playfully Deirdra punched him softly on the arm. 'You big baby. This little walk is doing you the world of good.' She glanced at the Sun. 'Come on, let's get on with it. We might push through another few kilometres before we eat. Josh, you come walk with me . . .'

The group broke. Deirdra walked briskly off to the scattered gear. Josh followed her, as if hypnotised.

Malenfant said, 'She'll break his heart some day.'

Emma laughed. 'Oh, she's already done *that*. Come on, let's get on with it.' She turned away, to their heaps of belongings.

29

The pass out of these Rim Mountains descended pretty sharply.

Aside from when forced to it during his bouts of survival training, Malenfant had never been much of a mountaineer. Now he was reminded that climbing *down* a slope was almost as hard as climbing up – indeed, more difficult in many ways. Though they mostly had to drag their luggage as before, there were places where they had to lower it on ropes, or pass it hand to hand. The fundamental difficulty with a descent was often that you couldn't quite determine where to place your next step – from that point of view working your way down a slope was more hazardous than climbing up it. Some of the time they were walking, sometimes scrambling, and on frost-shattered ground they indulged in 'scree-sliding', as Emma called it, which was pretty much what it sounded like. Josh in particular, who seemed utterly to lack physical coordination, and whose eyesight seemed poor to boot, struggled especially.

'It could be worse,' Irina said on the second day. 'I, we, have done this passage many times, and I'm taking you by the easiest route I know. Not the shortest . . . There are places around here where the only way down is rappelling. Fixing rope to the rocks with pitons, and clambering down one length at a time. Laborious and dangerous.'

'Especially if you haven't got any pitons,' Emma pointed out. 'Or the right gloves, or boots. Or decent mountaineering rope. Or—'

'Oh, I expect we could improvise,' Bartholomew said pointedly. 'As when we climbed the Chester Pylon. Remember that, Malenfant?'

Malenfant, with Bartholomew, dragged his travois over a couple more metres of rocky ground. 'Your finest hour, Spider-Bot. Shut up and pull.'

By the end of the second day the worst was evidently over. Though they were still stumbling down a respectable slope, the pass had opened out to a broad swathe of lichen-crusted rock. The Rim Mountains had receded to a barrier behind them, no longer looming presences all around them.

As the group broke up for the night, Malenfant, briefly alone, walked a little way further north, the way they would travel tomorrow. It was the first time he had taken a good look at the caldera itself, from the ground anyhow. From this slight elevation he made out craters, circles drastically foreshortened: each the mouth of a major volcanic vent, dormant or not. The ground was too ruddy to be moonlike; perhaps this was more like Mars. And he saw water – a big stretch of it, what looked like an inland sea.

Far beyond, more mountains, almost lost in the thin mistiness of this high air, under a blue sky.

And he thought he saw a single spark of fire. The gas plume, he guessed, burning steadily, just as Lighthill had spotted from orbit.

The Russians.

He turned back to his companions.

*

The next day they descended at last to the flat: a plain of rock and moss, and odd-looking mushrooms, and what looked like stunted, dehydrated grass but probably wasn't, with small clumps of low, wind-bent trees in the distance. Malenfant took big lungfuls of the air, longing to believe it was perceptibly thicker, moister, richer.

They found a south-facing bluff for a shelter for the night.

At about noon of the following day, the fourth since they had started down from the top of the pass, they came to a mass of bones, scattered over the plain.

Malenfant thought he recognised the bones, some intact, some shards – ribs and vertebrae, shins and shoulders. Human, he thought with a shock. Maybe the remains of some of the Russians up here? But there were surely too many individuals here. And the skulls were – distinctive. Different.

'Runners,' Irina said bluntly.

'Another kind of human, then,' Deirdra said.

'Small crania,' Bartholomew murmured. 'Not modern humans.'

'But not Hams either,' Josh said. 'The bones are hard to identify. But the skull shape is all wrong, yes.'

'Runners,' Irina repeated. 'Not Hams. Another sort. We call them *Runners*.' She knelt down and touched the bones, what looked like the ribcage of a child. It was an oddly tender gesture, Malenfant thought. She said, 'This plain looks empty, but it has its share of predators, scavengers. There is little meat left, as you can see. A few weeks, months, the bones will be broken up, gone. Nothing will be left of this – obscure tragedy. The wild is a tidy place. But not a sentimental one. Of course there are other causes of death for these creatures, in this place.' She stood, brushing dust from her hands. 'Come. We must walk.'

Following her lead, they pressed on.

And Malenfant puzzled over that final remark. *Other causes of death*. Hams, forced to migrate. These Runners, dead in the dust.

He sensed they were getting close to the mystery of Irina, and her Russians, and the displacement they seemed to have caused.

Towards the end of the next day – it had been an easy few hours' walk – they came to the shore of a lake.

Malenfant dumped his travois and walked forward, followed by the others.

The lake, a greyish blue under Persephone's reduced sunlight, stretched from a ragged shore of coarse sand to the horizon, and from left to right, as far as he could see. At its shore the water looked greenish and cloudy. Life in there, of some kind.

The others glowered out at this latest obstacle. 'Well,' Emma said, 'it didn't look as big as *this* on the maps.'

Irina pointed east. 'We go that way. A detour of a day, no more.'

Malenfant suppressed a sigh. 'And what's one more day? OK. What's it doing here, though? Some kind of spring?'

'There is plenty of water up here,' Irina said. 'Even if there is little rain, or snow, little precipitation. Ancient water, in aquifers, even in permafrost.' She smiled. 'We called the permafrost *frozen mud*. And this is a complex landscape, though it may not look it. The lake nestles in an old, eroded volcanic vent, yes. But, consider the sand at this shore, which has eroded from sandstone, which in turn—'

'Ah.' Josh stood, grinning. 'So how did the sand get here? Once all of this was under the sea. Must have been. Sandstone beds. Then the whole lot was lifted up into the sky by the great mantle plume.'

Irina said now, 'True enough, but you miss the detail. The geology was complex, and the biology. Before the uplift, life had been trapped here, or the remains of it, as those sea-bed sediments were formed. We, the Russians, have found widespread oil reservoirs. The relics of oceanic life. And—'

Malenfant snapped his fingers. 'And coal? Coal beds, two kilometres high? Well, I guess that explains the gas plume, the burner you guys set up. I know natural gas is associated with deposits of stuff like coal and oil.' That was a faint memory of a rare conversation with Michael, his son, the coal-industry junior exec. He set that aside. 'Well, it makes sense to me.'

Irina shrugged. 'The landscape is richer than at first glance. Come. We should make camp.'

They stayed one night where they had come to the lake.

The next day they pushed on, rounding the shore.

The day after that, following Irina's lead, they left the shore behind and headed steadily north, their travois leaving deep scrapes in the dry, sandy ground.

And the day after that, the one hundred and eighth day of the trek, for the first time since they had descended from the Rim Mountains, Malenfant once more glimpsed the gas flare that burned steadily over the Russians' camp.

THREE

On Her Time at New Akademgorodok, and Her Subsequent Ascent

30

The Russian settlement was dominated by the wreck of a spacecraft.

A white hull, it was like a vast fallen building on this tabletop of a landscape. That was the only thing Malenfant seemed to see, at first. After all, they had come a thousand kilometres basically seeking a way off the planet, and that meant a spacecraft. Well, here they were, and it was one hell of a spacecraft, but it was wrecked. It all depended, he supposed, on how badly wrecked it was . . .

As they approached, Malenfant was peripherally aware of the wider settlement, spread sparsely over this huge plain. Fencing. Structures of wood and what looked like brick, and glass – greenhouses? Spherical tanks that might hold water or gas, tanks scavenged from the ship maybe. What looked like fields where some kind of raggedy crops were growing. In the further distance, off to the east, that spark of a gas burner, and a silvery glitter on the ground – solar panels?

Bricks, though . . .

But, for Malenfant, all of this was in the background of his awareness of the ship itself. Irina had said little about it – least of all about its condition, its spaceworthiness. Well, now he could see it for himself.

The mighty wreck must have been a hundred metres long. It was a spindle-shape, he thought, a rough cylinder fatter at the centre than at the ends, wrought in silver and white. Set upright it would have been taller than most of the booster stacks produced by American industry up until Malenfant's day – well, a Saturn V might have just topped it out. But a Saturn was a stack of throwaway boosters; Malenfant could see immediately that *this* was a spacecraft whole and entire, with a massive engine block at one end, and windows and ports of various sizes set in the hull, amid clusters of subsidiary rocket nozzles. A craft you would launch and land in one piece, like the all-in-one direct-ascent craft imagined in old movies such as *Destination Moon*, that took off from Earth, landed on its tail on the Moon, and flew straight back.

He could even see a name, proudly emblazoned beside what looked to him like a Russian eagle: in Cyrillic lettering:

ЭЛЕКТРОД CMIX

His bangle subtly showed him an English-alphabet overlay, transliterated – ELEKTROD, electrode – and then, presumably, the Latin numbering CMIX – nine hundred and nine.

But that mighty back was broken. This huge, evidently supremely capable craft had fallen down onto Persephone's unforgiving ground just as hard as had the much lesser *Charon II.*

Movement, from the wider camp, distracting him.

A handful of people came out to meet them, or challenge them, perhaps. Three adults plus a small child, held in the arms of one of the adults. Three against six visitors, including Irina who they presumably knew already, and one increasingly battered-looking automaton in Bartholomew. As far as Malenfant knew Irina had not had any recent radio contact with these people, any more than Lighthill had, and so the party was just showing up without any warning. He suspected that a lot of tact was going to be required, and everybody would have to be kept calm. *And you're just the man I'd choose as ambassador, Malenfant.*

He looked back at the mighty ship.

Emma nudged him in the ribs, none too gently. The Russians were close now, and were studying their visitors warily. 'Malenfant,' Emma hissed. 'Pay attention.'

'Doing my best . . . Look at that beast. Nuclear propulsion. Just as Irina said. Has to be, right?'

'Malenfant—'

'*Look* at it. I'm in hog heaven, Emma. It looks like a *Star Wars* prop dumped in the middle of the set of *Little House on the Prairie* . . .'

A dig in the ribs from Deirdra this time, hard enough to hurt.

Because now the Russians were here. Two women, one man, that frail-looking kid in a woman's arms.

The two parties faced each other. Malenfant was aware of his own tattered state, his much-repaired coveralls, and the dust of the journey clinging to his skin. These Russians were none too neat either, but they had another kind of griminess, deep in their hands, the skin of their faces: they had the look of farmers, to Malenfant.

The woman without the baby stepped forward. Malenfant saw that her hair was blonde, tied back from her brow; her eyes were a startling green. She faced Irina.

'*Khoroshego dnya, Anna,*' Irina said.

'*Ya skuchai po tebye, Irina . . .*'

Through his bangle Malenfant heard the Russian exchange under a murmured English translation. '*Good day. I have missed you . . .*'

Bartholomew stepped forward. He held out bangles. 'Irina. Please explain that these will help us understand each other.'

The Russians stared at Bartholomew. He was clothed in the same style as the rest of his companions, but after multiple scrapes and self-repairs, his scuffed, friction-polished skin no longer looked entirely natural, Malenfant perceived now. It wasn't as if steel ribs and pulleys and glistening electronics were exposed to view, but maybe something in his manner had changed too – a discarding of comforting pretence.

But that very artificiality seemed to encourage the Russians to take the bangles, to accept an advanced-tech miracle without demur. Or maybe, Malenfant thought, given the Russians must have encountered the super-advanced technology of the World Engineers to have got here at all, one way or another, a mere telepathic bracelet was nothing.

With growing confidence, the blonde woman, Anna, faced her visitors, evidently forcing a smile. 'You have come far. Of course we were aware of your approach . . . Welcome to New Akademgorodok.'

'An ironic name,' Irina said. 'After a place where we once lived, ate, worked together, full of hope. For who would call this place a hopeful home? My companions, who survived the wreck of the *Elektrod*. Anna Filosofova.'

The blonde-haired woman.

'Vasily Georgievich Kravets.'

The solitary man, dark, squat; he grinned. 'My father was Ukrainian, not Russian. I have my own name for this place, and it is not a polite one.'

The other woman, her hair a rich black, stepped forward. 'And I am Nadezhda Stasova. My baby, Maria. Named for Maria Trubnikova, the third of the Triumvirate. As we called ourselves, three women of five in the crew. Died in the crash.'

Emma stepped up and went through a round of introductions of her own.

The little girl, safe in her mother's arms, stared at each newcomer, Malenfant saw. She smiled at Josh, and he waggled his grimy glasses at her. But, wrapped as she was in a blanket, Malenfant thought she looked pretty sickly, her body undersized, her head lolling. The skin of her cheeks creased when she smiled, like the skin of an old person.

Bartholomew saw him looking. 'As soon as we can, I want to get a good look at that child.'

'Noted.'

Anna stood back. 'We will make you welcome, of course. We are all humans, stranded in this place, and we must help each other as we can, yes? . . .'

Emma murmured to Malenfant, 'Which shouldn't need saying. Plenty of tension here, Malenfant. Well, I guess Irina wouldn't have left otherwise.'

He nodded.

'So,' Anna Filosofova said. 'Come. See our home. We have salted meat — pterosaur flesh rather than pork, as would be the tradition — and tea, brewed from nettles. Well, we think they are nettles . . . Call me Anna, by the way.'

The heart of the homestead was no more than fifty metres from the wreck of the *Elektrod*. They walked over, the newcomers following their hosts. Malenfant noticed that the one guy, Vasily Kravets, was keeping an eye on the android.

The positioning of the settlement made clear sense to Malenfant. The ship must have been the source of much of their raw materials and means of survival, especially in the early days here. But by now there was a considerable infrastructure away from the ship, spreading east, off towards that gas flare.

Malenfant was starting to understand, on some visceral level, that these people really had been here years. They had spread out.

The main dwelling place was a hut, a sturdy frame of wood and metal, lashed to the ground with cables – Malenfant guessed there could be strong winds up on this plateau. The Russians called this their yurt. The walls were of wood and mud, covered with sheets of what looked like pterosaur leather. But Malenfant saw there were a couple of courses of brick acting as foundations for the wall, and he wondered about that now, and the bricks he had seen earlier. You weren't going to carry bricks on a spacecraft, so where had they come from? In fact, he saw now, the bricks looked rough enough to have been home-made.

You keep being distracted by detail, Malenfant.

He tried to take in the bigger picture.

The yurt turned out to be at the centre of an open area surrounded by a sturdy-looking fence. Bits of metallic junk had been hung from the fence, maybe acting as a crude alarm in case anything came climbing over. There must be unwelcome visitors, then. Aside from the yurt, in the fenced-off area were a couple of smaller buildings, rougher – one maybe a toilet. And a couple of big spherical metal tanks, evidently cut from their frames in the ship, resting on wooden trestles. Piping, also clearly scavenged, snaked away from the tanks and through the fence, heading east.

Malenfant tentatively knocked on the tanks, making them ring.

Anna approached him. 'You are an engineer?'

'Partly. Pilot. Astronaut.'

'You are more interested in the engineering than in the people. A common syndrome.'

He smiled back at her. 'Sorry. Bad habit.'

'I would not say so. We all have multiple skill sets here – all of us survivors in New Akademgorodok. Some we have acquired since being stranded here; some, more in fact, are the result of our education, our training. Surely it is the same for you – wherever it is you came from. A spacecraft is a complex entity with a small crew, who must necessarily bring a variety of expertise types.'

'True enough.'

'But I too, you see, am more an engineer than anything else.' She glanced up at the tanks. 'If I were to happen on this place, the bits of robust engineering would catch my eye too.'

'I can see you have built a respectable home for yourselves here.'

'Respectable.' She raised an eyebrow at the word. 'We do what we can. A respectable stockade, you mean? Perhaps you compare us to the achievements of your own ancestors on the American frontier.'

Malenfant felt confused; he couldn't read Anna, this stern, tough person. This evident survivor. 'I'm sorry. Anna – we just met. I didn't mean to cause any offence, to – to judge. As you say we're all just humans here. All strangers.'

Emma overheard, and, walking up, laughed. 'It's also possible that the American frontier worked out some different way in Anna's world . . .' She looked at Anna. 'Sorry. I have no idea if any of that translated or not, through the bangles.'

Anna pursed her lips. 'Different timelines. Different reality strands. That has long been evident to us. In one is our Earth, a teeming population, and this world, this planet, does not exist. In this reality strand – well, here we are. A living planet, an empty Earth.'

Malenfant sighed. 'And we came from a third strand. No giant life-giving planet for us – but no twentieth-century Tsarist empires either. By the way, we call this world Persephone.'

Anna nodded. 'That will do. We have not named it, actually. We only named this patch of ground, which we call New Akademgorodok. A very Russian joke. Bitter! But still, we have done our best to make this a home. To carve ourselves a place in this . . . timeline.'

Malenfant slapped the side of one of those big tanks. 'I can see that. Took some work to haul this out of the wreck, I bet.'

'Well, we have the workers to do it,' she said, a little enigmatically, and Malenfant wondered what she meant. 'The tanks hold water and methane.'

'Methane?'

She gestured to the east, where the pipes snaked out of the compound. 'The pipes reach to the wells we have dug: water from deep aquifers, and the gas from what appears to be a kind of coal seam.'

'The flare,' Malenfant said. 'That's the methane source?'

'Yes. We burn off most of what is released. With time the pressure dwindles, of course. The methane we do capture serves only as a backup to our solar cell farm: as in space, on this high plateau sunlight is a key source of energy for us, just as Tsiolkovsky and others foresaw. But still, with this system of wells, we have water, and energy to heat it.'

He felt a deep, visceral longing. 'Hot showers?'

'Don't push your luck, Malenfant,' Emma murmured.

Anna now led them a little way deeper into the compound, where simple stones, roughly carved, marked what were evidently graves. Deirdra was already here, silently studying the little cemetery. Three of the graves were adult-sized mounds of earth, and the fourth was heartbreakingly small. Another child, then. This simple cemetery was in the shadow of the looming wreck of the *Elektrod*.

Anna said, 'We tried to build a home here. A homeland, yes. Even for the generations to come. Even though we were so few in number. For we cannot see a way to escape this planet, you see . . .'

Malenfant's faint hopes that he had got closer to a way off this rock shrivelled a little more. That was, after all, why they had come here. And if these Russians hadn't figured it out, in years long enough to have borne children . . . *Well, nobody said it would be easy, Malenfant.*

'A rescue mission from our own people is unlikely any time soon.' Anna smiled. 'Perhaps Irina has spoken of this. We were pioneers; we penetrated the strangeness of Anteros where none had gone before us. We lost our way. Others may follow, more cautiously, one day, perhaps – we may hope – even if we, the first generation, do not live to see it.'

Deirdra said gently, 'The first generation? So you hoped to found a colony. To have children who could follow you—'

'Yes. Despite this planet's perils, the harshness of its conditions – the gravity above all – and the lack of an enthusiastic welcome from its inhabitants. It is a big world; we hoped there would be room for us. Why not?

'But the first thing we had to do, as you can see, even as we emerged from the wreck, our first act in creating this New Akademgorodok, was to bury our dead in its cold ground. There were seven of us, aboard the *Elektrod*. Now four survive, plus the baby, Maria. She was named for Maria Trubnikova, who died in the crash. Maria, Nadezhda and I had called ourselves the Triumvirate. For the purpose of the mission we had adopted the names of the early pioneers of women's rights in Russia – perhaps you have heard of them, they worked together in St Petersburg in the 1860s.'

'I'm ashamed to say I haven't,' Emma murmured.

'Well, Maria did not survive the landing, as I said. Nor did one other woman – Valentina, a close friend of mine. There was another man, the father of baby Maria in fact. He was killed later, and is lying here with the others. This world is full of perils. As you no doubt know by now.'

All this was new to Malenfant. It struck him now that in the weeks they had travelled together, Irina had said very little, really, of her time with these people. She hadn't mentioned what unnamed menace had to be excluded from the compound with fences – the same menace that had killed one crewperson, the father? And, as Deirdra must be thinking too – who occupied the final grave? That tiny mound, covering what must have been a child born before little Maria, daughter of Nadezhda. Whose child?

Emma's hand slipped into his, and not for the first time in their relationship he had a sense of what her advice would be. *Give it time, Malenfant. These are lost, traumatised people, and we just walked in on them, out of nowhere. Let them keep their secrets a while longer.*

And in time, he suspected, they would all learn far more about each other than they wanted to know.

31

Josh shook Malenfant awake.

Malenfant could tell it was Josh, even before he rolled on his back to see. Josh's shyness came out strongest when he actually had to touch a person physically. So Malenfant's waking was a matter of a grab at his shoulder that startled Malenfant out of vague dreams of being a tiny Christ climbing a huge crucifix . . .

Malenfant reluctantly sat up.

Bright morning light cut through the imperfectly sealed flap of the door – cut into the gloom within this pterosaur-leather yurt. He could make out the sleeping forms of Emma, Deirdra – Deirdra snored softly – and Bartholomew, sleepless of course but lying down like the rest in order not to spook anybody by sitting up all night. Malenfant rubbed his eyes; they felt gritty, sore, as they had been since they had all climbed up to this dusty high country.

Even though it had been a week now, a week since their arrival at this camp.

Josh was squatting by Malenfant's bed, wearing those owlish, precious spectacles, carefully tended by their owner, but now with scuffs on the glass and one broken arm repaired with a bit of wire, like the bridge.

'Josh? What?'

'Vasily wants us to go for a walk.'

'Who? All of us?'

'Just the three of us. You, me, him.'

'The three males.' He glanced over at Bartholomew. 'Present company excepted.'

'He wants to show us some stuff, I think. Stuff I've been talking over with him. And discussing with Commander Lighthill over the radio.'

'Just us three guys, though? Do you think Vasily has been missing male company?'

Josh frowned. 'I don't understand.'

And Josh, Malenfant reminded himself, came from a thoroughly patriarchal culture, just like Vasily. Naturally Josh would see nothing unusual in an all-male gathering.

'Well, OK. As long as he doesn't crack the vodka, start telling dirty jokes, and get maudlin over the motherland.'

Josh thought that over. 'There are times when I feel I understand only about ten per cent of what you say, sir.'

Malenfant sighed. He swung his legs out from under a patched woollen blanket – a loan from the Russians – and began to rummage in the sack of clothing he used for a pillow, seeking clean socks. Or cleaner anyhow. 'Why now, though? Just because the rest won't be awake yet? What the hell time is it?'

'It's local six a.m. Or just after, now. And it's the first day of Long May, here in Persephone Year Five.'

Malenfant glared at him. 'What the hell does that mean? As you are probably aware by now, I'm not at my puzzle-solving best when just woken from a sleep on a heap of dirty laundry.'

'You'll see.' Josh just grinned. 'I think that's part of what Vasily wants to show us.' He stood up. 'We've got an hour before Vasily wants to set off. You want breakfast? I've put some nettle tea on to boil.'

Malenfant had felt hungry ever since the crash of the *Charon* on this huge world. He thought bleakly of pancakes, maple syrup, bacon, a gallon of coffee – caffeinated. He knew he was facing nettle tea and a baked potato. It would have to do. But at least the showers were indeed hot around here.

Sighing, he got unsteadily to his feet.

By the time Malenfant was ready to go, the rest of the camp was starting to stir. He avoided conversation as he hauled on his much-patched boots.

Then he headed out of the central compound – the big main yurt, the outhouses with shower and lavatories, the kitchen with its separate hearth – and met Josh and Vasily Kravets outside the east-side gate of the spiky wooden fence.

The three of them, in the light of the diminished Sun of a Persephone morning, cast long shadows back towards the compound. And beyond loomed the crashed *Elektrod*, its skin pale white, like a stranded, broken-backed whale. Still magnificent.

Vasily looked the part, Malenfant thought now as he studied him in the low morning light. Vasily was maybe forty years old. His clothing was a patchwork of fur and woven vegetable fibre, all based on a kind of coverall – originally perhaps not unlike a NASA jumpsuit – which was now, after a decade of mending and reinforcing, little more than a palimpsest covered by patches. His boots too were multiply patched, slathered with a kind of tar for waterproofing, and stuffed with fur. His headgear, like a broad-brimmed coolie hat, would have served as a prop in any stage production of *Robinson Crusoe*. And he had a hefty-looking revolver stuffed into his belt.

Whereas Josh, in his own much-patched clothing and his round glasses, looked like a kid who had fallen out of a treehouse.

Yes, Vasily looked the part. But, even though much of his expression was hidden behind a very Slavic-looking grey-streaked black beard, there was doubt in Vasily's eyes. Indeed he had a way of avoiding eye contact altogether, Malenfant had observed before.

See how robust *your* personality is after ten years in this wilderness, Malenfant. And remember what Anna told you. You don't know what these people have gone through. Pray you never learn.

Vasily smiled now. 'We walk. I will show you some of what we have built here. Much of it you have seen. But it may be you will bring a different expertise to our own – well, that must be true, if some of you actually do come from a future age – perhaps you will see alternatives, ways we can achieve our goals better.'

Malenfant nodded. 'Sounds good to me. Let's go.'

They started walking east, into the sunlight – towards that gas flare, a brilliant spark against the gathering sunlight of the morning sky.

Malenfant asked, 'You mentioned your goals?'

Vasily shrugged. 'The most elemental being to survive, of course. As individuals. Already a partial failure so far given those we have lost. And in the longer term, perhaps, to establish a permanent human colony on this world. If that is possible.'

'Hence, baby Maria,' Josh said.

'Indeed. And – other experiments. We did what we thought we had to. It is a matter of regret. Even if we had succeeded, I would regret. All of it.'

Malenfant sensed his sincerity, even if he didn't go into

detail. Maybe he was referring to whatever had been done to the Hams, to drive them out of here. Maybe these Russians had turned on each other, even. These weren't evil people. Just desperate people, who had been driven to desperate measures.

Not for the first time in his life, Malenfant was glad he wasn't expected to give absolution.

But Vasily hadn't mentioned escape, Malenfant noticed. Or even hinted at it. Nothing of attempts to get off this planet and back to space. That knot of anxiety tightened inside Malenfant. If these Russians really thought it was impossible to fix their ship – and they should know – what the hell could *he* come up with, that they had missed?

Josh said now, 'I told Malenfant today is the first day of your Long May.'

'Ha! Yes. We have always tried to keep track of time here. We began simply by scratching a day count into the hull of the crashed *Elektrod*. But the days, you see, are themselves longer than the days of Earth, and the year too a different length. Persephone is a world bigger than Earth, and deserved its own big calendar. And at length I, we, devised a solution.'

I, we . . . Malenfant suppressed a grin. *You mean 'I', Vasily. Working out calendars is so a guy thing.*

'Persephone's day is twenty-five hours long; its year is seven hundred and seventy-eight days long – Persephone days – around two and a quarter Earth years . . .'

Malenfant was well aware of the longer day, that extra hour. He had felt as if he was oversleeping every day since they had crashed at the coast, like a lingering jetlag.

'How are we to count time, then, in an intuitive way? An Earth-based calendar is an obvious bad fit. Well. We decided to take the second, the minute, as our base units. The beat of a second after all is comparable to the pulse of a resting human, a natural interval. But we defined a new long "hour", consisting of about sixty-three minutes. That way there are twenty-four long hours in a Persephone day. Oh, the calculation is out by a few seconds here and there, and a further complication is the slight ellipticity of Persephone's orbit, which leads to an irregularity in the year length. Future generations, if there are any, will need to apply a few fixes. Perhaps there will be a pattern of "leap days", added or omitted from the calendar every few years – no matter. Leave that to a new Pope Gregory!

'But the big advantage of our sixty-three-minute hours is that the twenty-four-hour "clock" feels the same as it does on Earth. Every day, six a.m. is very early morning, here as on Earth. You see?'

Malenfant grinned, and he saw Josh smiling too. 'OK. I'm nerd enough to admit I'm enjoying this. So, months?'

'We have seven hundred and seventy-eight days to assign. So we chose to define twelve long months: ten of them of sixty-five days, two of sixty-four. Which adds up to—'

'Ha!' Josh said. 'So you could have the forty-third of July . . .'

'Again you see the intuitive advantage. We did consider thinking up our own names for the Persephone months, perhaps based on national heroes. But none of us could remember them. So we used January, February . . . We fixed January 1 as the winter solstice here in the northern hemisphere of the planet. The world's axis is tipped, you know – not so much as Earth's, but enough for perceptible seasons. Long January lasts nine weeks! But, you see, when Long March and Long April come along, you know that spring is near, just as on Earth.

'As to a year numbering, we retrospectively defined Year Zero as the year we landed here – and worked out, again retrospectively, that that had occurred on the thirty-second of Long July of that year. And all that is how I can tell you that today is the first day of Long May in the Year Five.'

Ten years, Malenfant thought. Ten Earth years, human years, in this place.

Josh had listened intently to all this. Now he pushed his glasses back up his nose, and applauded slowly. 'That, sir, is magnificent.'

Vasily smiled politely.

He slowed as he brought them to the water pump.

Vasily said, 'We must discuss water. This pump was Yuri's design – Yuri, who died. I was a pilot, you know, in as much as I had a specialism. A pilot is no use without a functioning ship to fly.'

'Tell me about it,' Malenfant muttered.

'But I contribute as best I can . . . By building Yuri's pump, for example, and maintaining it.'

Which was more than a simple pump, Malenfant quickly learned.

Inspecting the rig more closely, he saw a hefty-looking drill: a long metal thread with a spiral screw, presumably scavenged from the *Elektrod*, set vertically in a frame of steel and wood. Two wooden bars stuck out from this arrangement, and Malenfant saw that if you and a couple of buddies grabbed these bars, and pulled or pushed, and walked in circles around the drill tower, then the screw could be made to dig into the sandy ground, and whatever lay beneath.

There were rusty stains on the turning handles, Malenfant saw. What might have been dried blood. He imagined human hands grabbing those bars – they did look the right size for the hands of humans, or near-humans, hands without any protection, hands that were made to push or pull at this bit of apparatus until the palms bled.

Ham hands? Runners?

It was evident that the screw had already been used repeatedly. Ragged holes pocked the ground, most of them capped with lids of metal. But one well was open. A fat pipe had been forced down it, with a right-angle bend attaching it to a feed to what was obviously a water tank standing on the ground, another spacecraft relic presumably, complete with a couple of taps. Wires trailed down into the hole too, attached – so Malenfant saw, peering down – to what looked like a small, portable electricity generator, which in turn was connected by pipes and trailing wires to another tank, of what turned out to be fuel: methane, extracted locally and burned in this generator.

Malenfant saw the principle behind this tangled, half-improvised heap. This elevated landscape lacked precipitation and surface water; rain, even mist, was rare. But it was cold enough to preserve layers of permafrost in the ground. Frozen mud. And there were ways of extracting such water. But first you had to drill down through the ground to get to the ice, then *melt* it – hence the generator – and only then pump the liquid water up.

Drill, melt, pipe, store.

'Good piece of kit,' he murmured.

'Of course we needed to find the water in the first place,' Vasily said.

'But you must have expected it,' Josh said.

Malenfant frowned. 'Why?'

'We are sitting on top of a huge mantle plume here,' Josh said. 'The rising heat from underground must force water up to the surface rock layers, until it finally freezes – and it's cold enough up here for it to stay frozen, through the long summers.'

'Correct,' Vasily said. 'So we surmised. We used radar reflections, in fact, to seek out such water. To confirm its presence. We found it, liquid, under a cap of ice or permafrost.'

'Yes,' Josh said, evidently thinking fast. 'I can see how that would work. A hundred-metre pulse – three megahertz – would penetrate to, what, ten times its wavelength? So down a half-mile or more. Any liquid water would reflect a strong signal.'

Vasily nodded. He smiled. 'That's it. We improvised the technology; our antenna looked like a huge television aerial. But it worked, as you can see.'

They straightened up and walked on.

Malenfant said, 'I vaguely remember looking at a technology like this in my space entrepreneur days. The Rodriguez wells that the US Army used to drill in Greenland. Same idea. Maybe we could adapt that technology to use on Mars someday, we thought. As I recall you would need something like a kilowatt per person to sustain a daily supply of permafrost melt.'

They had to talk around the unit, the kilowatt; the bangle translation wasn't clear.

'We get away with a little less than that,' said Vasily. 'But then we Russians are a frugal folk, unlike Americans.' And he winked at Josh.

'Don't look at me,' said Josh. 'You ought to try out the water supply in the average English public school. You'd need a kilowatt per person to heat *that* . . .' Then he stood stock-still, staring ahead. 'Wow. Bricks!'

Malenfant got his bearings.

They were still walking east, roughly, towards the flare. Now they walked past a big solar-cell spread, to the north, shiny black sheeting pinned to the ground. And, to Malenfant's right, the long pipeline that carried gas back to the camp.

And, yes, here was a heap of bricks, golden-brown in the

gathering sunlight. Nearby stood what looked like a kind of oven, a big iron chamber with a swing door at the front – presumably another scavenged adaptation from the *Elektrod* wreck. And a heap of rough-cut wooden logs, evidently fuel for this oven.

'Bricks,' Josh said again.

Vasily smiled. 'Yes, we experiment with brick-making. Like the Mesopotamians we have only dirt and water to work with. But we make mud, and bake it. Well, the Mesopotamians built civilisations with such materials.'

He picked up a brick; it was rougher in shape and finish than Malenfant had realised.

'Sun-dried,' Vasily said. 'Which takes a while, given the low intensity of the sunlight here. Mixed with straw, as you can see. It is good enough for now – you have seen how we use such bricks, courses of them as the bases of our structures. We experiment with kilns.' He indicated the oven-like improvisation. 'For fuel we use charcoal. We have the Runners return wood from forest clumps on the slopes of the Shield – possibly you saw the trails. We have experimented with mortar of different kinds, but for that we would need chalk, or something similar. We have lots of half-finished projects, experiments, under way. Sometimes I think we have achieved little in our decade here – sometimes a lot.'

Josh and Malenfant shared a glance. Another mention of the mysterious 'Runners'. And Malenfant's head filled with a picture of those desiccated corpses, out on the plain.

'Just surviving is a heck of an achievement,' Josh murmured.

Malenfant nodded in approval. Focus on the tech, for now.

'I suppose so,' Vasily said. 'We have been pinned in place to the crash site of our ship, of course. Our discovery of accessible water was fortuitous. And when we drilled deeper we soon struck the methane. If not for that we might have moved to some other, richer locale . . . I am no more a geologist than I am a hydraulic engineer.'

Josh looked around, his eyes magnified by his glasses, giving him an absent look. 'You did fine. And the methane is significant, in terms of the geology. *I* can tell this land was once sea bed. I could tell from space. So there could be chalk strata here. A couple of miles deep. And limestone below that. There are probably many layers of geological processing below that, given the energies of this giant planet. When sea bed is subducted – taken down beneath continental plates by tectonic movement – the organic sludge that lies on top of it is baked to produce oil, along with methane and other gases. All of it trapped under caps of limestone, waiting to be tapped.'

Vasily gestured. 'You can see we burn off most of the methane, but we do store some of it for power generation, along with the solar power we tap – we have efficient batteries from the *Elektrod* . . .'

Malenfant glanced up at the unwavering flame. Seems kind of a waste, he thought. He wondered what order of volume of gas came out of there, hour on hour. How much volume, if liquefied – given nothing but the technological resources he had already seen, *could* you liquefy it? . . . So what if you could?

There was an elusive chain of thought in there that he deliberately let go of; he knew it was sometimes best to let his own cavernous mind echo with such ideas for a while.

Like ocean-bottom sludge turning into methane, Malenfant. Suitable comparison.

They turned back. Malenfant's shadow, cast by the rising Sun, was still long before him as they walked.

'You must have big plans,' Josh said to Vasily, a little hesitantly.

'Big plans?'

'If you're making bricks. Are you going to put up more substantial buildings?'

'Well, we cannot live off the carcass of the wretched *Elektrod* for ever. There may be more than five of us in the future.'

Malenfant said evenly, 'More of you. From three Eves and two Adams? One Adam dead already.'

Vasily looked at him bleakly. 'There were other . . . experiments. You speak of Adam and Eve. I am not religious . . . but I understand the allusion. I am assured that genetically we are a diverse crew . . .' He shook his head. 'The moral qualms are overwhelming. Sometimes I have wondered, what right do *I* have to father a race? How could I . . . protect them all? And yet if we do not try, then what is the point of all our striving? For we can never leave here.'

Neither Malenfant nor Josh had an answer to that.

And Malenfant knew they were going to have to wait for the truth about what had already happened here to come out.

They spoke little as they returned to the centre of the compound, where the others were stirring, and threads of smoke from the fires looped into the air, and the thin crying of baby Maria could be heard.

And, restlessly, Malenfant thought about methane.

32

Good morning, Wing Commander Lighthill. Well, it's morning down here at New Akademgorodok . . .

Ah! Good day to you, Miss Greggson, if we are going to go all posh. Geoff and Deirdra will do! Thank you for calling. And it's morning too, I suppose, up here in synchronous orbit. Always morning, or mostly; the Sun is eclipsed by Persephone for perhaps an hour a day . . . I'm sorry. I'm waffling.

Waffle away, Commander. Geoff! That's as much the point of these regular calls as anything else. I wouldn't enjoy being stuck up there on my own. Even if you have got a whole interplanetary spacecraft to play with.

Hmph. And I am planning, tentatively, to do something with my big roomy spacecraft, rather than just sit here and watch day and night wash over this version of Persephone, entertaining spectacle though it is. A spaceship of one's own, though! A boyhood dream, but not one that one would seriously want to have seen fulfilled. To zip around the Solar System quite alone – well, it was good enough for Butch Breakaway, but he was made of sterner stuff.

Who?

Sorry! Funny how the mind works. Too much time navel-gazing up here. And how has Joshua endured his own jaunt? My last living crewman, of course.

Well, the trek didn't suit him at all.

Ha! I'll bet it didn't.

He survived it. He was very brave. But I think he was more bored than anything else. That was worse than the physical stuff for him. Frustrated, at not being able to do stuff. His stuff. Study and take samples and make notes and draw up hypotheses. He did his best, but . . .

I can understand that. You can't make a lot of notes when you are dragging a travois across a rocky plain, alongside a man-ape or two.

Well, they are more than man-apes . . .

As long as he didn't break anything, it probably did him the world of good.

Which reminds me. Bartholomew has a list of health questions for you to answer, Geoff.

Wilco. Nice to know my own battered carcass hasn't been forgotten. Put him on later.

Anyhow Josh is a lot happier now. He's busy, all the time. Either studying the environment, or working with Malenfant and the Russians on their technology—

Ah, yes. The magnificent *Elektrod*! Have you had a chance to see it yet? I can make out its carcass from up here, through a telescope at least. I wish I had seen it in action – in space, in its element. But what of your Russians? What do *they* want?

They only meant to explore, as far as I can tell. And they got themselves stranded just as we did.

Explorers, yes, as we are – with what purpose, ultimately? I suppose we could all ask that of ourselves. We British explore for the science, but also for the discovery of new territory, new resources. We are an empire – but we are on a civilising mission.

While extracting enormous wealth.

Undeniable. And as for this 'Cosmism' you have spoken of before, I've heard of Tsiolkovsky – everybody in the industry has, if only for his rocket equation – but all the mystical stuff behind him? Something to do with the resurrection of the dead, I'm told?

Who told you that? Malenfant, probably. I don't understand either, Geoff. But I do think we have things in common. Under the surface, there's a basic curiosity. What is the universe for? Why does anything exist at all – and why do I exist, here and now? Ultimately, what is the place of humanity in all of this? We all have the same questions.

Umm. Truth is – you know, Deirdra, I often feel humbled when speaking to you. You are one of the deepest people I have ever met, young as you are. Given my own background that's probably not saying much . . .

You're embarrassing me.

Sorry. Again.

We are trying to find a way to get off this rock. I think Malenfant may have some scheme boiling up in his head. But if the Russians haven't made it off in the ten years they've been here . . .

Not like you to be downbeat, Miss Greggson.

No. Sorry.

But I do understand.

One feels so helpless. I look down on your travails and can do no more than a bit of orbital scouting . . .

I do find myself turning inwards. Not surprising, really. Alone far too much.

I was a boarder, you know, at prep school. Linbury Court Prep on the South Downs, I doubt you know it. Oddly enough, spent a lot of time alone there. Both my parents worked, my father in the air force, my mother in the civil service. So, you see, there were times when I had to stay over at school in the summer vac. Often the only boarder left. A handful of staff who were kind enough – I played with their children sometimes, or children from the village. Term times were a lot more fun. But still, in the hols, age eleven or twelve, one was thrown on one's own devices. That was when I discovered Butch Breakaway and the rest, I think.

Who?

In the scientific comics. Space heroes. The masters turned a blind eye when I found a stash of confiscated material: a stack of Jules Vernes that might have been there since before Hitler's war, all these battered old comics. I have often heard that an intensive course of reading at a young age because of some confinement, an illness perhaps, shapes one for life. It certainly did me. And then the hols would be over . . . Listen to my maundering.

You can maunder all you like. Although I'm not sure what 'maundering' means.

Well, look, we have some business to progress. Relevant to our various missions, in fact.

Business?

Business. Look here, I feel like I'm wearing a groove in the sky just turning around and around this planet, while you crowd are scrabbling away down on the ground. I am, after all, sitting here in a high-performance spacecraft, which is pretty well fuelled, and more propellant can be obtained from the ice moons which litter this system—

You're thinking of making a journey? Of leaving Persephone?

That's the general idea.

I'm not the person to ask this, but is that safe?

For one person alone to go wandering between the planets? Of course not! If I had a medical emergency, for example – well. We must hope it doesn't come to that. But, though the control systems of the dear old *Harmonia* are nowhere near as sophisticated as your bangles, Deirdra, they can be set to bring the *Harmonia* back from wherever I choose to take her. So there will be a backup strategy in place. I will talk to Josh about that.

Where would you go?

I talked this over a little with Malenfant. One day we need to take a closer look at that anomalously hot moon of a ringless Saturn, I think . . . For now, though, it may be less ambitious to explore the inner Solar System. I have in mind a closer look at Venus and Mercury, first of all; later I may go to Earth. All of these worlds appear quite different, in this reality, from our own. To understand this system fully, including Persephone, we may need to understand those differences. The visits will be brief, although I may stop to refuel at the moons of Venus.

How long would all this take?

Are you in a rush? Sorry . . . You know that at cruising speed the *Harmonia* can cover an astronomical unit, the Earth–Sun distance, in a few days.

I flew two thousand AU in the Harmonia.

Indeed. Persephone is a little less than two AU from the Sun. I think these tours would each take a month, perhaps a little more. I will work all this out with Josh before I go, prepare a flight plan, make regular reports.

I think . . . it seems a good idea. And I also have a feeling you need to do this, Geoff.

True enough. Though I mustn't make such a venture just to relieve my own half-crackers state. And speaking of careless accidents, I hope you are being careful with poor Josh's heart. It is a fragile thing, and not used to strong emotion.

I . . . don't think I know what you're talking about.

Oh, come on. It's obvious he has an immense crush on you. I can see it from my twenty-five-hour orbit! Well, do be kind, my dear. If he gives you any trouble, mooning over you and such, tell him to buck up and play the game. That's an order.

Now, about this jaunt of mine . . .

33

Ten days after Irina had brought them all here – ten overlong Persephone days – Anna invited the newcomers to come and take a proper look at the wreck of the *Elektrod CMIX*. Maybe it had taken that long for them to be trusted with the colony's main treasure, Malenfant thought.

Josh jumped at the chance, and Malenfant could see why. Josh, the science geek, was enough of a space traveller himself to be drawn to go gawk at the wreck of an exotic nuclear-powered spacecraft from another timeline, whatever the excuse.

Deirdra was a more complicated case – as ever – and Malenfant, talking it over with Emma, was trying to track her reactions to New Akademgorodok. She seemed fascinated by everything she encountered on this huge enigma of a world. So she showed up to see the *Elektrod*. The wreck of a great gaudy space-opera whale of a ship would have intrigued anybody sentient enough to have an imagination, he thought. But she was a lot less interested in the Russian technology than Josh and the rest. What evidently intrigued her most was the Russians' backstory, just as she had been intrigued by Malenfant, a man out of his time, and the other manifold wanderers she had encountered.

And, he thought, right now she was disturbed by the clash

between the Cosmist values which seemed to attract her so much and the grubby compromises forced on these Russians in their attempt to survive here. Well, that was all part of growing up, he guessed.

She seemed distracted. Lacking eye contact. Searching the camp, looking to the dusty horizon, the glimpses of the Rim Mountains – even the spark of the methane flare – as if searching for something else, something missing, a lack she couldn't even define.

Malenfant reminded himself to keep an eye on her.

And to follow her lead, if necessary. Her instincts, after all, had brought them all this far.

Emma, meanwhile, wasn't coming today. She had other priorities, she had told Malenfant.

'The baby,' she had whispered to him that morning, over their one precious cup of coffee of the day, courtesy of the *Elektrod*'s dwindling ten-year-old store.

'Little Maria? What about her?'

'Bartholomew's concerned. So is Nadezhda, the mother. Her development isn't as it should be.'

'Well, this is a super Earth—'

'Yes, thank you, Doctor Malenfant,' she said heavily. 'I think Nadezhda has figured all that out for herself. But I think she is having trouble accepting Bartholomew. With letting him get close to the kid, anyhow.'

Malenfant thought that over. 'So you're staying close, to mediate.'

'For now.'

He nodded. 'What the hell, this great white whale of space isn't going anywhere fast, and neither are we. You know, if people weren't so darn complicated—'

'Life wouldn't be so darn fun. Go on, shoo.'

So he shooed.

And walked, with the others, into the shadow of the spacecraft.

Even fallen, the *Elektrod CMIX* was magnificent.

Anna stood back and let the visitors take a first good look in their own time, with cautions about residual radioactivity, particularly in the engine compartment.

The first thing Malenfant did was to pace out the ship, end to end. A hundred good steps with his own long legs from blunt prow to the big engine bells at the base: a hundred metres, as he had thought. Much of the hull was hidden in the dirt into which it had crashed, and from which tough-looking grass had evidently sprouted in the ten years since.

Then he walked back up the broken-backed carcass, this time counting the secondary rocket nozzles that stuck out of the craft's sides: twenty in all, it seemed, though that was a guess based on symmetry; with the ship lying on its side he couldn't see them all. Back at the prow, he looked into what were evidently the remains of cabins, and presumably a control deck.

More slowly still, he walked back down the ship's length once more. Behind the bridge and crew cabins in the prow, amidships, clearly visible through surviving glass panels, he could see that the central section of the ship had been given over to what looked like a greenhouse. Trays of dried soil, displaced and broken. Pipework everywhere. Much of the glass had gone, evidently shattered in the crash, some of it replaced by tarpaulins of pterosaur leather to keep the weather out.

And, in the section behind that, where hull panels had ruptured or fallen away, he saw structural beams supporting a series of huge tanks, spherical – each about five metres across, he guessed, pretty much filling the hull side to side, lined up like peas in a pod. These were presumably intended to hold propellant to feed the great engine: some gas to be super-heated by the fusion energies and hurled out through rocket nozzles to drive the ship onward. And beyond *that*, he assumed, at the stern of the ship, the engine compartment itself, behind solid-looking hull plate.

All this time, Anna watched him. Watched the others too as they made their own exploration.

Eventually he joined Anna back at the nose, where the name of the ship was emblazoned in metal letters:

ЭЛЕКТРОД СМIХ

She smiled at him. 'You said you were a pilot yourself.'

'You're being polite. You know by now that my shuttle was a chemical-propellant ship. Although I have the feeling that we may have been more advanced in some ways.'

'Really?'

'Electronics. Control systems. The material sciences.' He waved a hand at the greenhouse section. 'Maybe the life support.'

'Our purpose was the greening of space. The way one designs a craft must reflect one's goals, as well as the available technology.'

'Well, you would think so,' he said wryly. 'Let me tell you about the NASA subcontractor bidding process sometime.' He waved a hand at the name. '*Electrode*. Right?'

She smiled again, a little thinly. 'A name chosen by schoolchildren. Readers of a magazine of weekly super-science stories, in fact. Why? Because the name sounds exciting. Super-scientific, you see? Even if it has nothing much to do with spaceflight . . .

'Ah! If only you could have seen this sorry ship at her best, on the launch pad in deep Kazakhstan. The ranks of children indeed, watching, waiting for the launch. The great Tsiolkovsky himself was a teacher, you know. He lived just long enough to see Russia's first high-altitude liquid-fuel rockets, the *Cosmist* series, based essentially on his design, his theory, flying in 1935. He always insisted that our space developments be explained to the children . . .'

So Tsiolkovsky, in Anna's reality at least, had experimented with chemical propellants. Probably he had in Malenfant's reality too. The thought stuck at the back of Malenfant's head; it seemed significant.

Josh came pushing through the clinging grass. Deirdra followed him, more distracted.

Josh said eagerly, 'Malenfant – the big engine compartment at the rear of the ship, the base—'

'What about it?'

'It's quite empty!'

Anna glared at him. 'I told you to keep your distance back there. The relic radioactivity—'

'Oh, I was cautious,' Josh said. 'I've flown nuclear-powered ships myself, remember. I just looked, there were gashes in the hull . . . But that was enough to reveal that there's pretty much nothing left in there. Stubs of piping, electronics on the walls. Nothing to salvage, Malenfant!'

Anna seemed irritated, still. 'What did you expect? We followed emergency procedures when it became clear that the *Elektrod* had been badly damaged by its encounter with the blue hoop in the sky . . .'

Josh pushed his dusty glasses up his short nose. 'I've been thinking about that. We know the blue hoops bring life forms here, mix them up. But maybe they have other functions. *Maybe our crashes weren't accidents.* Maybe the hoops are also trying to exclude – technology. Anything advanced, anyhow. *They*, your Engineers I suppose, Malenfant, whoever is behind the operation of the hoops. So they have the hoops patrol the air, destroying what falls through. To maintain a kind of quarantine.'

'Yes,' Anna said. 'That makes a sort of sense. They are interested in *us*, as life forms, as components of an ecology. Of a system of life. Our technology might compromise that.'

Malenfant turned to Anna. 'So, your landing. You hit the blue hoop. And I'm guessing from what Josh saw that you dumped the nuclear core? Emergency procedures?'

'We did that over the sea – the deep sea to the west, between the continents you call Caina and Judecca, not the shallow continental shelves. Of course we must have done harm even so; radioactive materials will seep out of the wreck for years, decades to come. If we had not ejected we probably would not have survived the crash ourselves, and, probably, done more damage to this world. As it was we did not even have a means to steer as we fell, for the atomic engine had powered our attitude control nozzles too.'

Malenfant thought that over. 'You mean those lesser nozzles on the flanks of the cylinder?'

'Yes, I noticed those,' Josh said. 'Hefty pieces of engineering themselves, aren't they?'

Malenfant frowned. 'But useless without the atomics. Like the rest of this hulk.' He felt a crushing disappointment. A wrecked engine was one thing; you could fix that. An engine dumped at the bottom of the sea was beyond salvage. So was he trapped here on this world after all – after a thousand-kilometre trek to here?

He stayed composed. Find another way, Malenfant. Visualise the goal.

'You know, if we ever plan to fly out of here, we will have to watch out for the gatekeepers. The hoops. Whether they are purposeful or not. Maybe they will shoot down launches as well as new arrivals. Perhaps if we set up some systematic scouting we might spot patterns, anticipate their arrivals—'

Anna shook her head, irritated. 'You speak nonsense. Of irrelevant hypotheticals. We can never leave this place. Come. Follow. Let me show you the rest of what has become of my *Elektrod*.'

34

They entered the hulk at the nose, through a rip in the ship's skin.

From there, Anna led them through a jammed-open hatch into a kind of corridor, from which cabins could be accessed through round airtight internal doors, like a submarine's, Malenfant thought. They didn't enter any of the cabins, but through open doors Malenfant made out what looked like stripped-out bedrooms, heavy fixtures like tables and bed frames still bolted in place, anything that might be useful long removed.

Josh looked back into the nose of the ship, which was accessible through another hatch, with a stepladder. 'If the ship were vertical,' he said, 'the way I presume it was launched, then *that* way would be up.'

'Correct,' Anna said. 'The ship is a skinny cylinder, a hundred metres tall but no more than seven metres in diameter at its widest – you have seen its spindle-shape. A magnificent sight at its launch base on the Kazakh steppe! And, as you are guessing, Josh, the bridge, the control cabin, is in the nose. When we attempted to land I was up there, with Vasily, main pilot. The non-essential crew at that point were ensconced in these cabins, at the launch.'

'Makes sense, of course,' Josh said. 'You keep your crew as

far from the atomics as possible – as shielded as possible. Our own *Harmonia* has the same design principle.'

Deirdra snorted. 'The *Harmonia* is just a big dumbbell. This is *class*.'

Josh looked absurdly hurt, Malenfant thought. He tried to move the conversation on. 'So tell me when you got here, Anna. Irina told me you left Earth in 1981.' He grinned. 'And you landed here on the thirty-second of Long July in Year Zero.'

She raised an eyebrow, and smiled back. 'Do you mock my dear friend Vasily? Well, so do I, at times. We launched from Earth in 1981. 20 October. We were not the first humans to have been sent to Venus, but we were first to Anteros. On 8 March 1982, a week after arrival at Venus, we approached Anteros, and entered that strange tangle of tunnels it contains. Once we emerged in this system, we headed for this world – the most obvious target, rich in life signs – and when we got here, well, then it became 32 July, retrospectively at least.

'Once we were down we had to begin the business of survival – and in the earliest days we had to rely on the corpse of our ship, of course. In particular we plundered our greenhouse. Come and see.'

They passed along a tilted, broken-backed corridor that ran down the spine of the ship, away from the control cockpit and the accommodation cabins. Heading ultimately for the engine compartment at the base of the ship.

They reached another propped-open hatch, and entered a big, roomy, glass-walled compartment, that evidently spanned the width of the ship. The place was bright even in the wan Persephone sunlight, and basically warm, though Malenfant detected cooler draughts. As he had seen from outside, some of the glass panels had been lost, with some replaced by sheets of stretched pterosaur leather, some left as gaping wounds in the walls.

Still, the nature of the place was obvious. This was the greenhouse he had glimpsed from outside. He moved on, cautiously. He saw rows of trays on trestles, loosely attached, some with covers of glass or what looked like clear plastic. Some of these trays were over his head, easily accessible in zero gravity, so he guessed. Water pipes and electricity cables connected the trays – but likewise he could see gaps where equipment had been ripped out, even, evidently, lengths of fat water pipe. He could see no green in here now, but some of the trays had what looked like dried residual muck clinging to their inside surfaces.

Through scuffed glass, he saw the disc of a pale Sun.

'Our farm,' Anna said.

'Hydroponics,' Josh said. 'You suspended your growing plants in fluid. Pipe in nutrients, pipe out waste.'

Anna frowned. 'Your bangle gives me a convoluted definition of that word. Hydroponics? We call this a Vernadsky farm.' She waved a hand. 'I do not know how you live aboard your own ships. We build our ships as miniature Earths. We tend our garden, our farm, even in the depths of space, and in turn the farm, fed by sunlight, supports us. It feeds us, cleanses the air – the plants give us back our oxygen, and so on . . .'

Josh was intrigued. 'It's all disused and dismantled, but I think I can see the logic. A range of provision types, much as aboard our own *Harmonia*.' He pointed to relic equipment. 'A salad farm, correct? Green plants. And a yoghurt box, as we call it, where you grew algae. And a sushi farm, to cultivate fish – well, eels in our case. Same basic human needs, subtly different solutions.'

Deirdra broke in. 'All this is the basic principle of Cosmism, right? That we should learn to live in space – to expand beyond the Earth, and live on sunlight.'

Anna smiled back. 'I am glad one of you is sensitive enough to understand. Yes, we escape the bounds of Earth. For now we need atomics to escape the gravity well. But once in space – well, all you need is the energy of the generous Sun to build an infinite civilisation. We have – wings, like a pterosaur's, that we unfold to capture solar energy in space. Here, we have spread them over the dusty ground, and connected them to our batteries and other energy stores.'

Malenfant thought of the glimpses of silvered ground beyond the central compound.

She looked around at the dead growing trays. 'I wish you could have seen this in bloom. I wish you could see the greater Vernadsky gardens we have built, orbiting our Earth! Each a kilometre long, turning end over end for gravity – spinning so they always face the Sun. And within, people move like fish, or birds. A green belt of life around the Earth. You can see it from the ground . . .'

'You would love *Silent Running*,' Malenfant said.

'What's that?'

'Never mind.' He felt dissatisfied. He paced around the dead greenhouse, running his fingers over the grimy, empty cultivation trays. He came to a place where, presumably during the crash, one of those secondary rocket nozzles, a big piece of engineering in itself, Malenfant saw, had smashed through the greenhouse's glass wall and come to rest in the ruin of half a dozen trays. 'So,' he said, 'you Cosmists dreamed of ascending from the Earth and becoming one with the cosmos. And you ended up here, on this dismal plain, scavenging the wreck of your rocket ship to survive. How close is that to your goal? You even split up. Irina walked away.'

227

Anna stiffened. 'You know nothing about that.'

'Look – I'm sorry. I do admire how you have survived here. Despite some evidently tough choices. It's – heroic. But it's not enough.'

'Then what else would you have us do?'

'Isn't it obvious? Find a way to get off this rock.'

Anna sighed, and spoke patiently. 'But we have no atomic engine. One cannot escape a super Earth without a spacecraft equipped with an atomic engine. Therefore escape is impossible.'

But Malenfant found himself looking at that big attitude-control engine bell, busted through the glass.

And, turning his head, looking east, he saw the pinpoint glare of that methane burner, twinkling through the scuffed greenhouse glass.

Something stirred in his hind brain.

'Actually,' he said, 'I'm not sure that's entirely true.'

35

A couple of days later, Malenfant was itching with unresolved ideas about methane. He needed to find out more, but, he sensed, without giving away too much too early. He didn't want to get laughed out of court before the basic feasibility of his nascent idea was proven – or otherwise.

So, with Deirdra, he approached Anna, and pretended to be interested in the plumbing.

'I find I'm buzzing with curiosity. As you say, I'm a tech buff. And Deirdra, well, she is just generally curious.' And he wondered how the bangles would translate all that. He smiled. 'Can you show us some more? Where all the pipes lead, for instance? . . .'

It seemed a simple, even innocent request, but Anna hesitated. Malenfant sensed some inner struggle. Something she was motivated to hide?

Then she forced a smile. 'I like to think I would feel the same curiosity, about the engineering. Yes. And, why not? The sooner you see the truth, the better. Come. In a moment, follow me.'

Moving quickly, impulsively, she ducked into the main yurt.

Deirdra murmured to Malenfant, 'What truth?'

'I have a feeling we are going to find out soon enough.'

Anna emerged carrying, in one hand, what proved to be a key for a hefty padlock that secured an equally hefty gate in the stockade – and in the other, unremarked, a whip.

Once out of the main compound, Anna, Malenfant and Deirdra followed the pipelines roughly east, heading for another fence, a dark line across the landscape. The day was hazy, not hot.

'Not helping that she's stretching her legs,' he muttered to Deirdra, as Anna Filosofova receded into the distance. 'For her this is an afternoon stroll. For us, a route march.'

'Oh, stop complaining. Your body should be used to it after the hike. We ought to grab our opportunities to see stuff. While the goodwill lasts. Think of it. These characters have been totally isolated here since they crashed.'

'Yeah. Secrets have a way of building up when people are stuck together for too long.'

'But right now, Anna – well, she seems eager to talk.'

'So you're saying we should exploit this person's loneliness ruthlessly, while she's in the mood.'

'I'll leave the choice of words to you, Malenfant.'

Still following the pipelines, presumably all scavenged from the wreck of the *Elektrod*, Anna brought them to the second fence, a locked gate. The fence itself was very crude, just stakes roughly sharpened and hammered into the ground. As Anna worked the lock, Malenfant vaguely wondered why you would carry padlocks on a spaceship in the first place. Maybe on a weapons store? Or just to keep out the kids. Yeah, he could imagine Cosmist kids running around their big, light-filled craft . . .

He was distracted by a dazzle of reflected light, off to the north, to his left. Those big solar-cell wings, he thought, meant for space, now pinned to the dusty ground.

Anna locked the gate behind them, and they walked on.

Beyond the fence, they came to a tilled field, not all that large, where greenish plants topped ridges of sandy earth.

'Potatoes,' Deirdra said immediately. 'I grew them as a kid.'

Anna nodded. 'Then you will know potatoes are simple to grow, highly nutritious, and very effective in terms of yield per unit area. Our staple, I suppose. Which is why they were present in the greenhouse of the *Elektrod*, of course.'

Somehow all this homestead agriculture was hard for Malenfant to take in. He glanced around at the field, trying to work out what he was missing – what questions they weren't asking.

'Who tends all this? There are only three of you, three adults . . . What about pests?'

'For now the local insects seem to find our crops too strange to be palatable. There are no birds up here, you know. Sometimes we get a visit from a pterosaur, from the Rim Mountains. Quite a sight! Worth it for the loss of a plant or two. They are chased away.'

'The passive voice.'

Anna glanced at him. 'I'm sorry?'

Malenfant prayed that the bangles were up to translating the subtlety of what was troubling him. 'Anna, you say the pterosaurs are chased away. *Who* chases away the pterosaurs?' He waved a hand. '*Who* set up that long fence, who dug out this field, who tends the potato crop? Not just the three of you.'

Her expression in response was reserved, pinched. At length she said, 'I am reticent. I apologise. But our situation here is complicated. Logistically, even morally. We could not have survived without . . . making compromises. Ethical

231

compromises. Now all this is presented to strangers, to you, for the first time—'

Deirdra laid a hand on her arm. 'We know you now. Just show us.'

Anna seemed to think that over, and nodded. As if seeking to renew her purpose. 'That is my intention, today. If not now, when? Follow me.'

And she turned on her heel and headed north, cutting across the rows of potatoes.

Deirdra and Malenfant shared a glance, and followed as best they could. Looking to his right, further east, Malenfant made out that pinpoint flare of flame. The gas well. Some other time.

And as they walked, that dazzle of reflected light from up ahead grew brighter.

They came to another fence. Here there was a simple gate, which Anna led them through.

Beyond the fence, the shimmering silver solar-energy blanket reflected the weak, hazy sunlight, and some folds and ripples were bright enough to dazzle, even under the pale Sun of a Persephone midday.

'Come along,' Anna said, briskly walking over the silver billows. 'The blanket is tough stuff; you won't harm it. It does need to be cleaned of dust, dirt – pterosaur droppings, though that is rare – ha, that passive voice again!'

Malenfant and Deirdra followed, Malenfant feeling reluctant to step on the billowing silvered fabric – it felt like parachute cloth underfoot – despite Anna's reassurances.

Deirdra whispered, 'Why not leave a path?'

He just shrugged.

'So. Solar power,' Malenfant called to Anna. 'Also scavenged from the ship?'

'Indeed. And it is clever. A feedback loop enables the blanket to know how full our storage batteries are, and how much energy needs to be gathered. Just now the blanket is repelling most of the light that falls on it. Reflections are feared. When necessary, it will turn black – like an immense flower unfolding black petals, perhaps – to absorb the solar energy. Actually it is not when the blanket is black or silver that it scares them the most, but when it turns from one to the other; *that* seems to baffle them. And, usefully, keeps them confined. So the blanket serves as a cage without bars.'

'At last,' Malenfant said. '*Them*. A subject for all these verbs, which is a line my old English language teachers would have had to beat into me. *Who* is kept in a cage here?'

'You will see.'

They walked a little further to the north, and no matter Anna's assurances about the robustness of the blanket, Malenfant couldn't help but wince every time he made a footfall on it.

Then he saw who.

Anna slowed.

Malenfant and Deirdra stood at her side. Squinting north, against the glare of the blanket.

Malenfant saw people, a group of them, some moving around, more of them squatting on the ground. There was a fire burning; a thin thread of smoke rose into the air. Fire whose light glistened on naked flesh. All this in a kind of island of open ground surrounded by the sea of solar-energy sail.

They were seen.

Faces turned to Malenfant, and he strained to look back in turn. Bodies like athletes. Faces that might have been human. But the skulls—

'Runners,' Deirdra said. 'Like the skeletons we saw,

233

Malenfant. Irina called them Runners. They had skulls just like that, the small face, the big brows, the small cranium. Seems obvious now. *Homo erectus*, I think Josh would say.'

'Yeah.' Malenfant saw it. 'Or a close relative, a subspecies. More primitive than the Neanderthals?'

'You can see the efficiency of the arrangement,' Anna said. 'The solar blanket serves its primary purpose, while also confining the Runners without the need of more fencing.'

And that was presumably the main point of all the fencing they had seen so far, Malenfant realised now. To contain, control these Runners.

'We establish a clear corridor when we need to bring them out, and they are docile enough if you know how to handle them. As we have learned, not always easily, over the years.'

But Malenfant noticed how she fingered the whip she carried.

'You're holding them captive, then,' Deirdra said. 'I don't see how else to describe it.'

'Oh, you need not apologise for that. That's precisely what we are doing – of course we are.' She faced them. 'I am not without conscience. None of us is. Perhaps my evasive speech gave you a hint of that. They are not suffering materially. They have food; we let parties hunt. They bear children.' She seemed to hesitate on that point. 'But I am well aware that they are not content in confinement. There is a reason we labelled them *Runners*.'

Malenfant said gently, 'You can't get away from it, surely. They have needs that are denied, while you enslave them and put them to work.'

'Enslave,' Anna said coolly. 'A word of judgement. No, don't apologise. And don't take it back. That's what it amounts to. And we certainly do put them to work, as best we can. Otherwise we would not have survived here,' she said defiantly.

Neither of them responded.

Anna turned away. 'They are only capable of simple tasks, though. They can't use any tool save their own hand-axes – every one of which, chipped out of basalt, *is the same*, differing only in size. A Runner could no more use a different tool, a hand-saw or a spanner, than a bird could build a different kind of nest. But you can get them harnessed to a plough, or on a treadmill. They can even be trained to drive in fence posts. But they are human enough – genetically, even – to be close to us, to show a very human distress at times. I admit that.'

Her expression was blank, and Malenfant sensed that this woman, still more or less a stranger to him and from a different timeline to boot, was struggling with her own conscience.

And then he got it.

'*Oh*. I just worked it out. Genetically close, you say.'

Deirdra frowned. 'Malenfant? You worked what out?'

'*The other grave*, Deirdra. The child's grave.' He looked at Anna.

Who turned away, then looked back and faced Deirdra. 'Yes,' she said. 'I think you understand.'

'I talked it over with Vasily. Partially. But I didn't think it all the way through. He talked about founding a colony here. Generations of humans to come. But I was – sceptical. Three Eves and two Adams, and you lost one of those. It didn't seem feasible. But you had another option.'

'Yes. It was a kind of experiment, I suppose. Look – believe it or not, we acted on the best of motives. We did not wish to grow old and die here, to no purpose – if rescue never came. As Vasily told you. *We wanted children*. We wanted a colony. We wanted to raise future generations. But the gene pool—'

'Was unlikely to be adequate,' Malenfant said. 'It's not impossible, historically there have been extreme cases of isolation . . .'

Anna said hastily, 'One of us, Nadezhda, did become pregnant, with Maria. Gave birth. But her father – Yuri was killed even before Maria was born. And so, you see, we with our tiny gene pool had just lost half our male input. Vasily is not a bad man.' She forced a smile. 'For a Ukrainian. But he was not enough.'

'But,' Malenfant said, 'you found yourself surrounded by hominin genes of a different sort.'

Anna nodded. 'We could not use the Hams, though they are clearly closer to our human stock than . . . They would not have allowed it. They are too strong. So – well, Vasily went to the Runners. The first mother was an experiment.'

Deirdra glared. 'Easier to force a female to have sex than a male.'

Anna turned away again. 'That would have been tried later. Perhaps we could have achieved some kind of artificial insemination—'

'Forced, though,' Malenfant said.

She nodded. 'That was how it was, I am afraid. Vasily is not a bad man,' she repeated, more strongly. 'He hated what he did. But he did it for all of us, you see. We helped.'

'"Helped"?'

'Tried to soothe the female. The woman.'

'The rest of you held her down,' Malenfant said bluntly.

'Oh—' Deirdra touched his arm. 'I feel like I've been punched in the stomach.'

He put his hand over hers, and held it tight.

And he took a breath. 'OK. Anna. Sorry. Who am I to judge? Do Cosmists have consciences?'

'We were trying to survive, that's all,' Anna said.

'Sure. So did it work?'

Anna said bleakly, 'The birth killed the mother. The head, you see, close to the proportions of a modern human, was far too large for the birth canal. The baby was a boy. He lived only hours, though we tried a wet nurse – another Runner . . .'

'You buried the baby,' Deirdra said.

'We called him Yuri. A boy. Yuri, after Maria's father. Well. You saw the grave. We are not evil people, Deirdra, Malenfant. We were just desperate. That's all.'

Malenfant felt a kind of dull fury. He meant what he'd said to Anna. Who was he to judge? But did it have to be this way? Did mankind have to spread out over the cosmos, indeed the manifold, spreading murder, slavery, rape?

And he could see Deirdra struggling with this. He knew about the Cosmism she had absorbed, and now she was confronted with this gross contradiction.

But it was Deirdra who reached out and touched Anna's arm now. 'We haven't dropped out of the sky to criticise you.'

'Believe me, we judge ourselves. *I* do, every day. Well – I think that's enough for now. Shall we head back to the house?'

'Irina, though,' Malenfant said now.

'Irina?'

'We know she left the caldera, took the Hams, walked down to the coast and lived there for – what, years? Was this incident, of the Runner hybrid, what caused her to do that?'

'Oh, no,' Anna said, with a kind of bleak humour. 'Something *much* worse than that. I expect you'll find out soon enough. Come.' She faced west, and led the way.

Deirdra and Malenfant, holding hands, followed. Deirdra murmured, 'I know you came out here hoping to find stuff out, Malenfant.'

'Yeah. But not *this*.' He shook his head, turning away.

Thought about getting out of this hell-hole.

Thought about methane.

While Deirdra began to weep, silently.

36

It took Malenfant a couple of days to work out the preliminary plan to his own satisfaction. He wouldn't tell the Russians what he was up to, not until he was ready.

Nor Lighthill, stranded in deep space.

And he wouldn't tell his own companions either. Not Josh who was probably a far better engineer, even part-time, than Malenfant would ever be. Not Emma who had relevant expertise in the field, in addition to being an avatar of his ex-wife. Not Deirdra, though in this she had been, as ever since his waking from a long coldsleep under drowned London, his inspiration. He truly believed that the only way to test a crazy and potentially lethal plan like the one he was cooking up was by having as critical an audience as possible. Everybody looking for the holes. And if his scheme got through such a test, well, maybe it would fly.

Literally.

He did take Bartholomew aside. 'I need some advice about using the bangles.'

'What advice?'

'Can they be made to work like an overhead projector? A real comfort blanket of a thing from my NASA days . . .'

The concept took some explaining. But it turned out that, in a sense, the mind-writing bangles could.

Malenfant spent a couple more days polishing his argument, and checking his figures.

He set up a blank screen, just a sheet of leather, dangling from the wall.

Bartholomew had assured him that, though the bangles wouldn't literally project images onto this thing, they could make it *seem* as if they did, by writing the appropriate shared images into the viewers' heads . . . Malenfant just got on with it. Generally, even though he used his bangle every waking second of every day, he didn't like to think too hard about this kind of stuff.

When he'd got it working, he called them all in.

Before the screen, they sat together in their tribes, as he had expected.

To his right, the companions he had brought here. Emma with a cautious look, as if she feared Malenfant was about to make a public idiot of himself, and after all it wouldn't be the first time in her experience. Josh looking curious, anticipatory. Deirdra calm, alert. Largely silent and withdrawn, since Anna's revelations.

Russians to his left: Anna, Nadezhda with baby Maria, Vasily. Irina, as always, sat glum and silent, somehow apart from the group even in this small, crowded space.

It was hard to read their expressions. He sensed a kind of resentment, and wasn't surprised. The Russians had after all been surviving here for years, and here was Malenfant after a couple of weeks about to lecture them on – well, he conceded, how they had got everything fundamentally wrong. And maybe they sensed that.

It only added to the tension that the Russians were guilty

of awful crimes, though they denied it; the newcomers were judgemental, they could hardly not be, though *they* denied it. Not a happy camp.

And maybe Malenfant was the one who could get them out of this hole.

Everybody was staring at him, as he stood there.

The baby laughed, and gurgled. Laughed at the crazy man, he thought.

Her mother, Nadezhda, glared at Malenfant. 'Maria here ought to be asleep by now. Shall we start this some time today? Or—'

'I'm sorry. Gathering my thoughts. I have . . . a modest proposal.'

He paced.

'Look. Before I start in on this. You all, the crew of the *Elektrod*, have done a good job of survival here, stranded on Persephone. Stranded as *we* are now. You've made – compromises. I'm not sure if, in your shoes, I could have kept sane, let alone survive at all.

'But whatever the past, now I think we should *get off this planet*. Build, not a settlement in this terrible place, but a way out of here. OK. Sceptical faces already. Tell me why that's impossible.'

A brief silence, shared glances.

'Our ship is broken,' Anna said, sullen. 'I showed you its ruin. We scavenge it in order to survive.'

'More fundamental than that.' He looked around at the group.

Vasily actually put his hand up, then, glancing around, sheepishly grinning, pulled it down. 'Schoolmaster Tsiolkovsky, we have no atomic engine. We dumped it in the ocean before we crashed.'

'More fundamental than that, even.'

Josh tentatively put his hand up. '*And* we have no atomic engine fuel.'

'Right.' Malenfant shrugged. 'So what?'

Josh blushed and looked away.

'Sorry, Josh. It wasn't a dumb remark. Not meaning to pick on you.' He looked around at the group. 'You're wrong about all of it. You're making the wrong assumptions. It's just a question of looking at the situation a different way.

'Start with the fuel. Actually you have plenty of fuel. You've just been burning it off, or most of it.' He glanced at the blank screen – a screen of *flying dinosaur leather*, he reminded himself, and just for a heartbeat he was disconcerted by the strangeness of all this – and snapped his fingers.

On the screen appeared an image of the Russians' gas tower, over at their experimental drill site, with a flare of burning methane bright at the top.

The Russians just stared. At what was, Malenfant reminded himself, a mental image of his own projected into each of their heads.

'Come on,' Malenfant said. 'Think about it. I know you siphon off a little of the gas for use as a backup energy supply – you get most of your energy from your solar-cell farm, right? But – tell me. How much gas escapes per day?'

Anna shrugged. 'Around ten thousand cubic metres. Mostly methane. Six or seven tonnes, by weight. At that the supply has gone down; when we first tapped the well – and by accident, we were looking for oil or coal, not gas – the well released five, six times as much. Evidently we are depleting the reservoir. But this, I believe, would be typical of mining operations on Earth also.'

'Ten thousand cubic metres,' Malenfant said, pressing. 'But

a single cubic metre of methane, if burned, can yield around thirty-five megajoules of energy. If you tapped all that stuff you burn off and used it efficiently, you are looking at a power supply of around four *megawatts*. Even depleted as the well is. Whereas in fact you take enough for just a few hundred kilowatts, right? Even that is just a backup for the solar power plant.'

Vasily snorted and waved a dismissive hand. 'Ah, you exaggerate. Everything we have here is improvised from the wreck – you have seen that. The efficiency of any such process would be hopeless.'

'Well, maybe. Lousy efficiency or not, what I'm pointing out now is just how much untapped energy you are wasting there. And I'm thinking about alternate uses to which all that beautiful, stored, containable, transportable energy could be put. With a little imagination.'

Of which quality the Russians evidently needed more. Malenfant shut up for a moment, watching Josh nod his head – *he* was getting it – but the Russians, from an entirely different cultural tradition, indeed a different engineering tradition, looked baffled.

He waited. Keep your mouth shut, Malenfant. Best to let them work it out for themselves—

'Propellant,' Irina said at last. 'You are talking about using the methane as propellant. Rocket propellant?'

Eureka.

Vasily turned to her. 'Propellant? What propellant? To propel what?'

'Rockets.' She looked at him. 'Malenfant here is proposing to use this gas, this methane, as a rocket propellant. He will *burn* it, to get us off this planet.' She stared at Malenfant. 'Correct?'

'Correct.'

The one thing it would never have occurred to them to try. To these Russians, rocketry had always meant atomic rocketry. Now he had to get them thinking in a different category. And maybe Irina had been around the crazy westerners long enough to have picked up on their way of thinking.

Still he kept his mouth shut, beyond that one word of reply. *Let them work it out.*

It was Anna who laughed first. 'You can't be serious.'

'Never more.'

'You spoke of the energy potential in the gas . . . Yes, but you cannot use such energy to escape this planet's gravity well! The very idea is absurd.'

'Why absurd?'

She said heavily, as if explaining the obvious to a child, 'Because the feeble chemical energy released by burning methane – it is physically impossible; even Earth's gravity is too high for the energy density of your propellant.' She laughed again. 'And speaking of gravity, here we are on a super Earth with a higher gravity than Earth – and so a higher escape velocity – which would make the very idea of riding a methane rocket even more implausible.'

Pick on a detail, Malenfant. The rest will follow. 'We don't need to reach escape velocity. Low orbit will do – even a very low orbit, a decaying orbit. Lighthill in the *Harmonia* would be able to pick us up.'

Josh leaned forward, pushing his spectacles back. 'And with respect, Anna, I think you may be speaking from . . . a narrow perspective. It's *not* physically impossible. Even if, compared to the great *Elektrod*, any such ship will look like a travois. Anyhow, even you Russians must have flown chemical-propellant rockets at one time.'

Anna waved a hand. 'Well, of course. Tsiolkovsky's own

experiments – his early writings when atomic power was not understood, and as he worked on his derivation of his rocket equation, which applies to any propellant system – of course we flew chemical rockets, with solid and liquid fuels, gunpowder, various chemical combinations. For scientific purposes. For development! As educational toys for children! Just hops in the low atmosphere! But it was always clear that the energy densities affordable by atomics were much greater, much more plausible for propulsion beyond Earth. And by the time we were ready to go to orbit the atomic technology was mature.'

'Mature it may be,' Irina said calmly. 'But our *mature* atomic engine is right now at the bottom of the sea.'

An ally, Malenfant confirmed to himself.

Josh pressed his point. 'Perhaps it was so for you. And our own technological trajectory seems to have been similar; we built the nuclear-powered *Harmonia* after all. But it need not have been so. I *know* that in the realities from which Malenfant and Emma came, liquid-chemical rockets were used to reach orbit, by crewed craft – why, they went all the way to the Moon.'

Emma smiled. 'Actually, to Mars too. It was the slow boat to China, but it got my crew there, to Phobos.'

Malenfant took a breath. *Draw it together*. 'Yes. Josh is right, liquid chemical was the basis of *our* space propulsion technology. American. We used small nuclear power plants, yes, but generally for energy in-flight. Our atomic rocketry was always less mature. We did have a nuclear rocket prototype: nuclear-thermal, a fission pile heating up the propellant. That was taken along on the flight to Phobos made by my wife, Emma. In that timeline . . .'

He avoided everybody's eyes, including Emma's – the Emma

in this room, the Emma he had retrieved from a different Phobos.

'In that timeline the technology was called Ares-Apollo N. The nuclear stage failed; it killed one of the crew, stranded the rest.' He sighed, pressed on. 'So, yeah, I guess I'm prejudiced. I come from a different technological regime, more backwards in some regards if you will.

'But as Josh and Emma said, our liquid-chemical-technology regime enabled us to send people to the Moon and Mars, and to send robot probes out through the Solar System. So I guess that's why I find myself seeing chemical-propellant solutions to the problem of getting off this planet, where most of you see no solution at all.'

A pause.

Vasily was the first to speak. 'I sympathise, my friend. You speak of your lost wife. I lost contact with my own family, when we crashed in this place. They have been as dead to me, and I to them – unless we escape. And if we need a miracle to do so, that is what we must seek.'

He stressed the word *miracle*, Malenfant noticed, as if to emphasise he was in no way endorsing Malenfant's vision. Not yet.

But he was still talking.

'So,' Vasily said, waving a hand at the image on the leather sheet – an image they all saw but which did not really exist, Malenfant reminded himself. 'A rocket is more than its fuel. Even if I concede that methane – where my grandfather came from, that was cow farts! – can be used to propel a rocket, in principle, we do not have a rocket that will *work* on methane and oxygen, in practice.'

Perfect cue.

'I know,' Malenfant said. 'So we need to build one.' A fresh image, of a battered engine bell, still attached to the hull of the *Elektrod*. 'We have these to start with. Side-rockets. Right? For attitude control. *They* aren't nuclear. '

Anna snorted. 'They are little more than steam vents.'

'But they are engine bells, expansion nozzles, tough enough to withstand pretty high temperatures, right? I've checked that out. So that's a start. Oh, we'll have to build the rest of the engines, improvising with whatever the *Elektrod* can provide.'

Josh grinned, very boyish. 'Gosh. What a project that will be! We'll need propellant pumps, ignition systems, combustion chambers . . . And there will be no rules; we'll have to put it all together any way we can. I can't wait to start on *that*.'

'We'll need more than one rocket, Josh. Based on the size of the bells alone and extrapolating performance, I'm guessing maybe nine, ten rocket engines. That's flight articles, maybe another two or three for development purposes.'

Josh's mouth was round. '*Gosh*.'

'Never mind toy rockets,' said Vasily, a little testily. 'I am a pilot. Tell me about the performance of this rocket ship of your dreams.

'Let us get back to basics.

'Here is a key number. Escape velocity from Persephone is fourteen kilometres per second. That is the velocity at which any rocket must ultimately throw you, if you are not to fall back. Correct? Which is more than Earth's escape velocity of eleven kilometres per second.'

'All true,' Malenfant said. 'But I told you. *We don't need to escape*. We just need to make orbit around Persephone. Even a low, decaying orbit. Lighthill can pick us up from there in the *Harmonia*. And the velocity we need to make to achieve that, starting from down here, is just *ten* kilometres per second. Again, that's more than on Earth. But Persephone's *orbital* velocity is only a little less than Earth's *escape* velocity.

'So in principle a rocket powerful enough to enable us to escape the Earth altogether could at least put a package in orbit around Persephone. And, like I told you, back home *we* have built such rockets, with liquid-chemical technology. If not I would not be here.'

Vasily stayed silent this time. Malenfant felt another tingle, an anticipation of success; Vasily was at least not disagreeing with him.

'But let us move to practicalities,' Anna said now. 'Performance issues. Now, I know that the exhaust velocity of the nuclear rocketry of the *Elektrod* was nine kilometres per second. Only just a little less than orbital velocity here—'

'So the *Elektrod* could have made it off this planet easily. Well, with a decent fuel load.'

'Very well. Now. Tell me about the performance of your methane, as a rocket fuel. I presume you would burn it in oxygen—'

'That's the idea. Look – the optimal chemical-propellant combination is hydrogen-oxygen, which gives you four kilometres per second exhaust velocity. The faster you throw your exhaust out the back of your ship the faster you go, right? Methane-oxygen is pretty good; you get a little less than that maximum four klicks per second.'

Anna snorted. 'If you understand the rocket equation at all you will understand that a rocket performs best when striving to achieve velocities not much more than its exhaust velocity – less, ideally. To achieve more than *twice* exhaust velocity, as you propose here, would require a rocket whose fuel load would be, what, ten or twelve times its dry mass? More?' She laughed. 'Absurd. The thing would collapse under its own weight, even on Earth.'

'Not so,' Malenfant said calmly. 'Our engineers learned how to build big, because they had to. Look at this.'

With a kind of effort of will, he changed the 'slide'.

A Saturn V sat on the pad at Cape Canaveral, a cylinder white and black, with the silver thimble of an Apollo spacecraft perched on the top. Vapour vented, rising to a blue Florida sky.

Malenfant was pleased at the gasps he won from his sceptical audience. A dream of antiquity now, the Saturn brought a lump to his own throat.

Nadezhda, who had said little, got up from her seat, leaving Vasily holding little Maria, and walked closer to see. 'It is beautiful. Like a Kremlin spire.'

'Over a hundred metres tall,' Malenfant said now. 'About the size of your *Elektrod*, end to end.'

Vasily grunted. 'But most of the *Elektrod*'s volume was useful. A greenhouse, for example.'

'Point conceded. Most of *this* is fuel tanks,' Malenfant said. 'And most of it emptied out in fact, discarded, in the first few minutes of the flight. Three stages – look, you can see the engine bells of the first stage down here. And under the escape tower – see the little silver cylinder with the cone on the top, and there's more equipment in the fairings below and above? *That's* the payload. The Apollo spacecraft, destined to take three crew to the Moon. The system sent about thirty tonnes to escape velocity, and en route to the Moon. Getting back was easier,' he said drily. 'Take off from the Moon's low gravity, lose your incoming velocity through braking in the Earth's atmosphere . . .'

'It is insane,' Vasily said.

'It worked.'

'You should have waited for a more mature technology,' Anna said.

Nadezhda smiled at her. 'Are you saying *you* would have waited for some future generation to take the prize, Anna? Would you have been content with that?'

'To practicalities,' Vasily said. '*This* is what you intend us to build. Here, from the wreckage of the *Elektrod*.'

'Something like it, yes. Now tell me why it's impossible.'

'All that tankage,' Nadezhda mused. 'Anna pointed out that the initial fuel load would need to mass many multiples of the payload. And the structural mass – all those tanks, all those girders to hold those heavy tanks and engines, all of *that* must be hauled up off the ground too, at least at first.'

'Very true. That's why it's so big.'

'And the fuel?'

'The Saturn's big first stage burned hydrogen and oxygen. A mix of fuels elsewhere.'

'And it is stored in gaseous form?'

'No, no,' Vasily said. He got up and walked to the image, pointing at vapour plumes (and Malenfant had time to marvel afresh at the miraculous capabilities of the bangles, as Vasily's heavy form blocked Malenfant's own 'view' of the Saturn). 'It cannot be gaseous, of course. The fuel is stored as a liquid. It would be much too voluminous otherwise—'

'Of course it would be,' said Nadezhda. 'I wasn't thinking. I am not used to considering tanks of this – monstrous proportion.' She laughed. 'I could not estimate the orders of magnitude. Of *course* it must be liquid.'

'And stored cryogenically,' Vasily said. 'That is, stored at the very low temperatures at which hydrogen and oxygen liquefy.

Hence these boil-off plumes. That itself would be a tremendous technical challenge. Though we could of course salvage tankage from the *Elektrod*.'

'A challenge we don't have to meet,' Malenfant stressed. 'Not the whole way anyhow. Yes, we will need some lox. Liquid oxygen, which you get at a relatively moderate low temperature – moderate compared to liquid hydrogen anyhow. And methane can be liquefied and stored at the same kind of temperature.'

Anna stared at him. 'You say that very glibly. Granted we have gaseous methane pouring out of the ground, and oxygen in the air around us. Now we must trap and liquefy great volumes of the stuff? *How* much? That ten to one mass ratio – we must be looking at tonnes of methane alone.'

More like tens of tonnes, Malenfant thought. Or hundreds. He kept that thought to himself, for now. No point frightening the children.

'And the energy required to liquefy all this material?'

'You have the power,' Malenfant said calmly. 'Your big solar-cell farm.'

Vasily said, 'Yes, but even so, it will take days – weeks? To extract so much.'

More like months, Malenfant thought. He kept that to himself too.

'Well,' said Anna heavily, 'before we start liquefying the very air we breathe, let's think about this a little more. You speak of harvesting methane; very well, but there is more to a rocket than that. Malenfant, this monster Moon ship of yours looks barely capable of getting off the ground, even from the ground of Earth. So tell me. What of its thrust?'

'At take-off, a little less than three thousand tonnes.' By

which, as he hoped these spacegoers would understand, he meant the force of the engine's thrust was equivalent to the weight of that much mass, under gravity.

'Fine. And the take-off weight?'

'Twenty-seven hundred tonnes.'

'Ha! So the thrust exceeded the weight by a mere few per cent. Enough to get this monument off the ground – just.'

'You're right,' Malenfant said, grinning at the memory. 'It barely moved in the first few seconds; if you watched it launch you could *feel* it strain against gravity, almost. My own shuttle system wasn't much better. But it did get off the ground, every damn time. And then rose faster—'

'Very good. But, look, here we are on Persephone. *Higher gravity*. If you built such a thing here – even if it didn't collapse under its own weight first – the thrust is unchanged. But that higher gravity gives your fixed mass an increased weight, of . . .'

'About thirty-four hundred tonnes,' Malenfant admitted.

Anna sat back and folded her arms. 'There. Your thrust is less than that. This beautiful artefact could not even lift itself off the ground of Persephone. The triumph of my logic gives me no pleasure.'

Maybe not, Malenfant told himself. But you're hitting us with the logic of holding us down, here on Persephone. Not the first time you held somebody down, he thought viciously.

'True enough,' he said aloud. 'So we don't build a Saturn V. After all, we aren't going to the Moon. We build something smaller, more capable.' He nodded at the screen.

The rocket he showed now was evidently smaller than the Saturn V. But you could see the common ancestry, Malenfant thought, the slim lines, the narrowness of the second, upper stage over the big bulk of the first stage.

'So this is the Saturn I,' he told the group. 'Designed by the same team. Part development vehicle, part delivery system in its own right. It and its derivatives delivered Apollo spacecraft to Earth orbit for various test flights, and for access to the Skylab, an early space station. A little more than half the height of the Saturn V . . .'

Vasily nodded. 'It looks more . . . plausible. Its capability?'

'It could launch a tonne to Earth escape velocity. So, a useful size of robotic interplanetary probe. And, in our case, a useful mass to send into low orbit around Persephone.' He looked around the room. 'We build a small capsule. Just big enough for all of us to cram in there, survive for the brief time it would take Lighthill to come pick us up. And, hell, if we can't make the capsule light enough for us all we just build another damn rocket to take the rest.'

Vasily grunted. 'Before we arrange the seating plan, tell us about the performance of this Saturn I.'

'Seven hundred tonnes thrust. Mass five hundred tonnes. So a Persephone weight of six hundred and twenty-five tonnes. And therefore thrust *exceeds* weight by about ten per cent.'

Nadezhda grudgingly nodded. 'He's right.'

Malenfant exulted, inwardly. It was the first backup he had had. An ally at last.

Out of the corner of his eye Malenfant saw Deirdra, who had silently been following every word of the discussion, pumping a fist. Probably a gesture she had picked up from Malenfant himself.

Vasily snorted. 'So this beast gets off the ground. So what? Let us refer again to our friend Tsiolkovsky and his rocket equation! Surely the structural mass of such a beast *cannot* be less than, what, ten per cent of the launch weight? So that the final velocity could not be more than eight, nine kilometres per second – less than the ten minimum to reach Persephone orbit.'

Anna leaned forward. 'All right. I imagine the answer to that is to stage.' She glanced at Malenfant. 'Can you show this? . . .'

He smiled at her. 'I can.' If only because he had been visualising the revised image that came up now.

The rocket split in two, an upper stage lifting from the lower, revealing another engine bell. The lower stage theatrically tumbled out of the picture.

Malenfant pointed. 'I figure we will need one of our side-rocket motors in the upper stage, versus eight in the lower stack.'

Deirdra was frowning. 'Maybe I'm the only person who doesn't get this part,' she said ruefully.

Emma patted her hand. 'The rocket equation is about the dead weight you have to haul along as you try to get into space. Staging is a way of . . . getting around that darn equation. Once most of the fuel has been used up, you see, spent to get the stack off the ground, you can just throw some of that stack away – that big cluster of engines, the empty fuel tanks. Just keep what you need for the last push. It's not cheating, exactly.'

'You can't cheat mathematics.' Deirdra grinned. 'But you can use it smartly.'

'Exactly.'

'Look, we can go further,' Malenfant said. 'Remember we only need to do this once, so long as it flies. So we strip it down to the bones.' He waved a hand.

Whole chunks of the rocket's skin disappeared, revealing a stack of spherical tanks held in a stout metal frame.

'Ugh,' Emma said. 'Looks like an anatomical diagram.'

'Well, we don't need to look pretty,' Malenfant said. 'And saving every bit of weight will help. I predict we will end up shaving grams off our crew cabin, however we put that together.'

Anna sighed. 'I recognise those tanks. From the poor *Elektrod*, of course. Well – at least our ship will not have died in vain.'

Malenfant held his breath.

'*Eight engines*,' Vasily muttered. 'The stability issues alone . . .' Then he grinned. 'But then it is not as if I have anything better to do!'

Deirdra twisted to look at Anna. 'So does that mean we are going to do this?'

The Russians exchanged glances.

'We must be insane,' murmured Anna.

'No,' Vasily replied. 'Insane would be to stay here. To doom our children, our children's children perhaps, to a dwindling life, and final extinction. And not to mention the dreadful moral choices we have had to make to survive at all.' He glared around as if challenging them to comment. Then he reached out and let little Maria hold his finger; she gurgled. 'Our mission was *not* to give up our lives for no reason. If we can save ourselves – let's try it. And maybe if we are lucky, and if this madman with his nineteenth-century rocket designs does not let us down, we may all see the true Akademgorodok once again.'

It took about a month before Josh and the others began test-firing their prototype methane rockets. And by that time the *Harmonia*, under Lighthill's command, had come swimming back out of the inner Solar System.

37

Methane rockets, eh? Ingenious, I suppose. And a strategy put together in the mere thirty-something days I have been away from Persephone orbit?

Of course I've tried to follow the discussion during my journey. And I see you've got as far as a test fire! Impressive. Ingenious and industrious, Deirdra – good for Malenfant, good for Joshua, and good for you all. And it might even *work*; it's not technically impossible, at least, and as long as that's true one always has a chance. Though I'm a chap who never expected to fly anything but nuclear rocket ships, just like dear old Butch Breakaway . . .

Who? Oh, yes. You mentioned those old comics before.

Did I? Ah. I'm sorry, Miss Greggson. I know very well that I have spent far too much time alone, and especially when lightspeed delays in communication have made it impossible for us to have anything like a sensible conversation. One does turn inwards on oneself.

Perhaps I might have borne this better if I had been, I don't know, a sculptor – used to working alone.

I had a cousin who painted portraits of cats.

I can see it has been a long trek for you.

Indeed. It's not just that, actually. It's the lack of – well, scenery en route. You know that I visited Venus and Mercury, in that order. Cunningly designed route, given the configuration of the planets. But my close encounters with the inner worlds were brief, really. Just flybys. Oh, they loom out of the sky during the final days of approach, you see the planetary discs – the sparks of the moons in the case of Venus – but not much else, not with the naked eye. Then the hours of closest approach, a brief interval where there is a landscape scrolling past the windows, and you are busy, busy photographing and training every instrument on the passing world, and peering down at wonders to be seen once only in a lifetime . . . Gone so quickly!

I can imagine.

And in the intervals between . . . Well, you've seen it. To be suspended between the stars, away from any worlds. One does not even feel as if one is moving at all – as you know the drive is inert, save in brief moments of thrust when one arrives at a planet or leaves . . . One hangs there, alone! Like an ornament on God's Christmas tree.

God?

Strange how one comes to think about these things. My own parents were not religious, you know. Church of England, of course, but one had to be, given the social circles we moved in. And one enjoyed Christmas and Easter and so forth. But I don't think my parents *believed*. Nevertheless the basic messages sank home into one's head, which I suppose was the purpose of it all. I try to keep the Big Fellow out of my conversation, and indeed my thoughts, but He does have a habit of knocking on the door . . .

And do you let Him in?

That's the thing.

No.

I hope that doesn't shock you.

It would certainly have shocked my mother!

It's just that – well, perhaps I know too much now. Rather as you imply about your own society. We did have Bible studies at school – at Linbury Court, my prep, as well as my first school in the village. Genesis chapter one, verse one, is clear enough: 'In the beginning God created the Heaven and the Earth.' Except that it's quite evident to all of us now – and to me in particular – that He did not. Or, at the very least, *others*, these World Engineers of Malenfant's, have meddled so much that His handiwork has been obscured. We have been left with solar systems buried under layers of artifice. His handiwork maybe, *their* fingerprints all over the place! Like cosmic crime scenes, as Malenfant put it.

Just tell me what you found, Geoff.

Ha! To the point, refreshing as ever.

So: In the beginning . . .

Actually, let's start with the theory.

Our own beginning was, I'm told, some eight or nine billion years after the Big Bang itself. There was a cloud in interstellar space: a big ice cream swirl of hydrogen and helium and carbon, ice, silicon compounds. Initially it was about the width of the Solar System's current comet cloud. And it was actually a fragment of a much larger, disintegrating cloud, totalling millions of solar masses.

Well – this swirl started to collapse, to rotate, to flatten out. Most of its mass would fall in eventually to the central knot that would become the Sun. The rest, just one per cent or so, whirled around in a protoplanetary disc, as it is known.

. . . Are you still there?

Still here. I know the planets would form from that disc.

Correct. Now, as far as the planets were concerned, everything was determined by a series of 'ice lines'. Too close to the Sun, within Mercury's eventual orbit, no solids could congeal – not even rock or metal. Further out you had metals condensing, particularly iron, nickel, aluminium. Further out still you had silicon compounds – the stuff of rock – and beyond that ices of water, ammonia, methane.

And those condensed fragments stuck together in loose formations, grains that gathered into pebbles that gathered into boulders and mountains and small worlds . . . There were always collisions, always a great grinding and smashing-up, but a few of these babies survived. To become what we call planetesimals. Big lumps of stuff, some of them hundreds of kilometres across.

From which the planets were born.

Remember the ice lines? Out beyond the point where water ice could form, it was easier for the debris to stick together, to form huge cores. And when those cores were massive enough to attract each other gravitationally you would get a feedback effect, a runaway—

The giant planets. Jupiter. Neptune.

Right. Giants of gas and ice. Actually, *five* of them, I think, not just the four that survived . . . We'll come to that.

But further in you had a slower consolidation of the rock and iron fragments that would eventually form the inner worlds. Slower, and much more violent. For a while you had a real rugger scrum going on in there, with maybe fifty planetary embryos, as they're called, sailing around the inner System. Each at least ten per cent the mass of the Earth – that's about the mass of Mars, by the way – and *they* smashed together to build the final planets. It's as if you were creating a sculpture by throwing lumps of molten iron around a studio.

259

It seems amazing that anything coherent emerged out of that at all.

Well, it did – somehow. And it would have, evidently, even if there had been no meddling. As far as I can tell, only the Hand of God was at work as far as the creation of the gas giants goes, and the inner planetesimal cloud.

But after that—

The fingerprints of the Engineers are all over the place.

Give me an example.

Mercury. I've been there. To the local copy of Mercury. And it's too big!

Too big?

And, also, it's too *smooth*. Lacks craters. Ask Josh to show you some of the images I scanned down. But that's a detail, by comparison. The main thing is – yes, it's too blessed big. Well, it was apparent from the first surveys I made . . . That *we* made on arrival in this System.

Look. Mercury, *my* Mercury and yours, had an anomalous composition. Like Earth, it is a rocky world, with a core of liquid iron, a covering mantle of liquid rock – silicates – and a solid rocky crust over that. It must have formed from a jumble of these materials, but eventually the denser iron settled to the core.

Now, on Earth the width of the core is about sixty per cent of the width of the planet as a whole. OK? Including a big, thick mantle over that core. You might expect two rocky worlds to have the same kind of ratio of structure, even if one is smaller than the other. But Mercury, *our* Mercury, had a core that was about seventy-five per cent the width of the planet. Much *bigger*, in proportion, and a much bigger component of the total mass.

That's how it is at home. But here — well, you know what? *This* Mercury *does* have the same proportion as Earth. Its core is about the same size as our Mercury's in fact, but with that thicker mantle the planet is bigger overall — half Earth's diameter, as opposed to about forty per cent.

Umm. Quite a dramatic difference. So you think there must have been some difference in its formation, here.

Correct! And, given what I told you about its violent formation, all those planetary embryos flying around, what difference might there have been?

Something about those massive impacts?

Correct again. So, yes. In *our* Solar System, Mercury seems to have suffered a late, devastating impact that stripped away much of its mantle, leaving the remnant with an apparently outsized core. Whereas that never happened here. Either something *here* deflected that final impactor from striking Mercury, or, alternatively, something targeted that impactor deliberately, in *our* reality.

Something, or someone. You think the Engineers did this.

Oh, I think the Engineers did this. Why? Who can say for sure? But I can see reasons why *our* smashed-up Mercury would be useful.

Mining. Malenfant has talked about that.

Yes. With that thin mantle, our Mercury would have been an ideal site to mine all the way down to the iron core — if you felt you needed to do that. And didn't we find traces of what looked like ancient mining operations there? But I can't be sure, we *can* never be sure, probably.

Anyhow, you see how the handiwork of God is left muddled and obscured by such actions?

More evidence, in this cosmic crime scene. Let me tell you now about Venus.

Look – we know that our own Venus, so-called sister planet of Earth, was never Earthlike in its rotation rate. Earth spins on its axis in a day; Venus spins *backwards*, with a 'day' as long as eight *months* on Earth.

And our Venus's other problem is that its geological engine has seized up. No plate tectonics; no drifting continents; no way of relieving the planet's inner heat – which builds up until everything lets rip at once, and you get what Josh would tell you is called a 'global event'. Which is as nasty as it sounds: world-wide volcanism, continent-sized flows of lava, and so forth.

Meanwhile the Sun is steadily heating up, you see, and putting pressure on the climate systems of all the worlds, including Earth. Long ago it got too hot for Venus – our Venus, whose geological recycling engine may already have jammed. The oceans boiled off, all the carbon dioxide baked out of the rocks, and the place turned into a kind of oven under a greenhouse atmosphere thick as an ocean itself.

But not here, I'm guessing. Is this Venus still rotating backwards, at least?

No! Good question, Deirdra. In fact the days *are* very long – not *as* long, around a hundred Earth days – but *this* Venus spins in the right direction. So it's different, as different as Mercury II was from our Mercury.

And, Deirdra, this Venus is not like our own. *This* Venus is a true sister of Earth. It may even be habitable!

Thanks to that slow rotation, in fact. Not so slow as our version, but slow enough for the planet to have a global weather cycle. There's a cloudy day side and a clear night side; some of the Sun's heat is reflected from the day clouds, and the rest is carried steadily over to the night side where it radiates away into the clear sky. Add to that an efficiently working tectonic cycle, the drifting continents processing the rocks, and you have a planet which, as a heat engine, is in good repair. There's even an ocean – a water ocean – across more than half its surface.

Deirdra – *this* Venus is as temperate as Hawaii!

In places anyhow. Some of the time. Oh, it's no paradise. During that long night it snows pretty heavily, everywhere across the dark side. There's a permanent wind blowing across the terminator. And when dawn comes there can be small, daily catastrophes – flash floods as the night's ice dams give way. Like a sudden end to winter, every day . . . It's different from Earth. But I can't see why life couldn't prosper there.

And you think the difference between the copies has the same cause? An impact? Or one deflected?

I think it's another big one deflected, yes. This one wouldn't have removed the mantle – maybe Venus's bigger size made that impossible – but knocked it spinning backwards. And, I think, maybe it did a more subtle harm. Maybe that primordial smash is what screwed up the plate tectonics, somehow. Venus is a smaller world than Earth, and the mantle currents that drive the drifting continents might have been weaker. More easy to deflect, to block altogether.

Oh. So you think that's why our Venus seized up, as you say.

It's possible. It's consistent. But not this Venus! Not here!

So, one or other copy of this planet has been meddled with, once again. I think I'd like to believe that *this* is closer to the true Venus, the virgin Venus – Venus as God made it, if you like. Because it's habitable, an arena for life. Even if—

Yes?

Even if there is *not a trace of life* I could detect anywhere, on land or sea, in the air. I'd have been able to detect almost any conceivable kind of carbohydrate-based life, you know, if only because of deposits in the atmosphere. Like the methane your pal Malenfant is collecting on Persephone, a relic of ancient sea beds seeping to the surface.

You've convinced me, Geoff. So remind me. If this is all deliberate − evidence of meddling, as you say − how do you stop one half-formed planet from colliding with another?

You know how.

You saw it, on the other side of the manifold portal.

By meddling with the formation of even larger planets . . .

As previously discussed, when the Solar System was born, the gas giants grew fast. OK? Maybe merely a few hundred thousand years or so for Jupiter to grow from an Earth-sized planetesimal to the monster of hundreds of times Earth's mass that it is now. It would take much longer for the rocky worlds to form.

Jupiter chewed up a lot of disc material, but there was enough left over to build a Saturn. And, further out, with a subtly different mix of material, you got Uranus, Neptune . . .

And Shiva.

And Shiva. A fifth giant. I know all about Shiva.

Huge as they were − are − the giants formed haphazardly, wherever they happened to start to coalesce. But all, at first, within fifteen astronomical units or so of the Sun. Fifteen times as far as Earth is from the Sun − today Neptune is *thirty* astronomical units out.

And once formed they started to tug at each other, gravitationally − or rather Jupiter started to tug at them all − and they suffered friction from the remnant disc. All that dust was still pretty dense. They slowed in their orbits, even Jupiter. And they spiralled in towards the Sun.

Where the disc was thicker, and the friction must have been greater . . .

Yes. This was all very early, you know. The Sun's core itself had barely ignited; the rocky worlds were not yet fully formed.

You might think the giants would spiral all the way in to the Sun. But they were saved by resonance.

The big planets like to fall into orbits that resonate with each other: the periods will be in a ratio such as two to one, or four to three, or some such. So that, every few orbits, the planets line up and pull at each other. All this produces dynamic stability: once you get locked into that kind of dance, you tend to stay in it.

So the planets trundled in towards the Sun – until Saturn fell into a resonance with Jupiter. And after that, Saturn pulled Jupiter back from the brink – Jupiter had got in as far as the orbit of Mars – and the two of them settled into a three to two orbital resonance further out.

In the meantime, though, the migration had caused a lot of damage: scattering the dust disc, and dragging planetesimals, even whole planets, all over the place. Some of the planetesimals were thrown out to what would become the comet cloud. And some were thrown into the inner System –

Where the young worlds were smashed and pulled around. Impactors the size of worlds themselves. And that was when we had the big impacts on Mercury, Earth—

Exactly.

You have it.

And *that* was what the Engineers meddled with. Amid all that instability, a small tweak here or there – a gentle push – could cause a dramatic difference to the outcome of a collision.

To the building of a world.

Quite. And it wasn't over yet. Much later the System was destabilised again. Now the dust from the last of the smashed planetesimals caused another wave of friction, and the giants started a *second* migration, outward this time. That threw a new hail of rocks into the inner System – the astronomers called it the Late Heavy Bombardment. Giant craters on the Moon, and Mercury, and Mars, and so on.

And at some point in *this* process the orbit of the fifth giant, Shiva, became destabilised. It seems to have looped around Jupiter and Saturn, until it was hurled out of the System altogether.

Ah. It became the rogue. And in my home system, Persephone was thrown out there too. We figured that much out.

Yes. We figured it out. This is a delicate process which could be perturbed easily – give Shiva a push just so, as it bounced between the big giants, and it flies off *that* way rather than *this* . . .

Deirdra, we speak casually of the World Engineers. We still don't understand the Engineers' agenda. But it does seem to me that we have identified their World Engine. Just as we saw in your home system, yes.

The World Engine is the primordial migration of the giant planets.

Quite a saga. And you tell it well, Geoff.

Thanks. You should have said that to Old Wilkie, my English teacher at Linbury . . . Never mind.

Meanwhile, onwards. We all have our duties, I suppose. And, ultimately, we reunite. We continue our mission. We find these World Engineers of yours—

And hold them to account. Look, you may not be alone much longer. Malenfant is hoping his methane rockets will be working in a couple of months—

Still a long time to be hanging around up here. I do prefer to be busy, you know . . .

You're considering another jaunt.

Yes. Even if it means another spell in lightspeed solitary. There is one more location I ought to take a good look at. Can you guess?

Earth?

Earth.

38

By midday of the following day, Josh and Emma announced they were almost ready for another attempted test-fire of their prototype methane-oxygen rocket engine.

As the two of them made their final preparations at the test stand, Malenfant, with Vasily, hurried back out of the cordoned-off area, at the heart of the Rocket Garden. Stepping quickly over the evidence of previous rocket blasts: scars in the earth, scuffed dirt, scorch marks, tangled bits of failed equipment which nobody had troubled to clear up so long as they didn't get in the way of further work. That was the philosophy here, as it had emerged in its rough and ready way, Malenfant realised. This wasn't NASA. They had to get this thing right, but it only had to work once. After all, they would be leaving all this behind. They didn't have to be *neat*. It wasn't NASA. It wasn't even Bootstrap, Inc.

Still, you had to take precautions.

Vasily and Malenfant made it to the safety cordon, which was just a rope lying on the ground in a rough circle around the test stand at what was judged to be a safe-ish distance, and looked back. This whole area of development, of fuel tanks and other components, and engines in their test stands – even a skeletal pre-build of the final ship itself – Malenfant had called the Rocket Garden. It was to the south-east of the area of the caldera inhabited by the Russians and their guests. Just to the north was the gaunt frame of the gas well, with the gleam of the solar-cell farm visible beyond. The yurt, and the wreck of the *Elektrod*, were visible away to the west.

Anyhow here they were, standing in pale Persephone sunlight. Malenfant carried a satchel with a couple of flasks of water. He offered one to the Russian.

Vasily refused. 'Still tinkering, tinkering,' he muttered. 'For such a primitive technology, your liquid-fuel rocketry is rather temperamental, it seems.'

Malenfant suppressed a sigh. Vasily was a dour character at the best of times. 'Give me a break. We're halfway there. Nearly. Well, maybe.'

'Halfway? From where to where?'

'Good question. Look, we know that even when we get the methane plant set up, it's going to take thirty-five days or so to extract the gas we need out of the well over there.' He pointed north. 'And store it. While in parallel we work up the liquefaction process, the freezers. *And* build our rocket. And as it happens it's already thirty-some days since I first stood up on my hind legs in the yurt and tried to convince you all we could build this thing. I guess we're about where I hoped we'd be by now. In the middle of stuff, as much ahead of us as behind us. With the skeleton of the ship standing in the dirt. With Josh building his rocket engines—'

'Engine,' Vasily corrected him. 'One test article so far. Which has yet to fire for more than a second.'

'OK, OK. But we're getting there. Have faith.'

'Meanwhile, here comes more rusty salvage.' Vasily pointed west.

Malenfant looked that way.

Between the solar farm to the north and the sprawling farmland and greenhouses to the south, a rough track led westward back to the yurt and the wreck of the *Elektrod*. That had become a well-worn route as heavy components were dragged all the way out here from the ship to the Rocket Garden. And even from here Malenfant could see what was being hauled out today: another spherical tank, a massive thing, five metres in diameter, torn out of the guts of the *Elektrod* and destined to be installed, one of eight, in the guts of the new craft, to hold propellant or oxidiser.

It was as heavy as it looked, as Malenfant knew from personal experience when they had all pitched in to start the break-up of the wreck. Now it had been rolled onto a kind of huge travois, a frame of wood and leather that scraped along the ground. And it was being hauled by brute power, by the only motive force they had available: Runners, a whole squad of them, straining at leather ropes which were attached to harnesses across their chests and shoulders.

With one very small and slim member up front, Malenfant noticed now.

Vasily marvelled. 'I sometimes feel I am dreaming. Even after so many years here. On any other day, in any other time or place, to see a component of a crashed spaceship being dragged across the dirt of an alien planet, by a squad of primitive proto-humans harnessed with flying-dinosaur leather – well, it would seem odd, wouldn't it?'

Malenfant frowned, deliberately deciding not to reopen the near-lethal argument that had erupted within the group once they had decided to go ahead with the rocketry project.

The newcomers had got together and talked it over, and tried to insist that they progress the project without further use of the Runners. To the newcomers the Runners were not draught animals. But the Russians refused to cooperate with that. Maybe, Emma murmured to Malenfant, to *stop* using the Runners after all this time would have been a kind of tacit admission that it had been wrong in the first place, and therefore psychologically unacceptable. This was the Russians' camp. The rocket would be built with their technology, even if with Malenfant's engineering – and using their practices. The compromise had been made. Malenfant thought it tore them all up, to some extent. Even the Russians. Especially the Russians.

And through it all, of course, he was aware that there was *still* some greater secret being hidden by the Russian group, the black sin that had driven Irina out of the camp altogether.

So Malenfant could have done without wry observations from Vasily.

Still, he looked that way. 'I can see something even odder,' he said now. 'That's Anna supervising the operation, isn't it? But – look, there in the front triple of Runners – who is that?'

'Ah. On the right-hand side as we look? Perhaps my eyes are better than yours. That is Greggson Deirdra, I believe.'

'What the hell's she doing? Damn it. Vasily, maybe you could stay here—'

'You go sort out your crew-person.'

Malenfant set off at a sprint.

'Get out of there,' he said to Deirdra.

The party of Runners stumbled to a halt. All of them naked, they were hot, sweating, dusty, panting. And they were silent, their eyes averted. As if they were barely present at all.

Deirdra glowered back at him, and wrapped her fingers around the harness straps across her chest.

Anna, supervising the operation, just shrugged. 'Don't blame me. I told her she must not do this. *Bartholomew* told her she must not, that she will damage herself.'

'Are you going to order me around too, Malenfant?'

Pick your words carefully, Malenfant.

'When the hell have I ever been able to give you orders? If I could, you would be safe at home with your mother in Birmingham right now, building houses for your buddies to celebrate the solstice or whatever. Instead of here, smeared across the manifold.'

'So how are you going to stop me now?'

He sighed. 'How about plain logic? You aren't as strong as the Runners. Not nearly. And also you're not used to this.'

'He is right,' Anna murmured. 'Your heart is strong, your conscience, but your body is not. You pull—' She mimed a stumbling, irregular gait, her hands grasping imaginary straps. 'Not regular. You weaken the team as a whole, and worse you make the pulling lopsided. Which will harm these Runners more than if you do not pull at all.'

Well played, Anna, Malenfant thought.

'Walk with me,' he said to Deirdra. 'Please. Come see Josh's test burn. When it works – OK, *if* it works – it will mean a lot to him for you to be there.'

Deirdra was stubborn, but not foolishly so. She thought it over, nodded, and ducked out of the harness. Then she walked to Malenfant, flexing her shoulders and rubbing the palms of her hands together,

Anna wordlessly started to sort out the Runners into a new configuration. They responded without resistance to her brisk touches to their shoulders – not quite slaps, Malenfant saw, uncomfortable.

Deirdra wouldn't meet his eyes. But she followed his lead, back down the track towards the test stand.

She said at length, 'It's just wrong, that's all.'

'I know, I know—'

She glared at him. 'Doesn't this remind you of anything? You and I share the same timeline, remember. It's in my history too.'

'What is?'

'The deep origins of your space programme. The technology. I looked it up in the bangle. The first spacegoing vehicles were based on war weapons. Missiles targeted on London, in fact. Built and funded by a Nazi regime who used slave labour to construct rockets.' She waved a hand at the party of Runners, still labouring along, slowly, behind them, under Anna's calm guidance. 'Aren't we doing exactly the same thing? It's worse, in fact. The Runners can't even *dream* of escape, or sabotage.'

This issue, he realised, had caused the nearest thing to a direct confrontation between the two of them they had ever had, in over six subjective Earth years since he had woken in that drowned hospital in London to find her waiting for him.

And so it should, he realised.

'You're right,' he said. 'Of course you are. All I can say is, the quicker we can get off this planet, and leave the Runners alone, the better. The only other option being walking off into the dirt, to starve—'

She glared back at him. 'And maybe that's exactly what we should do—'

That was when Josh's test engine misfired.

It was more of a bang than the roar of a healthy rocket. It died away quickly. Like, Malenfant thought, the echo of a thunderstorm rolling around the Shield caldera.

He glanced around quickly. He saw that the Runner party, still dragging their huge steel tank across the dust, were terrified, yet too cowed to leave their harnesses. Anna was moving among them, speaking calmly, evidently trying to soothe them.

Deirdra, meanwhile, was staring over at the rocket stand.

Which looked intact, at least, Malenfant saw, when he turned that way. He could see that scavenged engine bell still pointing up into the sky as if the rocket were trying to drive itself down into the ground, rather than up in the air. It was, Malenfant thought, a strange echo of the World Engineer rockets they had once discovered on another Persephone, in another timeline, rockets that had been *built* to push at the ground. But now, rather than the healthy glow of a sustained flame, only a plume of dirty smoke rose up from that engine nozzle.

Malenfant and Deirdra exchanged glances. Then Malenfant spotted Vasily running towards the stand.

They followed.

Long before they reached the stand they met Emma and Josh coming the other way. They were both grimy, tired, and smelled of smoke. Josh's hair was mussed, and the lenses of his round glasses were obscured by a fine layer of dust and soot.

Emma eyed Malenfant. 'Vasily is closing down the test rig. Evidently we had a "race track instability". So Josh diagnoses.'

'A what-now? . . . Never mind. You both look pooped.' Malenfant dug water flasks out of his satchel. Emma took one and drank deep.

Joshua refused, but Deirdra pushed it back at him. 'Take it. You need it.'

Josh accepted the water, but sighed. 'What I *need* is an intensive shop-floor education in the intricacy of liquid-chemical-propellant rocketry.'

'Your glasses are filthy,' Deirdra said gently. 'Let me . . .' She carefully lifted them off his face, dug out a scrap of clean cloth from a pocket, began to wipe the lenses.

Josh now had panda eyes, Malenfant saw, amused, affectionate. White patches around his eyes, within a mask of soot. Yet the dirt on his face didn't hide the blush at this bit of tenderness from Deirdra.

But he was evidently angry, impatient, and his head was still full of his technical problems.

'You would think it's simple. In principle all you are doing is burning propellant and oxidiser together inside a box, the resulting gases expand, squirt out through a nozzle, push back on that nozzle thanks to dear old Newton's third law of motion, and Bob's your uncle. *In principle*. In practice, we have high-pressure, high-volume pumps working on fluids at cryogenic temperatures – our engines will consume a tonne of fuel and oxidiser every *second* – pumps that we scavenged from a Russian ship that were not designed for the job, mind you – fluids which are then splashed onto an injector plate—'

'Which is a kind of sieve,' Emma said, for Deirdra's benefit. 'Holes to let a spray through into the combustion chamber, so that fuel and oxygen get thoroughly mixed up, before you attempt ignition.'

'And even that isn't the end of the story. Even if you get it right, the ignition is a controlled explosion, well, hopefully controlled, that delivers a big thermal jolt to our combustion chamber, and an acoustic one too, we belatedly discovered – that first bang is *loud*. Our first attempts just got shaken to bits. I feel as if we are having to invent whole damn disciplines from scratch.'

Malenfant forced a grin, and squatted down beside him. 'Well, in a sense you are,' he told Josh. 'Look, I was in the private-rocketry industry myself for a while, and I learned more about the nuts and bolts than I ever would have as a NASA pilot. Of course we have the wisdom in the bangles, such as it is. Where there are probably theoretical studies on how they built the pyramids. But all the technicalities, the nitty-gritty details – and adapting what we actually have to hand, to create what we need – that's the challenge you are facing.'

'I'll say,' Josh said wearily.

Deirdra looked lost. 'So what actually happened today? What is a race track instability?'

'Where the detonation pressure, in that expansion in the combustion chamber, isn't quite symmetrical – it's not centred properly. You can get an overpressure on one side that leads to a kind of swirling wave effect, and as more and more fuel and oxygen pour in and burn up the instability can grow, diverging until it becomes a force that can rip an engine apart. As we found out. At least we were able to shut it down quickly . . .' He stood up. 'Oh, I'm going back. My current theory is that we haven't milled the holes in the injector plate quite symmetrically enough. I have a replacement I've been working on.'

Emma frowned. 'I for one need a break. Josh, let's just go sit down for a while and—'

'No, no. I see it all clear.'

Deirdra said sternly, 'She's right. You need a break.'

He smiled at her. 'Isn't one supposed to get back on the horse after one falls off?' He turned, raised a hand to wave, and stumped off over the worn grass.

Deirdra was still holding his glasses. 'I worry about him,' she said.

'Me too, kid,' Emma replied. 'He will try to do it all himself. Comes from years of competing his way through an imperial-British education system, probably.'

Malenfant frowned. 'I don't mean to push him. It's not like we have a fixed deadline. We'll look after him – and so will Lighthill, when he's back from his jaunt to Earth.' He sought

276

a way to lighten the mood. 'Deirdra, you don't come out this way enough. Let us show you what we're building here. Good excuse to keep an eye on Joshua a bit longer.'

'Also he needs his glasses back,' Deirdra said with an exasperated grin.

So they followed Josh.

Malenfant walked them over to the fuel storage plant, such as it was. Tanks, roughly lagged for insulation by a kind of fibreglass they had dug out of the *Elektrod*, and pumps, and pipes that sprawled over the ground, most heading back towards the methane-burning tower. In fact an awful lot of what they were building, Malenfant realised to his chagrin, still consisted of nothing much more than big tanks and pipework lying around on the ground.

'More guts from the *Elektrod*,' Deirdra said.

'Yeah. Well, you can see that. I have a feeling we've hauled just about every tank out of that ship larger than the toilet cisterns . . .' He thumped one big tank with his fist. '*These* babies are too big to fit into our rocket ship, so we're using them to store propellant and oxidiser as gases until we're ready to liquefy them to load the ship itself. You understand how this works.' He pointed at the gas flare. 'We tap the well out there, pass natural gas through a couple of filters to concentrate the methane, and then store it here until it's time to liquefy it for the ship tanks. We have plenty of power, coming from the Russians' solar-cell farm.'

Deirdra said, 'And the oxygen? Straight from the air?'

'Correct.' Emma pointed to a small building constructed using panels from the ship. 'We thought of electrolysis at first – splitting it out from water. In the end we built, well, we *improvised* an air separation plant. More 1940s technology. You filter the air, then compress it, and filter again to remove the carbon dioxide and the water. Liquefy it to separate out the nitrogen from the oxygen – liquid oxygen and nitrogen have different boiling points, you see.'

Malenfant said, 'We've tested all this but it's not operational yet. Because oxygen is so freely available in the air we can extract our two-fifty tonnes in a few days, five maybe. Whereas it will take about ten days to liquefy the methane, even after the month it will take to collect it in the first place. So we will wait until we have almost gathered all the methane we need, then do a rush job on liquefying it, and collecting the oxygen at the same time. Reduces the time we need to keep everything cold, and avoid boil-off.'

Emma pursed her lips. 'It's a heap of junk, though. I say that, and I helped build it.'

Malenfant had to laugh. 'Oh, come on. It works, doesn't it? And, improvising a rocket plant? I know it's tough for Josh, but not having the right gear actually makes it more fun. Like our early days at Bootstrap. Hey, come on. Let me show you the spaceship itself . . .'

Deirdra seemed a lot less impressed by the half-finished craft than Malenfant might have hoped. Looking at it through her eyes, afresh, Malenfant could see why. It bore little resemblance to the slim Saturns he had shown them – more a kind of tower of scaffolding, with indistinguishable technological junk inside.

Emma nudged Deirdra. 'Be kind about his toy.'

Deirdra thought that over, then murmured, 'Well, Malenfant. At least it's the right . . . height.'

'Yeah, yeah,' Malenfant said, suddenly feeling unreasonably protective. 'You can laugh. Yes, it's the right size and shape at least. And remember we won't be bothering with a pretty outer hull. Look – we took all these girders and struts from the *Elektrod* — well, I guess that's obvious. And we built for strength.' He walked them closer to the stack and began to point out details. 'See the big cage at the bottom? That's the load-bearing assembly. Eventually we'll have six of Josh's rockets in there, all firing at once. The assembly has to have the strength to contain those raging beasts, and transmit the shove they give to the rest of the tower.' He pointed further up. 'And inside, see the spherical shapes? Fuel tanks. Or oxygen. So there are already a couple of tanks in there, taken from the *Elektrod*, just like the one you were hauling today. We are using tanks of a standard size, five-metre-diameter spheres. Eight of them in all. Four fuel, four oxygen—'

'Why that size?'

'Because they were the most usable size of spherical tanks available in the wreck, that's why. If you use smaller tanks you reduce the impact of a catastrophic failure by any one tank, but you get more overall weight, and walk into a nightmare of plumbing when you try transferring the fuel and oxygen down to the engines and Josh's combustion chambers. Six tanks in the first stage.' He waved a hand to the top of the stack. 'And up there is what will be the second stage, when all of the heavy lower stuff is dumped in the high atmosphere: two more tanks feeding just one Josh engine.'

Deirdra smiled, and that was a relief for Malenfant to see. 'You really are enjoying this, aren't you, Malenfant? All this gadget stuff . . . '

He felt embarrassed. 'Yeah. I know. I'm playing with toy rockets in the middle of the moral horror of this place. But if it brings all this to an end—'

Wham.

They looked at each other, alarmed.

Malenfant hadn't just heard a noise. He had felt a kind of shock wave in the air, pushing at his chest.

He stared at Emma. 'He didn't wait.'

'Josh?'

'Yeah. He didn't wait for you to come back, before he tried another test.'

She said, 'Those damn race track instabilities.'

Deirdra was already running back towards the test stand, Josh's glasses still folded up in her hand.

'Come on,' Emma said.

And they stumbled after Deirdra.

39

It was a full day later when Malenfant, Deirdra and Emma began the digging of the latest grave, in the shadow of the wrecked *Elektrod*, in the little cemetery that was growing in the ground of Persephone.

The earth was heavy just here, faintly moist, like clay. Malenfant seemed to feel the extra gravity with every shovel-full he lifted with his ageing back.

Shut up and dig, Malenfant.

'So no British at all left down here now,' Emma said as she shoved her own spade into the ground. 'Poor Geoff, stranded in space. The last survivor.'

Deirdra said, without looking up, 'Everybody's stranded. Up there, down here. We all are.'

Malenfant and Emma shared a glance.

Emma said to Deirdra, 'You know, it's OK to feel – whatever it is you are feeling.'

Deirdra frowned. 'Such as?'

'Grief. Loss.' She sighed. 'Even relief. I know your relationship with Josh was complicated.'

'My relationships with everybody are complicated.'

'You know what I mean. It seems crass to say it now he's dead. But he clearly had a crush on you.'

Deirdra half-smiled. 'Well, I know that. But I never took it too seriously. I mean, what choice was there? I'm the only person here remotely near his own age.'

Emma smiled, tiredly, as she dug. 'Be blunt, why don't you?'

'You and Malenfant are together.'

That caused Emma and Malenfant to share a glance. *Together?* Refugees from different realities? It felt like they were together, Malenfant thought, and yet not, at the precise same time . . .

He parked that.

Deirdra went on, 'And the Russians have their own little web of relationships that were established long before we came here. *That*'s not going to change . . .'

And now Malenfant thought about that, it was a puzzle. He'd seen no sign of sexual relationships between Anna, Vasily, and Nadezhda – of Irina with anybody. And there had been no tension since the westerners had shown up, as far as he could tell. You might think shipwrecked Vasily would be dribbling over Emma, or Deirdra. It had just been eroded out of them. Their humanity flattened on this super Earth. Like their compromised morality, he thought.

'So,' Deirdra said, 'Josh and I . . . It's hard to know how I would have felt about Josh, or he about me, if it hadn't been for this . . . situation pushing us together.'

Emma smiled. 'Oh, I think Josh would have liked you on any world you two happened to come together.'

Deirdra looked away. 'I suppose we are living more like a community of Hams,' she said now. 'The ones we encountered with Irina during the trek. A handful of people, adults and kids, an extended family, stuck together. Isolated. Though in their case by choice.'

'Yeah,' Malenfant said. 'But we humans generally don't choose to live like that.' He looked down at himself, at his battered, dirt-covered coveralls, the spade in his hand on which new calluses were growing over the old. 'If our Fourth of July rocket doesn't work after all—' He looked at them. 'We've not really discussed this. How do you think you would feel about that? About being stranded for good?'

Deirdra nodded. 'I've thought about it. We could have kids. Mix up the women and the men, just as the Russians seem to have started to do. It doesn't make me feel – enthusiastic.'

'Nor the Russians, I think,' Emma said drily. 'Little Maria doesn't seem to be doing so badly. But all Bartholomew's technology can't make us native to this planet. The gravity alone—'

'Even so I don't know if there would be any point,' Deirdra cut in. 'Oh, the children would give us some comfort.' She smiled. 'Like baby Maria. But, what then? The Russians have proved it. We're not going to found a new branch of humanity here. We'll just die off, one by one. Or kill each other. Maybe there will be one left, alone. Digging her own grave. Without even the comfort of knowing that a trace of her will live on in the Codex.'

Emma glanced quizzically at Malenfant.

'Twenty-fifth century. A kind of huge library of dead people. I told you about that.'

'Whatever.' Emma walked over to Deirdra. 'Come on. We both need a break, I think.'

'I'm fine. We have to finish the grave.'

'We've made a good start. Leave it to Malenfant for a while. And the others probably want to contribute . . . . I think I need to borrow little Maria for a while. And if I need that, so do you.'

Deirdra gave in, propped her shovel against the yurt wall, and, with Emma's arm around her shoulders, allowed herself to be led away.

Malenfant took a swig of water from a flask, and clambered back into the half-dug hole.

After a couple of minutes Anna came out of the yurt. She pulled off her jacket, took a shovel, clambered down into the hole. Gave Malenfant a curt nod.

Without a word, silently cooperating, they dug.

The grave was finished by the end of the day.

The next morning they gathered around the still open grave, where Josh's body, badly damaged, lay in a canvas sack. Maria, in her mother's arms, wrapped up in an adult's black jacket, was quiet, wide-eyed, curious – calm, if not solemn. Bartholomew discreetly stayed at the back of the group. Malenfant idly wondered if somewhere in his rule set there were specific guidelines on how to handle grief, which all doctors must face.

The ceremony was dignified, given how few they were, and comparative strangers. Malenfant wasn't surprised. Save for Deirdra, even though they were from different timelines they were all space travellers, and space travellers got used to the funerals of companions.

Of course Lighthill couldn't be here. The Wing Commander couldn't even follow all this in real time, he was far away from Persephone in the *Harmonia*, far enough for a significant lightspeed delay to isolate him. And he was a commander who had lost all his crew, one by one.

He had told Malenfant what he thought Josh would have wanted today. 'Though it's guesswork, old chap. I mean, what fellow of Josh's age plans his own funeral? He wasn't religious, if that's any help. "More of a philosopher than a cleric" – that line was actually on one of his school reports . . .'

Religious or not, Lighthill said Josh would have wanted the singing of a particular hymn, called 'Abide With Me' – as far as Malenfant could make out, a piece popular with the younger Brits, where Josh had come from anyhow, because of some kind of association with soccer. He fed words and music down via the bangles. Deirdra, keen to help, had scrawled out the words with charcoal on a scrap of hull-metal. Emma, with her Catholic background, was used to hymn-singing, and said she vaguely remembered the melody.

And, as they tentatively mumbled out the hymn, Maria gurgled and clapped her hands. People sang louder, and smiled.

After that, in his own words, Malenfant relayed what Lighthill had wanted said of Josh, in this alien grave.

How Joshua Philip Morris, son of an accountant, had been a distinguished scholar at Winchester and Southampton – Malenfant assumed they were his school and college respectively – and had soon shown a kind of polymath ability to excel in more than one field. Ultimately he had taken a first degree in mathematics, a masters in mathematical biology, a doctorate in fusion engineering, more post-docs in other subjects. And, still young, he had joined the RASF, the Royal Air and Space Force, as far as Malenfant could see because it was one of the few British employers who actively encouraged the development of expertise in multiple areas – and, of course, the Space Force could transport him to wonders beyond the Earth.

Then Deirdra spoke. Malenfant saw that she held Josh's mangled spectacles in her hand. She described how she, Malenfant, Emma and Bartholomew had first encountered Josh – at a base on a moon of a different Persephone, in a different strand of the manifold – and Josh, almost incidentally, had shown her and Malenfant his discovery of life in the unpromising ground of that frozen little world.

'It's not just the discovery I remember,' Deirdra said. 'It was his love of it. I think that's the right word. Being alive in this rich, complicated universe, and being able to figure out bits of it. He loved it all.'

Nadezhda smiled. 'A very Russian attitude. No, a very *Cosmist* one.'

Malenfant stepped forward. 'Well, whatever the hell else he achieved, he was brave as a lion. A British lion. He knew as well as any of us the hazards of rocketry – especially the improvised sort we are attempting here. I . . .'

I wish it was me lying down there instead of him.

Emma laid her hand on his arm. Not for the first time, as in all the timelines he had visited, she seemed to know what he was thinking better than he did himself. 'It isn't your fault,' Emma said.

'Correct,' said Deirdra. 'We all signed up to this.'

'*Da*,' said Anna, forcefully enough that the Russian word broke through the bangles' translation software. 'We all knew; we all accepted the risk. Josh understood.'

'I know. I . . .' Malenfant turned and faced them all. 'And the best way we can follow this up is to get back to work.'

'Yes,' Vasily said. 'This was a lethal accident, but it was still a rocket test. Those race track instabilities Josh was so concerned about – well, he was right to be concerned, wasn't he? We waste nothing of this, not a datum of learning, even from Josh's final test. And we go on.'

Anna murmured, 'You are right. But not today.'

Malenfant glanced at her. 'What do you have in mind?'

'Potato vodka. For special occasions only. You will be our guests.'

Now Emma stepped up to the grave, picked up a handful of earth, threw it down on the body, and made the sign of the cross. 'Goodbye, Josh.' Deirdra followed in her turn.

One by one the Russians followed.

Bartholomew came forward, after the rest, and threw in his own handful of dirt, his face solemn, all but expressionless.

When it was done, only Irina remained, who Malenfant had barely been aware of during the ceremony. Standing at the back, in the shadows, out of sight – out of mind. But now she came up, dropped in a handful of dirt, her face set. And then she grabbed a shovel, and was the first to push a blade into the mounds of earth removed from the grave.

Her expression was blank.

Malenfant asked, 'Umm, you OK?'

She glared at him. 'After another death in this place?' And she turned away, and shovelled, and shovelled.

Malenfant, hesitantly, joined her, taking his own spade.

40

When Malenfant and Irina finally got into the yurt, the vodka was still being served, from bottles that were chipped, even cracked, some with pale, stained remnants of labels. And the drink was poured into what Malenfant would have called shot glasses, themselves scuffed and chipped, but evidently cherished.

As they settled, Bartholomew discreetly murmured to Malenfant, 'I can give you a pill to keep you sober. Or another to fix the hangover later.'

'Ask me at the end of the session. Keep an eye on Deirdra.'

'Always.'

They drank a quick first shot, toasting Josh, in a mouthful. Malenfant quietly observed Deirdra. She knocked back the shot with the rest, and after that, to his discreet approval, went back to taking small sips with plenty of water.

Everybody else was drinking, save for Nadezhda who cradled a wide-eyed Maria, and Irina, who sat silently just outside the circle.

Anna said gently, 'I for one enjoyed working with Josh on our rocket ship. And I think he was attracted to our Cosmist ideas. Though he seemed to find them hard to grasp. After all you will know that the name is a western label for something which is hard to define, but quintessentially Russian.'

'Or Slavic,' Vasily said.

To Malenfant, he sounded drunk already.

'Or,' Vasily went on, 'Slavic *and* Russian. A mix of eastern and western influences. That and, of course, Eastern Christianity. Tsiolkovsky's rocket ships are only a first step to greater things. Omniscience, omnipotence. To be able to see, do all things, when mind covers the cosmos. And more.'

'More than that?'

'More,' repeated Vasily. 'Such as the conquest of death. *The resurrection of the dead*. All of them. What greater goal can there be? Here is the influence of Christianity, you see. If Jesus really did conquer death, then He is an evolutionary discontinuity. A jump – like the first lungfish to crawl out of the ocean, gasping for air. So Nikolai Fedorovich Fedorov taught. And Vernadsky—'

'I've heard of him,' Emma put in. 'In my version of Russian history. He was behind a lot of the biological ideas, I think.'

'Correct. He spoke of the biosphere and the noosphere, the planet as an integrated living whole – and, thanks to us humans, an integrated intelligence too. We should husband the planet, even as it supports us. But one day we would become "autotrophic", in his word, when we would pass beyond the need to consume living things to survive. We would live on air and the power of sunlight, like – like trees.'

Deirdra grinned at Malenfant. 'Or food printers.'

He nodded. 'Hate to admit it, but sounds like these Cosmists would approve of your Common Heritage culture.'

'Maybe.' She closed her eyes, sipped her drink. 'Maybe our values are like the Cosmists', but more – subtle. Indirect. We don't believe in literal resurrection, but we remember the dead in the Codex – all of them, as far as possible – so they live on in that regard. We don't believe we can become a . . . a transcendent living planet. But we know what we are and where we came from. We are made of the water that comes from the seas and rivers of Earth, and from carbon extracted from the air by the plants, and salt and calcium and iron that comes from Earth's crust. And when we die we dissolve back, all part of a grander planetary cycle.'

'Not Josh,' Emma said gently.

'No. Not Josh. But this is a living world too. All he was will merge with Persephone, I guess.'

There was a pause.

'That is . . . beautiful. And not a lie. From today we must tell each other the truth. No more lies.'

That was Irina.

She still sat alone, near the doorway of the yurt, away from the rest and without a drink in her hand. Silhouetted against the light of the wan, setting Sun.

Malenfant murmured to Emma, 'Shit. I forgot she was even there. Made me jump. She looks like Yoda on a bad day.'

Emma snorted a bit of vodka, but kept control. She whispered back, 'Hush. I think we suddenly came to the important bit.'

'The what?'

'There's something they need to tell us. Don't you get it? Keep quiet and we might find out.'

When Anna spoke it sounded like a warning. 'And what lies do you refer to, Irina?'

'You know very well. But these newcomers do not, even if they may have suspected it.'

Anna rolled her eyes. 'Then we need another bottle.'

Nadezhda passed Maria to Vasily, went to the store, came

back with a fresh bottle, refilled glasses. Still Irina refused the drink, and sat alone, glowering at the rest.

And began to speak.

'When we came here,' she said, 'when we fell out of the sky, there were hominins all over this plateau, the Shield. Mostly Hams and Runners, a few of the australopithecine types – though they seem to prefer the lower altitudes, to be close to forests. Too high for that here.'

'We were amazed, of course,' Nadezhda put in. 'Amazed and – thrilled, at such an encounter. As I imagine you newcomers were when you arrived in your turn.'

'"Amazed and thrilled",' Irina repeated drily. 'Very well. But the hominins themselves seemed less amazed. They after all were accustomed to – no, had *evolved* to cope with meeting people. Not just different people, different *kinds* of people. The Hams live in small groups that make occasional contact with other small groups. To them we were just another small group of funny-looking folk who had some interesting stuff to trade.

'But our contacts deepened. We traded, for food. We gave the Hams a few trinkets. We used our better tools, our steel blades to make stuff better than they could make themselves, and they soon learned what we could do. Word leaked out about that, and so did our goods, and before you knew it more bands showed up, asking to meet us, asking for stuff. Why not? If we were to be stranded here indefinitely it seemed good policy to make peaceful contact with the neighbours. The Runners were more wary, but we harmed them no more than the Hams do. Not directly, not at first. We left them alone, and they left us alone.'

'At first,' Malenfant said heavily. 'So how *did* you get cosy with the Runners?'

'Salt in their food,' Vasily said simply.

Malenfant frowned. 'What's that?'

'A bit of salt on the meat. Discovered that by accident – they love it. Soon we had them clustering around the camp.'

Deirdra pulled a face. 'Like bait.'

Vasily glared. 'As our equipment gradually broke down, we struggled to survive. We knew we had to create a colony here, sustainable for the long term. Which meant a lot of heavy work – construction, digging, even drilling for oil and methane. As you have seen. As you too have benefited.'

'So you started to use them,' Emma said. 'The Runners.'

'In the Runners we had a biddable labour force,' Vasily said. 'You know this. You have seen it. A Runner is much smarter than a horse, say, and more adaptable. An animal capable of using equipment meant for humans – very useful.' He spread his hands. 'You should understand that this happened very quickly. Within months – we could have had no idea of the consequences.'

Malenfant said evenly, 'I'm not following. You've hinted at this. Consequences *worse* than slavery? Worse than using the females as incubators?'

'Let me guess,' Bartholomew said, from his own station at the back of the yurt. 'What was first? Measles?'

And suddenly Malenfant understood everything.

Vasily looked back at Bartholomew, still defiant. 'Smallpox. The deaths began within twenty-four hours of the first symptoms being evident. It was inevitable. In retrospect, I mean.'

Bartholomew nodded. 'Actually the transmission of infectious diseases across the manifold must be common. In Deirdra's twenty-fifth century most such diseases had been eradicated. Strict controls must presumably have applied to Lighthill's British explorers too. As we have travelled the manifold I have done my best to inoculate my companions against the most likely diseases. Still, it was perhaps pure luck that none of you contracted diseases from the Ham or Runner populations.'

Irina nodded. 'Very well. But when we Russians landed here—'

'The native hominins can have had no immunity to such diseases as smallpox. Crowd diseases, herd diseases, prevalent in populations whose ancestors farmed.'

'Nobody farmed here,' Irina said firmly. 'Before us. And so, when we fell out of the sky among them—'

Emma frowned. 'It was another Columbian Exchange. As when the European explorers and colonists covered the globe. Taking with them their culture and technology, plants, animals, from horses to rats. And also diseases.'

Bartholomew put in, 'She's right. It's a good analogy. The native peoples in America, Africa, Australia and elsewhere had had no exposure to European herd diseases, so they had no such immunities. Populations crashed.'

Emma nodded. 'And that's what happened here?'

Anna said, 'Well, we don't *know*. We do know that most of the Runners just disappeared from the vicinity of the Shield. Yet there are still some here.'

Emma glared at the Russians openly. 'And you still put them to work? Even as they were dying around you?'

'Those here, the adults, were survivors of the first run through of the plagues,' Nadezhda said. 'Chance immunity, perhaps. But, immune or not, they will surely still be carriers.' She stared at Emma, as if seeking understanding, if not forgiveness. 'So we *had* to keep them here, you see, if only for fear of spreading the plague further.'

Emma shook her head. 'It might already be too late for that.

In the actual Columbian Exchange on Earth, the diseases ran well ahead of the conquistadors.'

Irina nodded glumly. 'Thus it was.'

Anna said, 'Anyhow it seemed the best way. They are fed, cared for.'

'And put to work. And the Hams?'

'Their case was different,' Irina said. 'As soon as the first plagues hit their population, they retreated, huddled in their small units, their isolated extended-family groups. Avoided contact with each other, and that, obviously, limited the spread. They are indeed much more intelligent than the Runners – in fact they seemed to have worked out the essence of the problem faster than an uneducated human population might have.

'I guessed that they would want to leave here. As did I, by that time, for I was . . . dismayed at what we had done.

'So I led them out. A large band at first.

'Out through the Rim Mountains, down the river valleys to the shore. As you observed as we walked back, they broke away, group by group, as we travelled. Until only Ham's group was left, and I lived with them until – well, until you came.'

Emma nodded. 'Right. Which explains why they seem to have high-altitude adaptations. Because their home *was* at high altitude, before you arrived.'

Irina glared at her fellow Russians. 'So. Do you dreaming Cosmists promise resurrection for the Runners, these people we have carelessly slain?'

Anna scowled back at her. 'Enough of the piety, Irina. We all understand what has happened. We all share the guilt. We do not need sermons, as if from a popish priest. Tell me now. Will you help us work on Malenfant's rocket? Because if not, perhaps it is better if you leave.'

Irina smiled coldly. 'Oh, I will help. Because I believe it will be better to get humans off this world altogether. It would be better, in fact, if we had never come.'

Malenfant, sensing the confrontation was done, suppressed a sigh. 'I'll drink to that.' And he held out his glass.

41

I do not need permission from you to grieve, Colonel Malenfant.

OK, I don't mean . . . I'm sorry. It's impossible to say the right thing. But, look, Geoff, I've lost people under my command.

Nicola Mott. Who died twice, under your command and mine.

Josh was his own man. He was smarter than me on the technical level, and he understood the dangers better than anybody down here, probably. Yet he went ahead with the project even so. He was no action hero. But he was a hero, for sure.

And yet I was not at his side.

Hey, you've been exploring a Solar System, alone. Hell of a thing. I know how much Josh admired that. How much he admired you, sir.

I . . . ah, damn it. I have spent too much time alone. Too much time to brood, you see . . . I'll tell you frankly, Malenfant. Sometimes I wondered if you were pushing him too hard. But it is also entirely possible that if I had been there, on the ground, precisely the same choices would have been made. And, before you say it for me, Malenfant, yes, the best way we can honour Lieutenant Morris now is to finish your damn rocket, and get you off that big pudding of a planet.

We old farts do think alike, don't we?

Old farts? You're the one who is building a spaceship *driven* by farts, sir.

Ha! Touché. OK, you got me. But I'll tell you what else Josh would have wanted to know about, if he'd lived to see you return. What you found at Earth.

Ah. The debrief.

Very well.

It is not our Earth, Malenfant.

Not in the most basic of its particulars. That is the first thing to say. It is slightly more massive than ours, to begin with. It rotates in just eight hours, not twenty-four. And − it has no moon. Well, we could see as much from afar.

I orbited the planet for some days, and gathered data in a variety of ways, including spectroscopic studies and the like − peering at the scattering of sunlight through the atmosphere of a planet at its horizon can inform you of the air's composition − and I made radar surveys of swathes of the surface.

It is a world of cloud, and of thick air. A hundred bars, Malenfant. That's the pressure of the atmosphere at the surface, a hundred times that at the sea level on my Earth and yours. From space it is very bright, actually, like Venus, but the surface is perpetually hidden.

But the air composition, below the clouds, is not like our own Earth's. Much of it is nitrogen, carbon dioxide, water. And there are very high, quite pretty clouds of methane, Malenfant! If we were there we could scoop up your propellant through dips into the air.

No oxygen, though. In the air. No free oxygen.

Correct. Another key divergence from our Earth. Still, I searched for life. If I had had Josh Morris at my side he would have been strongly arguing for me to do just that. There are forms of life which do not need oxygen – indeed, to which oxygen is inimical. And I thought I had good evidence, even from the orbital surveys, that life of that kind must exist down there. Down in that pit of an Earth.

What evidence?

You should know, Malenfant. I've already told you—

Methane. Those high clouds.

Indeed. Which were evidence of an ongoing production of the gas, even if just a trace, in the deeper air. Methane, you see, is unstable. Reactive. Meaning it will readily combine with other chemicals – which of course is the principle you will exploit to drive your stink-bomb put-put. So it *ought* to be depleted. Methane in the high air, therefore, was most probably evidence of life, methanogen life at least – something *producing* that methane – in the lower air, the shallow seas, the land – even underground, perhaps.

But what? Here I was orbiting helplessly, without a lander. One thing I have learned from Josh Morris, you know, is that unless life has enveloped a whole planet, as it has on our Earth, you have to get up close to be sure it exists at all.

Yeah. I remember when we arrived at Persephone – Persephone I, the version out in the comet cloud. And you had a base on Melinoe, that little moon—

And Josh, stationed there, had found life in the upper layers of that moon's ice. I know. *He* would have longed to be down there with his sampling kit and his notebooks, even if we had had to drop him by parachute.

And so – well, I pushed my luck. I took the poor *Harmonia* through an atmospheric insertion. A glide down as far as the stratosphere. In order to sample whatever life forms might be found in the upper air. I sampled that world directly, I mean; I used the docking scoop.

A descent into the air. Wow. Quite a risk.

Indeed. But I felt it was worth it.

I was cautious. The atmosphere was tall, and thickened only gradually – which helped me, as you can imagine, I was flying by the seat of my pants, largely feeling my way. There were, incidentally, brutally strong winds, pushing persistently from east to west. My pass through the high air lasted only a few hours. But I had every instrument on the ship peering out, as well as my own two peepers . . .

I saw land, I saw ocean, I saw volcanic provinces like great wounds, fiery red, belching out gases. The surface is hot, almost at the boiling point of water. But there is liquid water on that surface. Shallow seas – indeed much of the surface is covered in water. There are scattered continents, small, none larger than Australia, as far as I could make out, so that the face of the planet is more like a tremendous archipelago.

And I saw life.

Not animals, not even vegetation as we know it. No forests, Malenfant, no grasslands. Just – slicks. Purple smears across rocky ground. In the shallow seas too. Banks of it washing up against the slopes of some of the big volcanoes; perhaps it fed on their gases, or their heat, or minerals pushed up through faults in the crust.

Purple smears?

That's all. But it was everywhere. And more than smears, in places. Even from altitude, I thought I saw structure – traces of networks. Impossible to be sure, and nothing showed up in the rather blurry photographs I took.

But I did manage to harvest traces of that life. I flew over one volcanic province – a place of geysers, founts of water and steam. It is not unlike parts of Iceland, volcanic heat acting on underground water and driving plumes that rise high in the air. I swept overhead, flying through geyser plumes, you see, hoping that some of that steam, and whatever debris it carried, might rise high enough for me to garner a trace.

And did it work?

I'm proud to say it did. Well, I probably wouldn't have told you about it otherwise, would I? There was a very low concentration of biological material, in the lungfuls of hot, watery nitrogen I scooped up. But some of it was viable – I mean, alive.

Thermophiles. Heat-loving organisms.

That's it. Just bugs, but evidently highly adapted to their environment, able to withstand even a ride into the high air driven by a steam geyser. Tougher than thee or me, Malenfant!

And I think, even then, I started to see the truth. Maybe you have guessed it too.

What truth?

Malenfant, we speak glibly of 'our' Earths. My Earth, your Earth, as if they were the only kind possible. Now I began to think that what I was seeing was something deeper, something more meaningful than that. I thought I was flying high over a kind of *preserved* Earth . . . The presence of the Visitors on those bleak landscapes only reinforced that impression.

Visitors?

Ah. I haven't mentioned them yet. Thought it better to withhold the news. All in good time, Malenfant.

A preserved Earth? Preserved how?

An Earth without a Moon.

*

We're back to discussing the formation of the Solar System, Malenfant. This Solar System anyhow. I remember talking this over with Deirdra when I got back from my earlier jaunt to the other worlds, Venus, Mercury.

I remember. And the rest of us debating it later.

I suspect that in this strange Solar System the different destinies of all the inner planets must have been – adjusted – at the same time. And with the same *process* of adjustment. In an age when the inner planets were struggling to be born.

At that time there was a crowd of planetary embryos, Malenfant, swirling around the inner System, baby worlds, some as large as Mars would become. The planets as we know them emerged from a series of shattering collisions and coalescences.

Very well. So Earth emerged – an Earth, anyhow. A ball of rock and iron, all of it left molten from the energy of the great collisions. Quickly the interior settled out, the hot and heavy iron sinking to form the heavy core under a rocky mantle, a congealing crust. After the quick loss of a primitive atmosphere of hydrogen, a remnant of the formative protoplanetary nebula, a thick atmosphere would have been outgassed through immense volcanoes.

Now, life appears to have taken hold, on the Earth at least, very quickly after this preliminary process of formation. Josh was always keen to tell me how we have found traces of life in even the very earliest rocks we have discovered, on *our* Earth.

But where did it come from?

Perhaps it formed spontaneously, on Earth. Perhaps it was seeded from elsewhere – from the young Mars, perhaps, which would have cooled rather more quickly than Earth, and so become hospitable to life earlier.

There's no Mars in this System.

True enough. But if it *had* arisen elsewhere Earth could have been seeded by rocks blasted off one world or another by impacts. A random spraying of life-bearing fragments.

Or, you are implying, perhaps it was seeded deliberately. By some agency.

Well, it seems possible. We have speculated about this, Malenfant, about some celestial farmer walking among the young worlds, still glowing hot from their as yet incomplete formation, and sowing some kind of seeds of life.

And life is what I found on this Earth, in the end. And it is *our* kind of life.

You're sure of that, are you?

No, damn it, Malenfant. I am a jack of all trades – we all are in the RASF – but I am no specialist in biology, still less biochemistry. However, I am sure as I can be.

Look, I watched those little bugs I had scooped out of the air grow and reproduce in the nutrients I fed them – a soup of rock powder in an atmosphere of nitrogen and water. Of course they did not need light. They did not need the Sun. They were chemoautotrophs, deriving their energy from the heat and the mineral content of the rocks. And I learned that they were tolerant to heat – even quite high temperatures.

Naturally I only discovered these things by poisoning or frying large numbers of them to death.

I know enough folk biology to recognise what you're describing. We called them the Archaea. The oldest bacteria, the oldest living things on Earth. Adapted to great heat, a poisonous environment—

Poisonous for thee and me, indeed. Not for them. Well, that was what they *looked* like; that was how they functioned. But what were they made of? That was a question into which I dug, in my ham-fisted way, in my lonely spaceship-cum-laboratory.

Having killed a good number of my guests, now I brutally

took them apart, to see what I could make of their biochemistry. I quickly saw it was the same *sort* of stuff as us: carbon chemistry in water. I recognised proteins, lipids, carbohydrates, amino acids, even nucleic acids – Malenfant, this was clearly an instance of proteins-in-water life that was every bit as alike our own, at the component level, as it could be. But how alike at the level of deeper complexity?

And so I tried to find out.

Amino acids. Consider that. These molecules are the building blocks of how our kind of life works. There are over three thousand amino acids known to the chemists. Our kind of life is built from just twenty-one of those varieties – and there's another selection, for left-handed orientations of their structures versus right-handed. So you're looking at a set of twenty-one out of over six thousand possibilities.

And I found that the same twenty-one-acid set that is used by *our* life is also used by the Archaeans from this Earth. *The exact same.* Think of the odds! Why, the number of all possible twenty-one-acid combinations—

Surely not all those combinations could produce viable biochemistries.

No, surely not. Perhaps very few. But it's hard to believe that, chemically speaking, there is only *one* possible amino-acid suite that would work. Not only that, at the higher levels, the nucleic acids, the protein structures—

Also the same as ours?

You guessed it. That is what I found.

And I went further.

I was able to separate strands of what looked to me like genetic material, DNA, from my hardy guests. And I tested them against strands of terrestrial DNA, samples taken from what I imagined would be similar organisms on Earth. We have quite a library of specimens aboard *Harmonia*, all stored in tiny slivers . . .

The genetics are not identical – you wouldn't expect that. But clearly the basic genetic mechanism of DNA, RNA and proteins is similar. And the similarity of the genetic coding seems close to me too – given several billion years of subsequent evolutionary divergence anyhow. The genetics is conservative to some extent. You, Malenfant, share some sixty per cent of your genes with the average oxygen-hating, heat-loving underground bug on Earth.

And not only that -- the biochemistry, the amino suite, is also identical to that of life forms we have discovered elsewhere. I mean at the first Persephone, Malenfant. On Melinoe, its moon, as poor Josh discovered. Think about that. It's staggering!

Wow. OK. So you've convinced me that this heavy, choked, fast-spinning Earth, in the present day, is home to something like our Archaean bacteria – the first living things on our Earth. What we can't say—

What we can't say is whether *this* particular Earth originated this suite of life. Or whether it came from some other world, another Earth in some other corner of the manifold – your Earth or mine, perhaps – or somewhere else, a Mars perhaps. Even on Melinoe. But I am becoming convinced there could have been *only one* origin event. Somewhere out there, in the manifold. The odds against a life system, nascent, selecting precisely the same amino suite and so forth over and over again seem utterly ludicrous to me. One origin, either here or – elsewhere.

Umm. Fair point. The mystery deepens.

And we have a lot to learn, still. By the way I have called the local Earth Vanilla, Malenfant. The Vanilla Earth. In a Vanilla System.

Vanilla?

Because of what happened next, Malenfant. Or rather, what evidently did *not* happen next, to this Earth. It seems to have been left – untouched – by further cosmic evolutions.

I know this, for it has no Moon.

And that means there was no Moon-shaping impact, Malenfant. Just as there had been no final, world-moulding impact on Mercury. And perhaps Venus, here—

Let me guess. Somebody has been screwing around with the migration of the giant planets. Which flung all those impactors around the System.

Modified perhaps by the subtlest of nudges. Persephone rockets pushing some relatively minor world this way and that, to create a cascade of disturbances. That's my best guess. Because all the while the inner planets were forming, the outer planets were migrating like manoeuvring tanks, throwing the remaining swarm of planetesimals into chaos in the process. We have spoken of this before. That tremendous Jovian migration was the motor of the World Engine, and indeed was the motor for the displacement of Shiva and Persephone in Deirdra's timeline – the displacements that were going to cause the Destroyer, the end of her Earth.

Right. So in our System, Mars got a slam at its north pole, creating a crater that rolled down to the equator. Mercury had much of its mantle stripped off. Venus was clouted so hard it started to spin backwards. And our Earth got hit so hard, the Moon split off.

That's the model. I looked it up – though the conclusions in my time may have been different in detail from yours . . . Not here, though. Not here. Presumably thanks to the Engineers and their meddling . . . *none* of that happened, as far as I can tell. Of course the impact changed everything for our Earth. Our *Earths.*

The Archaean life survived, though, evidently. On our Earth.

But in a much changed world. The old Earth, the Vanilla Earth, home of the Archaeans, was gone. Even the atmosphere was lost, blasted away – replaced with a thinner air of nitrogen, carbon dioxide, outgassed by the volcanoes or delivered by comets.

After that, *our* Earth started to cool. Even that was bad for the Archaeans, when they crept out of their refuges; the old thermophiles had to retreat from the surface of a world they had once owned. But worse was to come. As the air cleared, sunlight reached the surface – and the first photosynthesising bacteria evolved. They used the energy of sunlight to crack the carbon dioxide air, using the carbon to build their bodies, and releasing oxygen, a waste, into the atmosphere.

Oxygen. Poison for the Archaeans. A double whammy.

Evolution proceeded apace after that. Soon there was something recognisable as plankton in the oceans. About a billion years ago, the first sponges – the first multicellular animals. And soon after that, worm-like critters with internal guts.

Our ancestors.

Indeed. While the Archaeans were reduced to traces, clinging on in the deep rocks. The geologists call it the Great Oxidation Event. They might have called it the Great Oxidation Extinction.

Not here, though. You mention extinction. I think I see the pattern.

What pattern?

You know, Lighthill, it really is a shame Josh isn't here to discuss this. Because, down on Persephone, he was the first to perceive what we were seeing.

And what's that?

Refuges. Sanctuaries from extinction.

*

Look — we know that extinction events on Earth have swept the planet clean, over and over. When the massive volcano erupts, when the dinosaur-killer impact comes. Whole families of life are eliminated, and the survivors spread, and evolution starts all over again, filling up empty niches in a changed landscape.

Ah. But on Persephone—

On Persephone, as I told you, we found dinosaurs. We found other, very exotic ancient biota — exotic according to Josh. We even encountered extinct hominins. We speculated about how maybe Persephone had once been empty, but then artificially populated by some kind of sampling — transfers across the manifold of endangered populations, species, into a place where they could linger.

Umm. I remember you talking about that. But it's not a simple refuge, is it? Not just a zoo. You told me you saw a Neanderthal riding a pterosaur into the sky!

So we did. So maybe part of the agenda is to mix stuff up. I don't know.

Experimental ecologies. Yes, I could buy that. A way of exploring the potential of the whole. But as for the Vanilla Earth — ah! I see what you mean. It fits the pattern.

Because that world, that version of Earth—

Is a refuge, not for cave men or dinosaurs, but for the planet's first inhabitants. The Archaeans. Who, here at least, have been sheltered from the first extinction event of all: the Great Oxidation. And you could only preserve such a fundamentally different biosphere as the true Archaean in its full bloom, dependent on a fundamentally different atmosphere, on a separate planet altogether. Just as we see here. Wonderful thought! It all fits, doesn't it?

It's a shame Josh isn't here to see that hypothesis confirmed. Not to mention how it links to his discovery on Melinoe.

Yes. But it does rather confirm a supplementary hypothesis of my own.

About what?

About the Visitors.

Ah. You mentioned them.

I will send you visuals . . .

Malenfant? Tell me what you see.

Umm. The images are pretty partial—

Well, I do apologise. They were, you know, taken from a low-flying spacecraft in an atmosphere worse than the thickest London fog.

OK, OK. You're a hero pilot, I know.

I see what look like – robots – rather than anything biological.

You have an image here of maybe a couple of dozen, working in a rough circle. Each has a boxy core – no, it's more complicated than that.

I believe the main bodies are icosahedral. Twenty sides. The most complex possible Platonic solid. Geometric perfection, you see, multiple symmetries . . . But I may be reading too much into the blurry imagery.

The scale is tricky, nothing to match them against.

Again, I have radar reflections which suggest they are a couple of metres tall, that's all.

They have limbs, right? Some for locomotion, some for picking stuff up? Those manipulators look very fine. See how they split – bifurcate – like twigs on a branch. I remember a speculative design for a multipurpose robot, not a humanoid form like Bartholomew . . . Many limbs, like this. Bush robots.

308

Evidently a very practical design. Very adaptable. And – symmetrical, can you see, Malenfant?

Yeah. They'd look the same if tipped on one side, even turned over, it looks like.

As if adapted for an environment without an obvious up or down.

Adapted for space, you mean.

I believe so. You sound oddly phlegmatic about this discovery, Malenfant.

Well . . . It's only technology. And we saw technology on the first Persephone, didn't we? Those impossible Towers. Maybe I'm getting blasé. So what are they doing down there?

Well, I wasn't sure. But now we have speculated, have we not, that this Vanilla Earth is a kind of reserve for Archaean life – so maybe they are gardeners?

Ha! Maybe so. Taking samples. Maybe weeding: plucking out any nasty photosynthetic oxygen-farters that might come drifting down as spores from some other world. And maybe as agents of – well, whoever set up all this stuff in the first place.

Yes. Malenfant, just to be clear – you don't think we are seeing the Engineers themselves here?

Well, do you? To me they don't seem advanced enough.

I bet they could construct those fusion-rocket Towers we found on Persephone I. And I bet they could construct *themselves* – reproduce, after a fashion.

But they look like they're just tools. Smart tools, but tools. Certainly not capable of delivering manifold technology – higher-dimensional gateways in Martian moons, or blue scooping rings . . . I have a feeling we have a lot more to discover yet.

Yes. But here, despite all the alien strangeness, I have come to – cherish – this world. Vanilla Earth. When I came here, Malenfant, I imagined there could never be a world so ugly, certainly not a distorted copy of Earth. Now, after this mission, I can only think this Vanilla Earth is in some ways the most beautiful imaginable – a preserve for life forms nearly five billion years old.

Well. That's my report.

Shall we talk about your rocket?

42

Malenfant saw Nadezhda coming from a way off, over the flat plain of the Shield caldera. And as he'd expected she brought little Maria with her. The child rode in a kind of papoose on her mother's chest – a papoose, Malenfant reminded himself with a wonder that was not yet dulled, made of pterosaur-hide leather.

It was the day before the test flight of the *Little Joe*, the second-stage test article – and a day on which, he knew, some difficult decisions would have to be made. So he had asked Nadezhda to come walk with him around the Rocket Garden. It was all calculated. He wanted her to see it for herself, the reality of this thing – and the contrast with the *Elektrod*, presumably the only kind of ship she was accustomed to.

He was always glad to see Maria, whatever the circumstances.

The child had just passed her second birthday, and had been the subject of a joyful Russian party, complete with a 'cake' of rice sweetened with a little of a much-treasured hoard of sugar. Yet Maria still showed no signs of walking, and crawled only with difficulty. She was a lot happier to just sit in a corner, ideally propped up against a wall, and have people come to her rather than her toddle over to them. Well, for now Maria had no shortage of attention, from among seven more or less guilt-ridden, more or less lonely human beings, all of them far from home and, Malenfant suspected, scared most of the time. Looking after somebody else was a way of coping with all that.

Bartholomew was the exception. The robot medic was unfailingly calm, competent, kind, soothing. But Maria didn't like him, and when he tried to examine her she would only allow him to approach when in the safety of her mother's arms.

Malenfant wasn't particularly surprised. 'Kids have a knack of spying out fake humanity,' had been his diagnosis to Bartholomew when they had discussed Maria the day before. 'In my time we called it the uncanny valley.'

'Gosh, Malenfant, if only you had been there when the twenty-fifth-century experts were designing me.'

'You're concerned she isn't walking yet? The high gravity?'

'Essentially that. And probably other, more subtle environmental factors. But this is guesswork to some extent. By the time space exploration was abandoned in the twenty-third century, there had been no great experience of long-duration living in *higher* gravity fields than Earth's. Whereas there were masses of data on living in partial gravity, with experience from the Moon, Mars, space habitats.'

'What you're telling me is that you don't *know* what the high gravity is doing to little Maria.'

'Correct.'

Bartholomew had fallen silent at that, but Malenfant knew him well enough to understand what he had left out. *It's doing nothing good.*

Which was one reason why he had asked Nadezhda and Maria to come visit the *Little Joe* today, the day before the test rocket's one and only launch. Nadezhda had her own decision to make, about whether to subject her child to a ride in Malenfant's home-made spaceship. And the only way he could help her with that was to show her.

Not that baby Maria cared about any of that. Right now, as Nadezhda walked up, here she was reaching out to Malenfant, laughing. He had learned to lean down so she could pat his bald scalp.

'She likes you,' Nadezhda said with a grin. 'Heaven knows why. As Emma says.'

'Hmph. Another vote of confidence from my ex-wife . . . However, we are here for *Little Joe*. Come see.' He pulled away from Maria with an apologetic smile, and they turned to look at his craft.

His and Josh's.

Little Joe, its name wryly taken from a test rocket in the early days of the US manned space programme, was an open, roughly cylindrical frame of metal girders and struts, around fifteen metres tall – seven, eight times the height of an adult human being – a frame dominated by two big spherical tanks of steel strapped inside its core. At its base, below the tanks, was the thrust assembly, a flaring cage containing a single rocket engine bell, with the complexity of an ignition chamber dimly visible in the technological tangle above. At the top of the cylinder sat a rough cone, sheet metal roughly bent, hammered and riveted into shape.

That was pretty much it. Smaller rocket nozzles poked out of the flanks of the beast: attitude control. Big stabilising fins – a couple more were yet to be attached – flared at the base of the cylinder. And around the main structure was a horrible mess of pipes and ducts and wires and cables, connecting this test article to the wider infrastructure of the Rocket Garden.

All of this, every bit of it, had been scavenged from the much-plundered wreck of the *Elektrod*.

'So,' he asked Nadezhda, 'what do you think?'

She pursed her lips. 'I think it's a mess.'

He had to laugh.

'And scary. Can this thing possibly fly?'

'Well, I hope so.'

'Now I wish I had seen more of the construction process.' She sighed. 'I am, was, an engineer too. For now I am a parent who makes meals for engineers.'

'But that's precisely why I wanted you to see this, Nadezhda.' One reason, Malenfant. Not the only one. 'You haven't been involved in the build. So you have an independent view. Tell me what we missed.' He grinned, rueful. 'Everybody around here thinks I am gung-ho. A risk-taker. In fact I came from a very risk-averse culture in my own space agency, and I learned that an independent inspection—'

'Never did any harm. You have no argument from me,' Nadezhda said gently.

So they walked, keeping a good distance away from the rocket stack – even though it had yet to be fuelled.

'So what can you tell me about the *Little Joe*?'

'The design isn't merely a test article. It's also a prototype. This is pretty much what the second stage of our final rocket is going to look like, we think. The first stage will look like this thing on steroids – I mean, pumped up bigger. Here we have two tanks, propellant and oxidiser. In the first stage we will have *six* tanks. That stage will be about thirty-five metres tall, twice the height of this – *and* with a clone of this baby sitting on top. You see, the first stage will burn to get us off the ground, and when the tanks are depleted it will be dropped off and—'

'I understand the rocket equation,' she said mildly. 'So, this second stage will take us from the high air to a low orbit.'

'Where Lighthill is already waiting to pick us up in the *Harmonia*.' If all goes well, he thought, and if that lonely, half-crazy guy can manage, alone, to bring off the most tricky rendezvous he has ever attempted. All you can do is get everybody up there, Malenfant. 'So what we're planning to do now is to launch *Joe* solo, from the ground, and see how it performs. We'll be testing everything about the stage, save for its performance at high altitude, and the booster stage separation technology.'

She smiled. 'Two rather major omissions.'

'True, but what can you do? And we will be testing the rocketry systems and guidance, which will be pretty much the same on the big bird.'

'Talk me through the features of this stage, then.'

He nodded, and they walked on.

'Everything is salvaged from the *Elektrod*, of course. The engine bell – just one here, there will be eight of them on the first stage – was scavenged from the attitude control systems. We do have our own attitude control, from the fins you can see here, and those smaller nozzles fixed around the hull. They were taken from the *Elektrod*'s on-board ventilation system, would you believe. Gives you a sense of the scale of that baby compared to *this*.'

'I am told the control system is to be based on your bangles.' She raised her right wrist, where she wore her own bangle.

'Correct. You can thank Bartholomew. He was able to reprogram the bangles to – well, to fly a spaceship. The bangles are designed to read from and write to the human brain. Bartholomew adapted a set to read sensors such as attitude and altitude gauges and accelerometers, and write back to our rudimentary control system.'

She nodded, looking doubtful. 'And our backup if that complicated set-up fails?'

He pointed to his own chest. 'Me. With co-pilot to be decided.

I do have experience of flying big chemical-propellant rockets, after all.'

She smiled again, not unkindly. 'I thought you crashed your last command. The shuttle booster you told us of – the *Constitution*.'

'Well, there is that. Put it down to experience. Anyhow, this is a simple enough flight plan, and hopefully we will have every contingency covered in the programming of the bangles.'

'Every contingency you've thought of, you mean.'

'That's why we test.'

She nodded. 'Perhaps our traditions are different. We Russians test, and retest, of course. But mostly we *fly*. I know that the *Elektrod* is a novel technology to you. But to us it is old, old and proven, and based on technologies that are older yet. Perhaps we may be accused of a lack of innovation. We prefer to build on what works – to make that better, rather than to discard it in search of novelty.'

He thought that over. 'Yeah. Interesting. It was the same in my timeline, more or less. The Russians – the Soviets, the heirs of Stalin – built a superb missile, meant for intercontinental nuclear strikes, in the 1950s. And they were still flying that baby by the time I – well, when I had my accident. Still flying in 2019, so over sixty years later. Whereas in that time we Americans had gone from flying astronauts on repurposed missiles, to a whole suite of dedicated heavy-lift launchers, the Saturns, that we then threw away in favour of the space-shuttle system . . .'

She smiled. 'Western rationalism versus Slavic intuition.'

'We'll have to leave that to the comparative historians. Which is going to be a whole new academic discipline sprouting in the manifold, right?'

They walked on, around the rocket stack. Nadezhda jiggled

the child, who was squirming a little, restless, growing bored by all the talk.

'And the cone at the top is the crew module?'

'Just a mock-up of it, but, yeah. We'll be adapting what used to be an internal depressurisation shelter on the *Elektrod*. So, hopefully, airtight, you see. Room for nine couches.'

He left it at that. Nine couches. Including one child-sized. Enough to accommodate everybody. That was the necessary design; they'd had to anticipate taking *everybody*. And everybody would fit in there, if not comfortably.

But that nine didn't necessarily reflect the number that would actually fly. As Malenfant knew, and, possibly, Nadezhda already suspected.

Which was the real reason he had brought her here today. To make her *see* the reality of this crude thing they were planning to fly out of here on.

'Well,' she said now, 'you pass the inspection. And now we launch this thing. Yes? Tomorrow? Whoosh! Off into the sky.' She mimed this with one hand, and made Maria laugh. 'Whoosh! *Off* into the sky!'

'Yeah. But first, I'm afraid, we have to hold a meeting.'

'A meeting? To discuss what?'

'Those nine couches.'

'Ah. Whoosh! Whoosh!'

Maria gurgled and clapped.

43

They gathered in the yurt.

Malenfant counted the group as they settled, on home-made stools, heaps of blankets. The survivors of the *Elektrod*: Anna, Vasily, Irina, and Nadezhda with her child. And the survivors of the *Charon II*: Malenfant himself, Emma, Deirdra, and Bartholomew. Seven adults, one kid, and one robot: nine in all. They sat there waiting for him to speak, some cradling cups of tea, some water. Little Maria gurgled, snuggling her face against her mother's chest.

Malenfant was hardly the leader of this group.

But it's your ship, Malenfant. Your dumb idea. Although maybe it shouldn't be your responsibility for life and death in such a stark manner.

'You play the cards as they're dealt,' he muttered to himself.

Emma reached over and touched his arm. 'You OK?'

'No. But who is? Let's get this done.'

He stood up, and spoke to the group. 'Look. You all know, I think, what we have to decide today. If all goes well, tomorrow we will fly the *Little Joe*, and if that works as planned we can immediately start construction of its big brother, the ship that will take us to orbit around Persephone and to rendezvous with Lighthill in the *Harmonia*. And, you know what? I figure construction shouldn't take long. We will have proved our technology, scavenged and second-hand as it is. We know how to use it to put together rockets. This *works*.

'But you can't design a ship if you don't know what cargo it's going to carry.' He glanced at Nadezhda. 'Since we lost Josh, we've designed for nine.' He grinned. '*These* nine passengers. Including one robot that's heavier than he looks, and a little one who wouldn't take up much space at all. Nine. Why, I know all our weights, I can put that into the calculations.

'The question we have to decide today is, will it be nine that we carry after all?'

That didn't even seem to shock them.

Predictably Irina spoke first, smiling bleakly. 'And if not nine, who stays behind? And why?'

Malenfant avoided eye contact, letting the interval stretch.

In the end, as he had hoped – or maybe dreaded – it was Nadezhda who spoke first.

'I know what lies behind your question, Malenfant. Probably we all do.' She held her child at arm's length, and jostled her gently; Maria laughed. 'It is the issue of whether Maria, who was born on this world, can ever leave it.' She glanced at Bartholomew.

Bartholomew hesitated, though Malenfant knew very well the pause was artifice, precisely timed by some algorithm or other running on his crystalline soul.

'I am technology,' Bartholomew said at last. 'You are human. This is a human decision. I cannot—'

'You are her doctor,' Nadezhda said. 'Since you walked in here, doctor to all of us. Give us your recommendation, Doctor. Please speak freely.'

Bartholomew inclined his head. 'Very well. My

recommendation, and I am sorry to make it, is that little Maria should not be taken away from this world. The very launch would be trying for her. And aside from that – I've thought hard about this, though there are few precedents for her case – it is clear to me that Persephone's high gravity has had a profound effect on her.

'The human embryo was not evolved to develop here. No human child has ever before grown up in such a gravity field. There are a number of developmental effects: her bone thickness and structure, her blood volume, her heart rate, even the functioning of her immune system. No doubt there are other effects I have yet to spot, or that have not yet developed. She is still growing, of course. Look – she is too frail. I believe that for better or worse, by far the least harmful course for Maria is *to stay on Persephone.*'

Anna and Vasily seemed motivated to argue. 'Are you sure?' 'Are there other tests to be made, aids we could give her? . . .'

Bartholomew handled these responses calmly and competently. And he was convincing, to layman Malenfant's ear.

Malenfant let the discussion run on for a while.

In the end it was Nadezhda herself who cut it short.

'I have spoken to the doctor separately. He has not presented his conclusions so starkly before, but the evidence he showed me before today . . . And of course I have seen the rocket on which we would have to fly. It is clear to me. Maria can never leave this place. Maybe not ever, certainly not in some experimental rocket.' She smiled at her child, who smiled back. 'Look at her! She is always so happy when we are all together, like this. She will miss you all. But Maria cannot leave. Not in your crude rocket ship. And, therefore, I cannot.'

Silence followed, heavy, sad. Vasily dropped his head,

scowling, but did not contradict her.

Nobody was about to argue, to Malenfant's relief. *Nine candidates. Two down, seven to go*, he thought bluntly. This painful drama wasn't done yet, he knew. After all, Nadezhda and child couldn't survive here alone.

And now Irina was leaning forward.

She said, 'In fact we have other dependants here.'

Vasily, clearly disconcerted already by Nadezhda's statement, glared at Irina. 'What are you talking about? What dependants?'

'She means the Runners,' Anna said. 'Those we have kept here, in their stockade.'

Vasily thought that over. 'Ah. Yes. I had not thought of them.'

'I bet you didn't,' Deirdra muttered. 'Irina is right. They've clearly become . . . domesticated. Your captive herd. You can see it – they have to be *told* to eat.' She seemed to struggle with what she had to say next. 'I know it's not your fault. But it just *is*. And we have to find a way to deal with it.'

Malenfant and Emma shared a glance. More wisdom. From a young woman who was fast outgrowing them both, Malenfant thought.

'Exactly,' said Irina. 'If we wish to leave, what are we to do with *them*? Let them starve in their stockade? And probably hunger will take them, especially the young, before the predators find them—'

'Enough,' Nadezhda said. 'Your point is made, Irina. If we abandon these creatures they will die. Therefore we must not abandon them.' She glanced around at her fellows, Irina, Anna, Vasily. 'Some of us must stay. Conversely, some of us must go, go with these people. Try to find a way home, tell of what became of the *Elektrod* and her crew. Ensure a second ship is sent back to retrieve those who remain. So we separate, here. I will stay, of course, with Maria.'

'And I will stay with you,' Irina said. 'So that I may tend to the Runners. And we may both tend to the graves of those we have lost. You two,' she said to Anna, Vasily. 'You go with these westerners.'

Anna exchanged a glance with Vasily. To Malenfant, their expressions were unreadable.

Vasily said, 'Very well. If this is acceptable to Malenfant and his people.'

Malenfant nodded curtly.

'Then that's the plan,' Vasily said.

Anna frowned. She seemed neither elated at leaving, nor disappointed that the others were staying. 'We will come back. I promise.'

Nadezhda, looking weary, smiled. 'Then I promise that we will survive, and hold you to that—'

'Leave us the doctor,' Irina said abruptly.

Bartholomew turned, frowning. 'What was that?'

'You. Stay with us. You have treated us since you arrived here—'

'For which I am grateful,' murmured Nadezhda. She cradled Maria, who seemed to be falling asleep.

Irina said, 'Think how our chances of survival will be augmented if you stay here. And you can do much more. Why, you could study the Runners, their different physiologies. You could even compile learning on the response of the human body to higher gravities.'

Bartholomew said blandly, 'You tempt me with an appeal to curiosity. I have no curiosity. I do have a mission.'

Irina was unfazed. 'Is it not your mission to save human lives?'

'No. I am not a human doctor, who swore an oath. I have no duty. I am a machine programmed for one mission, essentially.

To preserve *her*.' He glanced at Deirdra.

To Malenfant's surprise, Deirdra actually blushed.

'And as a secondary consequence her necessary companions, whoever they may be at the time.'

Emma caught Malenfant's eye, and he knew what she was thinking. *Nice use of the word 'necessary'. Who says who's 'necessary'?*

Irina thought that over. 'But if *she*' – nodding to Deirdra – 'were to order you to stay with us, would you comply?'

'I would not,' Bartholomew said calmly. 'Before we leave I will do all I can to help you to prepare for the future, Irina, you and Nadezhda and Maria. But I must leave with Deirdra.'

Irina sat back. 'An admirably clear statement of the position. But you can't blame me for trying.'

'Of course not,' said Deirdra in a small voice. 'And I can't stay. I'm sorry. Wherever I end up . . . My destiny isn't here.'

There was a long, awkward silence.

Then Malenfant stood up. 'So I think we're done with the difficult stuff. Let's fly our rocket.'

44

After that, with the big decision made, the technical stuff went well, from the test launch of the *Little Joe*, and into the construction of the final craft. There were no more arguments, no drastic changes of plan. The ship they had built was big and heavy, but simple enough to assemble, now that, thanks to Josh's experiments and tests among other inputs, they knew what the hell they were doing. It all came together.

Until, Malenfant realised, a few weeks later, they were ready to fly – or die in the process of trying.

In the evening of the day before launch, Malenfant and Emma stayed behind in the yurt.

Everybody else had preparations to make, and were away making them. Malenfant knew that Anna and Vasily were running last-minute technical checks of the *Joshua Philip Morris*, on its launch pad on the other side of the settlement. Even Bartholomew had gone for a walk with Irina, Nadezhda and baby Maria – Deirdra too – the medic going over once more the medical knowledge and expertise he had tried to pass on to them.

Malenfant suspected Deirdra would find it even harder than the rest to say goodbye to little Maria.

Meanwhile Malenfant and Emma were packing up their own small bits of kit, a last few items. They'd had little enough to begin with after the crash of the *Charon II*, and still less by the time they had got here, to New Akademgorodok. The effort of having to drag everything across half a continent on wooden travois had been, as Emma had drily put it, a strong incentive to declutter. But still, what they had they cherished. Much-repaired underwear. Carefully tended boots. The bangles, of course. They had acquired little more since they had been here. There was the old-fashioned barber-shop razor that Malenfant had inherited from a dead Russian, the father of Maria – a man he had never even known. Malenfant rather treasured this. It had a mother-of-pearl handle. Beautiful thing, and it needed no electrical supply to work . . .

They were alone in the yurt.

The realisation seemed to hit them both at the same time. Malenfant looked at Emma. Her eyes were wide in the shadows.

'We're on our own,' Malenfant said.

'State the obvious, why don't you? More to the point we know where they all are. We won't be disturbed. For once.'

'Not unless a rogue pterosaur lands on the yurt.'

'Don't even joke about it . . .'

They moved at the same time, almost colliding. Their lips pressed. She dragged at the zipper of his worn British-made coverall.

'Hey, take care with that,' he said breathlessly. 'Even Bartholomew couldn't fix a zipper, I don't think.'

'Which is why,' she said, pushing the coverall back from his shoulders, 'the Russians use buttons. And you take care with my underwear. That's pretty much all I have too.'

'You know me. Always too conventional to go ripping it off with my teeth.'

She snorted a laugh, her face pressed into his chest. 'No, and now you haven't got the teeth.'

'Shut *up* . . .'

They fell in a heap onto her bed. The air in here, in what was essentially a heavily layered tent, was always cold, and they pulled blankets, furs, over themselves.

And fell into each other.

Afterwards they snuggled.

Emma lay beside the taller Malenfant. One leg crooked over his upper thigh. Her head on his chest, his arm around her.

'When we lay like this,' she murmured, 'it always felt like we were a match.'

'Yeah. Like we fit together. Or wore grooves in each other.'

Even if, he thought, this wasn't the Emma he had snuggled before.

She must be thinking the same thing.

'I'm scared, Malenfant.'

'Of the flight? Me too. Who wouldn't be? Look — we were both victims of terrible accidents, equipment malfunctions, in our other lives. A balky reaction-control thruster in the nose of my beat-up old *Constitution* nearly did for me.'

'And for me, our nuclear Saturn-N stage at Phobos. Simple faults with catastrophic results.'

'And *those* failures came in pieces of kit that were the result of investments of billions of dollars, had been tested for years by expert engineers every which way up, and had even been proven in flight. Spaceflight is *hard*. That heap of junk outside — let's face it, we'll be lucky if we get off the ground at all.'

'But it might work.'

'It might.'

'And we don't really have a choice,' she said flatly. 'We can't stay here. This world isn't for us. This high-gravity cage. All we could do is sit here and kind of get eroded into the dirt, like these poor Russians. We wouldn't even dare go exploring, would we? Not if we were going to slaughter whole populations with the bugs we carry, like the conquistadors heading up the Amazon.'

'No. We didn't come here for that. We came chasing the World Engineers. For sure Deirdra deserves more.' He breathed a sigh. 'Even if we are risking her life to give her the chance.'

'She understands the odds – intuitively, anyhow.'

'I know.'

She tugged at the hairs on his chest – silver grey, he knew, though it was too dark to see. 'Malenfant?'

'Hmm?'

'Why didn't we do this before?'

He thought it over. 'We barely had the chance.'

'We could have made the chance. We're on a super Earth, for God's sake. Plenty of room to find a bit of isolation. Why, we could have found a corner even on the *Harmonia*. It was a damn big ship. So, why not?'

'Maybe because—'

'Yes?'

'You're thinking it too,' he said. 'You are Emma. But not *my* Emma. I'm Malenfant. Not *your* Malenfant. We are a damn multiverse tangle. We *feel* we know each other. We don't, we're strangers. In my reality we, Emma and I, had a kid. Here – well, this was the first time. For *us*.'

'Yes, I was thinking it too.' She hesitated. 'I guess I was scared it would feel different.'

He sighed. 'Well, it did, didn't it? Look – there was a ten-year age gap between us, before. In all the worlds, as far as I can make out, I was born ten years before you. But now, because of the muddled timelines we came through, there's more than twenty years between us. That much sure as hell feels different, doesn't it?'

She shifted, raising her head. He could see her eyes, glinting in cracks of daylight admitted by the yurt's wall. 'Look at it this way,' she said. 'You're not *my* Malenfant. But you're the Malenfant I called out to, when I was stuck on Phobos. You're the Malenfant who came to save me. And I'm the Emma Stoney you saved. We're here now. And you know what? That's good enough for me.'

He grinned. 'I love you.'

'And I love you. Now let's get on with stuff. That backyard rocket of yours won't launch itself . . .'

45

They all said their final goodbyes to Nadezhda and Maria at the yurt. It was thought best to keep parent and child as far from the launch of the *Josh* as possible.

It was a difficult moment for the Russians, Malenfant observed. These dour, earnest people, dreaming their Cosmist dreams of the uplift of mankind, had inadvertently caused some terrible things to happen here on Persephone – hell, among other horrors, they'd inflicted a kind of extinction event on the local hominin population. And they had had their own differences over the years. But they'd come here for the right reasons, to explore, to learn. And they'd survived their stranding as best they could, endured the loss of several of their own, and made welcome Malenfant and his group, strangers to this world as much as they were themselves. It was complicated. But life always was, he reflected.

They kept it light for the sake of little Maria. Lots of hugs, kisses, jokes, laughing. Even so Maria seemed to sense that something was changing. As they finally left for the launch pad, walking away, carrying their bits of gear, Malenfant's last memory of Maria was of her crying in her mother's arms, calling for Deirdra.

*

At the launch site, they suited up, with the aid of Irina, ground crew for the day. She went to them, one by one, checking zippers, buttons, boots, hats.

Suited up: all they had were crudely padded coveralls, and heavy felt caps on their heads, and gloves if they possessed them. These were not spacesuits, Malenfant knew, they were not airtight – nothing but padding. Even their supposedly airtight cabin had been an improvisation from an internal component of the *Elektrod*. If it failed there was no fallback . . .

Stop thinking, Malenfant. Your dumb brain, always been your Achilles heel. To mix a metaphor.

When she was done with the crew, Irina checked over the crude pumps, driven by electricity from the solar-cell farm, that topped up the *Josh*'s eight huge tanks of cryogenic propellant and oxidiser – six in the first stage, two in the second – and glanced over the pressure gauges one last time.

Then she walked back to the crew. 'All satisfactory,' she murmured. 'Boil-off is some fifty litres per hour. A little less than we expected. A tonne a day, total, compared to the total of five hundred tonnes of methane plus oxygen. Acceptable losses, even if we didn't top up. Good Russian engineering, those tanks. Survived a spaceship crash without so much as a leak. A good omen for the day.'

'Let's hope so.' Malenfant shook her hand firmly. 'Thank you, my friend.'

Irina held on to his hand, but looked away. 'Tell our story.'

'We're coming back for you, remember? Or somebody will.'

'Of course. But even so.'

Malenfant nodded, and she let him go.

He walked back to the launch stand. Joined the rest at the foot of the rope ladder that dangled down from the conical crew cabin at the top.

Looked up at his ship, the *Joshua Philip Morris*, the fifty-metre length of its two stages. Even complete, the craft was still little more than a cage of crudely welded scaffolding, with the spherical tanks within visible in a row, like swollen peas in a vertical pod, and the ugly knots of engineering that were the rocket engines themselves at the base, inside their own, super-strong thrust cage. It looked powerful but somehow naked, Malenfant thought. Brutal.

Wisps of boiled-off methane and oxygen misted in the air. As if the beast was breathing.

Emma nudged him. 'You look scared. Don't frighten the children.'

'Hell,' he muttered. 'I am scared. Aren't you? What are we doing here?'

Bartholomew joined them. 'Malenfant, I've been asking myself that question since the moment we so unwisely thawed you out in that coldsleep ward in London. Let's get this done before all your precious fuel boils off.'

And Bartholomew pulled his cloth hat down over his ears, glanced up once at the long ladder, grasped a rung, and began the climb. Malenfant estimated it took him two minutes to clamber up the shaky ladder, reach the open crew compartment, wave, and duck inside. Then he dangled down a coil of rope, letting it uncurl all the way to the ground.

Deirdra went next, tying the rope around her waist before her own ascent. A little bit of backup: Bartholomew would pull on the rope as Deirdra climbed, so that he could save her from falling if she lost her grip. The rest would follow the same way.

Predictably Deirdra made it without difficulty.

Next followed Vasily.

Then Anna, who seemed to find it hard to make this final

331

break. She actually had a foot on the ladder before turning back, running over to Irina, hugging her one last time, stroking Nadezhda's arm, kissing Maria. Then she stalked back to the ladder, hiding her eyes from Malenfant and Emma. Malenfant realised he had never seen Anna cry, or Vasily come to that. And it seemed she was determined not to let him see that now.

Finally, the pilots. Emma gave Malenfant a brief hug. 'See you on board.' Then she turned and scrambled up the ladder.

Malenfant's turn. He took one last glance back at Irina. She nodded to him, calm, unsmiling.

Then he turned to the ladder, knotted the rope around his waist like the rest.

Missed the very first rung, slipped back one half-metre to the ground. 'Damn it.'

Tried again.

Succeeded this time. He started to climb steadily, one rung after another, trying to make it look as easy as the others had, though for sure it didn't feel that way now he was trying it himself. 'At Canaveral,' he muttered, 'we had elevators.'

Another rung and another. Quickly he gained height.

And now the experience was a little more like Canaveral, as the view opened up around him. But whereas at Canaveral you got a view of ocean and shore, of the row of launch pads on Merritt Island – you could see the sunlight glistening on the windscreens of the cars lined up on the roads, people come to see you launch – here he saw only a stretch of the bare, dismal ground of the Shield: the huge circular arcs that were ancient volcanic vents, the heart of this tremendous uplifted plateau. In the distance the Rim Mountains, through which he and his companions had climbed, it seemed an age ago.

A twilight scene under the dimmed Sun.

And, looking down, he was surprised by the extent of New Akademgorodok. The glass of the greenhouses reflected the weak sunlight like mirrors. The solar panels, turned to black to absorb the midday sunlight, were like a pool of oil on the ground, a slick with oddly regular edges. He saw the little compound of the Runners, trapped in that eerie black slick. He wondered what they would make of the launch today, when, if, it happened. Cower in terror, he imagined. Yet another great hole ripped in the fabric of their world by the humans.

He wasn't sure he could make out the yurt, off to the west; that part of the compound was a visual clutter. But he could clearly see the fallen *Elektrod*, a stranded white whale, looking again like the *Star Wars* prop it had reminded him of on first coming here. All of the settlement was built from that carcass, as if the contents of the great fallen corpse had spilled across the ground of Persephone.

And he saw, just as he reached the hatch to the crew cabin, a spark of light: the methane flare burning at the top of its drill tower, emissions burning off as waste once more, now that they needed no more gas for the flight.

He wondered if Lighthill saw the flame. From space Lighthill had been surveilling the area for days now, looking for any signs of intervention from the manifold and its technologies – any signs of the blue hoops in the air that had proved so lethal before. Any glimpse and the launch would be aborted. But there had been no alarms, so far.

And right now the *Harmonia*, with Lighthill on board, must be somewhere in the sky above, its own low orbit taking it to its rendezvous position – to where the *Josh* would ascend, if all went well. In just a few minutes, Malenfant realised.

If all went well.

He had reached the cabin. Bartholomew, grasping the door frame, reached out and took Malenfant's arm. 'Ready?'

Malenfant grinned. 'Always.'

46

He tied up the bits of rope that would hold him in his seat during the ride. The couches were more adaptations from the *Elektrod*, of course; their only harnesses were rope knotted around their torsos, padded with leather. Very rough and ready, like everything about this whole enterprise.

But here he was in a left-hand seat, the commander's seat, a position he would once have fought for. Where he belonged.

There was a countdown, of sorts. They had to launch at a precise time to meet the *Harmonia* − although, of course, Lighthill in the much more capable British ship would manage the final rendezvous of the two vessels in space. The crew of the *Josh*, earnestly strapping themselves in, would have very limited control over their craft from the moment of launch. Irina, on the ground and from a safe distance, would operate the crude controls that would ignite the first-stage engines − and when the first stage was expended and discarded, high in the air, electronic triggers would fire the single second-stage thruster.

If all went well.

Meanwhile the rocket's attitude in flight would be controlled by the bangles built into its rudimentary guidance system: they would squirt the crude steam rockets fixed to the hull that should keep the craft roughly on the right track, and from rolling, dipping, tumbling as it rose.

If all went well.

Malenfant, as nominal pilot, at least had a window over his head – a small porthole showing a slice of washed-out sky – and a joystick in front of him. That would fire the attitude thrusters selectively; if all else failed he could make the craft veer in its course, to some extent. But he had no control over the main engines. Now Malenfant looked at the joystick with a kind of trepidation. It was essentially a fallback, an emergency measure, in case the automatics failed. *He* was a fallback, not a true pilot. He knew he would hold on to the damn thing all the way through, until Lighthill met them in orbit. But he knew too that if he needed to use it in earnest, they were probably screwed anyhow.

At least he could tell the time. He glanced at the bangle on his wrist, which now showed a countdown, minutes and seconds ticking off on a conventional digital clock face of the kind he preferred.

He called, 'Two minutes to go before Irina lights the fire.' He twisted in his seat to look over his shoulder at his passengers. This crew cabin, adapted from that emergency shelter from the *Elektrod*, was a truncated cone, not unlike an old Apollo command module. The couches were arranged in two banks, four in the lower level, two in the upper. For now they were all lying on their backs, stacked up, crammed in. In the lower level, Malenfant knew, Bartholomew sat beside Deirdra in the central two seats, with the cosmonauts outside, Anna to Bartholomew's left, Vasily to Deirdra's right. He couldn't twist round far enough to see them all.

'OK down there?'

He got murmurs from Anna and Vasily, and a complaint

from Deirdra. She said, 'I can't see a thing.'

Vasily said sternly, 'Now, you know the logic. Bartholomew is central so that, as our medic, he can, hopefully, reach any of us if we have difficulties. Anna and I are the experienced crew, so if there is some other problem, a need for evacuation—'

'I know,' Deirdra said sulkily. 'I don't have to like it. I'll miss everything!'

Anna said, 'It's only a couple of minutes. You can last that long. We will either be docking with the *Harmonia*, or we will be dead.'

Malenfant imagined Deirdra trying not to laugh at that.

She said, 'Thanks for the pep talk.'

Emma murmured, 'Forty seconds, Malenfant. Irina ought to have thrown her switches and be clear by now.'

He sat back in his couch and glanced at his only instrument, the countdown clock on the bangle. Thirty-six seconds.

Thirty-five.

He tried to relax. Tried to take it all in. This was a unique experience, even for him; it wasn't likely to happen again.

'Twenty seconds,' Emma called.

He could hear the distant creaks and bangs of the cryogenic tanks, stacked beneath him like those peas in their vertical pod. He could see a scrap of sky, a square of it, through a small, tough window in front of his face. He could *smell*—

'Fifteen seconds.'

He could smell the welding, that burned-metal tang. Very raw, compared to the new-car scents of the repeatedly refurbished bridge of a shuttle booster, like his old *Constitution*. And he thought he could smell straw, or mud, as if walked in off the fields. An animal smell. The Runners, maybe, a lingering trace of the near-humans whose labour had helped build this thing. What an extraordinary thought that was.

'Five seconds.'

He grasped that joystick. 'This is it,' he called. 'Good luck, everyone.'

'Two.

'One.'

He felt the blast of the rockets as much as he heard the ignition.

A giant shudder.

And then a lesser trembling, a vibration – no, jerkier than that, the stack was tipping this way and that, as if drunkenly trying to stand straight. Well, so it was. Right now those auxiliary rockets, slaved to the bangles and simple attitude sensors, would be pulsing and spitting, trying to keep the ship vertical as it inched off its platform, driven by the uneven thrust of its inevitably mismatched engines.

But they were lifting. Light shifted across his lap, cast through the small window above by the distant Sun. Lifting, by God.

And the bangle on his wrist had started counting up from zero. The flight had begun.

'We're away,' he called back.

Emma touched his arm, and tapped her ear. *They can't hear you.*

She was right, of course. And he wasn't using the bangles. Save for an emergency, it somehow wouldn't have felt right.

On the engines roared, slowly the pressure seemed to build on his chest. He stared at that scrap of sky through his window, longing for a view of space. But he knew that was whole minutes away yet, that the main events of the launch – the main peril points – had yet to come.

A shadow crossed his window, briefly obscuring the light. Something *above* them.

'What the—'

He struggled to sit up a little more, straining his neck. He saw more shadows – no, translucent forms against the sky, huge wings extended.

Emma touched his chest, trying to push him back. 'Sit down! What the hell is it – blue rings?'

He could barely hear her over the engines' gathering roar. But he sat back and laughed. He yelled, 'No! Pterosaurs! The pterosaurs are flying around us! Following us up! Irina must be getting a hell of a view. Ray Harryhausen, eat your heart out. Spaceships and flying dinosaurs!'

Emma yelled, half miming, 'Will they hurt us if they hit us?'

'Doubtful. They are pretty flimsy. We're more likely to hurt them than the other way around, especially if they venture near the exhaust—'

She couldn't hear him. 'What?'

He shook his head deliberately, but immediately regretted it, as the thrust built and built, and the cabin rattled and clattered and banged, shaking Malenfant around like a dried pea in a tin can. He sat back and focused.

He knew the logic, of course. The rocket was burning its mass up fast, methane and oxygen, nearly a tonne a second lost to the fires of the combustion chambers. And as the stack got lighter, so the burning engines' thrust was able to accelerate it harder – and the more the whole contraption shook and rattled, along with its passengers.

From Earth, or from an Earthlike world in Persephone I, Malenfant had only ever flown to the edge of space in the massive, aircraft-like shuttle boosters of his own time, and a couple of times in a glorious spaceplane from the Earth of the twenty-fifth century. And even the shuttle had been nothing like this experience. This was very raw, very *real* – visceral. He wondered if some of the earliest space travellers had felt like this, Yuri Gagarin and John Glenn riding new-fangled ICBMs all the way to orbit.

Had they really built this thing? Had *he*? How had they even dared to climb aboard?

He checked his bangle. Only ninety seconds in.

And suddenly he was thrown forward.

Then shoved back again.

Then fore and back, fore and back, a rattling that threw him *forward* into the rope harness that cut into his belly and shoulders, then savagely *back* into the couch, ripped out of a lounge in the *Elektrod*, crudely welded in, and probably too small for him and definitely inadequately padded. And *fore* and *back*, over and again, melting into a rapid vibration, too rapid to count the beats.

He dared not turn his head. But he yelled, over the engine roar, 'Pogoing!'

A not uncommon phenomenon when you flew a rocket, a longitudinal vibration along the stack, instabilities in the exhaust flow mounting up. If you were unlucky it would just mount and mount until your rocket and its helpless crew would be shaken to pieces. Falling down the sky, in clouds of unburned propellant. But if you were lucky—

It stopped. Just like that. Malenfant was thrown forward one more time, against his rope restraints. He glanced at Emma. Her face pale, she gave him a thumbs-up.

And suddenly, another drop of the noise level. A smoother ride too, as more of the vibration died away. His hearing was dulled, but he could see Emma's lips move. *Mach One.*

He nodded; she was right. They were still deep in an atmosphere which resisted their efforts to push through it — but now, through the sound barrier, they were into a different regime of air dynamics. A gentler regime.

He glanced at his clock again. Still less than two minutes from the ground. But Malenfant let himself believe a little more. They had figured, on pencil and paper, that two minutes in would be the point of 'max q' – where a combination of their own increasing speed and the reduced density of the resisting air would combine to put maximum stress on the vehicle. Get through *that* . . .

They had, it seemed.

And the sky through the window grew subtly darker.

His altimeter was scarcely reliable, but he knew by now they must be about twelve kilometres up – about forty thousand feet high. Persephone's air, compressed by gravity, fell away with altitude faster than did the Earth's. So, already, the sky was turning a deep velvet blue, already the stars were coming out. Malenfant wondered if the *Harmonia* was visible yet.

And now, as the vessel shed more and more weight – as that tonne-per-second fuel usage became an ever greater percentage of what remained – the acceleration started to build up savagely. Again they had only rough, hand-crafted estimates of the maximum they would have to endure. Five gravities, maybe.

Malenfant was used to this, up to a point, though his shuttle boosters had only ever pulled two or three gravities – he had endured a lot more in the centrifuges in training. So he lay back and soaked it up. Tried to keep one eye on his bangle, without turning his head. Watched the timer clock hands click around to two minutes thirty—

Bang.

And the thrust died, as if someone had thrown a switch. He was shoved forward against his rope harness, and then bounced back into his couch. He wished they had given these tie ropes a little more padding; he for one was going to be bruised as hell in the morning. If he ever got to see another morning.

But he understood what had happened. And right on cue. Staging.

A second of silence. Two. He stayed still, said nothing. Silence, and a brief, blessed reprieve from the acceleration. Through his window he saw a spray of debris, glowing. Hopefully just a remnant of the discarded first stage, thirty-five metres of tanks and engines and girders, already used up, pushed away. Right now the second stage with the crew cabin, a reincarnation of the *Little Joe*, was drifting powerless in the upper air of a super Earth. But the very process of staging should have started the sequence in their crude automatics that would ignite the single rocket engine on that second stage. The methane and oxygen should be flowing from their tanks, just one tank each now, to the ignition chamber . . .

He imagined seeing the craft from outside. Falling like a thrown baton, above the curvature of the world, above the air. Brightly sunlit.

And in the very last second he saw a blue ring, surely enormous, hovering over the world. A star field beyond, with, somehow, a different quality of light shining through, as if it was an enormous lens. Had it come to obstruct their launch, after all? If so, it was not close enough.

He yelled, 'Can you see us? Can you *see*?—'

Thrust.

He was slammed back into his couch once more. The roar of the engine seemed louder than ever – but then, the second-stage engine bell was that much closer to the cabin. And once more the weight built up, fast and cruel, on his chest, and the whole ship seemed to rattle. It was worse, even, than before.

'Only a couple of minutes of this,' he yelled, in case any of them could hear. 'Just one engine burning now, but we are a much smaller mass to push than we were . . .'

Smaller mass, so higher acceleration. They had no G counter, any more than they had an altimeter or a whole bunch of other stuff that might have been useful. All Malenfant could do was to dig into his muscle memories of centrifuges, of the crash of the *Constitution*, and try to estimate how high the load was getting: six G, seven, even eight? *Curse you, Newton's third law of motion!*

Shutdown came.

Again he was thrown forward, and old bruises ached afresh as his restraining ropes tugged him back.

But this time he drifted back slowly.

And a washer floated up into the air before his face.

He turned to Emma, who looked exhausted, but grinned back.

'Weightless, by God,' he said. He tried to turn to see his passengers, but his head swam. 'Everybody OK back there?'

'Well, we lived through your piloting,' Bartholomew said drily.

'Did we make it?' That was Deirdra, sounding fresh enough. 'Did we make the right orbit?'

'Or any orbit?' muttered Anna gloomily.

You did just fine.

That was Lighthill's voice, relayed by the bangles, booming inside Malenfant's head. He glanced at Emma, who grinned; she heard it too.

'Geoff?'

Wing Commander Lighthill to you, if you want to be allowed aboard my ship, sir. Have you in visual. You're in orbit all right – just. Nearly six minutes from launch, you are five hundred and thirty miles downrange, and you have achieved Persephone orbital speed – just! And just as well. But I won't need long to come get you. My God, Malenfant, what a piece of junk that is! Only smart thing about it is its name.

'Thought you'd like that.'

So would Josh. And he would have been proud. Prepare to be boarded, gentlemen and ladies. But I'll just pop the kettle on first.

47

Under Lighthill's expert control, the docking tunnel, a wide, thin-walled, flexible snake, came squirming out of the flank of the *Harmonia*'s big, spherical habitable compartment.

Approaching, visibly quickly.

Malenfant had a sharp flashback to when he had first seen this particular piece of alternate-British kit in action. It had been at Phobos, moon of Mars, in the twenty-fifth century – by Deirdra's calendar at least. Malenfant, Bartholomew and Deirdra had gone out there on the trail of existential anomalies, seeking answers to the strange causal tangle of the manifold, still hugely ignorant of it all. There they had found a version of Emma – *this* version, Malenfant reminded himself, the Emma at his side, this Emma born into a different reality. And they had found a broken Russian, victim of a global war on his Earth that had erupted while he and his own companions were stranded in space.

And *then* they had met other travellers, in the tangled causal leaks that permeated Phobos. A crew of travellers under Wing Commander Geoff Lighthill, captain of the huge British ship *Harmonia*.

In the end, when the rendezvous of the ships came, it had been *Harmonia* that had come to the *Last Small Step*, not the

345

other way around. And so it was again, Malenfant thought now, as the great mouth of the access tunnel descended on his ship.

He reached out to his right, without looking, and found Emma's gloved hand.

She squeezed back. 'I know. Just like the first time around. Like we are being swallowed by some huge interplanetary basking shark. I wonder if the British designers ever stopped to think about how this thing would actually *look* in action.'

Malenfant had to grin. 'Probably not. That wouldn't have crossed anybody's mind at NASA, I don't think. And certainly not among these gung-ho British.'

'No. We space travellers were never too good at the psychological side, were we?' She turned her head, checking the rudimentary control panel before them. 'Geoff needs to get on with it, though. Our air pressure is dropping steadily. Has been since we cleared the lower atmosphere.'

Vasily, below her and to her right in his lower-tier couch, grunted at that. 'Tell us something we don't know. Not designed as an orbital capsule, this tank we ride. Inner refuge aboard *Elektrod*. Went through crash, then ten years rusting away on top of volcano.'

Malenfant said, 'Vasily, believe me, nobody is knocking your technology. It got us this far, didn't it?'

'So you never had doubts?'

'I never had doubts.'

'I accept your mendacious compliment,' Vasily said.

The light changed, became a little darker in the claustrophobically small cabin. Malenfant looked out through his window. A translucent sheet was occluding the sunlight.

There was a hammering on the hull, one, two, three.

'Got you,' Lighthill called over the radio. 'I am just outside the hull.'

'Yeah,' Malenfant said. 'We noticed. That's right by my ear, Lighthill.'

'Listen carefully. I will ensure the tunnel is sealed properly around your craft's hatch, with its rather irregular shape. Then I will transfer you one by one, as quickly as possible, into the airlock of the *Harmonia* itself. Bartholomew, I suggest you are the last out. Help your crewmates out as briskly as you can, and I will take over once they are through. All agreed?'

Malenfant growled, 'We're not a pack of novices, Lighthill.'

'Well, I'm a novice,' Deirdra said. 'I'm listening.'

'Good for you, Miss Greggson,' Lighthill said. 'Very well. Who's first out?'

'As I am right by the hatch, that would be me,' Malenfant said.

'Oh, joy.'

Malenfant winked at Emma. 'He loves me really.'

Once aboard the *Harmonia*, with the airlock safely secured and the access tunnel collapsed and stowed, the passengers gathered in the wardroom, the biggest single habitable volume in the craft. After the briskest of introductions for the newcomers to the facilities and their locations, Lighthill disappeared to the bridge, to begin the cautious manoeuvring of the *Harmonia* away from the abandoned *Josh* and the raising of the ship to a higher, safer orbit.

Malenfant went to a window, hoping to see the expended *Josh*, which, discarded, would begin its long fall to the ground – though it would probably land as a hail of heat-scorched fragments. But he couldn't find it.

The rescued crew stripped off their battered and scorched

launch suits. This wardroom, with its wood panelling and brass window frames, had always struck Malenfant as incongruously opulent for a spacecraft. The newcomers seemed grimy, smelly, out of place; they moved slowly, tired and uncertain.

But the Russians, accustomed to the still more spacious *Elektrod*, seemed only mildly interested in the décor. Anna had worn her hair long, down on Persephone II, but that wasn't going to be particularly practical in zero gravity. So she began to plait it, with practised fingers.

Then there were the supplies. Lighthill had set out bulbs of water and lukewarm tea on the big fold-out dining table that dominated the room. Food, too, greens and fruit and what looked like eel meat from the *Harmonia*'s own recycling system. Malenfant found he was hungry, suddenly, and fell on this. He couldn't remember when he had last eaten, in fact, given the rush of the final preparations before launch.

Emma joined him. 'I got sick of this stuff on the way to Persephone and back. Persephone I. I mean, *eels*, bred in low-grade sewage.'

'Me too. In fact, this time we *know* it must have been mostly Lighthill's own low-grade sewage. Right now, however, it tastes as good as a triple-decker cheeseburger.'

'I'll take your word for it,' she said around a mouthful. 'Preferring not to chew. Or think about it.'

Then, after eating, the crew dispersed slowly.

There was one zero-gravity shower aboard the ship, and after a brisk discussion, Vasily was chosen as the first in line. There was a scramble for the lavatory too, and they quickly rotated through that. Bartholomew commandeered an empty cabin as an instant medical centre, and invited – ordered – the crew to come see him, one by one. Malenfant recalled that, of the lost crew of the *Harmonia*, this cabin had belonged to Nicola Mott.

By the time Malenfant had taken his turn in the bathroom, Lighthill was waiting for him.

The Wing Commander grinned. 'You should have jumped the queue for the facilities, Malenfant. Rank has its privilege – and so does age.'

Malenfant grunted. 'Speak for yourself.'

He studied Lighthill close to, the first chance he'd had since the commotion of boarding. Lighthill's appearance was unreasonably smart, Malenfant thought, in crisp shirt and slacks and soft leather shoes that looked polished, and a shave that looked like it had been administered by a downtown barber. But his eyes were . . . hollow.

Too much time alone.

Lighthill's grin widened, a little forced. 'Don't worry about me, old chap,' he whispered. 'No more sign of those blue hoops, by the way. That big bugger appearing from nowhere during the launch gave me a shock, I'll tell you.'

'We got away with it, Geoff.'

'That we did.'

Emma joined them, and they talked about the fate of the *Josh*.

'It really won't last long, sadly,' Lighthill said now. 'In its orbit, I mean. Much too low, the atmospheric drag significant.' He glanced at the others, and said quietly, 'Possibly its eventual orbit was lower than you thought. My projections were that you wouldn't have survived a single complete circuit without unacceptable decay – by which I mean too much drag for the rendezvous and coupling to have been feasible. So I had to reach you on the first orbit. And I had to come down a bit further in than I was comfortable with, I can tell you.'

His voice sounded scratchy, Malenfant thought. Out of practice.

'But you did it, Geoff. You put your own life on the line to save us.'

'Just doing my job. I do admit I didn't much fancy the alternative.'

'What alternative?'

'That you might have failed. I had already lost all of my crew, remember. The original crew of the *Harmonia*. Every one of them. You, at least, are companions of some years. If you had been lost too—'

Emma gripped his shoulder. 'None of us is equipped to survive alone.'

'Your hair, Geoff,' Deirdra said, coming over to join them.

'What's that?'

'It's so – neat.'

'Ah.' Lighthill looked shy to be talking about this. 'Well, yes. It is such a fiddly business to cut one's own hair. But one must keep up appearances, you see; do that and the rest follows. My father served in India, in troubled times for the Raj. He taught me that.'

Malenfant shook his head. 'God, I've missed you. To me you always sound like some old black-and-white movie from around 1950.'

Lighthill grinned. 'Well, of course, Malenfant, I never doubted I would encounter you and your own gleaming dome again someday. I had to keep the old place looking spruce.'

'I can see that,' Malenfant murmured.

He wasn't lying. He glanced around the wardroom again, and Deirdra took the cue to go off and explore. Lighthill had been one man alone, but you would always get muck floating in the air, trapped by filters in the atmosphere circulation system, and mould of various kinds lodging in awkward corners. Here, everything looked as if it might have been scrubbed to a sparkle.

Emma frowned. 'With all respect, though, Geoff – it's *too* neat. You need other people to create a little chaos, I guess.'

Deirdra, rummaging through stuff, smiled. 'Josh Morris was always good at that. Leaving a trail of chaos, I mean.' She had found books, held in place on a shelf by loosely tied string. Evidently what Lighthill had been reading. 'A Jules Verne omnibus. Boyhood reading, right? *Just William*. I never heard of that.'

'Borrow it if you like.'

Emma came upon the record player, camouflaged inside what looked to the unwary eye like a kind of sideboard, of light wood. She opened the lid, looked at the fine acetate discs inside – a lightweight manufacture intended for spaceflight cargo, Malenfant knew, like everything else on the *Harmonia* – and flicked through the titles. 'These are all classical. A bit austere too. Beethoven string quartets . . .' She looked at Lighthill. 'Nothing with voices. I thought you liked the crooners, those old guys from the forties.'

'Found that stuff a little tricky,' Lighthill said stiffly. 'After a while. Even some of the classics. Beethoven's later symphonies, for instance. The Pastoral. Couldn't bear the silence, though. Or, worse actually, the sounds of an empty ship. Bangs and thumps that would wake me up. Bit hard to sleep. Odd visions out of the corner of one's eye. You know.'

Studying Lighthill, Malenfant felt like he was looking at a crumbling mask.

Anna and Vasily, on their own tour of exploration, drifted over.

Vasily said, 'Well, all *I* see is rather remarkable spacecraft. Of course, dwarfed by our own *Elektrod*, but still roomy. I think our. . . Roads? Our separate paths through history?'

Lighthill nodded. 'That's the term we adopted before encountering you lot.'

'Maybe your Road and mine have more in common than we understand, yet.'

Malenfant wondered if that could be true. 'Maybe this is how empires build their ships,' he said now. 'On a grand scale. Luxurious even.'

Lighthill snorted. 'Spacegoing *Titanic*s – I hear it in your voice, man.'

Vasily grinned. 'Sooner a bed in the *Titanic* than a hammock in the boxy little ships *your* people seem to fly in, from what you told me – yes, so long as you avoid the icebergs.'

'Odd you should say that,' Lighthill said. 'Because I have a feeling an iceberg of a kind might be our next destination. Let's sit. There is food left. More tea? Or cold water?'

Knowing where the water must have come from, Malenfant asked for tea. At least you could be *sure* the water had been boiled first.

48

After a couple of hours, they broke up and scattered to the private cabins, and as far as Malenfant knew they all fell into a long, exhausted sleep. Lighthill too.

It wasn't until eight hours later that, after they had cleared away the remains of breakfast from the wardroom table, they gathered to talk about their next steps. They all still looked ragged to Malenfant. As no doubt he did.

Lighthill opened the discussion. 'So here we are. Now we must deal with the issues of the day, and the days to follow.'

Vasily nodded. 'Persephone II over. Hairy-arse spaceflight over. Now, next steps.'

'Well said,' Lighthill said drily. 'Look – we all had different reasons to come here. I'm here because it's my mission, as it has evolved. Within the overall mission of the RASF. To explore, to establish the – geography – of this strange new realm we find ourselves in. This manifold, as Malenfant calls it. To try to understand. And to try to work out what *use* it might be for us, some day.'

Malenfant grinned. 'Like you Brits figured out a use for Australia and India and—'

'If you want a debate on the merits and demerits of the British imperial project we can have it, Malenfant. Though I would point out that the nation you come from wouldn't even exist if not for the British – those in your timeline, anyhow. Sooner that than a bunch of interdimensional Kaisers and Tsars.' He glanced at Vasily and Anna. 'No offence.'

Anna smiled. 'None taken. Since our own Tsar is not – expansive. We came here to understand, too. We are Cosmists. We are more pure explorers than you are, I think, Commander. We seek to understand our place in the universe – and now, it seems, in the multiverse. For only by embracing the sky can we fully understand ourselves.'

Vasily spread his hands. 'Perhaps. But remember the plagues and other horrors we idealistic explorers inflicted on the denizens of Persephone II, as our friends call that world.' And he looked Anna in the eye. 'Also, go to Kiev. Ask there about your not-expansive Tsars.'

Deirdra nodded. 'And I came here to understand, too. My world, my Earth, was doomed to destruction because of the approach of a rogue planet. I wanted to understand why that had to be so. Whether that fate could be avoided.

'Well, let's sum it up. We discovered the manifold, this big tangle of histories. And we found that the Solar System, in some of these reality strands at least, has been – meddled with. The formation of the planets, everything. That some agents, that we call the World Engineers, have been throwing the planets around for – well, for their own purposes.' She glared around the table. 'I want to find the Engineers. And I want to *ask* them why they do what they do. What gives them the right to decide life and death for whole planetary populations? Life and death for my own world, my Earth. My family. My mother . . . That's why I'm travelling.'

Malenfant looked around the table. Vasily nodded, seriously. The rest said nothing.

But Deirdra, Malenfant noted, had quickly and quietly imposed her authority.

'Well,' Lighthill said. 'As to our next steps – I think it's clear to me, at least. You are all familiar with the reports I have returned, of the nature of the worlds of this oddly sterile Solar System. And my reports of the machines I saw toiling on the local Earth, which I called Visitors. I did wonder if we should return there, but the machines seemed to be mere gardeners, tending the anaerobic biosphere that survives on that unmodified world. I saw no signs of any more advanced intelligence there – and no sign of manifold technology.'

'No blue hoops,' Malenfant murmured.

'Quite. I have my own guesses as to the Engineers' intentions here, Miss Greggson. You know that I have called this place a Vanilla System. For here, the Engineers seem to have more or less forestalled planetary development *before* the first round of massive impacts – the impacts that shredded Mercury's mantle, and knocked a moon out of the guts of the Earth, and so forth. But *not*, it seems, before life had a chance to develop – or most likely be seeded – on Earth itself. On Vanilla Earth, quite unlike our own.

'I cannot believe that this is *the* source, where life itself evolved through chance collisions of chemicals. But somehow that doesn't fit, for me. This system is too – engineered for that. Too clean. Like a vast laboratory, or a library of samples. Not a place of creation.'

'And maybe that was why we were brought here,' Vasily murmured. 'Nothing in the manifold happens without some purpose, it seems – even if the purpose is not always apparent to us.'

'Well said, that man,' Lighthill said with a smile. 'Quite so. Maybe this Vanilla System is – if not a source, then a hub, a junction in the network through which many paths cross. But I think that with these insights, we have learned all we need to know about this system, this manifold Road.'

'So we move on,' Deirdra said firmly.

'We move on. And we know, do we not, where we should look next? Aside from those elusive glimpses around Persephone – the blue hoops, even while the *Josh* was launching – there is evidence of manifold technology in only two places in this system: at Anteros, moon of Venus, evidently a misplaced Phobos, the gateway through which we all arrived. And—'

'And at Saturn,' Malenfant said. 'That anomalous moon.'

'Precisely. A moon furthermore that shines with the light of an ancient, young Sun – the lure that brought us here in the first place, a radiation we glimpsed, or thought we did, in those deep, impossible shafts in the Phobos gateway, the chimneys.'

Anna nodded. 'Good. Then we go to Saturn.'

'Of course the *Harmonia* is more than capable of taking us there.' Lighthill added, grimly, staring around, 'But as we leave this place, I only regret that there are so many comrades who will no longer travel with us.'

For a moment he seemed unable to speak.

Vasily rose from his chair, drifted over to Lighthill, and enfolded the Englishman in a big, enclosing hug.

Malenfant saw how Lighthill, little by little, softened in his embrace.

49

Lighthill insisted on a full week of shakedown before they went anywhere. And he backed up Bartholomew in insisting that all the crew who had lifted from Persephone II should have still more intensive health checks and treatments, to ensure they were ready for the rigours of a spaceflight, to Saturn, that was likely to last weeks.

But Bartholomew pointed out that Lighthill's own health was a concern too. He had been stranded in zero gravity, save for short periods of rocket thrust, for long months now.

Bartholomew said, 'You have all had either too much gravity, or too little. I prescribe exercise.'

'Just like my boyhood, actually,' Lighthill muttered to Malenfant, later that first day after the rendezvous, as, with Anna, they plodded side by side on treadmills – more gadgets fished out of the ship's capacious hold and fixed up in the wardroom. All three were strapped to their frames by elastic harnesses, which gave their legs an illusory gravity to push against. 'Up at six, and an hour's PT before breakfast as punishment for ragging the swots.'

'School again, huh, Lighthill?'

'Always a reference, in so many ways. Why, now Bartholomew is back I even have a matron!'

The other chore Lighthill insisted on during that week of shakedown was for the new crew to work through the *Harmonia* herself and her systems. He drew up a roster, and, after some predictable arguments about the appropriateness of the assignments, the passengers went at it willingly enough.

They would perform a thorough systems check, Lighthill decreed, from one end of the ship to the other, testing, adjusting, replenishing, repairing, from basic power and propulsion through to the tangled details of life support. A lot of supplies had to be brought out of vacuum storage, as the ship's habitability was upgraded from a single human passenger to six. And – as Lighthill confided to Malenfant – in the course of their work fixing the flaws and performing their bits of preventative maintenance, the newcomers would all learn a hell of a lot about the ship and its technologies.

Malenfant himself had a good therapeutic time doing it. It was a guilty pleasure being back in a technological environment, after so many months down in the dirt on Persephone. Actually living with Neanderthals, for Pete's sake.

He suspected Anna and Vasily felt some of that. But they did mutter a lot about comparisons with their own technologies. Malenfant had the impression that whereas the *Elektrod*, a kind of mobile greenhouse in space, had been a vessel of peace, they felt that the *Harmonia*, with its dense hull and hard lines, not to mention its weapons racks, was more a ship of war. And, of course, they were surely right about that.

The week went by quickly for Malenfant.

Then Lighthill gathered them together, told them he was satisfied with the state of his ship, and that they would be leaving for Saturn after two more ship's watches.

*

At the appointed hour the next day Lighthill took his place on the bridge, with Anna at his side as his chosen co-pilot in training. Malenfant and the rest sat strapped into their seats in the wardroom. Lighthill had withdrawn the covers over the wardroom's small viewing windows, revealing the looming super Earth below.

And as the ship went through a final high orbit, Malenfant looked down one last time at the huge face of Persephone II, dimly lit by the remote Sun. He saw the continent Caina heading for evening, with the river they had followed north from the coast a gleaming blue-black ribbon cutting across a flat, sparse landscape, and with the great upland of the Shield casting a shadow itself the size of a continent. Malenfant wondered if Ham was down there somewhere. Maybe flying his half-tamed pterosaur in the morning light. Or Nadezhda, gazing up at the sky, with little Maria. One day Anna or Vasily or both would return here; one day their different Russia would surely rescue its citizens from that world. Perhaps Lighthill's RASF would come here to commemorate those who had fallen. But Malenfant doubted he would ever come this way again.

And when the *Harmonia*'s mighty engines cut in, and the vessel swung away towards the outer dark, he waved a hand in farewell to the planet, his second Persephone, and those he had left behind.

Saturn, in this Solar System as in Malenfant's own, was ten times as far from the Sun as was Earth. As Lighthill had promised it took nearly a month, mostly of unpowered cruising, for the *Harmonia* to make the crossing.

Before the giant world filled their vision.

50

After the final orbit insertion burn, Malenfant and the rest of the crew waited in the wardroom while Lighthill and Vasily, his co-pilot for the day, performed engine shutdown checks.

Waited quietly for a scheduled thirty minutes, in the steady glow of electric lighting, the wardroom windows covered for now. This version of Saturn might have no rings, but Lighthill had been unsure about the debris density, even as far out from the primary planet as they were going to settle. 'Just because there are no bright, obvious rings doesn't mean the stuff that made them up isn't out there somewhere,' Lighthill had reasoned. 'So the windows stay covered until we know it's safe.'

Nobody was going to argue about that. It felt like a long thirty minutes, though. Even the wardroom's wall-mounted monitors, like ancient cathode-ray-tube TVs, stayed blank.

At last Lighthill came bustling in, followed by Vasily. Lighthill grabbed a bulb of tea. And he smiled.

Malenfant had to smile back. 'I recognise that expression. The monkey grin of an astronaut who did something right for once.'

Lighthill raised his tea bulb in mock salute. 'Well, it was a tricky burn, Malenfant. Or series of burns. Inserting the

Harmonia into planetary orbit, and *then* into an orbit around the ice moon itself. Coming in from out of the planet's rotational plane too. But, yes, we did it right. Behold Saturn.'

With a theatrical flourish he pulled a lever.

On one side of the wardroom, panels pulled back silently to reveal a starry sky – and a single, pale disc of a planet.

Much larger to Malenfant's eye than the Moon in Earth's sky, Saturn was nearly full. The colour was yellowish brown, perhaps, but the lighting, from a distant Sun, was dim. The disc seemed visibly flattened, presumably an effect of the planet's fast rotation: the waist of that fat ball of gas was thrown out further than the average diameter, and the poles correspondingly depressed. Cloud banks streaked its face, and as Malenfant watched carefully, he thought he could see change. Those cloud banks shifted, evolved. He couldn't remember Saturn's rotational period. Ten hours or so? And there seemed to be some kind of sparking at the upper pole. Electrical storms, an aurora?

It *looked* like Saturn, from what Malenfant remembered of space-probe pictures from his own time: *Voyager*, *Cassini*. It was all oddly disappointing, Malenfant thought.

He held out his hand; his open palm just about covered the disc of the planet. 'How far out are we? What, about ten diameters?'

'Something like that,' Lighthill said. 'Just about the orbital distance of Titan.' He looked at the Russians uncertainly. 'Which is the largest of Saturn's moons in our timeline.'

Vasily shrugged. 'And ours. Different name, though.'

'We are in orbit around a moon here, in fact. But it's not Titan. Not even close. No rings, of course.'

Deirdra swam out of her chair, and with practised, un-conscious grace in the microgravity, sailed to a window. She really was turning into an astronaut, Malenfant thought, with a kind of poignant pride.

She said, 'It's hard to see anything at all. It's all so – washed out.'

Lighthill said, 'Well, they don't get a lot of sunshine out here. I'll show you.' He threw another switch.

Deirdra turned now, and looked back through the corresponding window at the rear of the cabin, as the shields on that side were lifted. Malenfant saw pale light shine on the planes of her face.

Beyond that window he saw only a brilliant pinpoint – bright enough to cast sharp shadows across the cabin, not bright enough to make him squint.

'There's the Sun,' Lighthill said. 'We're ten times as far from the Sun as Earth is, remember. So you only get a hundredth the intensity of light out here. A lot less than at Persephone, even. Just a trickle of heat. Let's take a look at the moon we're orbiting.' He turned another switch.

Another room-wall panel opened. They turned to look.

At another sphere, silvery, hanging in the dim rectilinear light of the pinpoint Sun.

Unlike Saturn, it was not quite full in the sunlight – it was like a gibbous moon. And this world was much bigger than Saturn in Malenfant's field of view, like a large dinner plate held at arm's length.

Silvery, yes. All but featureless. So featureless that it looked almost artificial: a much more perfect sphere than Saturn, say, and with hardly a blemish on that smooth, aluminium-like surface. Ice, maybe? But it lacked the cratering of an ice moon, a Europa, say. As if it had been polished smooth of defects.

Not perfect, though. Malenfant, staring, searching for detail, thought he saw a pale trace of atmosphere of some kind, the slightest of arcs at that sunlit edge.

And there was one detail on the surface, he saw now, his eyes focusing. Something odd along the centre line, which he took to be the equator. It looked like a kind of stitching, as if this world was one big baseball.

Memories stirred.

'Behold,' Lighthill said. 'Not-Titan. And with this view, now you know pretty well as much about it as I do. Well, a little less. Its period in orbit around Saturn is the same as Titan's, at fifteen days – Earth days – but that's about all it has in common with *our* Titan.'

'Right,' Malenfant said hesitantly. 'Which is – orange. A big ball of water ice and rock, with that thick smoggy atmosphere of nitrogen and organics and methane and stuff . . . Well, this one has an exposed surface – of water ice, I'm guessing? Very smooth ice? And maybe a trace of air, judging from that arc at the sunlit edge of the face . . . How far out are we?'

'From the moon? Oh, around two diameters. I reckoned we should stand well away, while we decide what we want to do. A diameter being about two thousand miles.'

'Umm. About the size of Earth's Moon, then.'

'Yes, but about a quarter the mass of the Moon. Whereas Titan is about twice the mass of the Moon. Which makes the temperature anomaly even more difficult to understand.'

'What temperature anomaly?'

'Well, look at that Sun. A moon like this ought to be cold – very, very cold. That's true even of our Titan, as massive as it is, which is close to two hundred below the freezing point of water at the surface, even with all that thick air. But *this* little bugger is only about twenty degrees below.'

'Impossible,' Vasily said immediately.

'I agree.'

Lighthill looked around a little uncertainly, as if unsure of his own logic, Malenfant thought. But then he had been quite alone with all this stuff, and nobody to share observations, guesswork, conclusions.

'But,' Lighthill went on, 'the evidence is inarguable. The heat leaking from the interior is obvious, easily measurable from afar with the ship's instruments. Thermocouples. And that's presumably why the surface is so smooth, as you say, Malenfant. Any cratering or cracks would relax away. I also took spectrometry readings. The radiation coming from this little moon is dominated by waste heat – just a black-body curve. But it has some wrinkles. Notably, what *looks* like sunlight, in the visible spectrum range. As if leaking out from some inner source through crevices.'

'Yes,' Emma said. 'Of course. The reason we came out here in the first place. What looked like sunlight, but—'

'Anomalous. Remember? We could see that from afar. Passing through the deepest, most anomalous manifold portals on Phobos. Umm, Anteros – whichever. A glow which has a spectrum like sunlight too, but light emitted from, we concluded, a Sun much younger than ours – when the Sun was much cooler, its spectrum subtly different.' The uncertainty in his manner, even his speech patterns, seemed to increase. 'This was the lure we followed. Young sunlight. Well, we located the source – coming from this little body, this strange Not-Titan.

'And here it is. I've measured it precisely, recorded the results. But I have to admit that though we've come all this way to take a look, I still have no idea what these features mean. Nothing natural, surely. Though, of course, fundamentally speaking, if this little moon is so warm it must have some kind of source of inner heat.'

Deirdra nodded – reassuring, Malenfant thought, confident where Lighthill seemed to waver. She said, 'Well, it's just as well we're here to figure it out then, isn't it? But also, what's it *for*?'

It seemed a surprising question, and it shut everybody up.

She glanced around, meeting their gazes. 'I wasn't trained as a scientist. I know scientists aren't supposed to think that some natural phenomenon is *for* anything. It is what it is. But in this case why shouldn't all this be *for* something? We *know* this Solar System, probably like all the copies of it, isn't just the result of natural processes. You just said so, Geoff. Somebody has been meddling. And that meddling—'

'Is precisely what we came here to find out,' Malenfant said. 'Good point.'

'So maybe that heat source isn't natural. Maybe it's some immense engine. Or at least it's better to think of it that way.'

Lighthill nodded ruefully. 'But the situation is so extraordinary it is difficult even to frame the right questions. However, we might soon find some answers. The moon is featureless . . . almost.'

As he said this he winked at Deirdra.

Immediately Malenfant was on the alert. 'What's that supposed to mean? Look, I can see that equatorial feature, the line . . . Have you seen something else?'

Lighthill nodded. 'The equatorial line. Yes, interesting in its own right, and suggestive, isn't it? We must discuss it. But even *that* is secondary to the main feature.'

'What main feature?'

'Here's what's what. I've come up with something – or rather, I've set something in motion. In the last stages of our approach to this moon.

'I haven't been fully open with you. In my first survey of, umm, Not-Titan, yes, Malenfant, I saw something else. On the face turned away from us just now, but in the sunlight still, I imagine. I needed you to see it in colour, so I took some photos, pushed them through the 'fast-developer kit—' He dug into a pocket, pulled out plastic envelopes, each containing a wet-chemistry photograph. He passed them around.

When Malenfant got his copy, he grabbed it and stared.

At a blue hoop, the colour of the sky, perfect and whole.

It stood over a plain of silver-grey that itself seemed to curve away slightly. There was a gap between hoop and ground – if ground it was – so that the hoop seemed to hover, effortlessly, framed by a sky that was dark as night.

Emma's lips were pursed. 'Look, Geoff – you're feeding this stuff piecemeal, I think you've been over-planning this. You really have been on your own too long.'

Lighthill snapped back, 'Well, that's hardly my fault, is it? Oh – I'm sorry for the secrecy. The sudden reveal, as if by a conjurer. Rabbits from hats . . . I thought it best to let you soak in the context first . . . I'm sorry too about the quality of the pictures.'

'Good enough,' Malenfant growled. He tapped his image of the blue hoop. 'This thing is down on the surface of Not-Titan?'

'Well, not *on* it as you can see, but hovering a little way above. Needless to say there is no visible means of support. A minor miracle, it seems, when dealing with this technology, even on such a scale.'

'What scale?'

Vasily growled out an answer to that. 'The hoop is about a mile and a half across. More than two kilometres.'

Malenfant glanced at Vasily, who had been Lighthill's co-pilot during the orbital manoeuvres. He might have seen this for himself. A co-conspirator, knowing just a little more than the rest, then. He stood impassive, loyal to his new commander.

'This is what we came for,' Deirdra said, staring at the image. 'Right? The strange sunlight. We could see that even from Anteros, from Venus. That was the lure. But, manifold technology. *This* is what we came to find.'

'Maybe,' Malenfant said. 'You need to tell us what you're thinking, Geoff.'

Lighthill nodded slowly. 'Very well. I'm thinking that the portal down there is more than wide enough for us to fly the *Harmonia* through, intact and whole. If we choose.'

Malenfant saw Emma's eyes widen at that. But she, of course, was an experienced astronaut too and understood the peril. 'My God. You're not serious.'

'I certainly am,' Lighthill said. 'We could do this, in principle. No air down there – certainly no natural features to impede us. We could fly down and *whoosh straight through*, the only danger being a fouling on the hoop itself.

'It sounds outrageous. But what options do we have? We have no landing craft, as you know. It would not be impossible to jury-rig a lander to take a crew to the surface of Not-Titan, down from some high orbit. The low gravity, the lack of atmosphere – I've done some sketch designs, in fact. But – why wait for that? We could answer many of our questions more quickly. Well, perhaps.'

Emma nodded. 'By just flying the *Harmonia* through that manifold gate you found.'

'So,' Bartholomew said now. It was the first time he'd spoken since Lighthill had emerged from his cabin, Malenfant realised. 'We have just arrived here, after a month-long flight, and you are immediately going to fly this ship, our one and only functioning spacecraft, straight through the mouth of that interdimensional portal. Have you *any* clue what kind of health risks that might pose?'

Lighthill said drily, 'I will count that as an objection. Anybody else, ayes or nays?'

Anna grinned. 'Aye from me.'

Vasily nodded. 'I have talked this over before with the Wing Commander. Do it.'

'How long?' Emma asked practically.

'Before we reach the hoop?' Lighthill shrugged. 'Hours. Our orbit around Not-Titan has a twenty-eight-hour period.' He glanced around. 'All right, confession time. Here's the truth. *I've already done it*. Put us on an approach course. If we follow our current trajectory, to take us down to a graze of the surface – seven hours to closest approach.'

Stunned silence. Malenfant stared out at the moon, wondering if he could already see it loom closer.

Emma spoke first, glaring at Lighthill. '*Too long alone,* Geoff. You either over-plan it, or you let your impulses take over. And you don't consult others before acting. You've lost your perspective, your judgement.'

He met her stare. 'It would be easy to turn the ship away. If there are any objections—'

'Not from me,' Anna said.

Lighthill turned. 'Malenfant? What say you?'

Malenfant stared back at him, and tried to organise his thoughts. This whole process, driven by Lighthill's muddled mixture of urgency and over-planning, was happening too fast. He realised they hadn't even discussed that other feature down on the moon, that line around the equator, hauntingly familiar . . .

But maybe Lighthill was right. That haunting hoop was the

obvious next target. What good would it do to delay?

He shrugged. 'Let's do this.'

Anna grinned. 'The ayes have it. You crazy fools.'

51

As the time for rendezvous approached, Malenfant donned a slightly ill-fitting British-made pressure suit and went to the bridge of the *Harmonia*. He had pulled rank as best he could; *this* time he was going to be the *co*-pilot as Geoff Lighthill guided his ship through its latest unlikely adventure.

And Malenfant, like Emma, kept to himself the doubts he still had about the judgement of a man who had been alone for far too long.

In zero gravity Malenfant slid easily into the co-pilot's seat – the seat on the left, the right being reserved for the commander in the British tradition, the opposite of the American. It suited Malenfant; he was used to the left-hand side. The bridge was a small, dark, quiet cabin, smelling of the ozone tang of electronic instruments, the musty, scuffed leather of the acceleration couches. Big picture windows gave an expansive view of space – and, if you leaned forward out of your couch and craned your neck, of the outer hull of the *Harmonia* itself. After years out of its dock – in Lighthill's reality an expansive facility in high orbit around Earth, according to the Wing Commander – that hull was yellowed by the unshielded sunlight, pocked by impacts from the minor debris that littered deep space.

And, beyond that, he looked out on the dull, featureless,

almost metallic-looking surface of the ice moon, dimly lit by the remote Sun. He was still high above that surface, high enough for the moon's curvature to be apparent. It was, he imagined, much as the Apollo astronauts must have witnessed Earth's Moon as they approached, back in the 1960s. This ice moon was pretty much the same size as Luna. But the extraordinarily precise manoeuvre they were going to attempt – to slide this hulk of a ship through a hoop a mere two kilometres across, that stood just over the surface of this three-thousand-kilometre-plus-wide moon, from an approach at orbital speed, more than a kilometre per second – made the Apollo landing look like a walk on the Canaveral beach. He felt his stomach clench.

The only internal lights in the cabin were the glows of instruments. Malenfant saw Lighthill's face as a pale mask in the gloom, his eyes shadowed, his teeth gleaming white when he smiled.

'You're a crazy man,' Malenfant said. 'You know that? What happened to the cautious commander?'

Lighthill shrugged, strapping in, glancing over his instruments as he spoke. 'Still in here somewhere. Malenfant, I *have* spent too long alone, looping around this strange alternate Solar System. I admit it. Can you imagine what that was like? However, now I see no reason to hesitate. And, frankly, I have every confidence in the manoeuvre that is going to take us through that manifold portal. It is merely a matter of celestial mechanics—'

A radar altimeter pulsed, Malenfant saw, giving precise readings of their slowly diminishing altitude.

Lighthill said, 'Anyhow it's all moot, isn't it? We're stuck on this course for good or ill. And we ought to start thinking about *that*.' He pointed out through the window. Even as he checked his instruments, he started taking photographs.

Where the cold, blank ground of the ice moon was looming up, slowly, steadily flattening below them. All but featureless. Save for a line of darkness scraped across that ground, directly beneath them, pointing dead ahead.

Malenfant had glimpsed this feature as a fine trace from high orbit. Now he saw it close to for the first time, its details blurred by speed. *It looked like a fence*, a vast picket fence hundreds of kilometres long, erected across Antarctica – the icebound Antarctica of his own era – a meaningless demarcation between one chunk of frozen wasteland and another.

And he had seen something like this before, in another reality. He knew what it was. So did Lighthill, surely.

They said nothing, not for now. Malenfant just concentrated on the flight itself, on instruments showing the ship's attitude, its velocity, its slowly diminishing height from the ground.

'I'm registering traces of atmosphere,' Lighthill said at length. 'We have scoop samplers on the outer hull, feeding a mass spectrometer. Could hardly be any thinner . . . Water, hydrogen, oxygen . . . And just a trace of methane. A trace of a trace.'

Malenfant grunted. 'Even from high orbit, I noticed that fine layer of air at the horizon.'

'Yes, yes . . . I've seen geysers here, water squirting out of cracks in the ice, driven by that inner heat source.'

'Right. And then the Sun's radiation, feeble as it is, breaks up the water into hydrogen and oxygen. The hydrogen must mostly escape to space—'

'The methane is interesting, though,' Lighthill said. 'Organic molecules: some kind of chemistry going on down there. It's evidently warm enough for that, inside the moon at least, given a heat leakage that can create steam, drive geysers into space. *There could be life*. Like the purple mats of Vanilla Earth, perhaps. Life that never sees the daylight, under miles of water. Maybe strange sightless fish feeding off pale lichen, as in our own deep oceans. Could it be the same here? Oh, Josh would love this!'

'It explains why this surface is so damn smooth,' Malenfant said. 'There must be impacts from time to time. Craters must form. Saturn's moons do show features like that – back where I come from, I mean. The ice will be soft enough for such features to mostly relax away. But there has to be resurfacing. Aeons of fine frost cover, healing over the flaws.'

Lighthill nodded. 'You're surely right. But the resurfacing evidently hasn't been sufficient to cover up *that*.'

And Lighthill pointed to the 'fence', whose line they were still tracking. A fence that, as they dropped further, slowing, was now resolving in Malenfant's vision.

Into a row of towers. Tall, thin. And all lined up along the equator of this moon, a perfect alignment.

'It is just like Persephone, isn't it?' Malenfant said, wondering. 'I mean, the Persephone we found out in the dark, shoved out of Deirdra's Solar System to the comet cloud. Persephone I. The Towers.'

'As I thought when I first saw this, as the *Harmonia* approached. Just like it, yes. To a remarkable degree of precision . . .' In a screen, Lighthill brought up a magnification of one Tower. It was thin, a hollow shaft standing on its end. And Malenfant could see its top, gaping open.

'Twenty kilometres tall,' Lighthill murmured. 'The radar echoes confirm it.'

'Just like the Persephone Towers?'

'Indeed. And with the same geometry, as far as I can tell. Hollow tubes, like chimney stacks. Marching all the way around the equator. And, just as on Persephone, they are around three-quarters of a kilometre apart.'

'Umm. On Persephone there were sixty-five thousand of them, right? Striding across land and the shallow seas. Here, a lot less—'

'Fifteen thousand, I estimate.' Lighthill laughed. 'A *mere* fifteen thousand.'

'And you think they have the same purpose? What we guessed on Persephone I—'

He shrugged. 'That's the simplest hypothesis.'

The simplest hypothesis. That the Towers, as on Persephone I, were in fact the exhaust stacks of a global array of rockets. On Persephone they had been nuclear-fusion rockets, consuming water ice for fusion fuel and propellant, designed to push around whole planets more massive than the Earth . . .

'Why?' Malenfant mused. 'Why build all this here? We thought that Persephone I had been used as a kind of cue ball in a game of interplanetary pool, right? A comparatively easy deflection, that then caused a secondary deflection of migrating gas giants, that in turn shaped the formation of a Solar System for some purpose. A cascade of small adjustments. Planet-shifting.'

'Correct. As we surmised. The gas giant migration *is* the World Engine. But, you are wondering, why shove around a mere moon? The mass would be too small for such world-bothering purposes.'

Malenfant shook his head. 'Could this be some kind of test bed for the technology?'

Lighthill frowned. 'Doubtful. We determined that the Persephone I Towers had been built *billions* of years ago, remember – the geology showed it. All this tech has been around a long time. It seems unlikely that experimental rigs would survive.'

'OK. Point taken. So this moon has been made mobile for a purpose of its own – why?'

Lighthill checked his harness. 'A fascinating discussion, Malenfant. But one that will have to wait. Because the climax of this particular phase of our unlikely jaunt is almost on us.' He pointed ahead.

And Malenfant saw, far ahead, along the line of Towers, a flash of electric blue.

Lighthill opened the intercom to the wardroom, where the rest of their companions waited. 'Here we go, chaps,' he called. 'Strap in.'

Following the precise mathematical logic of orbital mechanics, without power save for the finest of last-minute attitude-thruster squirts by Lighthill, the *Harmonia* dipped out of the sky.

The very last moments seemed to flash by.

'Lucky for us,' Lighthill murmured, staring ahead, unblinking, concentrating ferociously, 'that the manifold portal is a little offset from the line of the Towers itself. So as we drop through the last kilometre or so we shouldn't hit any masonry.'

'*Shouldn't.*' Malenfant couldn't take his eyes off the approaching Towers. The belly of the ship seemed almost to scrape their tops. Their gaping mouths flashed past, Malenfant counted, two every second, like a rapid pulse.

Lighthill grinned tightly. 'If you want the truth, Malenfant, I wanted to go barrelling through the hoop as soon as we got here because I'm not sure I'd have had the nerve to do it, if we'd waited around a few days and I'd *thought* about it any more . . . Ten seconds. Hold on to your breakfast.' And, unexpectedly, he stabbed at a button. 'Bombs away!'

Malenfant, startled, felt no shudder.

But when he glanced in a rear-view monitor he saw an object, barrel-shaped, fall away from the craft, evidently released through the door of some bay. It diminished rapidly in Malenfant's vision – but as it dropped onto the pale ice, he saw a splash of red, white, blue.

'Shit. Was that a Union Jack?'

'Seemed appropriate.'

'You *have* gone crazy, Lighthill.'

'You'll see. All part of the cunning plan. Hold tight—'

Shadows flickered across the cabin now, a blinking light that made it seem as if Malenfant was sitting through some corny old *wet*-chemistry movie. When he looked to his right, he saw the shafts of the final Towers, pillars rushing by. He was actually *below* the tips of the Towers, then, less than twenty kilometres above the ice.

But, he knew, they needed to get lower yet, to within a kilometre of the ground—

In the very last seconds, he glimpsed lumpy forms toiling at the bases of the Towers, moving slowly, ponderously, like clumsy gardeners. *Visitors.* As Lighthill had seen on a moonless Earth, in this reality.

Blue light flared.

There was a *jolt*—

So they passed through another manifold portal.

As usual, everything changed.

And sunlight, seeming dazzling bright, splashed into the cabin. Malenfant heard himself cry out, and he threw his arm over his eyes.

Lighthill howled. 'Butch Breakaway, beat that one!'

FOUR

On Her Further Travels Across the Manifold And Her Descent Into Zeus, Moon of the Third Persephone

52

Lighthill reacted quickly.

Even before Malenfant had got over his dazzle, metal panels slid down silently over the big viewing windows.

'Doing the same in the wardroom,' Lighthill muttered. 'Go back there, would you? And tell your man Bartholomew to check over the crew. If he's not doing it already. You may tell them that there shouldn't be any significant action for several hours.'

Malenfant felt disoriented, bewildered. Slow to respond. 'What the hell just happened? I—'

'I have been through more of these transitions than you have, Malenfant. Remember that. When you first found us, by blundering through portals in the heart of Phobos, we, in the *Harmonia*, were already seasoned travellers.' A curt smile. 'I suspect there is, or can be, a jolt to the system. After all it's not as if we evolved to go hopping between timelines, is it? So, best to give people time to adjust.'

'But not you, right, Lighthill? You can keep functioning, even all alone, the captain lashed to his mast?'

'Well, that's a Navy metaphor but I'll accept it.' He glared. 'You still here, man? Go, go . . .'

Malenfant, seeing no choice, went.

*

Back in the wardroom he found Bartholomew was already working through a series of physical checks on each of the crew. When Malenfant floated in he was taking a blood-pressure reading from Emma – made by wrapping his robot hand around her upper arm.

Anna and Vasily moved from window to window, cursing in Russian at the covers that obscured their view of the new universe outside.

Malenfant saw cracks of light where the covers didn't quite fit. Cracks of that strange, brighter sunlight he had glimpsed on the bridge.

Deirdra, phlegmatic and practical, was making tea.

Malenfant drifted over and joined her. 'You really are British after all. When there's nothing else to do, have a cup of tea.'

'You want a cup or not?'

'What do you think?'

'What's going on, Malenfant? This is very frustrating.'

He shrugged. 'Just Lighthill being Lighthill. We'll have to wait.'

Bartholomew smiled. 'Well, I can make use of the time.' He came drifting over to Malenfant. 'Your turn. Roll up your sleeve.'

Malenfant held out his arm.

'You are taking this delay well, Malenfant.'

'Huh. Frustrating as hell.'

'I'm sure the über-experienced Commander Lighthill knows what *the hell* he is doing.'

Lighthill bustled in. 'I'll take that praise at face value. Indeed I do. Take a look at this for a start.' He passed around a small photograph, still wet from the developer.

Emma, Deirdra, the Russians, drifted over to see.

When he got hold of it – with his upper arm still enclosed by Bartholomew's grasp – Malenfant saw a Union flag, roughly unfurled, dumped on a pale surface, evidently ice. And a flash of electric blue at the side of the picture.

'Huh. Your parting gift to Not-Titan, right?' He glanced around. 'This flying ace here dropped a kind of bomb onto the ice, right beside the hoop, just before we went through. Needed a souvenir, Lighthill? One for the officers' club some day?'

'Oh, do shut up, Malenfant, you can be tiresome. You don't understand. This was no stunt. This was reconnaissance. Science, even. You see, this photograph was taken looking *back* – and *after* we had passed through the manifold portal.'

Malenfant took a moment to process that.

Deirdra was quicker. 'You dropped this on the ice before we went through the portal. After we'd gone through it, into all this sunlight, *then* you took the picture. So the ice moon we left behind, in the Persephone II thread—'

'Is the exact same ice moon as exists in *this* thread,' Lighthill said.

Malenfant looked around. Anna and Vasily, perhaps less accustomed to jaunts across the manifold, looked particularly baffled.

Whereas Deirdra seemed electrified. Ignoring the rest, she grabbed Lighthill's photograph and peered into it, almost hungrily.

Emma said, 'OK. Good thinking, Lighthill, I'll give you that, to have set this test up. Didn't occur to me. But we have seen this kind of thing before. On Phobos – the version of Phobos where you found me. Remember the Russian craft there? Which was buried deep in the ice and stuck out of the surface *at the same time.*'

'Yes. The manifold is a strange place,' Deirdra said slowly.

'It doesn't just link up different realities. It has the property that objects, even people, can be in two places at once. And so this ice moon is *simultaneously* back in orbit around Persephone II, and here – wherever we are now.' She looked cautiously at Vasily and Anna. 'It's pretty bewildering, even when you see it with your own eyes.'

Lighthill nodded cautiously. 'Some of our own theorists, at Cavendish and elsewhere, speculate that the nature of reality at the quantum level simply isn't like what we experience at the gross human scale. Why, I remember being taught the gas laws – the behaviour of gases, how their temperature and pressure and so forth are related – and the mathematical models we were given to think about *that* were very common-sense, all to do with ping-pong balls rattling around in a box. And it worked! On that scale anyhow. But there's no reason to think that it's ping-pong balls all the way down. In fact we know it isn't . . .

'And so, perhaps, you see, maybe with this manifold technology we encounter behaviours quite different from anything we are used to. If quantum effects are being magnified up to the macroscopic level. An electron can be in more than one place at the same time, effectively. Well then, with manifold portals around, so can a whole moon.'

Vasily listened carefully to all this. Then he said, 'I studied quantum mechanics in Kiev. Good teacher. Stupid subject. Cat dead, cat not dead. So what? Who cares? Not even cat. What's next? Open blinds, Commander.'

Lighthill grinned. 'Vasily, my friend, I like your attitude. All right. 'Ware sunlight.' He ducked into the bridge, hit a switch, returned quickly.

Around the cabin, the external window covers slid silently out of the way.

And sunlight shafted into the room, hard, bright, dazzling Malenfant.

The ship was evidently rotating, very slowly, on its long axis, and beams of light tracked slowly through the cabin, catching the dust in the air, bits of debris. A paperclip, floating, shone like a diamond. Malenfant noticed how the crew oddly cowered out of the way of the light, which was much brighter than at the orbit of Saturn, in a different reality.

And through the open windows Malenfant glimpsed space.

Distant stars.

The curve of a planet's limb.

What planet? Not Saturn.

Lighthill said, 'Careful with your eyes in the light – but, though the Sun seems dazzling bright, it's not. I mean, not compared to what we all grew up with—'

'We aren't at Earth's orbit,' Malenfant snapped. 'Is that what you're working around to telling us?'

'Quite so,' Lighthill said. 'And we are no longer at Saturn either – well, as you can see. I've already been able to determine the distance quite precisely from an examination of the sunlight itself . . . At Saturn we were ten times as far as Earth from the Sun. Here we are a little less than *three* times further than Earth. The sunlight is perhaps an eighth of Earth's intensity – not a hundredth, as at Saturn. So the brightness is something of an illusion; you will soon adapt—'

'And there's a planet out there,' Malenfant said, curtly. 'Not-Titan is still a moon, then.'

'Quite right,' Lighthill murmured. 'Though no longer a moon of Saturn. And now one of a pair of moons, in fact.'

'A pair?' Deirdra was evidently trying to remember. 'Help me out, Malenfant. My astronomy still isn't good enough. What planet is three times as far out as the Earth? Or was, back home. And, what two moons?'

He shook his head. 'No planet in our system. Well, a dwarf planet, Ceres. Big boss of the asteroid belt. But here . . .' He glanced at Lighthill.

'Here, something else,' Lighthill said, nodding. 'See for yourselves.'

They crowded to see.

The planet hung in space, face turned to the Sun. Malenfant tried covering the new world with his outstretched hand; his hand at arm's length just about obscured the full disc – just as he had been able to cover Saturn from the ice moon, he remembered.

And the planet itself, swathed in cloud, was a blue-grey disc, with land masses showing a pale brown, and water such a deep blue it was almost black. The reflection of the Sun off the water was brilliant.

'Remarkable,' Vasily murmured. 'Like Earth.'

'But it's not Earth,' Emma murmured. Malenfant felt her hand creep into his. She said, 'Is it? Not even an Earth in the wrong place.'

Lighthill said calmly, 'We are just inside the orbital distance of the ice moon right now. When we came through the portal, I quickly put us into a free orbit which will take us sailing down towards the planet for a close pass before bringing us back up again. We should be making our closest approach, what, twenty hours after we came through the portal? Plenty of time to prepare. As to how far out we are, Malenfant, the ice moon, with a companion moon in the same orbit, has a distance from its primary of about a third that of Luna from Earth, back home.'

Malenfant nodded, thinking fast, and held up his hand

against the planet, for comparison. 'All right. So that baby is some way bigger than the Earth, then.'

'Of course it is,' Deirdra called across from her own window. 'Malenfant – don't you get it? Can't you see? *That's Persephone.* Or another version of it. I'm right, aren't I, Commander Lighthill?'

'Looks like it,' Lighthill said grudgingly. 'Somewhat further out from the Sun than the world you explored – Persephone II, we called it. Though obviously not out in the comet cloud like poor, doomed Persephone I. Must we call this number three? But, yes, the mass and size estimates I've made fit that hypothesis—'

'You can *see* it,' Deirdra said, sounding excited. 'Look, Malenfant, Emma – that patch near the top of the disc – doesn't that look like Caina?' She crouched, twisting her head, as the ship rotated. 'It's passing out of my view. Damn it.' She hurried to another port, drifting with practised ease in the lack of gravity.

Emma crossed the cabin, following Deirdra's lead. 'You're right. There's the Shield. You can see its shadow. Of course it's Persephone – Persephone III. But it's different from our Persephone, isn't it? The thickness of the atmosphere – you can see it at the horizon. Much of the land looks . . . bluish? Purple? Water, life everywhere.'

Vasily said, 'Have to descend to see. Like angels from the manifold.'

'Quite right,' Lighthill said. 'Though we are likely to have a crowded agenda.'

Malenfant snapped, 'Enough of your drip-feeding, Lighthill. Cut to the chase. That's Brit-speak to tell us you've found out more stuff about this system. Correct?'

'Correct.' He sighed. 'Very well.

385

'For one thing, there is an Earth here. I mean, a living, human, densely populated Earth.'

That shut them up.

'Since we came through the hoop I have only dipped into the broadcasts I can pick up, the leakage of a radio-noisy planet, and have made little of what I have heard so far. All in good time, I suppose. Two things, though. *We have been spotted.* Already. The radio chatter indicates it. And I did hear dates. The year. I'm pretty sure that it's 2019 down there. Or at least, *a* 2019.' Lighthill grinned. 'You are halfway home, Malenfant.'

'Can't be a coincidence,' Emma murmured. 'Nothing about the manifold is coincidental.'

'There's more,' Lighthill said now.

'What?' Malenfant said.

'Somebody *else* has noticed us. More radio chatter. That second moon of Persephone, companion to Not-Titan. It's a big one – about the size of Mars – our Mars. Well, there is no Mars here; perhaps it *is* Mars. It shares the same orbit as Not-Titan—'

'Trojan orbits, I bet,' Malenfant said. 'Not-Titan is ahead of the Mars moon in its orbit by sixty degrees. Or trails it by sixty. A classic stable configuration; the Solar System, our Solar System, is full of examples. Correct?'

'Correct. But that's not the most interesting thing about it.' Lighthill hesitated.

'Spill, damn it.'

'Very well. In order.' Lighthill ticked off the points on his fingers. 'The Mars moon seems to be habitable. Second. There is a human colony there – at least one. Third. It was the humans there who spotted us first. We have actually been hailed, with a radio message. In the English language!'

Last finger.

'Fourth. This matters to both of us, Malenfant—'

'No,' Deirdra snapped, startling Malenfant with her interruption. *'None of this matters*. This, this stately strategy, your methodical explorations. Can't you see that we have found what we are looking for? And it was under our noses all the time.' She waved the little photograph, of the Union flag on the ice. 'This moon!'

Lighthill glowered, evidently offended at this breach of protocol, even of good manners.

While Malenfant held his breath. 'OK, Deirdra, we'll talk about it. Lighthill, your last finger—'

Lighthill looked at him steadily. 'The message is from Nicola Mott.'

53

You have to understand something of our situation here, Wing Commander Lighthill. New Paris is – a happy place to live, I would say. And a successful place, a thriving colony. Already we have first-generation natives – children born here, on Demeter, who have never known troubled old Earth. And Demeter itself is fascinating in its own right. It would be even if not for the native life forms, even if we only had its spectacular landscapes to explore . . .

It was going to take a couple of weeks, they were told by this new Nicola Mott, before the colony on Demeter could send up a ship to meet the crew of the *Harmonia*. The British ship had no planetary landers of its own, since losing *Charon* and the makeshift *Charon II*. The crew were stuck in space until the locals came to fetch them. If ever.

Lighthill groused, but parked *Harmonia* in a high, slow orbit about Zeus.

Zeus: the locals' name for the ice moon, Not-Titan, as it was manifested in this particular Road of the manifold.

Demeter: that was their name for the Mars-sized moon of Persephone III.

Malenfant had to put up with a schoolroom-classics explanation of the names from Lighthill. In Greek mythology, it seemed, Zeus, king of the gods, and Demeter, goddess of agriculture among other things, had been the parents of Persephone. If so, Malenfant thought, the child dwarfed the parents. But, given the apparent significance of the ice moon, a multi-reality enigma that seemed drenched in alien technology, and given the obvious evidence of vibrant life, human and otherwise, on the Mars moon, the names seemed fair. Zeus and Demeter.

To the locals Persephone III was just Persephone, a name that seemed to cling to the multiple versions of this giant planet across the manifold.

Agreeing on names was one thing. Otherwise it was clear from Nicola Mott's tone, when she spoke to Lighthill or Malenfant through radio links from the ground on Demeter, that the travellers were far from welcome here. She never said so out loud, but the message was clear enough. The Demeter colonists evidently had their own agenda.

Also she clearly had problems with Malenfant's, and Lighthill's, claims to some kind of relationship with her. These people were aware of the manifold portal on Zeus – of course they were – as well as the other alien technologies. But they didn't seem to have explored the portal – or if they had, they weren't sharing their results.

So Mott kept talking to them, but dismissed any mention of personal stuff. In fact, to her, the political background of her own culture seemed much more significant.

As, Malenfant thought glumly, he might have expected, of anybody, in any Road.

Lighthill, soon aware of the delicacy of their situation – and, as an imperial officer, more of a diplomat than Malenfant would ever be – began to make recordings of these conversations on magnetic tape, and listened over to key passages with the others, the better to interpret their subtler meanings.

Demeter, this version of Mars, Malenfant had learned, was something like the high Arctic. Pretty much habitable, though pretty chilly too – and with an atmosphere that was low pressure, but contained some oxygen. It was a world where a human being could walk around in the open with nothing but warm protective clothing and an oxygen mask. Some Earth plants could grow out in the open; many others, including crop plants, flourished in simple shelters or greenhouses. It was a hell of an improvement on the Mars Malenfant remembered, with its vanishingly thin air, deep cold, sleeting solar radiation and toxic, caustic dirt – a Mars which would kill you in minutes, maybe seconds, if you were unwise enough to expose yourself to it unprotected.

To him this was reminiscent of Old Mars, the more or less habitable sister planet everybody had once wanted to believe in, and explored in fiction by Weinbaum and Clarke and . . . Stuff he had just hoovered up as a kid, even if it was already well out of date. And here it was. He felt an odd, illogical envy.

But, Nicola said, her voice tinny on the tape, *our situation here is – fragile. The colony was founded by a coalition of nations, some of whom were at war very recently. In my lifetime. A war that almost tipped into global nuclear conflict, in which case – well, we would have lost far more than the chance to explore the wonders of Demeter. And so we here in New Paris are a kind of expression of that fragile post-conflict unity. Living here under multiple flags, including that of the UGE.*

UGE: the United Governance of Earth, Malenfant learned, as Lighthill made careful notes. A kind of beefed-up version of the UN, halfway to a world government, it seemed.

We are all aware of our symbolic importance here – of the scrutiny we are under. We are not just an example of peaceful international cooperation. One of our purposes here, which is rarely articulated out loud, is that we are a kind of fallback for the human race. Suppose war comes again? Humanity might be destroyed on Earth; the planet itself might become uninhabitable – but we might survive, and so the human race would persist. We are like a reserve colony of some endangered animal in a zoo.

'An old argument,' Lighthill murmured. 'An Earthbound mankind has all its eggs in one basket.'

Malenfant nodded. 'We had the same argument. Expressed pretty much the same way. We never did anything about it. But then,' he said, thinking it over, 'we never dropped any nuclear weapons in anger after the 1940s. Whereas I have the feeling things were different here. I guess we'll find out.'

. . . Why, there are German veterans working alongside Russians, without friction . . .

'Translation,' Lighthill murmured, listening to the tape. 'Don't rock the boat.'

'Yeah. And I wonder what war those Germans and Russians are veterans of,' Malenfant said.

Just as one example, Nicola went on, *even your orbit around Zeus could have been interpreted as a provocative act. Many accept your explanation that you represent no nation of our Earth. But you must understand that Zeus itself is essentially embargoed, for the foreseeable future. It evidently contains relics of extraterrestrial technology—*

'The manifold portal is more than a relic,' Lighthill muttered. 'Plus whatever is on and inside Zeus. Deirdra's lure.'

'Yeah. More diplomatic language.'

Also we have resource constraints of our own, Nicola had continued. *Our craft are propelled by nuclear-fission rockets. As is yours, yes? The propellant can be manufactured from local resources, particularly water from Demeter, but the fission fuel itself must be imported from Earth, at great cost. Demeter has many gifts for us, but uranium deposits close enough to the surface are rare . . .*

Malenfant, listening closely to her voice, imagined Nicola, the person.

'Of course hers *would* be the first voice we heard here – that darned manifold resonance again. Smart move for her commanders to use that to have a single point of contact to deal with an anomaly like us. Quick thinking. But it's actually a hazard, for us. This must be hard too on Nicola. I think we got landed on her on top of other responsibilities. And when you think about it she is serving as a kind of capcom for us. Capcom for a whole world. A whole reality. Tough on her personally. But she's doing a good job.'

'Quite so.' Lighthill snapped the recording off. 'Well, you know the rest. Nevertheless, we have an opening. Nicola tells us that these utopian Demeter colonists have a mission planned in their own nuclear-rocket spaceships to send a crew down to the surface of Persephone itself, to inspect the local life forms – and, I suspect, to seek out uranium deposits. This is in a couple of weeks. They are prepared to divert to meet us here in Zeus orbit – evidently their little ships are capable of *that* – and they will even take one or two of us along with them. Down to the surface of Persephone III, I mean. All a goodwill gesture – and a means, no doubt, to keep us distracted and under control, while they give us a good look-over.'

'Yeah. Before we are allowed anywhere near this Demeter base.'

'It's an offer we should accept,' Emma said. 'Obviously. Whatever covert motives they might have.'

Malenfant nodded.

But Deirdra broke into the discussion, frowning. 'You want to go to Demeter? But that's a distraction. So is Persephone.

392

What we really need is a proper look at the ice moon. Zeus. *The moon itself* is the thing. Can't you see? It exists in two places at once. It's another paradoxical manifold artefact, but on a scale we haven't seen before. A whole world transformed. And now we know there's a heat source at the centre—'

'Yes?'

'Maybe you missed it, Malenfant. But in my history the biggest heat sources of all were the big AI suites. Remember all those chimneys around the suburbs?'

That made him think. 'Good point,' he conceded.

'Right! *That's* what we need to be exploring. The people on Persephone and Demeter − even on Earth, here − I'm sorry, Malenfant. It just doesn't matter.'

He paused before replying, thinking hard. She was obviously right that the ice moon had to be a key focus for them. But he was concerned. It seemed to him that Deirdra was changing. Becoming harder, more determined, clearer in her own goals. She was exploring the manifold in order to understand the means and motives of the entities, still hypothetical, that they called the World Engineers. Everything that deflected her from that goal, such as engagements with the colonists on Demeter, was increasingly no more than a distraction.

But, wherever she was going, she had to take others with her.

'I agree with you,' he said. 'But we have to work with the locals, Deirdra. We need − well, I think we need their permission to descend to the ice moon. If not their cooperation. We can't defy them. For now we should take their offer of a ride to Persephone III. Find out all we can. But—'

'But it's complicated,' Lighthill said, scowling. 'The situation difficult to read. Nicola herself is difficult to read, even for us, who knew her before. Even if we can convince her that *that's* true.'

'Right,' Malenfant said. He felt oddly weary. Maybe he had had too much of wandering through a kind of gallery of mirrors containing alternate copies of people he had known. And loved. 'Right. This is a different Nicola. Not the RASF pilot-scientist you trained with, Lighthill. For one thing she is forty-nine years old, in her timeline – so several years older than *your* Nicola when she died in the lander crash on Persephone. I mean, Persephone II. In fact she's about the same age as the Nicola *I* knew when she died, in the shuttle booster crash that nearly killed me too – in a different 2019 to this one.

'We think we know her, just from the tone of her voice. We don't. We knew her avatars. *This* Nicola is the product of her own life, a history we still know virtually nothing about. She doesn't know *us* at all. And, frankly, from her tone, she doesn't want to know us. To her we are a huge distraction from – well, whatever her own goals are here.'

Deirdra said, 'You think Nicola doesn't *want* to know about other versions of herself.'

Malenfant looked at her. 'Well, would you?'

Deirdra pondered that. 'I guess it would depend on whether I could work with her. Another me. If she shared my goals.'

'A very pragmatic answer,' Malenfant said drily.

She smiled at him. 'Come on. Let's get to work.'

Lighthill frowned. 'Get to work doing what exactly?'

'Well, we have two weeks before Nicola and her crew get here. We have to work out what we want to achieve – and how much of it we need to get done before these UGE people show up and stop us, for the sake of the unity of a planet we'll probably never get to set foot on.'

Lighthill laughed. 'So much cynicism in one so young.'

'If that's true I learned it from you, oh empire builder. Come *on.*'

And, somewhat to Malenfant's surprise, Lighthill followed her out of the cabin.

Emma drifted over to Malenfant, and took his hand. 'You feel you've lost her.'

'I . . . Something like that. I haven't felt so, umm, redundant, since she defrosted me. She's leaving me behind. She's right, of course, in terms of her own motivation, her goals. I only hope I haven't led her into harm.'

Emma squeezed his hand. 'I don't think you have led her anywhere, Malenfant. Come on. Let's find something useful to do.'

54

Two weeks of waiting for the arrival of the UGE intrasystem ship, which would deliver, presumably, a disgruntled, uncomfortable copy of Nicola Mott.

In the meantime, the surviving crew of the *Harmonia* split to work on various projects.

Lighthill stuck to his command tasks, at first, anyhow. Bartholomew made his regular medical rounds. Malenfant, like Lighthill, floated around, looking over shoulders, lending a hand if he could.

Vasily and Anna seemed fascinated by Persephone III, and from this orbital platform studied it intently. Malenfant reminded himself they had spent many years trapped on Persephone II, with the Neanderthals and the pterosaurs, and had lost many companions down there. Now they were drawn to this manifold clone of that super Earth.

'Basic geology the same,' Vasily said. 'Being further from the Sun makes no difference to *that*. But everything different here.'

'Well, some,' Anna put in. 'This world's continental map is a little different. No surprise. And it's colder here. We will have to go down to be sure what this implies.'

She produced photographs, taken from orbit, for Malenfant to study.

Malenfant found himself peering through what looked like thick soupy air, a brownish layer, at unpromising landscapes, plains and mountains, rivers and ocean shores. He saw nothing that looked like advanced life to him: no herds on the plains, no schools of dolphins breaking the waves. Nothing even like forests, which he knew could look like clumps of greenish moss from space. But here and there he saw smears of purple-grey, or green-grey, or . . . just grey.

'Doesn't look too exciting.'

'Doing our best,' Vasily growled.

'It may not be "exciting". Exotic, yes,' Anna said. 'The energy budget for life is *different*. We are that much further from the Sun, so the heat received from that source is less. But the leaked inner heat flow, from the warm interior of planet, is the same as Persephone II. A lot more than Earth's inner heat. So, different energy ratios, external versus internal, from what we found at Earth. Therefore different life forms, possibly. Different life strategies, certainly. A different balance between the domains of life, perhaps, bacteria, plants, animals. We need to be down there testing, collecting samples, analysing. We do need to hitch that ride down there with Nicola Mott on her nuclear cab service, when it shows up.'

'Or you could just ask her about it,' Malenfant said. 'They've been studying this system for years.'

Vasily raised his eyebrows. 'Where's the fun in that?'

'And what's the use?' Anna said. 'No guarantee of quality.'

That was, Malenfant knew, an expression of a common cynicism among the crew about the UGE colonists and their motives, and it was understandable. Reading between the lines of what Nicola had had to say, it was clear enough that their 'New Paris' was as much a political stunt as it was a scientific endeavour. Not unlike the Apollo missions in Malenfant's own timeline, then. So maybe the quality of the science here would indeed be similarly compromised.

But at least they were here, Malenfant thought, these New Parisians, having evidently weathered some kind of threat of disastrous war. And maybe here, whatever else they discovered, they might find unity, which would be more important than any specific scientific result.

And while he was thinking about that, Emma had started to take an interest in Demeter, Nicola's moon-Mars.

Malenfant recognised the habit. This Emma had come from a subtly different timeline to his own, in which she had followed more of a scientific course – it was her grasp of the geology of Phobos that had got her a seat in an American-Russian venture to that enigmatic moon in the first place.

Now, lacking easily used cameras – she longed for digital, hated all the primitive wet-chemistry developing of the British gear, distrusted the over-advanced twenty-fifth-century bangles – she was making her own telescopic observations, he found. And she was now recording her stuff by hand in neat British RASF-issue notebooks, a precious and diminishing resource gifted her by a grudging Lighthill, notebooks now filling up with sketches of global images and specific bits of terrain, all carefully annotated. Malenfant remembered Josh's carefully kept journals – journals he and Deirdra had made sure had been collected before they left Persephone II, now tucked into a safe aboard the *Harmonia*, his home ship.

Emma's single most spectacular image was a double globe, showing her impressions of the two hemispheres of Demeter, east and west, with arrows leading to more detailed notes.

'So,' she said, when Malenfant looked over her shoulder. 'Don't patronise me over my graphic skills.'

'Wasn't about to.' Actually, he had been.

'Tell me what you see.'

Two hemispheres of orange-ish ground, the unmarked white of polar caps, the grey-green of open water. An asterisk, marked 'New Paris'.

'Umm, like they flooded Mars. Planted a few trees—'

'Wrong-o,' she said. 'You missed the most basic feature of all.'

'Now who's patronising who?'

'Whom, as Lighthill would say. Well, you are an easy target, Malenfant. Look – Mars, *our* Mars, isn't symmetrical. North to south. The whole of the northern hemisphere, pretty much, is – squashed. Lower than the mean elevation. The terrain is younger too, than the southern half. Younger geologically.'

'Ah. I remember. The hypothesis is some massive impact hit Mars, back in the day—'

'Probably at the same time of rough-housing that a baby world the size of Mars itself hit the Earth, and the Moon was born of the big splash.'

'Or not, in Lighthill's Vanilla System. Whereas our Mars took a mighty blow around the north pole.'

'Right. The whole crust was half-melted, or shaken to pieces. And when everything had calmed down, and the molten rock solidified again, you were left with one huge crater that covered the whole northern hemisphere. Biggest in the Solar System, it's believed. If you flooded *that* planet you'd get a vast northern ocean – that and a few crater lakes in the south, like Hellas. That was *our* Mars.'

'OK. And there was no Mars at all in the Vanilla System.'

'Well, there, it looked like a version of Persephone took Mars's place. Persephone II, where we landed. There, maybe Mars didn't get a chance to form at all. But *here*, I guess, all that planetary migration went another way. And Mars ended up a moon of the big intruder.' She held up her notebook again. 'Now tell me what you see.'

'Polar caps, and seas – ah, but no big Martian flooded hemisphere in the north. Just smaller seas scattered over the planet. So no big impact.'

'Correct. This *is* Mars – or what Mars might have become if it had avoided the big boreal-basin impact, and had ended up as a moon of a super Earth. It has the same parameters as our Mars – mass ten per cent of Earth's, gravity forty per cent. But it also has that thick atmosphere, around seventy per cent of Earth's surface pressure. Orders of magnitude more than *our* Mars. Oh, and it's tidally locked to the primary, Persephone.'

'Like our Moon. One face always turned to Earth—'

'Right. Well, you'd expect that with Demeter being so close in, only a third the Moon's distance from Earth. The tides, in those seas and in the rock, must be ferocious, by the way. So it's Earthlike – a lot more like Earth than our Mars, by the way – but with differences. That hundred-hour orbit dictates a hundred-hour "day", given that one-face lock, and the air is thinner than Earth's too, so less of a heat trap. That makes for a big temperature swing over that day-night cycle. Looks like it drops down to freezing in the middle of the "night", but back up to maybe twenty-five Celsius at "noon".'

'OK, but that's warmer than I was expecting. Tidal flexing, do you think?'

'Maybe. I'd have to go down there with a few thermocouples and such to see. Or I could just ask Nicola.'

He spent some more time with her; she showed him more results. He was quietly glad to see her so immersed in the work. It was what she was best at, damn it, across her manifold iterations. It was pleasing to see her get the chance.

But while Vasily and Anna were studying Persephone III, and Emma was thinking about moon Mars-Demeter, Malenfant discovered that down in the basement Deirdra was building a spacecraft.

55

Not really a basement.

But it really was a spacecraft.

Deirdra was working in the main cargo hold, a huge chamber near the base of the big sphere that was the *Harmonia*'s habitable compartment. And Lighthill was here helping her, with every expression of enjoyment.

Malenfant had come to know this space well, and its purpose. *Harmonia* was a vessel equipped for deep-space missions lasting years. Like the sailing ships of the first decades of oceanic exploration on Earth, if anything went wrong she could not expect to find a friendly and well-equipped shipyard to help, or even any raw materials – only what she carried herself. All but empty now, the hold had once held a variety of heavy-engineering components, from tools and small spare parts all the way to items such as complete spare attitude thrusters, replacement fusion-engine combustion chambers and engine bells, and various kinds of exotic fuels, lubricants and power packs. Malenfant recalled how, when they had needed to land on Persephone II to investigate the smoke that turned out to be rising up from Irina's hearths, a nearly identical copy of the *Charon* planetary lander they'd lost on Persephone I in the comet cloud had been put together from spare parts.

And now – though Malenfant wouldn't have believed it possible – from what had been left over in here Lighthill and Deirdra were putting together another landing craft.

If you could call it that. It looked like a dining table with a rocket engine fixed to the underside. And two broom handles protruding above. That was pretty much it.

Malenfant, weightless, drifted around this thing. 'OK. I see a platform to stand on. These two uprights with handles – I imagine they'll have controls built in. That main engine used to be a spare attitude thruster, right?'

Deirdra seemed excited but defiant. Lighthill was a little shamefaced, though pleased with himself. 'You'll see we are still missing a few details,' she said.

'Right. Such as fuel tanks. And any kind of control system: instruments, guidance. Oh, how about a hull?'

'No hull,' Deirdra said. 'We'll be in our pressure suits. Who needs a hull?'

'So, what – you're just going to stand on this thing and ride it down?'

Lighthill leaned forward, stroking the stumps of the control columns. 'I'm thinking you can guess down where.'

'I can guess. I hope I'm wrong. You're going to try to land on Zeus, the ice moon, aren't you?'

'Of course Zeus,' Deirdra said.

'And it has to be you to go confront it, does it?'

She faced him, and grinned, fierce as a lion. 'You know it, Malenfant. I was just a kid when I hijacked the *Harmonia*, more or less, and had us fly off to the outer System to try to deflect Shiva, avert the Destroyer smashing my Earth.'

'You don't need to remind me—'

'So now, again.'

'I'm trying to understand.'

'Well, try harder.' And she turned away.

Lighthill meanwhile was evidently concentrating on the technicalities, rather than existential puzzles or evolving personalities. Probably wise, Malenfant thought.

'Look, Malenfant,' Lighthill said, 'you may mock our efforts, this is an exotic body we're looking at here, but it has familiar features that make it perfectly accessible. It's an airless ball with roughly the same size as Earth's Moon. In fact, even gentler gravity. Yes? Now, where I came from, we first landed on the Moon in a ship with an atomic engine of pretty much the same class as the *Harmonia*. But we didn't have to do it that way. *This* is closer in spirit to your – Apollo, was it? A very light lander, a couple of crew, an engine the size of a suitcase sufficient to get you down there and back up again. And even that was over-engineered, arguably, if you went for the absolute minimum.'

Malenfant hesitated, then admitted, 'OK. I do remember some design studies that had this kind of minimal approach. A guy, or two guys, in pressure suits, standing on a single rocket. But even so – jeez, they would still have had NASA engineering behind them, to design and build such a thing and test the hell out of it—'

'I don't need all that,' Lighthill said calmly. 'I know my technology. All I'm doing is solving a known problem.'

'And besides,' Deirdra said with a trace of impatience, 'we're running out of time.'

'Before what?' Malenfant asked.

'Before the New Paris people get here. They already said that Zeus is embargoed. Malenfant. I . . . know you want to think well of Nicola Mott. I even think she means well, they all do, in their own terms. They might stop us. They will *probably* stop us.'

He faced her, over the framework of the ridiculous toy lander.

'Is it really so serious that you need to take such risks? Are you sure you need to get down there?'

'Of course I am. It's the centre of the mystery here. You've trusted my instincts before.'

'Yeah, but . . .'

He glanced over at Lighthill, but Lighthill, wisely, hung back. But Malenfant knew he would back Deirdra. Not for the cosmic consequences, not even as a consequence of his own impulse to command, but just because this technical challenge, building a lunar lander out of the junk in the basement, was *fun*.

Butch Breakaway, you have a lot to answer for.

Deirdra, suddenly seeming very young, drifted over and hugged him. 'It's not as if you're never going to see me again.'

But he had his doubts about that.

Eventually he gently disengaged. 'I know when I'm outnumbered. So. Pass me a spanner. What needs doing next on this heap of junk? And you do know you'll have to persuade Bartholomew to let you go, don't you?'

'Working on it.'

That turned out to be a good question, though.

And it turned out that Bartholomew would consent to the mission only under one surprising condition.

Just two days later, the scratch-built lander was ready to fly. They wasted no time in bundling it into an airlock, and launching it out over the ice plains of Zeus.

With Deirdra and Bartholomew aboard.

56

'Down at one kilometre per hour,' Deirdra murmured. 'Lateral three kph. We're doing fine.'

Malenfant was on the bridge of the *Harmonia*, currently in high orbit around Zeus, thousands of kilometres away from the little drama being played out above the surface of the moon. Helpless to intervene. As he always had been.

An Apollo echo.

He could only picture them, side by side on that little platform, clumsy in their unaccustomed pressure suits. On the right, in command of the spidery little craft, in her own pressure suit, stood Greggson Deirdra, as the half-improvised lander descended, cautiously, cautiously, towards the icy ground, and a picket fence of twenty-kilometre-tall Towers. And at her side Bartholomew, in a pressure suit he didn't strictly need, standing at the left-hand station of the *Flying Bedstead*. The two of them working through procedures the professional astronauts on the *Harmonia* had drummed into them.

Meanwhile the rest of the *Harmonia* crew had crammed into the ship's bridge to follow the descent: Malenfant, Lighthill, Emma, Vasily, Anna.

Deirdra's tone was calm, controlled.

'Now down at forty kilometres per hour. Lateral three kph,

still. We have a good radar lock; we're about forty kilometres up from the ground. We'll be below the height of the Towers in thirty minutes, at this rate. Heading right for the gap between towers A and B as we planned . . .'

Two towers picked at random as a target, with the one criterion that they should lie on the other side of the moon from the manifold portal. For reasons of safety, caution, they were attempting the landing about as far away as they could get from that particular hazard.

'Your abort options will soon start closing down,' Malenfant said. 'Don't forget your decision points, Deirdra.'

'I'm on it.'

A pull on his arm.

Emma was glaring at him. 'For God's sake. Let them get on with it, Malenfant.'

'I do understand,' Lighthill said, a little more kindly. 'I've run crew before, you remember. I've found it hard to let the chicks fly the nest. But we have given them the best chance we could. We did design and build the *Bedstead* as professionally and as well as we could in the circumstances.'

'I do know that.' It was true enough. Once the performance required of a Zeus lander had firmed up, and once Deirdra and Lighthill had proved their concept would work, the multinational, improvised crew of the *Harmonia* had worked together to perfect the thing.

It was Lighthill who had named it the *Flying Bedstead*, apparently after some development vehicle built – in his timeline at least – by Rolls-Royce, back in the 1950s, as a way of testing the performance of then-new jet engines. But Malenfant was reminded more of NASA's Manned Manoeuvring Unit, a similar rig developed before his own time, in the 1960s, to allow the astronauts to practise the skill of landing on the Moon in a rocket ship lowering itself down on its tail. Famously, Neil Armstrong himself had been piloting the MMU when it crashed . . .

The *Flying Bedstead* flew just fine. Malenfant himself had taken it for test jaunts outside the *Harmonia*. Fine, especially given the fact that they had hurried like hell to build this thing and get it launched before Nicola and the emissaries from New Paris came hauling ass up here, presumably with their own agenda.

The technology wasn't the issue. The issue was the crew.

Deirdra had insisted on going, with that eerie determination. Bartholomew had tried to argue her out of it – and when that failed, he insisted that the only way he could fulfil his primary mission, the care of Deirdra, was to accompany her himself.

Malenfant had almost laughed. 'To ride an experimental spacecraft down to an anomalous, unknown body, out of a crew of experienced professional astronauts, we select a robot medic? Are you serious?'

'It's my duty, Malenfant. And you know that I am, frankly, as capable of managing such a craft as any of you. More so. I will be like an extension of the machine. But, regardless of anything else, *Deirdra is my priority*.'

They had argued and argued.

In the end Malenfant, agonised by a thwarted sense of responsibility – not to mention a secret, thwarted desire to be riding the latest mission himself – was reduced to letting them go.

And, now, watching and waiting.

Deirdra's calm voice called up. '*Harmonia, Bedstead*.'

He snapped back to the present. 'Go ahead, Deirdra.'

'We're below the top of the Towers. Thirty minutes to the ground . . .'

*

Now the imagery was extraordinary, Malenfant thought, even at second hand.

Towers passing to either side of the drifting lander, each twenty kilometres tall − maybe twenty times taller than any building human beings had ever attempted on Earth, even by Deirdra's twenty-fifth century. Close together too, less than a kilometre apart.

They looked technological, as opposed to anything natural. The best guess was still that these structures had to be identical in purpose to the copies the crew of the *Harmonia* had encountered on that other Persephone, version number one, out in the remote comet cloud in another timeline. These Towers, so like chimney stacks, were the exhaust vents of some kind of rockets.

But the travellers on the spot, it seemed, who were like mosquitoes flying around a picket fence, had different impressions.

'We're falling. Slow as a snowflake, it feels like,' Deirdra reported. 'And now we are in among the Towers it all feels too *big* to be something made, something technological. Does that make sense? Malenfant, it reminds me of the forested Sahara. When we went to find the *Last Small Step* in that dusty archive of obsolete spacecraft, do you remember? All those trees, millions of them, growing thick and even, capturing all the carbon from the air. And all the trees looked the same. Living things but halfway to engineering. Whereas this is engineering that feels halfway to something living. A rocket forest.'

Bartholomew put in, 'Well, if this is a forest, maybe we're starting to see the foresters at work. Look down . . .'

The visuals were a mess, briefly, as Deirdra turned her head, and looked down the length of the chimneys to see the ground.

The bangles, worn now by all the crew in the *Harmonia*, were only short range. So they had rigged up a system: what Deirdra saw was transmitted to the bangles, and then uploaded as a TV signal to be transmitted back to the ship's cruder monitor systems.

And she was indeed seeing a new strangeness. Movement and manipulation of a quite unnatural kind.

Toiling machines, dozens of them, crawling around the Tower bases. A strange, unearthly sight. And yet familiar, to Lighthill at least.

'Visitors,' Lighthill murmured tightly. 'As I witnessed on Vanilla Earth.'

But he had never had such a clear view, Malenfant knew. Those angular bodies, each about two metres across, each core blurred by a forest of manipulator arms sprouting from corners, edges, even through what looked like open faces. He could see now that many of those limbs clearly had lesser limbs sprouting from them, bifurcating, splitting, and ending in finer and finer manipulators.

Lighthill murmured, 'Handy beasts, aren't they?

'Maybe they can work all the way down to the molecular scale,' Emma said now.

'Why not? On that other Earth, you'll remember, I did see them mucking about with what appeared to be life forms, of a primitive kind.'

'In the garden of the anaerobes,' Emma said.

Lighthill grinned. 'I like that.'

Malenfant frowned. 'Wow, think of it. A robot capable of nanotechnological manipulation. You could splice genes, maybe.'

Bartholomew said, 'Sounds like showing off to me.'

The crew looked at each other.

Then Vasily laughed out loud. 'Your robot has a sense of humour, Malenfant.'

Malenfant snorted. 'It thinks it has.'

Deirdra said now, 'I said the Towers could almost be natural, like trees. Well, from here, it does look like the Visitors are *tending* the Towers somehow. As opposed to building, or maintaining, renovating. Working away at the bases . . . Like feeding the roots of trees. I used to see people doing that back home in England. That might be just an instinctive impression, but—'

Malenfant said, 'If anyone ought to follow their instincts at this point, it's you, Deirdra. Yes, like trees. But what are they being grown out of? What raw materials?'

Bartholomew put in, 'I think I see some of the Visitors working around a kind of well, in the ground, the ice. Like a drilled shaft maybe.'

'So,' Vasily said, 'maybe Visitors are using stuff from inside this moon to build their Towers. Or grow them. Makes sense. What stuff, though? Maybe some deep-buried rocky core, inside this moon of ice?'

'Maybe,' Lighthill said. 'Our intrepid explorers may get more data when they land.'

'A landing we ought to be concentrating on,' Deirdra said impatiently.

Lighthill murmured, 'Or rather, on which we should be concentrating—'

'Can it, Butch,' murmured Malenfant. 'OK, Deirdra, copy that. We'll keep quiet. Call if you need us.'

Silence for a while, as the two astronauts worked.

The primitive telemetry aboard the *Harmonia*, scrolling numbers and cathode-ray-tube graphs, showed clearly what

411

they were doing. The *Flying Bedstead* slid easily away from the flank of the nearest Towers, away from the fence alignment altogether. And, over open ground, their descent quickened.

'Disparate technology,' Anna murmured now.

Malenfant turned. 'What's that?'

'Just thinking aloud. This strange moon. It's like a museum of machines. The fusion-rocket Towers. Not sure if I ever believed what you told me about these things you found on a different Persephone. Even the pictures you showed. Now, here we are; now I believe. But this is crude technology, isn't it? *We* understand it. We could almost build it.'

'Almost,' Lighthill said ruefully.

'Next, those robot serfs. Autonomous workers that must be at least as smart as your pet doctor, Malenfant. We could not yet build such a mechanical mind. Perhaps in Deirdra's twenty-fifth century. But I would be surprised if even they had nano-scale manipulators, as we speculate. The robots as a whole are more advanced than the Towers, that's for sure.

'But then you have the manifold interface. Big blue wheel, hovering over the ice, and whatever is lodged in the heart of the moon. Another scale of technological achievement. So what is the ring? What's it made of — let alone, how does it work? Spacetime twisted and bent like steel, perhaps, to make a pucker through which a whole spaceship can pass, to another universe. Technology that even seems to enable objects the size of moons — like this moon — to be in two places at once. Disparate technology again. As if from different cultures, even, not just from different eras.'

Vasily nodded. 'Perhaps all this is just very *old*. I grew up on a farm, far from the city. Replacing stuff was difficult. What you had, you kept. So we had a radio set, bought in Moscow by myself after I joined the air force and started to travel. And we had a tractor dating from around 1920, my grandfather's. And my father always worked the potato fields with a big shovel, blade of cast iron, that he swore came from the nineteenth century, when they were laying the great railways across the continent, and they made steel as hard and pure as ever you would find.'

Malenfant nodded. 'OK. So maybe this place is old, like your farm. Picking up stuff from different ages, from different cultures. But what's the purpose? What's it all for?'

'Well, Malenfant,' Lighthill said heavily, 'if we knew that already we wouldn't be wandering around a multiverse in search of answers, would we? But answers there may be soon. Because our intrepid explorers have just touched down.'

57

A couple of TV cameras had been fixed to a leg of the *Flying Bedstead*, and these returned a view of Deirdra and Bartholomew at work.

On the ice of Zeus, moving around. The images were not much better than those returned by the first Apollos from the Moon, Malenfant thought.

Bartholomew was fixing up a shelter of treated cloth over the lander base. They weren't expecting to stay long, but having an airtight refuge ready in case of some medical calamity was an obvious precaution to take.

Deirdra, meanwhile, was already exploring. Bounding around on the surface in her pressure suit, in slow, dreamy hops.

Emma had made coffee, and handed a lidded mug to Malenfant. 'Just like the old Apollo footage.'

'I was thinking the same thing.'

'Of course I wasn't born in 1969; I grew up watching reruns. That scratchy imagery, just like this. Armstrong and Aldrin making the first Moonwalk.'

Or not, in Malenfant's reality. *Aldrin labouring to dig a makeshift grave, with tools meant to retrieve geological samples.*

Deirdra's voice came back. 'I'm very light on my feet here. Even compared to the Moon, and I always felt like we floated around there, when we went to that Japanese base. I know the gravity is a fraction of the Moon's . . .'

Just as Malenfant and the rest had anticipated, Zeus was about the same size as Luna, but around a quarter the density – more like the density of ice than the silicate rock the Moon was made of – so the gravity was only a quarter of Luna's, a mere five per cent of Earth's.

'And it reminds me of the upper levels of the space farm, Malenfant, remember? You had Earth gravity at the rim of the turning wheel, fading to nothing as you climbed . . .'

'So what is the surface like?'

'Ice.' In the images, he saw her pause, stand still, scrape the grains with a toe. 'Not solid, and not like frost. Like old snow, maybe. Under a few centimetres it's compacted down.'

Vasily grunted. 'Impact gardening. Constant peppering of micrometeorites. Smash surface to splinters.'

Bartholomew put in now, 'I can confirm it's *warm*, as well. You may not sense that, Deirdra; I can feel it through my boots. My skin is pretty smart.'

'Like your mouth,' Malenfant murmured.

'Big shout-out to you too, Malenfant! Shouldn't be as warm as this. Well, we knew that. Give me a hand with this stuff . . .'

He lumbered into view. He was carrying a compact package of equipment that must have felt light in the five per cent gravity, but Malenfant could see that it was awkward to handle. In low gravity weight went away, but not inertia, nor the sheer clumsy bulk of stuff.

So Deirdra took hold of the package too, and the two of them tipped it over, set it down, and began unfolding flaps and lowering attachments. They were clumsy, but they had at least practised these manoeuvres in zero gravity.

This was what the crew had come to call their 'science stuff'.

It had been cobbled together from junk cannibalised from *Harmonia*, much as had the lander itself, and it was designed for what Lighthill had called a 'smash and grab' scientific exploration of Zeus. They hadn't known what problems or threats the crew might face down there, and while it was possible for them to stay for days, the package was intended to maximise the science return if they had to lift off in a lot less time than that – hours, even.

So probes were plunged into the loose ice – shoved in manually by Deirdra and Bartholomew, like pushing spears through Arctic snow – spears bearing geology probes: seismometers, thermal gauges, samplers designed to extract any biological traces found in the ice. There was even an independent subsurface explorer, little more than a self-propelling drill bit. When Deirdra stood it up on the ice, point downwards, this mechanical mole whizzed and whirred and plunged down into the ice, seeking data from deeper layers, spinning out a super-long monofilament comms cable: a gift of Bartholomew's medical pack, meant for stitching wounds.

Meanwhile, more cables were pulled out of the package to be connected to ports on Bartholomew's own arm, exposed to the vacuum and the 'skin' peeled back for the purpose. The most advanced and sensitive instruments they had available, miniaturised, were contained within Bartholomew's own body; he wasn't just a nurse simulacrum, Malenfant had long ago learned, but a walking talking biomedical science lab.

And so it was Bartholomew himself who was soon delivering the preliminary science results.

'OK,' he said. 'I can tell you that this ice is indeed mostly ice. Water ice. But it's not pure. For a start there are traces of minerals – olivine for one thing—'

'Rock,' Lighthill said. 'Silicate rock. What Earth is made of, I believe. The mantle and crust at least.'

'Correct,' Emma said. 'So maybe it does have something in common with the ice moons we're used to. A water-ice crust, maybe a water ocean under that, wrapped around a rocky core. But . . .' She consulted her bangle. 'Given the overall density that core can't be more than a few kilometres across. Tens of kilometres at best.'

'Deep buried,' Anna said. 'So there must be some kind of process to bring minerals up to the surface. Convection?'

'Which,' Vasily said, 'is probably least mystery.'

'Correct,' Emma said again. 'My bangle is giving me direct heat readings from Bartholomew's instruments now. Also radiation at other wavelengths. There may be structure in some of these emissions. Like partially scrambled signals. Also – and even the bangles aren't quite smart enough for this – there may be gravity-wave emissions too.'

They were detecting gravity waves? Malenfant frowned, wondering how they were managing that. Maybe the bangles networked, those down on the ice moon and up here on the ship – acting together to detect very small displacements, the minute shudders of spacetime that occurred when a gravity wave passed. If so, he was officially impressed.

Vasily grunted. 'Gravity waves? Caused by what? Some kind of massive flows in the subsurface ocean?'

'Doubtful. Not massive enough. We need to follow this up,' Lighthill murmured calmly.

Emma reported now, 'And the surface is hot. As Bartholomew said. Only about fifteen degrees below zero – I mean, the freezing point of water ice.'

'*Lot* of heat pouring out of this thing,' Vasily said. 'As we knew. Of the order of a couple of hundred watts per square metre.'

Lighthill had his slide rule; he did some quick figuring. 'So if that's typical of the whole moon you are looking at a heat output of a few thousand terawatts.' He glanced up. 'Which is a few hundred times the power output of all of human civilisation where I come from. And I imagine that's similar for you, Malenfant.'

'Yeah. A lot less in Deirdra's day . . . So there's one heck of a power source buried inside that moon somewhere. But − what for?'

'Perhaps,' Bartholomew said, 'to support a giant incubator.'

Frowns all round, Malenfant saw, as they absorbed that.

Malenfant leaned forward. 'Bartholomew, say again?'

Deirdra laughed. 'You should see his expression. I think he's telling you he's found life. Life in the ice of Zeus.'

Cue a stunned silence on the *Harmonia*.

Malenfant was the first to speak. 'For a purely algorithmic intelligence with no identity of your own, you're quite the showman, Bartholomew.'

'I exist only to serve.'

Anna growled, 'Tell us of this "life", please.'

'I'm finding bacteria − structures too, perhaps, hints of colonies, mats, films − but nothing more complex. Certainly no multicellular life. But they are like the bacteria you found on Vanilla Earth, Commander Lighthill.'

'Anaerobes.'

'Yep. Archaic forms − archaic in an Earth context anyhow − simple creatures living off the heat flow and traces of minerals in the ice. As well as near the surface, they are evidently colonising deep down, as our probe is finding − it's descending faster than I thought − the ice must be softly packed, porous, with lots of cracks, even hollows, for the bacteria to survive inside. Even so I think an Earth-based biologist would call these extremophiles. Tolerant of heat, pressure, salt, acidity . . .'

'I can tell you about the biochemistry,' Deirdra said excitedly. 'Well, I think so, if I understand what my bangle is telling me. It's more CHON life, Malenfant. Carbon, hydrogen, oxygen, nitrogen. Organic chemistry. It's life like ours.'

Bartholomew said with evident patience, 'Not just like ours, Deirdra. It *is* ours. Remember, I'm a walking biochemistry lab myself. I don't recognise these species, the extremophile bugs. But I can tell you—'

'No,' Lighthill said, sounding excited. 'Let me guess. I'll wager it's just as I found on Vanilla Earth. The gardens of the anaerobes, remember? Not life that's merely *like* ours, at the molecular level. Life that *is* ours – life identical to ours. With the exact same selection of twenty-one amino acids—'

'Correct,' Bartholomew said. 'Though there are some differences at the higher levels of structure, the nucleic acids, the protein structures . . .'

There was a faintly stunned silence.

'Well, we learned a lot,' Malenfant summed up. 'For one thing, given you landed more or less at random, this whole moon must most likely be infested with life. Life like ours. The surface layers at least.'

'Not just the surface,' Bartholomew said. 'The drill is already several hundred metres down – no, more than a kilometre now – and is still finding the ice full of life. Richer actually; there is more mineral-rich grit down there.'

'Noted.'

'And I'm not sure "infested" is the right word,' Bartholomew said.

Emma nodded. 'Yes. You said "incubator". You really think

419

this could be some kind of breeding vat? The whole moon, maybe?'

'Fits the facts. You have a sphere of slush, kept warm by some mysterious internal power source, and laced with organic chemistry . . .'

Emma smiled. 'It's how I'd design it, I guess.'

Lighthill glanced at a clock. 'All right, you two. You have the science package set up and functioning. You haven't stopped moving since you left the *Harmonia*, several hours ago now. Back to the surface shelter with you. Suits off, bathroom breaks, food – for you anyhow, Deirdra. And try to sleep.'

'That's impossible,' Deirdra said. 'I'm all keyed up. This is great! No wonder you all became astronauts. OK, I'll take a break. But I'll never sleep, not here.'

'You'd be surprised,' Malenfant said gently. 'Anyhow we have stuff to do ourselves. Nicola's on her way up from Demeter . . . Do as Geoff says, Deirdra. Good advice for once. Grandad over and out.'

The orders were obeyed. As Malenfant had expected, once her hammock was set up inside the shelter, Deirdra had no trouble sleeping, even with Bartholomew on his usual sleepless watch.

Before she woke again, though, more data came chattering into the *Harmonia* from the subterranean probe. As deep as it plunged, spinning out its superfine cable like some mechanical spider, the independent probe continued to find traces of life, extremophile bugs tolerating more and more hostile conditions.

About a hundred kilometres in, though there was no clear boundary, the ice turned increasingly slushy.

At two hundred kilometres down the probe was navigating through liquid water. The little probe swam on, Malenfant thought, like a blind deep-sea fish, heading deeper and deeper.

They had designed it for this circumstance, liquid oceans under ice crusts being common in the moons of their home Solar System.

Still it found traces of life, sparse in the water. There were clumps of it, like islands, biofilms clinging to bits of rock.

And the water grew increasingly hot, the deeper the probe went. Deeper and deeper. Hotter and hotter.

More than a thousand kilometres down, as the water approached boiling point, the plucky little probe failed at last.

That was when Nicola called to say that the *Starry Messenger* was closing for rendezvous.

When he told Deirdra about that, her reply was blunt. 'Keep her talking until we're done here.'

58

Well, Colonel Malenfant. This is awkward.

Doesn't have to be, Nicola. Look, I've been through this kind of encounter before. Let's just talk, and see where it takes us.

But thanks for the basket of fruit.

Ah! You're welcome, Colonel. I imagine after so long in space you will be glad of a break from stored food and strict recycling. This is just a sample of the produce from our greenhouses on Demeter. You do need the glass cover, and of course the Sun is feeble and so the ground is less productive per acre, but with patience and some inventiveness . . .

Can't wait to see those greenhouses. Thank you. Just call me Malenfant, by the way.

Malenfant. Did *she* – the other Nicola Mott—

Yah. We were one hell of a team. Even when things went wrong for us on STS-719. As I told you.

I – how can I put this – close as colleagues, but no closer?

She was married. To a woman called Siobhan Libet.

I . . . know no Siobhan Libet. I have to tell you, Malenfant, that same-sex marriage is – not unknown – but rare in Britain. My Britain. Outside the remit of the churches, certainly. Between us, I have had partners. I have a partner here. I mean, at New Paris, on Demeter. It pays to be discreet, however.

It's very difficult getting my small brain around all this. History is evidently complex, with unexpected consequences of small perturbations. I mean, I do believe you, implicitly. This tale of exploring the manifold, your account of a portal on Zeus – well, we have footage of you bursting out of that object, an anomaly we have yet to examine close to ourselves. One thing at a time.

As to the veracity of what you have been able to tell me about – well, myself. Even of a second version from yet another twist of history, who flew for a British space force with Geoff Lighthill—

I would advise calling Wing Commander Lighthill 'Wing Commander Lighthill'.

Ha – thank you.

You might have met her, I guess, if not for misfortune. Lighthill's Nicola. Twists of fate. She might have travelled with us, here.

But, you say, she died on Persephone – a different Persephone.

We call this stuff resonances. Across the manifold, you keep encountering the same elements – people, locations – sort of drawn together.

Commander Lighthill has been able to show me . . . relics of her. That's the wrong word to use about oneself, surely! He seems to have kept the personal effects and so forth of each of his lost crew, promising to return them to the families some day. Bits of clothing, family photographs. It is very odd, Malenfant, to have one's own face peering out of photographs, taken in places you never visited, caught up in events of which you have no experience.

I can imagine. But as I said there are commonalities. You became a space traveller, evidently. In this timeline. As did my Nicola in hers, and Lighthill's too.

I'm drawn to it, it seems, aren't I? Whatever the

circumstances, whatever the background – whether or not a war or two has intervened. For that does seem to be the main divergence between our timelines, doesn't it? Our Nearly War of 1985.

. . . Maybe. We didn't have a 'Nearly War', I don't believe. But I suspect there has to be a deeper divergence – something that caused your war as a by-product. Something more fundamental. And I suspect that has to do with the different astronomy here. The obvious difference.

Yes. So I'm told. You have no Persephone—

Not in the inner System, no.

But, Malenfant, even only a decade before I was born, say, Persephone, and Demeter and Zeus, were still little more than points of light in the sky. What difference can they have made?

I don't know. So just tell me about you. I think you mentioned you were born in Cambridge. Cambridge, England, right? As was the Nicola I knew, at least.

Correct. In 1970. Born in the city hospital, grew up in a village on the outskirts. Commuter country really. I was an only child. My father was a property lawyer, my mother a parish councillor. She was American born, by the way.

I knew that. It helped my Nicola get into NASA in the first place. The American space agency.

We were a small family, as were my parents' families. My only close cousin was Sarah, who was born when I was twelve. It all seems very old-fashioned now.

Very English. Lighthill will love hearing you talk about it.

I think it was because I was a solitary child that I became so fascinated by space – and Persephone in particular. And it was a local thing, in a way. We had nothing to do with the university, but every so often some glamorous visitor would come to the city for a conference, or one of the dons would surface in the national news, and so we had the odd celebrity visitor to my school. And I became aware that people were studying Persephone right there, in the city where I lived.

So, as I grew up, I found out all about the planets, and so on. And what I learned, I suppose, is quite different from your background, where Persephone was, you say, lost in the outer Solar System.

Right. In what Lighthill calls the comet cloud. Not even detected until after my shuttle crash.

Well, our Persephone certainly is visible – to the naked eye, I mean, one of the planets known to the ancients, along with Mercury, Venus, Jupiter, Saturn.

No Mars – of course not.

Mars?

Your Demeter. We think. In your System a moon, in ours an independent world.

Really? I had not known that . . . Well, we had Persephone, dimmer than Venus or Jupiter, closer in than the first of the giants . . . A wanderer on the edge of the dark, which is why, I always imagined, the planet was named after the queen of Hell.

It was Galileo with his brand-new telescope who first saw the planet's face in the 1600s. There was a gleam, which he correctly inferred was the reflection of the Sun from an ocean. And he discovered Demeter, the larger of the moons, lost in the glare of the primary to the naked eye.

From the 1650s Huygens observed the polar ice caps, the continents, not well enough to map the world reliably, but enough to measure its rotation. The second moon, Zeus, wasn't discovered until the 1870s, by Schiaparelli. Who also mapped

Persephone for the first time, showing continents and seas and what he thought were seasonal waves of vegetation. His results were attacked; Persephone was thought to be too cold for life, and any air too thin. Maybe his results were an optical illusion. Eye strain. Ha!

Well, Schiaparelli lived to be vindicated when modern astronomical methods started to be used. In 1909, an American astronomer called Wallace Campbell took a spectrometer up Mount Whitney, to analyse Persephone's light without any filtering from Earth's atmosphere. And he observed a thick air, a cold but liveable surface.

The sensation, though, was his observation of the big moon, Demeter, which had, he thought, a transparent atmosphere maybe a tenth as thick as Earth's, and a surface temperature that was well above freezing at any given location for much of the year. Turned out that was an underestimate, of course; Demeter is actually *more* hospitable than that. Even so the results brought controversy, retractions, confirmations . . . In the fuss, nobody noticed Campbell's radiometry measurements of the surface temperature of Zeus, the other moon, which was just an ice ball – but looked much too warm, even then.

I think the astronomers got stuck then for a few decades, arguing over confusing results returned by inadequate instruments. It wasn't until the first space-probe flyby, by Mariner 4 in 1964, that the first close-up photographs were returned of the dense air, the oceans, the banks of life on Persephone – and even more sensationally the glimpses of what looked like forests on Demeter. That moon in particular, which turned out to have an atmosphere orders of magnitude more massive even than had previously been estimated by Campbell and others, was suddenly a viable target for human colonisation. So the expansive dreamers had been right.

Yeah. Not where I come from. I'm ten years older than you, Niki—

Niki?

Sorry . . . A nickname for somebody else. I remember the images returned by our Mariner 4, of our Mars. My father showed me these grainy images in the newspaper. Craters. Virtually no atmosphere. No visible life. Our Mars suddenly looked much more like the Moon, say, than Earth. I think in retrospect it was a downturn in the prospects for human spaceflight. There seemed to be no pressing reason to go on beyond the Moon. We did send limited expeditions to Mars in the end, in the 1980s, but—

It was very different for us. I was six years old when they landed the first Pilgrim probe on Persephone. They went there first because it was an easier target, thicker air for aerobraking, no complicated orbital mechanics as would be required to reach a moon as opposed to the primary. The lander had no movie camera, but I remember how the still images captured that strome as it washed towards the lander like an incoming tide, and just swallowed it up! 'Welcome to Persephone' – that was the headline the next day.

Strome? What's that, some kind of life on Persephone? . . . Never mind. We'll get to that.

I think maybe it was the Pilgrim results above all that fixed the trajectory of my own life. I was six years old, and I just knew I wanted to *go* there.

And there was some momentum about that. I remember seeing Wernher von Braun making his famous speech, just a few months before he died, about the significance of the new findings. If Persephone had life, and if Demeter was probably habitable too, the system was a new destination for mankind, another New World, a high ground. And whoever got there first could be in a position to dominate human history for good.

The logic seems crazy now, in retrospect. But it was enough to start a new space race, I suppose you'd describe it. A race for Demeter, especially. Huge new launchers were planned on either side – and space-based weapons were developed in earnest. There were to be orbital weapons platforms, even battleships, capable perhaps of taking out surveillance and communications satellites – even the enemy's crewed space platforms. All because of this fantasy of the 'higher ground'.

Yeah. We had scares like that. In the 1950s it was going to be Russian nuclear bases in orbit, or on the Moon. And in the 1980s, 'Star Wars', we called it. Advanced space-based weapons destabilising a decades-long nuclear stalemate. The technology didn't progress too far. But it did put the Soviet Union under a lot of economic pressure, which led to glasnost. *That's a very simple summary, but—*

Glasnost? A word I don't know.

Ah. A kind of thawing of relations, east and west. The Soviet satellite states declared their independence. Ultimately the Soviet Union itself collapsed, politically. What followed was far from utopian, but at least it spared us a major east-west war . . . But you never heard of glasnost.

I'm afraid not.

But, thinking about it, you had heard of the Soviet Union. Believe me, that's not a gimme.

Perhaps we have found what I believe you call your jonbar hinge, Malenfant – at least, the divergence as it affected humanity. Up to that point, the late 1970s, the existence of Persephone-Demeter-Zeus rather than your Mars evidently made no significant difference to human history, overall. Not until von Braun's inflammatory speeches, anyhow. Which certainly worsened tensions on a heavily armed planet.

And you went to war. Your 'Nearly War', right?

Yes. Which I understand you did not suffer.

Well – all I can say is it could have been worse.

59

Look, I was fifteen at the time. And I paid about as much attention to world politics as any fifteen-year-old. It was all just scary stuff on the TV news. Until it wasn't. So I learned a lot more about it later, from histories, documentaries – memoirs of veterans, after the secrecy restrictions were lifted. Fascinating, really.

My mother was involved, though – did I mention she was a parish councillor? That job became more of a burden after Thatcher passed the civil emergency acts, oh, this would have been the early 1980s. So every local authority had to lay in stocks, of food and medicines and such, sufficient in our case to cope with isolation for a certain period, and to manage a certain number of refugees from the city – Cambridge, I mean, and, at our location, maybe people coming out of London too.

They built a nuclear bunker under the council offices. My mother had a key! All of which seemed comical rather than frightening. Have you ever heard of *Dad's Army*, on the TV? Oh, well.

But I do remember the news being scary, if I paid attention to it. Lots of instability in the world, especially in the poorer south, South America, Africa. Southern Africa in particular was disintegrating into war. There always seemed to be tensions between China and Russia, as well as between Russia and the west. Unrest in places like Poland and Yugoslavia. I remember images of massed columns of Soviet tanks rolling through city centres.

Lots of flashpoints, then.

Yes. And I think in retrospect there was a lot of pressure on the leaders of the USSR to act.

It was rational in a sense. Even before the new space war, their big strategic fear in Europe was West Germany – well, only a generation before, the Second World War had resulted in an invasion of Russia and the death of tens of millions. In the 1980s, even without any direct threat, the very existence of such a huge, wealthy, democratic state in the heart of Europe was destabilising the Soviets' own imperial project.

So West Germany had to be – eliminated?

That was the logic. And if they were going to act at all it might have to be soon, before a rising China had to be dealt with, before unrest in other parts of the world threatened other strategic interests – and before there were nukes in orbit or on the Moon, offering their enemies the ultimate second-strike capability. This was the Soviet government's point of view, you see. The Soviets weren't crazy, or suicidal. They knew there was a chance of triggering a global nuclear war. But they hoped to achieve what they wanted in Europe with conventional means.

They hoped? Jeez.

Well, that was evidently the plan.

So, in the summer of 1985, things started to happen. There were huge military manoeuvres all over the eastern bloc. Supposed uprisings in places like Czechoslovakia, which resulted in huge columns of Soviet troops and tanks being pushed westward.

All of which was covert mobilisation, I guess.

I knew nothing of this. I found it frightening but – irritating

431

too, you know? It was summer. I was fifteen years old. I had other stuff to do.

But then, this was June, we were still at school, we all got scary leaflets pushed through our door. 'Protect and Survive'. Instructions on how to build bunkers and stuff. You packed the shelves with tinned food, and filled suitcases with soil to serve as sandbags, and made toilets out of planks and buckets. And you had to make ID tags to label the dead! It was ridiculous, and it was gruesome, and it was useless, you could *see* that. Which made it all the more scary. I can remember my mother telling me that if the worst came to the worst I was to forget about the house, take the key she had for the parish council bunker, and get to that.

The next day they closed the schools, which we enjoyed, until we found ourselves loading up the sports centre with blankets and so forth in case of refugees. Oh, they cancelled the Test cricket, which made my dad fume.

It was still hard to take it all seriously. I think the older generations rather enjoyed it, actually. It reminded them of the war – Hitler's war. We even got ration cards.

Then in July the Soviets attacked.

It all seemed chaotic at the time. But the historians pieced it all together later, and the Soviet strategy actually made a lot of sense. From their point of view.

Their plan was to take West Germany, basically. So they would cross the East German border, to north and south, and push across Germany to the Rhine, in seven days. But they wouldn't cross into France, because France wasn't in NATO, and they hoped to split the opposition that way. France had its own nuclear arsenal, and that would be a big loss in terms of the potential opposition to the Russians. That was the strategy.

So the day before the invasion proper they made softening-up strikes on West Germany, hitting airfields, transport and communications hubs, government offices. They kept declaring this was a defensive move, to eliminate supposed interference by the West Germans in the Soviets' own domain. And there were strikes in space too, against the surveillance satellites.

Then, the next day, came the invasion.

Well, back in Britain it wasn't even on TV. Although I do remember the Queen telling us war had been declared on the Russians. Her words became famous, like Churchill and his beaches: 'Not for a single moment did I imagine that this solemn and awful duty would one day fall to me . . .'

Eventually I met veterans, survivors who later made it into the space programmes, and learned more about what really happened. It had begun with a massive advance all along the West German border, with T-72 tank regiments, infantry carriers, attack helicopters, MiG planes. It was a multiple thrust, aiming at Hamburg, Hanover, Frankfurt, Munich. Pushing hard from one preplanned tactical position to the next.

No nukes at that point.

No, but the Soviets did use chemical weapons, napalm. The allies were prepared to an extent. You had tank regiments meeting the enemy, US Sheridans and German Panzers among others. Squadrons of Tornados and F-15s in the air.

All of central Europe was a battlefield.

My mother knew a neighbour with a son in a Royal Artillery gun detachment. And he would later say how overwhelming it all was, the shock of it. The explosions, the flames, the smoke, the reek of blood – a huge barrage of noise, from the air, the ground – in terms of the human experience it was an order of magnitude harder even than the Second World War battlefields, it seems.

The allied forces were outnumbered. That had always been the issue with their strategy for the defence of Europe. But they fought well, that first day. They used a lot of recon, and struck back intelligently and flexibly. Whereas the Soviet front somewhat disintegrated, what with the differing speeds of the units in their massed formations, tanks outrunning infantry on foot, all hard to manage under their monolithic command system.

It was a day of hell, for sure. The Soviets advanced far into West Germany; there were mass casualties, huge refugee flows from the cities.

But there was no easy breakthrough. And, though it wasn't clear to the allies at the time, the Soviets were already falling behind their strategic objective of reaching the Rhine in seven days.

It bogged down that quickly.

Yes. It was all very different from even the Second World War, that was clear from the start. Hugely consuming of resources and very fast moving. It would be a war of days, not years. You either won quickly, or not at all.

Back at home we were all a bit bewildered, I think. There was a news blackout, though my mother heard some of it through her local government channels. A state of emergency was declared; I remember that. Roads were closed – blocked.

The second day was even scarier, I think. That was when we started to see a trickle of refugees driving in their cars out of the city centre, and even from London, despite the roadblocks. A few days later there were more, coming out on foot, even on bicycles. It was like something out of H. G. Wells.

And Britain was coming under direct attack, already. The Russians were taking out the airfields and the ports, which were being used to resupply the war effort on the continent.

We thought we heard some of the strikes, like thunder in a cloudless sky. The old folk went on about the Battle of Britain.

Also, it turned out, the Soviets were attacking targets in France, which had declared war on the Soviets along with NATO.

But the Soviets had hoped the French would stay out.

Well, they didn't. Another strategic setback for the Soviets. The French didn't fight, but they offered support – bases, reconnaissance, logistics.

I think it was on the third day that the sirens first sounded, in the village. It had been a bad day already. Outages of power and water. Police chasing a few looters. I spent the night in that council bunker with my dad. Mum was in the sports hall helping supervise the latest refugees from London. It was hard to sleep, and scary when we came out in the morning to see if any damage had been done.

That morning was when I first saw the Air Bridge, I think. That was what the news started to call it, when we got any news.

Resupply convoys?

Yes, coming from the States. When the weather was clear – and it was mostly clear all through the conflict, it was like the Battle of Britain in that way – you could see the lanes of contrails draped across the sky, like Bifrost. They were using civilian 747s as carriers, as well as military craft. And they were accompanied by fighters, F-4s and F-111s and Tornadoes. We didn't see anything of it at the time, but there were also convoys coming by ship across the Atlantic. There was a major battle going on in the region of Greenland, as the allies tried to keep the Soviet submarines from coming down into the North Atlantic.

But I think when I saw that Bifrost in the sky – all those

resources pouring in from America – well, I believed we would win, in the end.

In the end. But if you thought that, the Soviet commanders must have thought so too.

Indeed. Well, they were stalled. West Germany itself was a tough nut to crack, it turned out. There the emergency preparations hadn't been like ours, my mother with a key to the town bunker and leaflets delivered by the postie on his bike. *They* had a reserve army, huge bunkers, stores of food and medical supplies, hardened communications and power systems, detailed plans for civilian evacuations – all carefully prepared, years in advance. So the Soviet front was rolling through all of that, but even as the shock troops moved in they started facing resistance at their rear. And there were opportunistic rebellions in their client states too.

OK. They needed to have won quickly, and they hadn't. But they still had nukes.

Yes. They still had nukes. Both battlefield weapons and strategic weapons – missiles that could take out cities in America. I've learned since that it was an extraordinarily dangerous moment. Some of the Soviet leaders had wanted to deploy tactical nukes in Germany. *Their* troops had been trained, even equipped, for nuclear battlefields, as if it was just another class of armament, and you'd carry on fighting. But NATO saw it differently. In their doctrine, *any* use of nuclear weapons would have meant escalation. A global war, with strategic strikes on Soviet homeland cities, and all the rest.

I believe the nearest we came to true calamity was the sixth day.

By then we were – well, I think we were bored. We kids. We were hardly let out of the house. Even when the power was on, there was no news – only the odd emergency proclamation – nothing but reruns of *Coronation Street* and *Doctor Who*. And then there were rumours of evacuating us kids – and at fifteen I was still a kid – out of there to the west, to Wales maybe. Wales! My God, we thought, it's getting serious.

In the end, and I guess it was a last gamble, one faction in the Soviet hierarchy – presumably the leading warmongers – came up with a plan. They would fire off one strategic nuke. A kind of symbolic strike. Almost a diplomatic gesture.

Diplomatic?

They would take one city. Paris was mooted. And they would expect the allies to take out one city in return. Leningrad, maybe. And then both sides would declare an honourable draw. Like a rained-off Test match, my dad said.

Some diplomacy. But that never happened, I'm guessing.

It never happened. There was some kind of internal coup in Moscow. And then, later that day, through the Swiss, Soviet envoys started putting out feelers about a ceasefire.

Well, it was over.

The next night my mother took me to a choral thanksgiving service at King's College Chapel, in the city. I remember they said the choir was scratch, put together from residents and refugees. And the chapel roof had been blown off, a stray bomb from raids on the local airfields.

The allies had no interest in pursuing the Soviets once they had withdrawn from West Germany. Nobody wanted an imperialist war in Russia, like Hitler's – and of course there was still the possibility of all-out nuclear war. Besides, even once the Soviets had withdrawn, a massive relief effort was required in central Europe.

A Marshall Plan for the next generation.

Something like that. After the war there were a *lot* of

international conferences. Even more boring than the war-war build-up before 1985, for a teenager like me. But a new organisation emerged, a kind of stronger version of the UN: the UGE, the United Governance of Earth. In fact the UGE is our own political master up here – no one nation has sovereignty on Demeter, or indeed on Persephone. Maybe there will be some kind of genuine world government one day, even as we reach out off planet . . .

You ought to speak to Deirdra. Greggson Deirdra, one of my companions here. From a history – well, actually, my own future – which went through a process like that. A lot later than you, though.

The Soviet Union survived, you know. As a kind of core. But it shrank back, lost its European client states, the Baltics – even the Ukraine broke away. And it's given up its plans for global conquest, so far as I can see. It's *very* wary of China. But it still has its space programme. And, guess what – there are Russians up here with us, in New Paris.

So you fulfilled your own dreams, then.

Sort of . . . I never met *you*, though, Malenfant. Not like those other versions of me.

Maybe I'll look myself up some day. I – this version you're speaking to – did fly tanker planes in lesser wars, regional wars. Maybe in your world I got sucked into the military effort.

Ha! Maybe you flew in the Air Bridge, over England. If I'd known I'd have waved.

So, all that history already, and I was just fifteen. After that I followed my ambitions – and I felt grateful for the chance to be doing anything at all, to be alive. I mean, as I studied the war more as I grew older, I realised how close we had come. That was a common perception, I think. Nobody wanted to come that close to annihilation again.

And then there were Demeter and Persephone, living worlds far from Earth.

Right. So you spread out. It's the old saw, you don't keep all your eggs in one basket. And maybe a habitable world like Demeter can be a second basket for mankind's eggs, in case we ever do get around to blowing up the Earth.

Indeed, or when the comet comes. But it wasn't just that – Demeter is a world in its own right, not just a lifeboat – and the science of it is fascinating.

OK. Anyhow, in the middle of all that – we show up.

And you've given me a lot to think about. Given what you've told me about your own history – maybe you're right, Malenfant. It seems clear to me now that it was the existence of Persephone in our skies that tipped *us* over into a nuclear war you seem to have avoided. The planets influencing human destiny – it's almost astrological, isn't it? And maybe this world is well named for the queen of Hell.

Anyhow, Malenfant. Would you like that ride down to Persephone?

60

Malenfant, Emma, Vasily and Anna were all loaded aboard the *Starry Messenger*, Nicola's intrasystem transport ship. Lighthill stayed aboard the *Harmonia*, out of sight of Nicola's people, responding to concerns expressed by UGE medics about the care he needed before being brought down to a super Earth after so long in space – and quietly acting as capcom for the Zeus expedition, of which the UGE people were not yet aware.

As the *Messenger* drifted through its eighteen-hour transfer orbit to Persephone III, Malenfant and his party happily explored. A transport ship evidently designed for interplanetary crossings as well as jaunts around the Persephone system, the *Messenger* was a blunt cylinder, with passenger compartments in the prow, a fission-reactor engine the size of a small car at the stern, and a long mid-body that was mostly tankage of water for propellant – a mass that also served to shield the habitable quarters from the engine. A simple but robust and efficient design, Malenfant concluded.

But it was while they were still en route down to the huge, dark mystery that was Persephone III that the storm broke over the landing on Zeus.

*

A furious Nicola rounded up the visitors, bundled them all into the *Messenger*'s tiny passenger lounge, closed the door, and scattered satellite images and a fat text report, weightless, in the air, where they drifted, accusing.

'I've been told your people have *landed*. On *Zeus*!'

Malenfant found it difficult to answer. As it happened this was only the second time he had met her face to face. And she looked so like *his* Nicola – short, slim, even the same dark cropped hair.

The others, though, waited for him to speak.

'Caught red-handed,' he said at last. 'Although, to be fair, whether this news is bad or not depends on your point of view, I guess.'

Emma gave him a covert kick in the shins. It *hurt*, and he wondered how she managed that in zero gravity with no obvious handholds to brace against. Years of practice, he supposed.

'Point of view,' said Nicola coldly. '*Point of view*. Malenfant, my point of view is not just mine. It's the UGE's. It's my national government's. Even my university's. And, do you want to know my point of view? I'm appalled. Simply appalled, at what your people are doing down there. Why, if we had known you were building that improvised landing craft in the first place—'

'You'd have stopped us. I know. Well, we did it anyway, and in a rush, so we could launch before you got here.' And Deirdra's instinct had been right, he thought in retrospect, to get this done before the locals stopped them. 'But they're not *my* people. Strictly speaking, Bartholomew isn't people at all.'

'Don't get smart.'

'Sorry. But, look, I don't command them. None of us do.'

'Maybe. Maybe not. But, Malenfant, you can be sure I will pressure you personally to any extent I can to resolve this situation.' She grabbed images out of the air, leafed angrily through the text report. 'Why, the planetary quarantine protocol violations alone – oh! What a mess.'

Malenfant thought she had never seemed more imposing – and, in a way, more unlike the Nicola he had flown with. Who, for better or worse, had been shaped by years spent inside the very American institution of NASA. Aboard a craft in flight you followed what the ship commander or mission control said to the letter – but on the ground, you were given a lot of independence of thought. If you didn't like the way some manufacturer was fixing the rim attachments of a heatshield, it was your duty to speak your mind. And certainly, in the end, it was the independent spirits who rose to the top. So you had a unique mix of authoritarianism and individuality – and all that had shaped the Nicola *he* had known.

But *this* Nicola had been a fifteen-year-old who had witnessed, if remotely, a near-nuclear war in Europe. And, he knew, she had had a different shaping from that point. She had never been military, strictly – so not like Lighthill's Nicola either, who had worked for the Royal Air and Space Force. The British space organisation this Nicola had been part of, developed mostly after the European war, seemed to have been a little more like NASA. But under the auspices of this UGE, as a kind of senior manager, her work was diplomatic, an endless negotiation through what seemed to be a slew of international protocols and agreements governing crew procedures, disciplinary matters, the handling of science results and samples – even issues of sovereignty and national accountability.

The result was a very different Nicola from 'his', or even 'Lighthill's'.

He had tried to discuss this with the Wing Commander. Lighthill had just shrugged. 'Nature and nurture, Malenfant.

What do you expect? That's the whole point of the English public school system.'

Well, Malenfant was pretty sure that he and his companions represented a challenge that *this* Nicola could have lived without. The bureaucratic overmind wasn't about to comprehend a manifold of parallel universes, let alone spooky cross-reality ties, but it had seemed quick enough to grasp that in Nicola they had a patsy ideally placed to take charge of the whole peculiar mess whether she liked it or not.

And now, he saw, Nicola was brandishing long-distance images that clearly showed their probe on the surface of Zeus.

'And you're actually drilling. *Through* the ice crust. My God. Look, Malenfant – we have strict planetary quarantine protocols. We are *trying* to protect the native life forms here – on all three worlds in this system. Oh, on Demeter – though that will always be controversial – it's just *so* Earthlike that it's hard to contain our crops, our trees and flowers, even the bugs we carry. On Persephone, as you'll see, it's all so different that contamination, in one direction or another, isn't an issue.

'But on Zeus, we've imposed quarantine. The life forms we see in the upper ice are so primitive – why, we have only made one landing ourselves, with an automated probe. Mostly, all we do is fly probes through the geysers. Highly sterilised probes at that!'

Just as, Malenfant remembered, Lighthill had sampled the life forms of a different Earth, back in the Vanilla System.

Nicola went on, 'And now your people down there are just ripping everything up. So what are you going to do about it? Order them to stop?'

Malenfant felt like laughing. 'Nicola. Believe me. Deirdra hasn't taken any orders from me since the day I met her, when I woke up in a coldsleep pod under a drowned London.'

Nicola frowned. 'Coldsleep? Cryogenic suspension?'

'Long story. Another time. Look, none of us can order Deirdra to stop what she's doing. Oh, you could land a few UGE goons—'

Nicola said coldly, 'The UGE is an organisation of international cooperation and peace. It does not employ "goons".'

Vasily grinned. 'I for one would rather not put that theory to the test.'

'OK,' said Malenfant. 'But my point stands. And even if you did send down a whole, umm, committee of diplomats – well, what good would it do? She's down there already. Maybe a lot of the harm, in terms of contamination, has been done. Besides – think of the potential science benefit you might reap.'

Emma touched Nicola's arm. 'It's not often I say this, but Malenfant is right. A geyser, even if it's natural, is only going to give you a mixed-up, random sample of whatever's going on down there on Zeus – or rather, inside it – and a sample that I guess must have to go through a flash-freeze process out in space even before you get your hands on it. *This* way, whatever the risks, you might retrieve orderly samples – maybe even get a precise assay of the biochemistry down there, all the way down through the ice, even down into the liquid ocean itself. You ought to know that Bartholomew incorporates a very advanced biochemistry analysis facility.'

Nicola visibly hesitated. 'The android?'

Malenfant had to smile. 'Twenty-fifth-century advanced.'

Emma said, 'Be pragmatic. You may as well exploit this if it's happening anyhow. And, let's face it, you might do even more damage by going down there and shutting it all down forcibly.'

More inner struggle showed in Nicola's face. But at last she gave in. 'Very well,' she said. 'What's done is done. As you say we may as well make the best of it, scientifically. But I'm still conflicted about this. I will have to justify this up my own chain of command. And I *still* wish you hadn't gone down this road at all. Certainly, I doubt very much that any of you will be allowed anywhere near Zeus again.'

'Point taken,' Anna said a little coldly. 'Even if we are not ourselves citizens of your wonderful UGE, and are not bound by its laws.'

'Even so,' Nicola said. She glared at them. 'I need to make some calls. Don't leave this cabin. And make sure you call me before your team down on Zeus pulls any more stunts.'

Given she was moving in zero gravity, she did a good job of slamming the door behind her.

Anna turned to Emma, and applauded, a slow, sarcastic hand-clap. 'Expertly done, Madam Stoney.'

'I do my best,' Emma said, though she seemed distracted. 'But it was mostly bullshit.'

Malenfant was vaguely shocked.

'Come on, Malenfant. So Deirdra and Bartholomew have drilled down to the base of the ice cap, down to the liquid ocean. What then? You really think they will be content with scooping up a few samples in a bucket?'

Vasily nodded. 'I have wondered. Surely they will not stop. This is their one and only chance to see this. See what lies deeper in that ice moon. What I'm unsure of is how they will proceed.'

None of them were, Malenfant thought. He could make only confused guesses himself. As ever Deirdra was far beyond his control.

So he said nothing. He expected he would find out in time.

A few hours later, a message came in from Deirdra, through the bangles. And they found out.

*

445

'If you're going to argue with us, Malenfant, get it over with,' Deirdra snapped. Her voice came through the bangles and sounded in his head – not through any radio link to ensure the UGE people couldn't eavesdrop. 'We just spent a day drilling a two-hundred-kilometres-plus hole in this ice. This is a stable, static little moon, as moons go, but not entirely. This shaft, that we just elaborately dug out, could close up any minute. But, look, all Bartholomew needs to do is to drop down this shaft—'

Malenfant exploded. '*Bartholomew?* He needs to do *what*?'

'If he does it freefall, all it need take is fifteen or twenty minutes,' Deirdra said. 'In practice he will brake against the walls . . .'

'Shit, Deirdra!'

Emma squeezed his arm. 'Just listen, Malenfant. Tell us the plan, Deirdra.'

It was Bartholomew who replied now. 'So I will descend the shaft relatively cautiously. I'll take samples of the ice en route. And I'll be trailing monofilament cables, so even if the ice closes up after I've passed we will still stay in communication. And after that—'

Malenfant snorted. 'Yeah. After that. After you've fallen through a couple of hundred klicks of ice. Then what, Bartholomew?'

'After that,' Bartholomew said, 'at the bottom of the shaft, I'll have to break through into the liquid ocean beneath. It's a smooth temperature gradient. Given what the probe found, we are anticipating layers of thick slush rather than a sharp interface. I think I'll be digging my way through.'

'Oh, fine,' Malenfant said. 'And then what, you go swimming? *Inside a moon?*'

'Well, actually – yes. Heading straight down, of course. It'll be dark but I can follow the gravity gradient.

'Look – don't be concerned for my welfare. I wouldn't recommend a human do this. In fact I'd forbid it. But I am a pretty sturdy mechanism. And I will be wearing a pressure suit, I have layers of gloves, some pretty robust tools. The point is – if you think of me not as a medic bot but as a candidate probe for this expedition, I'm pretty well equipped. It's not even a question of my having to return; I'll be able to sample and analyse the organic soup that seems to fill this little moon all the way down, and feed back the results—'

'Enough,' Malenfant snarled. *'It's not even a question of my having to return?* What the hell kind of language is that? Screw the science. Some kind of dumb probe you ain't.' He deliberately left the rest of that unsaid. *What you are is a friend.* 'Tough you may be, but you're *not* some piece of spacebound dedicated hardware. You're a medical robot designed to work in environments where humans are comfortable. You have to be vulnerable if you venture too far outside those limits.'

'Says the man who had me climb out of a skyscraper?'

'Yes, and you came back damaged, didn't you?'

'Never mind *if* he could do it,' Anna said. 'Why *would* he? Bartholomew, I thought your programming was about preserving human life, specifically Deirdra's. What's that got to do with this ice-fishing stunt? How is that helping Deirdra's health?'

'Indirectly, perhaps.'

Malenfant snorted. 'So your algorithms determine, right?'

'If you want to put it like that. Malenfant, you know as well as I do that Deirdra is driven above all by one obsession: to understand the truth of the universe into which she was born. That has taken her a long way – you'll admit that.'

Emma nodded. 'Malenfant, you wouldn't have found the

manifold at all if not for her drive. Her intuitive leaps. I think I see where you are going, Bartholomew. She now thinks the secret, or the next layer to be uncovered anyhow, is somewhere deep inside this strange little moon. And so—'

'And so it is my studied opinion that the best way to treat her — to advance the health of the whole person, psychologically at least — is to help her explore this moon.'

Deirdra spoke. 'We worked all this out since we landed. We didn't mean it to happen this way — we weren't deceiving you — but now that we're here . . . Malenfant, I care for Bartholomew as much as you do, and don't bother denying it. But I appreciate what he's doing here, what he's risking, as much as I've appreciated anything anyone has done for me, my whole life.'

'Which I think is enough talk,' Bartholomew said now.

Malenfant leaned forward, longing for a microphone to yell into. 'If I had the slightest inkling you were planning a jaunt like this, I'd never have let you go. Bartholomew, you idiot—'

'If you start me crying I'll rust up. Good luck, Malenfant.'

'Bartholomew!'

'*Geronimo!* . . .'

'And he's gone,' Deirdra whispered.

61

Nicola insisted on staying with the *Harmonia* crew – and, when it was explained to her, using the bangle link. She went through reactions Malenfant remembered of his own first exposure to the technology, a start at the expensive-headphone sound apparently booming inside her own head, and a bewilderment at the capabilities of the twenty-fifth-century technology. But she was pragmatic and calm – *his* Nicola always had been – and soon she was as bound up with the science results as the rest, Malenfant realised, her innate curiosity, and postponing for now, at least, the wrath she would deliver when this was all over – and the wrath of the authorities over her too, he thought.

In the end, though, Bartholomew's fall through the ice shell of Zeus, extraordinary venture though it was, became almost routine. After a few hours of it anyhow. You could get used to anything, Malenfant concluded.

After he jumped down the hole in the ice, it took mere minutes of his airless, frictionless fall for Bartholomew to reach his target velocity of somewhere over a hundred kilometres per hour. After that he kept his velocity steady with gentle scrapes of boots, gloves and padded knees against the walls. Malenfant knew he had internal accelerometers to help him judge the speed.

Two hours to get through the ice crust, then.

On his way down he used a bare fingernail to take samples of the ice, with any biological traces. A quick assay soon showed he continued to detect extremophile bacteria, or their relics, as the probe had in the upper layers.

The crew on the *Messenger* quickly confirmed that the life traces he was finding had a biochemical basis identical to terrestrial life. Even at extreme depths.

'Just as at the surface,' Emma murmured. 'And just as Lighthill found on Vanilla Earth, in that other manifold strand.'

'And,' Nicola put in reluctantly, 'on Demeter.' She stared around. 'Persephone too, come to that. It's remarkable you people have discovered this so quickly. Maybe we have been too cautious, too slow. But we could not have suspected this . . .' She shook her head, evidently still thinking it through. 'So what is the wider pattern telling us? Lots of worlds – one form of life . . . and not just in my Solar System, so you say, but across this manifold of yours—'

Malenfant had no response. All this was over his own head, for now. For the descent itself was a compelling adventure, even without the existential dimension.

Even the visuals were striking, if disturbing, thanks to the bangles. If he closed his eyes, he could see through Bartholomew's eyes as he gazed down at the shaft below. Or up at the dwindling circle of light above, where Deirdra's face, behind her visor, had quickly become invisible.

After a period of intense monitoring Malenfant started to feel tired. Almost dizzy.

He took a break, not expecting to sleep, but leaving orders to be woken before the descent was over. As it was, he slept dreamlessly until some internal clock woke him up.

Two hours had elapsed. Bartholomew had to be nearing the end of the ice shaft.

Malenfant visited the head. Called by the galley, grabbed globes of drinking water.

Made his way back to the lounge. All his remaining companions from Persephone II were here, still; Nicola was away.

He listened to the monitor. Bartholomew's voice, crackly and faint: '. . . The slush is getting thinner, I think. I have a feeling I will break through soon to more open water . . .'

The visuals were worthless now, Malenfant saw. Bartholomew, alone, was falling into dark and cold. But data on his immediate environment chattered in. Water, full of mineral traces and organics, the temperature hovering around freezing. Emma made quick notes as the descent continued.

'Obviously the comms rig with the bangles is still working fine,' Malenfant murmured to Emma. 'That's miracle enough.'

She nodded agreement, but her attention was focused on her notes, the science. 'They were right that there is no smooth interface,' she told him. 'The ice turned into slush a while back, which in turn is loosening up as we get closer to authentic liquid water . . . I've been thinking while you were asleep, Malenfant. Nice to get the chance in peace.'

'Yeah, yeah.'

'I think Nicola has missed a point about those geysers of hers. Remember? The plumes of organics-laden steam that come shooting out of Zeus? Or, no, that's not fair to her. We have seen more of the wider multiverse than she has. Maybe it − opens the mind.'

'What do you mean?'

'Well, the geysers. Think about it. What are they *for*?'

'They're geysers. Do they have to be *for* anything?'

'That's the question. Maybe they do. We have learned to think that way, haven't we? There is conscious intention here. The Builders at work, somehow. So to keep asking what stuff is *for* is perfectly valid, rather than to assume it's all some natural phenomenon. If we don't ask, we'll miss stuff.'

'So, the geysers—'

'Look at the wider picture. The functioning of the moon as a whole. You have life, incubating away under that lid of ice. And "incubate" is maybe the right word, just as Bartholomew said, given it's all conveniently driven by some mysterious inner heat source that nobody knows anything about. Yet life that is identical to our own, at the biochemical level at least. So we have learned.

'And what happens to it? It gets thrown out by "geysers", that's what, spraying out the good stuff into space. The life-laden water turns quickly to ice, no doubt, but it must surely be drifting like snow towards Persephone III, and Demeter. Maybe even the other worlds of this System.'

'Such as Earth,' Lighthill murmured. 'And has been for billions of years, perhaps.'

'Ah,' Anna said. 'I see it. We know that some bacteria, extremophiles, can withstand the conditions of space – the radiation, the vacuum, for long periods. Centuries, even millennia—'

'Millions of years is what I recall from the theories I studied,' Vasily said. 'And after they do land on other worlds, seeds of life are sown. This is panspermia. The universal self-scattering of life.' He grinned. 'A pleasingly Cosmist idea. Of course that does not deny the utility of a helping hand.'

'A helping hand.' Malenfant frowned, thinking that through. 'OK. OK. So, Emma, are you saying this ice moon is a, a panspermia machine?'

Emma hesitated. 'Well—'

Vasily put in, 'If so, couldn't be better designed for job. Warm, moist interior, full of resources from the rocky core, all churned up by convection in the water – ideal to incubate life. Then, low gravity and natural cannons to fire the products off into space.'

A brief silence. That thought hung in the air. That word, *designed*.

Malenfant tried to process the idea. This moon *wasn't* a natural object. Emma was right to ask what it was all for – all its features. It was a made thing; it had a purpose. They had come here on the track of the destructive, or constructive, planet-building agency they had called the World Engineers. And if this speculation panned out – maybe Deirdra's instinct, mysterious but always sound, had directed her straight to a home run.

He glanced at Emma, and thought he saw the same notion reflected in her expression. 'Somehow this life-infested little moon is central to the whole project.'

'I guess so.'

'Which,' he went on, 'in some spooky higher-order manifold way, is why Deirdra has been brought to it.'

'Maybe.'

'And you don't think Nicola's people have thought of this?'

'I guess not,' she said. 'They clearly aren't thinking in the same – categories – as we are. In terms of design, of intention – of World Engineers with some agenda of their own. To Nicola, it's still a naturalistic interpretation that she'll reach for.'

'Then there's a lot she has to learn.'

That was when Nicola herself came bustling back into the cabin.

'He's pretty much there,' she said now, sounding excited. 'Bartholomew. We've been listening in to the radio feed. At

453

the bottom of the shaft in the ice. Right on time. His movement is becoming freer. He's falling faster too.' She looked up, and grinned. 'Through the slush, and falling into an ocean with a roof. God, you are breaking rules we haven't even thought of yet, but I am coming to love you people.'

And that, Malenfant thought with a stab to the heart, was the Niki he knew.

He closed his eyes to study such visuals as Bartholomew was returning. Nothing but the glow of a head torch, shining through a metre or so of murky water. That murk, Malenfant supposed, was all they were going to see of the life down here, and the mineral debris, stirred up from the rocky core, that it must feed on.

Emma said, 'I'm guessing we are only getting glimpses here. Glimpses of a whole sub-ice world . . . Surely evolution won't have progressed far, in these conditions. The geyser samples we've seen have contained only simple bacteria – simple meaning no internal cell structure, let alone multicellular forms; no animals or plants. It's probably bacteria all the way down.'

Vasily murmured, 'Archaean bacteria, though. Tough beasts. Resistant to heat, radiation, vacuum, desiccation. Hardy little space travellers. Panspermia agents.'

Malenfant glanced uneasily at Nicola, but, staring at various readouts, she seemed not to have picked up the remark. Too out of left field for now, maybe.

'How much further?' Nicola snapped now. 'So he has reached the ocean. How far is he intending to go?'

Bartholomew himself answered now, oddly toneless, Malenfant thought, the voice booming inside his own head, lacking even a patina of humanity. 'Well, Deirdra and I didn't put a limit on it.'

'He's keeping up the pace he had when passing through the

ice,' Deirdra said. 'A hundred klicks an hour or more. He's *swimming* down.'

Malenfant tried to picture it. Bartholomew must have shed the last, obstructing scraps of his human clothing. Maybe stripped down his own structure somehow. So he would be swimming, down through that spherical shell of a global ocean, legs thrashing, maybe too fast for the human eye to follow . . . And reporting as he did so.

'I'm keeping my speed constant, but I expect things will get interesting soon. The physical conditions are already changing, slowly. Pressure rising. And, significantly, the temperature is rising. About one seventh of a degree with every kilometre. We expected that, of course; I swim closer to the heat source at the heart of this moon with every stroke. And already the populations of bacteria around me are changing. The cryophiles, the cold-lovers in the ice, gradually thinning out. Also the nutrients available here – essentially bits of dissolved rock – are growing thicker.'

Emma was frowning. 'That seventh of a degree per klick – keep that up and you'll reach boiling point in, what, seven hundred klicks or so – halfway to the centre of the moon itself. Or maybe a little further, depending on the pressure. Six or seven hours from now. What then, Bartholomew?'

Malenfant leaned forward. 'That's when you turn back. Right?'

Bartholomew said only, 'This is a unique exploration. Possibly never to be repeated. I intend to go on as long as I am capable of it.'

Malenfant sighed. 'Yeah, right. I just knew you would say that. Well, just take care of yourself down there, Aquaman. OK. Six hours, huh? So this is going to be a long watch. I had a break already. Whose turn now?'

'Mine, maybe,' Emma said. 'And – Nicola, I think we ought to bring you up to speed. About what we're all thinking. Do you know what I mean by "panspermia"?'

Nicola looked faintly alarmed, Malenfant thought. But – intrigued.

And Bartholomew said, 'The light around me. It grows stronger.'

Malenfant and the rest took turns eating, sleeping. As did Lighthill, up on the *Harmonia*, with a couple of UGE medics.

And, by turns, Anna, Emma and Malenfant quietly took remote charge of Deirdra, now alone on the surface of the ice moon. Made sure she slept, ate, and took bathroom breaks.

While Bartholomew just swam down, on and on. Tireless. Mechanical.

As the hours wore away, so conditions gradually changed around Bartholomew, just as predicted. The temperature rise hastened, from a fraction of a degree per kilometre just under the ice, up to one degree per kilometre and beyond. Malenfant imagined the conditions inside that ball of water and ice and rock, the heat energy pouring out like a slow, unending explosion from the fierce, still unknown heat source at the moon's heart, growing more intense as Bartholomew battled his way deeper and deeper.

The light here was like sunlight in a shallow ocean, where the plankton grew. This was the light detected from afar, leaking out through the moon's ice crust. But the interval of brilliance was brief.

After that the density of life petered out, slowly but surely, as the extreme-environment adaptability of the underlying biochemistry was tested to its limits.

At last, after eight, nine hours of descent from the surface, the water-boiling-point mark approached.

Just as at the liquid ocean's interface with the ice shell, however, there was no clear boundary, no simple surface. At some point, liquid water full of steam bubbles phased into a kind of gas full of remnant droplets of hot liquid water, and laced with a sparse rock dust.

For a while, even beyond the nominal boiling point, some hardy extremophile bacteria clung to life. But there came a point where no biological traces at all could be detected by Bartholomew's internal instruments.

And still Bartholomew fell.

It was an extraordinary thought, Malenfant reflected, that Bartholomew had now passed through a surface *below* an ocean. Below, and into a great internal bubble of superhot steam, holding up that ocean. An inside-out world.

Bartholomew said in that odd flat whisper, 'Of course it is a testament to those who designed me that my instruments and other systems keep functioning at all in these conditions. My inner workings, my skeleton, are not organic at all. Constructed of high-grade steel, and more exotic metals. In fact—'

'*In fact* even steel has a melting point,' Malenfant snapped. 'What is it, a couple of thousand degrees? And are you telling me that the rest of you has, what, burned off? All your soft parts? What the hell do you *look* like now, Tin Man?'

'More tin. Less man.'

Deirdra put in, murmuring in all their heads, 'He understood all this, Malenfant. The cost of the descent. It was . . . his decision.'

Malenfant snorted. 'Like hell. He's a robot, Deirdra. Programmed to serve humanity. For all his bullshit he does what we want him to do, whether we say it out loud or not.

Two thousand degrees, where steel will melt. When will he hit that?'

'Close to the centre,' Emma said. 'That's based on heat-flow models. There's a rock core down there, Malenfant. We know that from studies of the gravity field, as well as seismic soundings and such. About sixty kilometres in diameter, no more. Presumably enclosing the central power source, whatever it is. And the surface of *that* is where steel will melt.'

Vasily nodded. 'Agreed. Given the power output, temperature of central source must be five thousand degrees. As hot as the Sun's surface. Around that there must be a bubble of rock vapour, maybe twenty-five kilometres across. And above that a layer of liquid rock, and a solid crust over *that*. Maybe not a crust, maybe a layer of loose fragments. Cloud of boulders.'

'Shit,' said Malenfant. 'Vapour, liquid, solid rock. It's like the steam-water-ice stuff further up. Made out of *rock*.'

Nicola nodded. 'So Bartholomew might survive as far as the surface of that rocky core, maybe. But not much further.'

Bartholomew said now, 'I will go as far as I can. For this may be our only chance.'

Malenfant shook his head. 'Bartholomew. After all we've been through—'

'As far as I must.'

'You can't sacrifice yourself like this.'

'As far as I must.'

'Deirdra! Shit, you started this. Call him back. Maybe even now . . .'

Emma touched his hand. 'I think she's crying, Malenfant.'

All they got from Bartholomew now was that one repeated phrase, every few seconds, like an automated call sign.

'As far as I must.

'As far as I must.

'As far as I must . . .'

Malenfant couldn't stand it. He walked out.

'As far as I must.

'As far as I must.'

The next six, seven hours, as Bartholomew fell slowly through a steam-filled cavern eight hundred kilometres deep, seemed interminable.

Again Malenfant tried to keep up some basic discipline, a rota of breaks for food and napping, as much for his own benefit as the others'.

As the end neared, they all huddled in the passenger lounge.

Patchy readouts from some of Bartholomew's instruments – not all – kept coming through. He still responded to vocal messages only with a mantra that sounded pre-recorded now.

'As far as I must.

'As far as I must . . .'

By the time the fifteenth hour of the descent was reached, and Bartholomew reached the nominal radius of the rocky core surface, Malenfant was wrung out. He imagined what must be left of Bartholomew now, a kind of endoskeleton of high-grade steel, falling in the superheated, rock-laden gloom, only a few of its components still functioning at temperatures now measured at well over a thousand degrees.

Deirdra, alone on the surface, had been silent for a long time.

Every few minutes, Malenfant tried calling again. All he got was the mantra back again.

'As far as I must.

'As far as I must.

'As far as I must.'

And then, a change. 'As far as I. As far far as I. As far.'

Malenfant closed his eyes. 'Bartholomew? Are you there?'
'As far as I *can*.'

Silence.

And a different voice spoke in Malenfant's head.

This little one has fallen far enough.

A neutral, machine-like voice . . .

Hello, Bartholomew.

You are safe now.

Emma glanced at read-outs. 'He's stopped falling. I *think*. The data is too flaky to be sure . . .'

Malenfant yelled, 'Who's speaking? Who the hell are you?'

Hello, Greggson Deirdra.

Hello, Emma Stoney.

Hello, Malenfant.

My name is Michael.

Michael?

Listen now.

Michael. My son was called Michael. You are not—

Listen now.

FIVE

On Her Final Ascension to the Far Downstream

62

Malenfant only glimpsed the exterior of the Persephone lander attached to the *Starry Messenger*, a hurried glance through a scuffed porthole. The lander looked like a big, fat Apollo command module to him, a squat cone with a thick heatshield attached to its base, and connected by a docking port at its nose to the body of the main ship.

'Which is no surprise, I guess,' he murmured to Emma, as they, with Arkady and Vasily, trailed Nicola and a couple of UGE crew through a short docking tunnel into the craft's snug-looking interior.

They found two rows of couches on hefty frames. The space below was crammed with cargo, anonymous-looking crates held down by buckled straps. The four of them in their pressure suits were a crowded tangle of arms and legs as they sorted themselves out.

Emma asked, 'No surprise?'

'Since we know Nicola's history took a decisive divergence from ours with that 1985 war. So *after* Apollo. Hey, I wanted a window seat.'

In the lower row of seats, Emma had already squirmed into the left-hand couch, by a small window, and Anna the right.

Nicola looked over her shoulder, from her own seat in the top row. 'Less chucklin' and more bucklin'. And that's a line I generally only need to use on the few kids that have made this journey so far. Separation in five . . . three, two, one.'

There was a rattle from the nose as clamps unlocked, and then a bang, as if the outer hull had been struck with a spanner – as, Malenfant guessed, manoeuvring thrusters pushed this lander away from the main body of the *Messenger*.

Sunlight, through the window, slid across Malenfant's lap.

Nicola called back, 'OK, now the retro thruster pack will fire. In three, two—'

A jolt, then a steady thrust that drove Malenfant back into his seat.

Nicola kept talking over the dull roar of the rocket. 'Obviously Demeter is the more equable world. But Persephone is habitable – clearly, as it's already inhabited by life not unlike our own. The gravity is high, but not that high. The air is thick, without enough oxygen . . .'

'We know,' Anna said. 'Our Persephone, gravity the same. Air sounds the same. A challenge but it can be borne. Humans can live down there.'

'And that's what we're trying to prove. Burn-out in five, four, three . . .'

When the thrust stopped Malenfant was thrown forward. The sudden silence was startling.

But almost immediately he started to feel a steadier push at his back. Already they must be hitting the upper layers of the thick air of Persephone.

'Here we go. The deceleration is gentle at first, but don't be fooled by that. I'm sure you are all capable of enduring the ride.'

'Colonising Persephone,' Anna prompted.

'We see it as an . . . opportunity, I suppose. Remember, we have that shock of war in our near past. The further we spread out, the less chance there is of any single event, such as a global war, eliminating us all – all of humanity, I mean. And indeed our culture, our civilisation. We suspect Demeter is an unusually Earthlike world, if you look on a galactic scale. Persephone is a tougher challenge, but a more common planet type. And if we can live *here*, we can live anywhere.'

Malenfant butted in. 'Let me say it first. Good Cosmist thinking.'

Vasily grinned. 'You learn well from us, Malenfant.'

Nicola called back, 'OK, the Gs are building up now. We will aerobrake down from interplanetary velocities. You know the drill. Don't fight it. When it gets too heavy fill your lungs with air and take short panting breaths . . . Once safely in the lower air we will descend on a parachute. Persephone is easy to land on, given the thick air, in terms of fuel consumption at least. Not so easy to launch from.'

'We know.' Malenfant, thinking of their travails on Persephone II, shared a rueful smile with Emma.

And the deceleration suddenly upped in intensity, quite savagely. Malenfant groaned, and braced himself, filling his lungs as advised, taking short panting breaths. Through the window, beyond Emma, he could see a glow building up as the atoms of the upper air were smashed aside by their passage, a light that was cast into the cabin.

'This colony,' Vasily shouted now. 'Named what? New Paris on Demeter . . .'

'New St Petersburg,' Nicola called back. 'After what would have been the first target in retaliation for Paris. Given that history, what else could it be?'

And the load on Malenfant's chest spiked again, making him cry out.

63

Michael. You say your name is Michael.

He was called Michael. He is in me.

I . . . *in* you. Where is Bartholomew?

He is in me. He is safe. We speak through him.

Who else is in you?

Many. Merged. As many rivulets become tributaries of a great river.

Rivers. What do you know of rivers?

I saw rivers in Africa. Michael saw rivers. Michael was born in Africa. Do you have any baobab fruit?

Baobab?

I remember baobab fruit. Michael remembers baobab fruit.

No fruit. I'm sorry . . . I don't understand. You asked for Malenfant. Did you know Malenfant? And Emma?

Michael knew Malenfant. Michael knew Emma Stoney.

Michael is, was, the name of their son. Well, in some realities. Maybe this is another of those weird cross-manifold resonances.

I was not their son. But Emma saved me. She came to Africa, where I was born. Later she came to a school where I was contained, and saved me again.

Saved you from what? Why did Malenfant or Emma, uh, find you, seek you out?

Because they wanted to know.

Know what?

What you want to know. What the downstreamers wanted to know.

Downstreamers? Downstream of what, time? Are you talking about the future?

In a sense. A far future. Very far.

Are the downstreamers descendants of mankind?

Yes.

What did they want? What *will* they want? What could they possibly want?

What you want to know. In a sense.

They asked the same question you asked.

Why the world was coming to an end.

64

On landing, they were all made to sit in the lander for an hour, to allow their cardiovascular and other systems to adapt, at least a little, to the higher gravity. They were able to open up their suits. Nicola passed around bulbs of water.

The light through the windows was murky, a kind of orange-brown. Wind howled; once or twice the massive lander shuddered.

'You're quiet,' Emma murmured to Malenfant.

'Giving these elderly bones a rest.'

'You're thinking about Deirdra.'

He glanced at her; she was right, of course. 'Since there's not a damn thing I can do for her. And still less for that idiotic machine Bartholomew, or what's left of him.'

'It's just all so strange,' Emma said. 'Whatever the hell I expected – it wasn't some kind of *mind* down deep inside that thing.'

'Maybe should have guessed,' Anna murmured. 'Deirdra did guess. Should have listened. I mean, all that heat – turns the whole inside of the moon to superheated steam – just leaking away. *Waste heat.* And what do we know, in all our worlds, that have a problem with waste heat? Computers, that's what.'

'True enough,' Malenfant said. He thought now of Deirdra's twenty-fifth century, an England pocked by the huge ruins of AI cooling stacks, like enigmatic lunar craters. She had grown up knowing what those stacks had been for.

'And just think,' Emma said. 'All that power. Ten thousand trillion watts of it, is what we now estimate from the heat output Bartholomew experienced. Remarkable. The human brain runs on around a hundred watts. By comparison, you know – I asked him this – Bartholomew's central processing required around a kilowatt.'

Malenfant was interested. 'I never thought to ask.'

'So Bartholomew's brain was a pretty smart piece of kit, but only a tenth as efficient in power use as a human brain. Which, given its shaping by evolution and all, may represent some kind of optimum. If all you have to work with is wet chemistry anyhow.'

Vasily pursed his lips. 'So this big heat source in Zeus. Equivalent to ten thousand billion Bartholomews. Or a *hundred* thousand billion human brains. One smart fellow, if so.'

Nicola looked back, having listened to all this. 'Fascinating. I don't think we ever got that far in our speculations. Well, of course we never had the temerity to drop in a probe. But – *Zeus*. King of the gods. Maybe we picked a good name.'

'Maybe,' Malenfant said. 'Anyhow, I guess the destinies of Deirdra and Bartholomew are in its hands now. Metaphorically speaking.'

'Umm,' Vasily said thoughtfully. 'Then I wonder what *it* wants.'

Emma grasped Malenfant's gloved hand. 'It already spoke to us, remember. Through Bartholomew. And it *named* us. It knows us, somehow. This isn't over yet, for better or worse.'

'Maybe so,' Malenfant said. 'But I have this feeling I'm never going to see Deirdra again.'

Emma squeezed his hand harder. 'Her mother will never forgive you.'

He shrugged. 'I'll never forgive myself.'

Then an alarm chimed. 'That's it,' Nicola called back. 'This bus has reached the end of the line; everybody out . . .'

They were led, slowly, in their sealed suits, through a translucent access tunnel towards the nearest of a series of robust-looking domes. Now, as he cautiously moved, Malenfant could feel the familiar heavy weight of Persephone. Another Persephone, he reminded himself, his third. He ought to get some kind of loyalty card.

Looking back through the tunnel wall, he saw how the squat cone of the lander sat dead centre on a big green-painted cross on what looked like a concrete pad. He was impressed that the landing, presumably under some kind of steerable parachute, had been so precise.

Beyond that, the Sun was halfway down the sky – he knew it was afternoon here, in this part of Persephone – a Sun just visible, through a sky cover of what looked like thick smog: an orange haze, murky, light-obstructing. The only green he could see at first glance was that marking on the landing pad, standing out against the gloom, a defiant Earth colour . . .

No, he saw more scraps of green in the distance. They looked almost like pitchers' mounds in baseball, he thought. Some other artefact of the colonists here, no doubt. Were there Americans here? Maybe they actually *were* pitchers' mounds.

'Almost nostalgic,' he murmured.

Nicola walked at his side. 'What's that?'

'The smog. Back where I came from – when I was a kid,

anyhow, before the cleaner air legislation started cutting in – this could have been the Bronx, say.'

Vasily looked back as they trudged slowly through the tunnel. 'You should live in moment, Malenfant. That thick air. Not pollution – natural! Antique!'

'Quite right,' Nicola said. 'You've evidently been looking us up. This isn't so glamorous a place as Demeter, but the atmosphere is "antique", yes. Maybe "primordial" is a better word. The air, we think, is like that of all the terrestrial planets when they formed. The first atmospheres, outgassed from the molten interiors of very young worlds. On Earth it was probably all blasted away by the big impact that created the Moon. Here, though, on Persephone, the primordial bombardments seem to have served to thin out the first air rather than detach it completely. Several bars of carbon dioxide, nitrogen, water vapour – and some free oxygen. Not enough for us to breathe of course. But—'

'But life must be here,' Anna said immediately. 'Photosynthesising life. Using sunlight to crack carbon dioxide for carbohydrates, to release free oxygen you mention. Must be.'

'Correct. A recent addition, we think – recent in evolutionary terms. Meaning one or two billion years ago rather than four or five billion . . . You'll see. Sorry. Not far to a comfy sofa now.'

That had to be translated for the Russians.

The domes of New St Petersburg were heavily braced to withstand the strong gravity and powerful winds of Persephone. As a result the settlement was enclosing, somewhat claustrophobic.

The travellers were all assigned rooms – two to a cabin.

Then they were led to the nearest thing the Petersburg base

had to a communal area. It was a big lounge, with a serving hatch to the main kitchen, and a kind of bar – non-alcoholic drinks only, an official rule Malenfant would have been prepared to bet was broken frequently.

He admitted he was glad to get a chance to sit down, on one of the promised sofas.

Nicola briskly introduced them to the fifteen-strong current personnel, and left them to it as she caught up with other chores pushed down her schedule by the big interruption that Malenfant and his people represented.

Emma, at least, was polite, and worked her way through awkward conversations with curious colonists. They were a multinational crew who turned out to know little about the provenance of the visitors – or the existence of the manifold – save for gossip, or leaks. It made Malenfant wonder how widely their presence was known in the rest of this Solar System, especially on Earth.

Lately, Vasily and Anna returned from short walks of exploration, apparently impressed by New St Petersburg. To Malenfant, though, this was just more space technology, of which he had witnessed plenty before, in this corner of the manifold and elsewhere. He had learned there were only so many times you could ooh and aah over some guy's ingenious repair to a human-sewage processing system.

Persephone III, like its manifold twins I and II, turned on its axis every twenty-five hours. So a too-long night, day and night again passed for Malenfant while he and his crew went through their mandatory acclimatising. There were meals, more short walks around a base that seemed smaller on the inside than out. Sleeps, in small, quiet rooms.

Every couple of hours, he used his bangle to listen for updates from Zeus.

It was a relief when the second morning of their stay came around, and Nicola rounded them up for their first EVA. Out of here at last.

65

They had to wear atmosphere suits, of course – lightweight, easy to wear compared to the heavy armour of lunar or orbital EVA suits, but then these suits only had to exclude a thick but toxic atmosphere, rather than protect the wearer from hard vacuum.

But before they were allowed outside the suited explorers all had to go through a series of sterilising showers. Rough and ready planetary protection, evidently. Nicola even had a tourist-friendly slogan: 'What you bring to Petersburg, stays in Petersburg.'

They gathered outside the domes, not far from the landing area, which Malenfant saw now was a splash of crudely mixed concrete. Further away was another apron, scorched black and studded with heavyweight gantries. For cargo hauliers, evidently. There were other facilities out here, open to the unbreathable air. Blocky buildings, tanks, stacks of equipment. It was something like a small industrial park, he thought.

All of this under that smoggy sky, the strangely dim, almost autumnal light of a shrunken, distant Sun.

They walked forward, at a cautious pace, led by Nicola Mott.

'Impressed?' Nicola said drily. 'I can show you around if you like. Most of this is chemical processing, of course. Extraction plants for water, methane, hydrogen, oxygen – the stuff of life, and propellants for our rockets. Oh, and our surface rovers. Methane burners.'

'Sorry. Wool-gathering,' Malenfant replied. 'I – uh, yes, I guess I am impressed. This is a pretty extensive base for 2019. Well, compared to my 2019 anyhow.'

She nodded cautiously. 'I think with time I'll get used to sentences like that. But, as I understand it, we did have a more welcoming target to reach for than the "Mars" you describe. So we built faster, I suppose. Come, this way. You'll have noticed we're on foot. No coincidence we're so near our target; we set this base down close to one of the most promising manifestations of vent life.'

Malenfant frowned. 'Vent life?'

'The target for the morning's walk. Come.'

Vasily swung his arms around as he strode out, following Nicola. 'Just nice to walk like this again. You think, Anna?'

'I know what you mean. We spent years on our own Persephone. Now that gravity is like pulling on a comfortable old backpack. And, you know where we are, Vasily? The continental distributions are the same. *Caina*, as Malenfant calls it. We are near the southern shore of Caina. You can see it from the relief maps these colonists have compiled from space, the photographs . . . Even though there are no oceans here, of course. And different names.'

'No oceans, but plenty of deep aquifers,' Nicola said. 'We found that out through radar sounding, and direct drilling later.' She slowed her pace. 'Now. Take care. We're approaching the lip.'

Malenfant frowned. 'The lip of what?'

'A crack in the ground. See? The opening to one of the major vent systems around here. The reason our first landings

476

were so close by. This is what we came here to explore, first. Tread carefully. Trust me, you aren't used to the light yet, or the gravity, and the edges can be tricky, all but invisible, and every so often they crumble back . . . Here we are.'

The fissure itself, maybe a couple of metres wide, was a dark wound in the burnt-orange dirt. Malenfant made out traces of previous expeditions: pitons thrust in the ground, a coil of rope, frayed and abandoned.

Vasily knelt down to see, peering into the crack. He seemed to spot something near the rim. He reached out a gloved finger, thought better of it.

Nicola said, 'Not exactly spectacular, I guess. When we were working hard at this site you'd have seen bubble tents alongside the rim, and instruments and tools strewn around: hammers, picks, drilling rigs. Inside the tents, cores with labelled layers, scraps of discoloured rock being brushed, labelled, or tested in flasks of acid, examined with a binocular microscope. Back in the domes we have more extensive lab suites, of course. We use mass spectrometers, and X-ray and laser fluorescence; we look at trapped gases and isotopic combinations. Oh, and we have Wolf traps that use radioactive nutrients to trace any metabolic activity . . .'

She seemed nostalgic for the project, Malenfant thought. Better than bureaucracy, he guessed.

Both Vasily and Anna were kneeling by the vent now. 'But there is obviously life here,' said Vasily. 'Visible to naked eye.' Now he did, boldly, scrape a gloved finger across a surface a few centimetres below the lip of the vent; his fingertip came up discoloured – purple, Malenfant thought, though it was hard to be sure of the shade in the muddied orange daylight. Purple – and green.

Nicola grinned, as if they had passed some test. But she handed

477

out sterile wipes. 'Please don't handle the merchandise.'

'Sorry,' Vasily said as he wiped his gloved finger. 'Know better than that.'

'Don't worry about it. After all it's years now since we completed the preliminary analysis and genetic sequencing of all this.'

'Analysis,' Emma said. 'Of life forms down in these vents?'

'That's it. There are at least two great kingdoms of life on this planet, Emma. Oxygen producers near the surface, and, down below, anaerobes – oxygen haters – more primitive bugs that have pretty much retreated to the underground, through vents and cracks and so on, like this one. There's water down there, in the permafrost, even aquifers of liquid water, as I said. Surface ice at the poles. But the deep vents are a very comfortable place to be, for an oxygen-averse, chemical-eating bug. The vents are warm. And there is plenty of moisture – you sometimes see a kind of fog.'

Emma nodded. 'Right. I get it. This is a bigger planet than Earth, and the inner heat, the geothermal energy, is that much greater too. So the fissures, the vents must run deep.'

'True enough,' said Nicola. 'It is dark and static down there, and so the bugs organise themselves into great sheets – biofilms, or microbial mats – billions of individual cells. They self-organise, they cooperate. We even think they communicate, chemically, through what's called quorum sensing. As a result, if you go down there, you see these great sheets of slime that appear to – *contain* – the fog, or even direct it in useful ways. Manipulating their environment, optimising it for life. All slowly evolved, you see, over millions of generations. Or billions.'

'I like that,' Anna said. 'Cooperation on an immense scale, by the smallest of organisms. Planet-wide, even, maybe.'

Malenfant grinned. 'Let me guess again. Very Cosmist.'

'Well, so it is,' said Vasily.

Nicola sighed. 'You have to take all this as speculative, though. There's so much to study, so little data gathered yet – and not much comparison data from home. If our anaerobes do have close terrestrial counterparts they must be buried much deeper than on Persephone.'

'Right,' Malenfant said. 'Lighthill will have to tell you about an exception we found, Nicola. In another corner of the manifold. Vanilla Earth. A kind of museum of anaerobes . . . or a refuge.'

She looked interested, if puzzled.

'But here,' said Vasily, holding up the finger that had scooped up the green, 'there *are* also green bugs, living alongside anaerobes. Perhaps hard to find . . .'

Anna was staring beyond Malenfant, at something behind him. She stood up. 'Maybe it's not always so very hard to find. Malenfant . . .'

Emma turned to see. And yelled, 'Malenfant!'

Malenfant frowned, began to turn.

It happened in a flash.

All he saw was a mass, huge, heavy. Heading straight for him.

Anna leapt at him, with remarkable speed, strength and agility in the stronger gravity. She caught him around the waist, like a rule-stretching football tackle.

But as he fell backwards, he saw that the mass approaching him was fast too.

It was a green mound, sleek and moist, somehow rearing up, just where he had been standing. A motile blob, bigger than he was. He hadn't seen it approach, or heard it. But he recognised it, had seen this before.

He was being attacked by a pitcher's mound.

All this in a flash. Now, with Anna hauling him aside, he fell hard in the tough gravity. His helmet slammed against the ground, and his head rattled.

That was all he knew.

66

Tell me more. Please. I've rested, I promise . . .

I speak of your future. Of my future. Of possible futures.

Different futures caught in the manifold.

You, they, spread out from Earth, the Solar System. Through space and time. Humans did that, and their descendants.

Everywhere they found structure. Emergent complexity. Crude, chance-built replicators, of carbon or silicon or metal, churning meaninglessly in the dark . . .

Like Lighthill's Visitors?

Nowhere did they find true life. And nowhere did they find mind.

I'm trying to understand. No life? You mean, biochemical life? But there is life in the Solar System. In every variant I have visited . . .

Life is rare. No. Unique, in its origin, at least.

Unique?

Its emergence, from unlife. That was unique.

The first origin was the only origin.

The downstreamers came to see that.

It happened only once. Because it was all by chance, you see – all so unlikely.

Chance? You mean, life emerged on Earth? And it only

481

happened *once*? In all the universe, all that time? Only on Earth? . . .

Seriously?

I talked to Emma about this, a few times. And Malenfant. The Fermi Paradox, which Malenfant knew all about. If intelligence had arisen somewhere else, we ought to see them, or their artefacts. Starship wakes . . . The Galaxy is big, but it's older than it's big, he said, in a way. There has been time for civilisations to rise and come this way, over and over.

Emma had *studied* life beyond the Earth. Went looking for it on Mars, Phobos. And she talked about the apparent rareness of life in the universe. To her it was a biological puzzle. The principle of mediocrity, she said, was a basic principle of science. You shouldn't assume you are in some special position in the universe, in space and time. And if Earth was the *only* place life and mind had arisen, you would be violating that principle.

We ought to have found life on Mars, and elsewhere. But we didn't.

Very well. But there is a counter-argument. If life's emergence was rare enough, maybe it would only occur once in the universe. A strange accident.

And are you saying that's what happened?

Think of the complexity of the mechanisms of life, based on proteins in water. Think of it all gathering by chance, by accident.

Organic chemistry is common, of course. Amino acids, proteins, nucleic acids. These occur on many planets, even in interstellar clouds. Everywhere. But the biochemical basis of life, your life, based on these raw materials, is an exquisite mechanism.

A mechanism?

In a sense. Bartholomew is a mechanism. A mechanical exterior, and a computer decision-making system, and a data-processing system, and more. So is life a set of subsystems, of functions. But built of biochemistry. DNA structures host the software, an instruction set, which is read by RNA, which in turn controls the assembly of proteins, the hardware, the structural elements of life. It is a complex, intricate process, full of information flows and feedback mechanisms.

But some human made Bartholomew. Nobody made the machinery of life.

And even the raw materials from which that living machinery was made were themselves complex. The biomolecules underlying all this, that themselves had first to self-assemble by chance from a heap of random components.

I . . . see. It does sound unlikely when you put it that way. All of that assembling by chance.

The miracle of life, then. Not divine, but so unlikely it was unique. It need not have happened at all.

But once life did emerge — perhaps in some crater lake, full of organic compounds, still warmed by the energy of the impact that had created it — once even a rough draft of the essential processes had emerged, by chance — evolution took over. Natural selection, based on a competition for resources, picked out the best of random variants, so that the processes, the molecular machinery, the information flows, rapidly came to a kind of perfection.

Perfection?

Consider. A living cell in your body is full of tiny molecular motors and ratchets, which flawlessly read the DNA sequences and construct proteins. Over and over, flawlessly. The axons that pass information between neurons in your brain also do so flawlessly, and use virtually no energy. And so on. I am a made thing — I, the object into which Michael was downloaded before his biological death. I am as near perfect as my creators could make me — and I do have some qualities you lack, such as effective immortality. But even I have nothing like your exquisite precision, your remarkable efficiency.

OK. So the origin of life is vanishingly rare.

Unique. The downstreamers searched the universe. They found it only once. The accidental self-assembly of a life mechanism, in the murky puddles of a primeval planet.

Their own point of origin. Earth.

And so, OK, that one instance of complex life led to humanity. Who survived, and spread beyond the Earth.

Survived alone, for epochs far beyond the reach of your science.

Alone. A terrifying, wonderful thing.

Alone.

67

'We call them stromes,' Nicola said ruefully. 'The big motile mounds. I should have warned you. We got used to them – and we learned to keep them away. They are attracted by warmth. The heat leakage from your suit . . .'

They were back in the lounge of the New St Petersburg base. For now Malenfant's team were sitting around him, with Nicola, and a few gawkers from the resident staff. At least they had got rid of the smug, competent doctor with cold hands who had treated Malenfant as if he didn't deserve any attention at all, which, luckily for him, was all but true. Still, she had made him miss Bartholomew even more.

In the distance he could hear children playing.

Anna, rueful and regretful, kept bringing Malenfant cups of warm tea, even though he had told her more than once that he forgave her for saving his life. Then again, he couldn't see the bandage wrapped around his own scraped and bleeding scalp, as she could.

Her duties done, Nicola had come to sit with them.

'Stromes,' Emma prompted.

'Yes,' Nicola said. 'The most obvious manifestation we've yet encountered of the oxygen-producing half of the biosphere here.'

'I'll say they were obvious,' Malenfant said wearily.

Emma asked, '"Stromes" for stromatolites?'

'Well, that's the nearest analogy from Earth. A stromatolite, Malenfant, a very ancient form, is a big, static community of bacteria and silt layers. Photosynthetic, oxygen-producing bacteria. At any moment there is a living upper surface at the top, soaking up the sunlight and reproducing. That gets silted over, and dies off, and another layer forms on top. And so it goes, and grows. On Earth such things started fossilising – oh, before the continents formed. Well, a strome looks a bit like that. But it's actually a community of photosynthesisers and anaerobes – they inhabit separate layers within—'

'But your stromatolites are mobile,' Emma put in.

'And they eat people,' Malenfant said ruefully.

Nicola didn't deny it. 'They are motile, yes. We aren't entirely certain *how* they move. For sure, to make a dash across the landscape must consume a lot of a strome's energy store. But yes, they move. Mostly they don't actually attack each other, but we think they do compete. For heat sources. Geothermal, you see.'

Vasily was thoughtful. 'Think I understand. Studied this before; thought about it on Persephone – our Persephone. Two sources of energy for life.' Malenfant saw how he mimed light from above with one splayed hand, warmth from below with the other palm. 'Energy from sunlight above, or geothermal, from the ground. On Earth, geothermal is small compared to sunlight. One fiftieth of one per cent. So the fat, greedy photosynthesisers grabbed the upper world, and the poor old anaerobes struggle to survive on the gruel of that thin leakage of inner heat.

'Here, different. Sun further away, and planet bigger, hotter.

I figure geothermal is ten times as much, maybe a hundred, as a proportion of the total.'

'That's it,' Nicola said. 'We think. So the balance of energy is different, and life has evolved different strategies. You have a deep, rich underground biosphere – down in the vents, you saw some of it – and the beginnings of an oxygen-rich, light-driven biosphere up here. But the upper world isn't so dominant. The stromes are the most obvious example we have of a kind of cooperation between the two. A strome soaks up sunlight, yes, but it has anaerobes toiling in the dark in its inner structure. Not only that, a strome will seek out hot spots in the landscape, even if there is no direct access to the subterranean biosphere.'

Emma said, 'Malenfant, I think the stromes are a little like the electric cars of our day. They are mobile to some extent. But every so often – actually, for much of their existence – they like to settle on hot spots, and on the mineral seeps that come with them, to, well, recharge.'

Nicola said, 'We think there must be mutual paybacks. The deep biosphere is very static. Maybe the mobile stromes help spread genetic diversity around. Or some such.'

Malenfant snapped, 'And that thing that jumped me thought I was a hot spot. Right?'

'Don't flatter yourself,' Nicola said. 'You were just in the way. But the stromes do have form. We first confirmed there was life on Persephone when a strome ate our first Pilgrim lander. Yes, to the strome you were just a hot-spot curiosity, Malenfant. Although if it had managed to overwhelm you, and got through your suit, it could have eaten you without throwing up.'

Emma leapt on that. 'So they're made of the same stuff as us. Right? At the biochemical level.'

Nicola nodded. 'Correct. The basic biochemistry is the same. The same suite of amino acids, the same basic genetic code – the same biochemical pathways, much the same set of proteins, lipids, carbohydrates. So we can eat each other. Oh, Persephone life has evolved away from ours since the seeding, but—'

'What seeding?' Vasily leaned forward, intent. 'What do you mean?'

Again Nicola seemed to hesitate. 'Well, you see, life in this system at least is interplanetary. If you come visit us on Demeter you'll see the same thing again, another example . . . the exact same biochemistry suite as on Persephone, as on Earth, though with different expressions. Different suites of creatures. So it *must* originate from the same source. And the simplest explanation, the most obvious source, so we have always thought—'

'Is Earth,' Emma said.

'Is Earth.' Nicola took a breath. 'That's the best theory we have. Or had, before. I'm not a specialist in biology . . . Life evolves on Earth, is trapped in rocks, it gets blasted off the planet when the comet strikes; the rocks wander in space before falling on another world, like Persephone. Or Demeter.'

'So that's one hypothesis. But now—'

Nicola frowned. 'But now we have your results from Zeus. Once again, identical to terrestrial life, to Persephone life.'

Emma said carefully, 'Look, Nicola, I know we broke your rules by going down to Zeus. But maybe it's for the best. *We* are more used to thinking in a wider frame. For instance, it was always a natural assumption that life on Earth *originated* on Earth. I mean, ours or some other Earth. And if it spread through the Solar System through being blasted off by meteorite impacts, it's natural again that that should come direct from Earth. But in the wider frame there are other possibilities.

'Look – in terms of energy, it's *much* more likely that a package of chemicals, or of simple life forms, will escape from Zeus, say, rather than from Earth – you don't need impacts, it can just be thrown out, almost gently, by geysers from a weak gravity field – and end up on Demeter or Persephone. Zeus is like a custom-built incubator for life. Warm and wet inside. It's even equipped with a kind of delivery mechanism, in its geysers. It's almost ideally constructed to seed Demeter, Persephone.'

Nicola stared at her. 'Even so. That is -- startling, yet compelling. But could life *originate* there? On a low-gravity ice ball? As opposed to a planet like Earth, with its energy flows and mineral riches . . . And the language you use. "Ideally constructed." You have got used to thinking in such terms, I think. But it won't be popular.' She thought further. 'Perhaps there will even be a religious backlash. So much for the Creation story!'

Malenfant caught Emma's eye, and an unspoken message passed between them. Malenfant thought he understood the problem. Nicola's culture was scientific, used to seeing phenomena as natural, without conscious causes behind them. Whereas Malenfant's crew had had a tough education in the existence of conscious causes. *Let's not go into the whole business of the World Engineers. One shock at a time . . .*

And Malenfant was distracted by Anna and Vasily, who had broken away a little, and were gossiping in rapid-fire Russian.

Malenfant frowned. 'Hey. Keep it down, we're trying to have a conceptual breakthrough over here. What's the gossip?'

Anna glanced at him, and back at Vasily. 'Sorry,' she said. 'I think we've come to a decision.'

'Decision? About what?'

'Staying.'

Anna turned to Nicola. 'This base isn't full. Of people, I mean. Is it?'

'It's not at its full complement, no. Not that there's a fixed upper limit. There are plans to expand. Even found other colonies . . . You're asking if you can stay here? On Persephone?'

Vasily hesitated. He and Anna shared another glance, and both nodded, as if reaffirming. 'Yes. We wish to stay.'

Malenfant felt vaguely bewildered. Even betrayed. 'I hadn't seen that coming. Why? You're a long way from home here.'

'True,' Anna said. 'But we spent a long time on Persephone II. This *feels* like home. We adapted, I suppose. And this version is actually more interesting, you have a suite of life here that's like nothing anybody saw before. Fascinating to explore.'

'Also,' Vasily said, 'we know that, as you say, Nicola, super Earths are common – more typical of worlds beyond, in other stellar systems across the sky, than Earth. Learn to live here, live anywhere. *We* already lived on such a world. Cosmism! Let's get started. And we two can play our part.'

Anna glanced at Nicola. 'So what do you think?'

Nicola seemed taken aback. 'You understand,' she said carefully, 'I'm not the commander here. Even the commander has to report back to the UGE hierarchy on Earth.

'However.

'You are clearly capable workers. As you say, you are probably better adapted to the gravity than most of the existing crew. You do bring a remarkable science perspective from this other Persephone. And also,' she said more thoughtfully, 'you are of course our first visitors from – well, from across the manifold. A concept I admit I barely understand myself yet. This is supposed to be a multinational effort. On behalf of all mankind. Why not welcome people from beyond the walls of reality itself? . . .'

As she spoke, clumsily coping in her own way with this flood of extraordinary new ideas, Malenfant felt deeply impressed by this version of Nicola – as with all the versions he had met – for her flexibility and clearness of thinking. Her sheer competence.

Old regret stabbed at him once again.

Apparently impulsively, Emma leaned over to the Russians and grabbed their hands. 'But you'll be stuck here. Won't you? Once we're gone. With no way back home, to your own mother Russia . . . Or to Nadezhda and Maria and Irina on Persephone II . . .'

'Not for now,' Vasily said. 'Regretful. But, has not this journey of ours opened up the manifold to mankind? I can see future where there will be more visitors coming through Anteros and Phobos and Zeus and other portals, and manifold and connecting routes will be explored, the manifold mapped . . . One day, we will be able to go home, as easy as riding Kiev metro. But until then—' He spread his hands. 'We have work to do here. *This* is home.'

'And perhaps,' Anna said gruffly, 'what we build here may atone for all we destroyed on that other Persephone. The hurt we inflicted.'

Vasily bowed his head, and reached for her hand.

Malenfant became aware that Emma had been silent for a while. He turned to her. Her face blank, she was staring into space, evidently too distracted even to take in the news about Anna and Vasily.

'Hey. What's wrong?'

'Just trying to think my way through this. I guess I'm still getting used to life in the manifold. So, OK, life on Earth *here* was seeded from the ice moon, Zeus. I can accept that. And on Persephone III, Demeter. *But there's no Zeus in our Solar System.* So where the hell did *we* come from? Answer me that, Malenfant. Where?'

He thought it over. 'Maybe Deirdra, on Zeus, is finding that out right now.'

The next day, Nicola reported that Anna and Vasily were allowed to stay on Persephone, for now. Maybe for good. But she had been ordered to bring Malenfant and Emma up to the base on Demeter, the second moon. She hurried them along; the lander was due to leave soon.

And on Zeus, in her slow, cautious, bewildered way, Deirdra continued to communicate with the thing inside the ice moon.

68

Solitude, in the end, shaped everything about the downstreamers.

The first priority, of course, was to survive. For if they failed, perhaps none would ever replace them, in a universe already slowly dissipating, running down. The idea of that slow unfolding without even a mind to observe it was unbearable.

So they became farmers.

Your children. In the distant future. Farmers of worlds.

We had given up farming, in my time. In the twenty-fifth century. The only farms were museums. We tended the world we inherited. But I . . .

They had no choice. The universe was not as fecund as it had once been.

Farmers of worlds. As the stars cooled, and long winter of the universe closed in.

Then farmers of the last stars, when the galaxies themselves, all but exhausted of raw materials, began to dim.

Then, as the galaxies evaporated, the dead stars drifting away, the downstreamers became farmers again, of the great galaxy-centre black holes – sources of vast amounts of energy, if properly managed. Later yet, they farmed the still greater black holes that lingered at the heart of superclusters of galaxies: monstrous entities that were gathered, deliberately, in great slow fleets, gathered and merged. For, the more massive a hole, the slower it evaporates. And the longer it can sustain life.

Yet, ultimately, even the mightiest black holes dissipated. Like flaws in spacetime, slowly healing.

A new, darker, poorer age began. And the long-gone epoch when life had emerged – when the stars had shone – was known as the afterglow of the Big Bang.

Still they persisted. They found a way to preserve themselves in the foundations of spacetime itself. This was a lossless substrate, where no energy was expended to preserve their thoughts. It was a refuge.

But this was finite, a finite resource. It would hold only a finite number of thoughts. When it filled up, no more change would be possible. A nightmare prospect for such minds – a kind of stasis. A kind of living death.

And in the future lay a more profound loss. Dark energy, a kind of antigravity field, would tear it all apart – even the almost static, most conservative downstreamer communities, that had lasted so long.

Even their archives would be lost.

There was despair.

Libraries became bonfires.

I . . . understand. I think. I came from a time, a world that was going to end. Only a few thousand years ahead. Surely we, the last survivors, would have succumbed to despair in the end.

But *I* didn't give up.

No. And the downstreamers did not give up. They, or some of them, found a way to create a different story.

I don't understand—

They found a way to touch the past.

69

On Demeter, the main landing area was a high, arid plain, a safe ten kilometres from the main buildings of the colony, New Paris, itself. Malenfant had seen little of this when he and Emma had first landed here, with Nicola, having said their goodbyes to Vasily and Anna on Persephone.

Now, a few days later, he was getting a better look, as the two of them, once more with Nicola, were bussed back out to the landing site. They came here this time to greet Lighthill after his own descent from space.

The morning sky was spectacular, Malenfant discovered, on climbing out of the bus. The air of Demeter was tall – the low gravity gradient saw to that – but it was thin and, above the lower layers, clear and dry. There could be low cloud, but when that melted away you could often see stars, even in the fifty-hour daylight.

And of course the huge, complex face of the primary, Persephone III, hung stationary in the sky.

The landing area itself was splashed and scarred by the relics of multiple touchdowns, Malenfant saw. Bare of all but the most robust specimens of the local life, and yet to be colonised by the hardiest Earth species that were, in some places, as Malenfant had already seen for himself, spreading tentatively from the greenhouses of New Paris, and other settlements here on Demeter. Today another scar would be left on that much-abused ground, once the New Parisians had landed the shuttle bringing Geoff Lighthill down at last from his lonely vigil aboard the *Harmonia*.

Despite Lighthill's own protests, he would be accompanied by a couple of local medics; he had spent too many months in zero gravity.

Malenfant's own ride down from space to this place had been nothing like as tough as the Apollo-like descent to Persephone, a super Earth. Indeed the landing craft had been more like the old space shuttle once flown by Malenfant himself, but in conditions of low gravity and thick air better suited to the logic of the design.

Now Malenfant thought he could see that shuttle, returning once more, scraping a contrail across the sky. And it didn't surprise him to see the glider begin a wide, sweeping turn, still very high in the sky.

'Look at that,' Malenfant said to Nicola. 'Manoeuvres to lose energy. S-turns, we called them. I say *we* – you and I. When we flew space shuttle boosters.'

Nicola stared, curious, cautious, her face obscured by goggles and oxygen mask, a strip of flesh at her forehead exposed to the local air. 'Yes. You spoke of this. The other me who got to fly American spaceships. What luck.'

'Luck. Until that last flight.'

They had talked this through more than once, and Malenfant had become determined not to bring it up again. So much for that resolution.

But Nicola slipped her gloved hand into his, and squeezed, as they watched Lighthill's shuttle, still high, bank and turn again, shedding more orbital energy.

70

What do you mean, touch the past? Time travel?

Not that. Not physically.

Think of it this way.

The equations of physics are symmetrical, in time. A radio transmitter sends messages forward in time, in radiations scattering away from itself. But the underlying equations of electromagnetism have another solution which shows radio waves moving backward *in time, coming from across the universe, converging on the transmitter. Advanced waves, they are called, versus the more familiar retarded waves.*

The downstreamers manipulated boundary conditions to select reverse-time solutions to such experiments.

I don't understand any of that. But I have a feeling it doesn't matter.

We will have time to discuss it.

In short the downstreamers found a way to send a message, to their own deep past. Indeed, your past.

And the receptors of that message were the most sophisticated information-processing machines in all of creation at that time. And therefore the most – open.

Sophisticated. Given what you've said already – you mean, human minds? Human brains?

The brains of children. Growing, malleable. Receptive.

And they sent the message, their instruction set, as deep in time as they could – to the earliest point where the technology was available, as needed to achieve the downstreamers' goals.

It was as if the brightest of children, all across the planet, had the same waking dream. A vision, of what had to be done. What had to be built.

They were feared. When their abilities emerged, even individually, and especially when their joint projects began to coalesce, most were killed. Many killed by their own parents.

I . . . am sorry. I suppose I understand, but—

My name is Michael. I was born in the year 2001, in a village called Natakindi, in Zambia. It was a very poor place, where if you were lucky you got money from a relative working for the government, and the women foraged in the bush. We had nothing. I was an orphan. Yet I . . . developed. I understood later that, for example, I had deduced the principles of special relativity from watching the behaviour of light beams from an old flashlight.

A teacher spotted my potential and, seeking reward for himself, reported me to the authorities. At that time many children like myself were emerging, across the world.

You were dreaming the dreams of the downstreamers.

They called us blue children, among other names. We were gathered up and put in institutions, where we were studied, punished, exploited, contained. And ultimately we were to be destroyed. That was the plan.

For people feared us.

I would have died in obscurity. Unable to fulfil my destiny. Probably killed before adulthood.

Emma Stoney saved me. Emma Stoney who had come to my village, and cried. I saw many children cry. Before Emma Stoney, I had never seen an adult cry.

I survived Africa. I contributed to the project, and survived that. I saw what came next.

And what did come next?

We fulfilled our project.

Everything changed.

Have you heard of vacuum decay?

Vacuum decay . . . I think so.

The universe itself is unstable. Right? It's in a high energy state, but a precarious one, like, like a rock balanced on a thin pillar. Push it one way or another—

And it falls over, falls to a lower energy state, and smashes. The vacuum itself has many stable states which—

I get the idea.

This was our project. The transformation of the universe, through the provoking of vacuum decay.

It was a remarkable process.

It began in a much-damaged school. A mundane setting. The children's impossible experiments looked like so much junk to the watching adults. Home-made toys. But when they built their design from the future, when they triggered their technology, the effects, the destabilisation, spread out at lightspeed.

The school was destroyed in less than a millionth of a second. Earth in half a second, less. The Moon in a few seconds. The bubble reached the Sun—

I see. I get it. The end of the world. At the hands of children. You demolished the universe? So people were right to fear you, then.

But the way your balancing rock was pushed off its pillar, by the efforts of the blue children, was precisely done.

It was not a single new universe that emerged from the rubble, but a collection. A family, a brood of daughters bursting from the womb. All blank slates in the beginning. But each of them was rich in black holes, with rips in the fabric of spacetime. So the daughter universes were linked, causally. Like a tree, with branches and branchlets and twigs, budding one off another—

You are talking about the manifold. This – back-in-time gesture of the blue children – *created* the manifold? Whole spacetimes, splitting and diverging.

And the technology used to access it—

The blue hoops?

Artefacts of folded time. They were created in the same instant. Though it was an instant outside any spacetime. Your language is not sufficient.

The oldest technology in the universe, then. In all the universes. Quite a thing. No wonder we were baffled.

And I am the second oldest technology.

I survived because Malenfant had taken me into space, to Cruithne, companion of Earth, where a manifold portal waited. Once through there . . .

Once the manifold existed, the next phase of the project began.

I, and perhaps others like me, was projected back, to the beginning. Back through a splintered, bifurcating spacetime. Even beyond the antenna brains of the blue children.

I emerged in roiling turmoil, not long after the singularity itself.

I was then as I am now. A mind embedded in an artefact. A kind of knot of spacetime. A knot now locked up in the core of this moon.

The singularity? The Big Bang? And the power you put out – your heat suffuses the whole moon—

Comes from a link back to the singularity itself, through a spacetime flaw. A feed of antimatter. The nearest analogy in your physics is perhaps a 'white hole'.

OK. I'm not going to claim to understand any of that. We

thought the radiation of your moon was like – ancient sunlight. That was what drew us to you.

I, my casing, was designed that way. An oddly nostalgic touch by the downstreamers. A nod to the young Sun which nurtured their forebears. A kind of—

Signature?

Yes.

But you were still – you. In some sense. You remembered some of it.

The downstreamers were more like librarians, or museum curators, than any other human vocation. They thought of me as an archive. So I am, I suppose. But an archive that has grown with time. But I retained my identity. As Michael. Or – as I remembered it, at least. As I have observed, and learned. And fulfilled a greater purpose.

What purpose?

To spread life.

I could not create it, but I could disseminate it. Encourage it. Explore it. Record the evolution, the destiny of that life. Discover its full potential.

But in that age, when the afterglow was still bright, first I had to wait for planets to evolve that could host that life.

71

The shuttle swept down to an easy landing on fat wheels. In the thin air Malenfant heard a screech of brakes, and a roar of some retro engine, a rocket or a jet; he saw an exhaust plume near the nose.

Remarkably quickly, the stubby little craft rolled to a stop.

Ground crew, waiting behind Malenfant and the rest, hurried forward now. They fenced off the craft's nose and tail, wary of exhaust fumes and leaks of propellant, and then pushed access equipment up to the side of the craft where a hatch opened briskly.

Only minutes after the landing was complete, the workers scrambled up a rolling staircase and helped the flight crew, in bulky pressure suits, walk slowly down to the ground.

Lighthill was predictably a special case. He emerged from the ship already strapped into a wheelchair. A hydraulic platform lifted him smoothly down to the ground. Malenfant's first impression was that his head was too large for his body, and it lolled, until an attendant packed his neck with cushions.

'Shit,' Malenfant murmured. 'Worse than I thought.'

'Not a word,' Emma said. 'Not even your cherished banter, Malenfant.'

'Noted,' Malenfant said without resentment. 'He's been through hell.'

'No,' Nicola murmured. 'You told me his story. He has lost his crew. One by one. Most of them far from his ability to save them, or even join them in death. He is still in hell. And he will never leave. So, smile for him.'

A grin fixed on her own face, she marched forward. Malenfant followed.

Emma just ran. When she got to Lighthill, she leaned over and folded him in her arms, gently, Malenfant saw, as you would handle an old, old person.

72

So I saw it all. Almost from the beginning.

The birth of the universe: a flash of heat.

After just a second the familiar subatomic particles of our reality crystallised from a soup of energy. Then nucleosynthesis began – the gathering of those particles into atomic nuclei. Structure quickly emerged, on the small scale, as atoms formed and collected into molecules. Chemistry began.

And on a greater scale gravity began to accumulate those molecules into larger and larger structures. Huge, amorphous molecular clouds broke up into galaxies, which were incubators for generations of stars and planets.

It happened so quickly.

Just four billion years after the singularity, star formation peaked. The Sun was yet to be born; the universe will last a long time after the Sun has died. Yet never again will it be so full of light as it was then, as I saw it.

It must have been glorious. I can't imagine it.

No. You can't.

And the stars and planets were incubators for life?

Potentially. Potentially only. I travelled the new worlds. I sought life, or the beginnings of it. Perhaps Earth had not been unique

*after all. Perhaps things would be different in this new reality. So
I searched.*

*And there were some stirrings. As I told you, oddly, the most
promising in the beginning were more mechanical than organic.
In the right circumstances, complexity can emerge from accidents
of other kinds than the biochemical. And as I travelled I began
to take with me elements of this life. Elements, winnowed by a
different kind of evolution, but limited in potential.*

*Elements such as the memory-crystal material you call Phobos
glass—*

Yes. It lined the passageways we passed through.

*On its origin world, a cold, metallic place, this served as genetic
material, as the substrate for a kind of DNA.*

And, mechanical life.

You're speaking of the creatures we call the Visitors.

*And creatures like them. Not robots, in the sense of golems built
by other, superior sorts. A product of an evolution of their own,
though a dead end in terms of complexity. They can only advance
so far. They are useful. They survive with me.*

And the fusion-rocket Towers? Did the Visitors – umm,
invent them?

*Oh, no. The Towers were a relic of yet another mechanical life
form, long extinct. A migratory form, who pushed their worlds
from star to star. The Towers are cultivated rather than built.
Grown like trees on a suitable substrate, their natural root-engines
rationalised for efficiency.*

Ah. I think we speculated about this. The Towers, growing
like trees.

*Earth, the Solar System itself, was not created until some nine
billion years after the singularity.*

I watched, as the young planets coalesced.

Almost immediately life arose, on Earth. The First Earth.

CHON life, Emma calls it. Earthlike life. So that was its one and only creation.

It was. I saw it. Life was there, almost as soon as the rocky surface solidified. Yes – I saw that unique emergence. The origin of all of us, of everything meaningful in this universe. On just one world among trillions in this galaxy alone.

It was – surprising.

After all, early Earth was such a hostile environment. At a few hundred million years old, under a dimmer Sun, it retained its thick primordial atmosphere of carbon dioxide, methane, steam. It had a day of only a few hours. The continents had yet to form, and under brick-red skies, the global ocean was shallow, muddy, broken by a few islands. It was hardly a promising venue for life.

Yet life quickly emerged, self-assembled, became established. I saw it.

This was the First Earth, then. The only source of true life, of mind, in all of space and time.

And I was there.

And now my job was to propagate that life.

73

As the rover carried them back over the dusty ground towards New Paris, the first thing Lighthill commented on was the flags.

If he had noticed anything of the local life – the air pods, the coral-like trees – he didn't mention it. The flags, though, caught his attention. Malenfant had to concede it was a spectacular display. Set up over a field of solar-energy panels – across which a handful of workers were brushing away dust, probably an unending chore – a picket line of poles stood, each with a small, colourful flag held out by stiffening rods.

'Good Lord. A regular parade. Like Whitehall on Empire Day.'

Nicola, sitting up beside the driver, called back, 'Over a hundred and ninety flags, one for each of the nations of Earth. Well, on our Earth right now. Now being 2019. Sorry – I'm still getting used to this kind of conversation. I should say some of the flags are disputed – they don't reflect nations so much as peoples seeking independence from some other nation.' She looked back with a grin. 'You're British, as I am, Commander Lighthill. So you might recognise Scottish, Welsh, even Cornish flags up there. Others – Catalonian—'

'Good Lord.'

'Well, we went for inclusivity rather than categorisation.

Also, less easy to see, much of the lower section of each pole is plastered with corporate logos. If we have to make some kind of publicity broadcast, or even a private thank-you, we pick out the correct flag, the right logo, to frame the shot.' She shrugged. 'Otherwise we don't pay them much attention, to be honest. Here is *here*. The flags are just something else we have to keep clear of the dust.

'Nearly there.'

74

I, this form – as I told you, I am now an artefact of folded time myself. Primordial, if you like.

As soon as the First Earth formed, as soon as life began, I was dipped into the heart of a moon of water ice and rock. The Galaxy was already full of such objects. The ice moons themselves incubated life, from the seeds I gathered from the First Earth, using allies like the Visitors. Yes, I disseminated that life using the ice moons. And in such moons I was able to travel between the stars.

How? Never mind. For now. You spread life, then. Using the ice moons. With geysers? Spraying worlds with life-laden water?

It did not always work. Life did not always take, or survive.

You must understand that arenas capable of hosting life, especially rich, complex life are rare. Vanishingly rare. This is obvious. After all life arose only on one planet, Earth.

To nurture such life, a planet needs to be close enough to its star that liquid water can survive on its surface. The planet must be of the right size, not so small that it cools too quickly, not so large that its surface roils with heat, its gravity crushes, its air chokes. . . . The most common kind of rocky world is what you call a super Earth. Like Persephone, bigger than Earth.

Life is doing well on Persephone. Nicola Mott's Persephone, Persephone III.

But of course it cannot emerge there. On such worlds. We know that because it never has.

And even when, if, life is established on a suitable planet, there are many filters through which it must pass to survive. Some are cosmological – a nearby supernova or gamma ray burster could sterilise a world. The world itself could become unstable, through volcanism for instance. The climate could collapse into lethal heat or silent cold. An over-complex biota could collapse on itself, for example through some runaway pathogen. And if intelligence arises, such disasters as warfare or a catastrophic wasting of the environment—

I understand. But sometimes it worked. Once in a hundred?

Less than that. Far less. But, yes, it worked. And at a time when the universe was as fecund, potentially, as it would ever be.

A dead universe came, tentatively, alive. Thanks to the efforts of myself, and others like me.

That's . . . wonderful. Terrifying. And we did it all, we humans. What a responsibility.

But it was the Solar System that was always my primary target.

The System that had hosted the first, and only, spontaneous biogenesis. Of course it was the centre of attention, both my own and that of my masters in the far downstream.

Now my masters called me back to the Solar System. For they wished to explore other possibilities.

75

Arrival at the base was straightforward. The tractor just drove up to a port, from which attendants dragged collapsible tunnels and sets of steps to lock over the tractor's hatches. The passengers were moved seamlessly from one pressurised environment into another, with a little awkward handling of Lighthill in his chair.

They all kept their external suits on until the dome was sealed up around them. Even then they had to endure a short ritual as the suits were vacuumed, then hosed down, to remove any dust before they entered the main living areas. Then, naked, the travellers went through a series of showers themselves.

Malenfant understood all this, and patiently endured. Demeter's dust was not so caustic as that of Mars, its remote, arid manifold twin, but could contain contaminants such as peroxides. And, even after years of study, he knew by now, nobody on Demeter was quite sure whether it might be possible for native life to cause some kind of infection in the human population.

On the other hand Malenfant knew that already terrestrial plants, some genetically engineered, some not, were growing out on the open surface.

For all the short-term caution – for all the current language of contamination – everybody knew that a long-term mixing-up of the biospheres was inevitable, and to be welcomed. That seemed to be the theme of this post-war settlement, Malenfant mused, as much as it had one. A mixing. A cooperation. Of nations, and of biospheres.

Once they were released into a living area they paused, to let Lighthill take a look around.

After some days here, Malenfant had got used to it all, and now tried to see it through fresh eyes. This was the colony's largest unit, Malenfant had learned, and the oldest. It was a geodesic dome, double-skinned for safety, but translucent, and letting in much of the pale daylight while the remote Sun was up. The structure was much airier, lighter, than the domes down on Persephone itself. But the sunlight was just as wan, and fluorescent tubes glowed across the roof structure.

A big area of roof panelling was transparent, though. Full of planet, a huge crescent, unmoving, locked into its position in the sky.

Malenfant spotted Lighthill looking up at this.

'We call this little spot Persephone Park,' Nicola said.

Malenfant said, 'They wanted one place where you could just sit and see Persephone, motionless in the sky, going through its phases.'

'Ah,' Lighthill said. 'I wonder if I could spot my *Harmonia*.'

'You know we left a skeleton crew aboard,' Nicola said. 'Two of our best young engineers—'

'Who come from an entirely different technological tradition.'

Malenfant murmured, 'Not that different. I know how you feel, Lighthill. But they'll keep her safe for you.'

Nicola made to move them on. 'We've sorted out a cabin for you next to Malenfant and Emma, Commander. Why don't we—'

'No. Please.' Lighthill held up a hand before he could be rolled away. 'I know the quacks will want to prod and poke at me, and stick needles in wherever they can find a vein, and so forth. Plenty of time for that. But I've been stranded in space for far too long. Guided tour first,' he said, wheezing a little. 'And a bit of company, eh? Then off to Matron.' He looked up at Nicola, almost pleading. 'Why, I even emptied my bladder before the descent.'

Nicola glanced at her medics, who shrugged. She smiled and beckoned, wordlessly.

As they rolled off, with Emma now pushing Lighthill's chair, Malenfant saw that one of the medics followed, a short, discreet distance behind.

And as they walked a splinter of light in the sky, seen through a different window, caught Malenfant's eye. A bright double star, not far from the great bow that was crescent Persephone. Earth and Moon. The only moon in the Solar System visible to the naked eye across astronomical distances, like this. He felt an odd swell of pride.

Even if he had a sudden, odd intuition that he was never again going to see that double world up close. He shook his head, trying to get rid of the mood.

Then he turned away and walked after the others.

76

Once more I came back, to this part of the manifold, to this clutch of possibilities – came at a time when the Sun itself was very young, born from a collapsing interstellar cloud.

Before the planets had fully formed.

Already there was life, of course, on this young Earth. It had happened very quickly.

Now my project was to – explore – that formation.

OK. So I've had to learn something of how the planets formed. A big cloud of dust and gas and ice spun around the new Sun, flattening into a disc. The dust and ice stuck together in grains that became pebbles that became boulders—

That coalesced into planets, yes. Coalesced violently. But it was in the later stages of formation, when the giants had already emerged, and the inner system was still full of planetesimals, objects themselves the size of small planets, that I was able to—

Manipulate?

Manipulate. Yes, you know some of it. The giant planets themselves were migrating.

And by pushing around lesser objects, such as Persephone, you could tweak that process. To shape a whole planetary system the way you wanted it. The great migration was the engine of worlds. I think it was Geoff Lighthill who worked it out in the end.

You must understand that I was populating the manifold. Filling it with variant forms of the Solar System. Different arenas for the development of life. I tweaked, I experimented. That was my mandate. To explore what might have been.

I made copies. Copies of the whole Solar System.

My first experiment was to divert an impactor, a young rogue planet, so that it hit Mercury.

Why would you do that? To wreck a world—

Not wreck it. I needed raw materials for what came next. The iron of the exposed core of Mercury. For such purposes as cladding manifold portals in rock and ice.

You're talking about Phobos. And Anteros in this System . . . You *built* those objects?

The Visitors did on my behalf. The portals, of course, primordial objects of folded time, existed already.

So you meddled with Mercury, to turn it into a mine.

And you meddled with Earth too.

77

Away from the entry area, the artificial light inside the big dome became more dominant, the setting more functional. A base of Demeter concrete supported a series of blocky inner structures, some of which, Malenfant knew, were themselves capable of holding breathable air pressure – a backup in case the main dome ever failed.

The first place they stopped on Lighthill's tour was, to Malenfant's eye, a warehouse, full of shelves, neatly labelled, but stacked high with . . . junk.

'The swap shop, we call this,' Nicola said. 'A kind of temporary store. We are a long way from home here, and our native manufacturing facilities are minimal, still. And so we are always running out of stuff – or, more specifically, always missing the one crucial spare part you need to complete the job. So if you have anything that's broken or worn out or just don't need any more, you dump it in here – we have a catalogue, you index it under various headings. And then, when *I* need a spare part for my left-handed toilet flush, I have at least a fighting chance of finding what I need, or can improvise from, right here.'

Lighthill nodded, very cautiously. Close to, his neck looked distressingly scrawny. 'I understand why this is your most important place.'

'Yes. More so than First Landing, though we built a little monument there. The religious types would argue for one chapel or another. The hospitals have a claim, especially as we have had our first births in there, the first on Demeter. Others would argue for our first cemetery. But to me *this* sums up the spirit of the place. Making do. Getting on with it.' She smiled at Lighthill. 'What we British think of as our best qualities.'

Lighthill nodded in evident approval.

They moved on, Lighthill's chair slowly rolling. They encountered only a few people. One child, maybe four years old, who stared openly, before her father pulled her away. Lighthill, though, smiled back at her, and winked.

'Don't seem to be too many folk around,' he said in his wheezy rasp. 'I know your colony can't be that big, but . . .'

Malenfant said, 'There's something you're missing, Lighthill. At any one time half the population of this place is asleep.'

Lighthill thought that over, and gave Malenfant a weak smile. 'Ah. I imagine you are referring to the hundred-hour day. On this moon, with one face locked towards its primary, Persephone.'

'You'll like this, Lighthill. With your orderly mind. A hundred hours, equivalent to about four of the twenty-four-hour Earth days we all evolved in. Right?'

'"In which we all evolved" would be better. Very well . . .'

'So,' Nicola said, 'we call that a week. A Demeter week, of four days − but we break that down further into eight twelve-hour shifts. And at any moment, half the population is up and active, and the other half − well, not. You can imagine it's all a little more flexible than that. But it does mean we can hot-bunk. We don't need dormitory space for the whole population at once. And so we can support more people than the space would suggest, while giving everybody something like a normal sleep cycle.'

517

'And getting more done. Very good. You're right, that does appeal to my rather limited imagination. Although I think I would have devised a more complex scheme of overlapping eight-hour shifts, which—'

'You can tell us how we got everything wrong when you've had the guided tour, Commander,' Nicola said, not unkindly. 'Once we've shown you what we got *right*.'

They emerged from a passage, and faced a glass wall. Beyond which lay bright sunlight, and green.

78

I came back to Earth, the First Earth. Already rich with life, but which even now still had to face its greatest bombardments. The most significant was a collision with a protoplanet as large as Mars—

Malenfant says they called that event the Big Whack. When a huge impact caused a kind of giant splash, with Earth and Moon forming from the debris.

I was there.

I saw.

It was a remarkable sight to see. For a time Earth had a ring, like Saturn's, of glowing debris. A ring of rock and iron, though, not ice.

But life persisted, Deirdra. Even through that calamity. It may have emerged from the most unlikely of causal chains, but once established Earth life was resilient. Extraordinarily resilient.

I had studied the creation of life. Now my makers wanted me to study its potential.

79

'We won't take you through into the greenhouses for now,'
Nicola murmured to Lighthill. 'You'd need a facemask. The
doctors say that your breathing might be compromised. And
when you're a little healthier you'll be able to get up close to
the mining and manufacturing areas. Where we are extracting
iron ore and so forth . . .'

'No matter, no matter. Magnificent sight, under this clear
dome. And it's so bright! Given we are so far from the Sun.'

'Most of the tree species are from high latitudes, where the
light is low anyhow.'

'*That* one looks like an oak, though.' Lighthill pointed with
a bony finger.

'An oak it is, and growing quickly – too quickly.'

'Ah,' Lighthill said. 'That one-third gravity. Like Mars. Trees
three times as tall as Earth's – that oak will grow like a sequoia,
perhaps!' He laughed, but it trailed off into a cough.

'Maybe we'll do that one day. But for now we don't *want* all
the carbon in our air captured in trees.'

And Malenfant found himself thinking of an afforested
Sahara, in a different strand of reality, where the plan had
been the diametric opposite – to capture a significant chunk
of Earth's atmosphere's carbon dioxide component, by

growing a forest that spanned half a continent.

They moved on to a more expansive greenhouse, behind a sealed protective wall of glass. The area beyond had windows open to the air of Demeter, Malenfant saw, and the sunlight was more or less natural. Just a stretch of the sandy ground, fenced off by glass panels, at first glance, and littered with what looked like peculiar rock formations.

But were not.

'Tell me what I'm seeing,' Lighthill said a little plaintively.

By now Malenfant had seen it all before. He leaned down and pointed. 'OK, Lighthill. See that thing like a dead tree stump? Or maybe a termite mound—'

'Over there. Three feet high. Some geological feature?'

Malenfant shook his head. '*Life*. Demeter life this time. At the height of the day it opens up, and reveals – not leaves – panels of a dull green.'

'Photosynthesis?'

'Yeah. Not exactly like ours, different active chemicals, but the same idea. Energy from the Sun, used to crack the air and grow – taking the carbon and releasing a little bit of oxygen into the air. But at night it closes up.' He pointed again. 'That thing that looks like a fat pine cone? Same idea. They open up in the day, take the light and the moisture, and then fold up at night.'

Now Nicola pointed. 'And that growth that looks like a bit of coral?'

Bent over, twisted – quite ugly, Malenfant thought, looking at it afresh.

Nicola said, 'That's Demeter's equivalent of a tree. We think. It actually has rings, like a tree's, but very fine – we think that thing may be fifty thousand years old. Very old, very tough, very enduring.'

Malenfant patted Lighthill's shoulder. 'Not unlike us two, Geoff.'

Lighthill looked bewildered.

80

So you started to explore the manifold.

Indeed. If you close your eyes I can show you.

Inside my head? I . . . OK. I guess it's no worse than using the bangles.

Tell me what you see.

Umm . . . A planet. Like Jupiter, thick air, bands of clouds across its face, but the colours are pale, the sunlight bright. No Moon . . . Oh. *Earth.* This is how Earth would have been without a Moon at all. Like Geoff's Vanilla Earth. No impact.

Correct. Bigger, a thicker atmosphere – not as welcoming for complex life; ideal incubator for the primitive – the world on which that primitive life evolved, after all.

Another.

Oh. More bands of cloud. But this looks – tilted over. Like Uranus?

An Earth which was left tipped on its side by a glancing impact: the poles left resting in the plane of the Solar System. This one is a world of massive seasonal shifts, of huge migrations of life washing across the planet, from the winter pole to the summer. Here, the most advanced hominin is a Neanderthal-type. Robust, enduring.

Like the Hams of Persephone II . . . How did *they* get there? Or to Persephone, for that matter.

All in good time. More examples.

That moon is *bright* . . . A world with a larger moon than my Earth's?

Yes. Its huge tides made Earth's coasts uninhabitable, the seas savage. Here, there were no crossings of the great oceans until air travel was developed, and disparate cultures emerged on the continents. Disparate evolutions, in fact.

Now—

I see an even bigger moon, with seas and continents of its own.

Now—

Lots of moons, all of them small, like Jupiter's system of satellites.

Now—

An Earth with rings like Saturn—

Now—

Stop. Please. I can't take it all in.

Stop.

Bartholomew, the doctor, surviving inside me, chides me for tiring you.

But all these examples, you see, were generated by the manipulation of a single event: the Moon-creating collision. And I propagated life, in one alternate after another. One new destiny after another.

And I kept one Earth whole and entire, untouched by giant collisions. Indeed in a Solar System, similarly preserved.

The Vanilla System.

It was a kind of . . . reference point. Later I used it as a sanctuary. A reserve, if you will. It was useful, given wide projects.

OK. Let me sum up. So biochemical life was created once, on the First Earth. That was the womb. You create the manifold, all these alternate Earths. None have life of their own. And meanwhile this ice moon of yours, with its warm interior, its geysers – this is a machine for what Malenfant could call panspermia, I think.

So you scooped up samples, and travelled to alternate versions of the Solar System. Right? Where Earth *hadn't*, spontaneously, spawned life. And seeded them.

I did. I crossed the manifold. A tree of branching, interconnected possibilities.

But the seeding, usually, was indirect. In most iterations it was Mars – or Demeter, or an equivalent world – that was first to become hospitable. Before Earth itself, I mean. Being smaller, Mars lost its thick primordial atmosphere more readily, liquid water gathered on its surface first . . . Mars did not originate life, but it was a useful secondary incubator. But the tragedy for Mars, in most iterations, was that it was simply too small to hold on to its thick, moist air—

Aside from in special instances. Like when it was orbiting Persephone.

Yes. But by the time extinction had overcome Mars, natural processes would, usually at least, have carried the life I had seeded to other worlds.

I understand that much . . . I think. Meteorites slam into the ground, blasting off chunks of life-bearing rocks. Which then drift through space, until they land on other worlds – Venus, say? Europa? And deliver their passengers. So, what then? Did you just watch life spread – the Earth turn green, the air clear, and the oceans become blue?

But I don't understand why there should be *people* on all these different Earths.

I mean, if the divergence between the worlds is in 1969, like in Malenfant's Nixon Bundle, you'll get people in both . . .

Roads. Even the *same* people, like copies of Malenfant himself. But if the divergence goes all the way back to the creation of the Moon – wouldn't the drastically different conditions have led to different kinds of evolution? Why would any kind of people show up there? Even Neanderthals?

My makers wanted to study the potential of Earth life, and particularly humans, in a variety of circumstances. What might we have become? And so I was given additional responsibilities. New technologies.

Oh. *You* transferred them across. To different worlds.

There was an object Malenfant called the Red Moon – he witnessed it in some iterations – which I used to transfer human samples between realities. And there, under different physical conditions, the differently evolved human stock cross-bred, diverged. There was speciation. At times samples of the successor species were transferred back to Earth – the Neanderthals, for instance, who—

Whoa. Are you serious? You tinkered with human evolution to produce subspecies? And you dumped them back on the Earth? No wonder the fossils baffled the archaeologists.

It was my mandate. It was successful, in its own terms.

What about Persephone? That's been another useful, umm, *resource* for you, hasn't it? A tool to manipulate the evolution of whole planets.

Yes. But also a super Earth, with room for life, and in some iterations relatively close to the Sun . . . It is in this System – with the world you called Persephone III – that it is somewhere near its own optimum location, for life at least. As you and your companions have witnessed.

Yes . . . And Demeter—

Here, Demeter has been kept warm and active by the tides of its giant parent. Demeter is a Mars that was never allowed to die. And indeed in a sense Demeter is the parent world, for in this system it was life that developed there, planted from Zeus, that seeded both the local Earth and Persephone.

Ironic that the existence of this rich Persephone III ended up causing a war on Earth. But that's people for you. So what about Persephone II, in the Vanilla System . . . Neanderthals and dinosaurs?

It was a kind of reserve, and the basis of another experiment. A special one. A sampling across time. In this case not for the purposes of forced speciation, but of comparison. Or, combination.

A defiance of the extinction events.

OK. I think Josh Morris figured that out. Or guessed it, anyhow.

The history of Earth, fecund as it is, is punctuated by extinctions. Each leaving a world impoverished compared to the ecological richness that had been lost.

Right. So, the dinosaurs. A world full of creatures that had spent hundreds of millions of years evolving exquisitely to fit their roles. Most of which just vanished when the comet fell. But what if—

What if they had survived? What if, perhaps in a subtly altered world, they had come into contact with a later biosphere – say, with the evolving mammals?

You built an arena where you could see what happened when Neanderthals met pterosaurs?

Having encouraged speciation on separate worlds, now the downstreamers wished to mix, to combine – not to test strengths, but to see what new life forms, or life strategies, might emerge. What untapped potentials might be revealed.

Yes. Josh did figure it out. Damn it. If only he'd lived to know that. And on Earth, in that System, the Earth Lighthill visited—

On Vanilla Earth we preserved survivors of the very first mass extinction event, when oxygen-producing bacteria had emerged, filled the air with what was effectively a poison, and all but wiped out the archaic anaerobes from which they had evolved. Yes, Vanilla Earth, as a true copy of the First Earth, was used as a seed bed for the further propagation of life. But, yes, it also served as a refuge from that first extinction.

This is my mandate from the downstreamers. To explore the multiverse they created. To look at all the ways life could be played out, all the possibilities inherent in it. To let it run.

Even if people had to die to achieve that?

The downstreamers are not destroyers of worlds. They are creators. Enrichers — though it takes the sacrifice of individuals, even worlds, to achieve that. They are students of the life from which they themselves emerged.

Enrichers? You say that when they are prepared to destroy whole worlds?

My whole world, my Earth?

Did that have to die?

Michael?

81

Lighthill gazed at the enclosed greenery. His voice was a breathy wheeze.

'All this life. On Mars! Or, a kind of Mars. The tides kept it warm, yes? I suspect Josh Morris would have taken one look at this world and worked it all out for himself far more quickly . . .'

Emma put a hand on his shoulder.

'Not that it's a picnic for life here,' Nicola said. 'There is a daily – well, hundred-hour – temperature swing of forty degrees or more. From temperate warmth at noon, to below-freezing cold at night. Every day and night.

'And life has had to adapt. You have tough, deep-rooted plants with leathery skin, that can keep their water from evaporating in the heat of the day, or freezing in the depth of night. Demeter is not unlike a high desert on Earth, in some ways, and we see similar adaptations. Very tough, slow growths – or, in some organisms, a quick dash for the water when it becomes available.'

Lighthill nodded, if cautiously. 'What Mars might have been, eh? But I suppose all these leathery trees and so forth will be pushed aside when terrestrial life gets a foothold. The game's up now, is it?'

Nicola frowned. 'Oh, no. That's not the intention at all, Commander. We will be releasing Earth life, adapted and evolved, out into the landscape, yes. But we aren't going to eliminate the native life. If that looks likely, even locally, we won't release terrestrial organisms at all. We're quite determined about that, us here on the ground, and our governments, as well as the UGE, back us up.' She looked around at them. 'I think I see scepticism. Even surprise. I'm quite sincere.'

Emma nodded. 'I don't doubt it. And I've been trying to puzzle out why. I think it may be your war, Nicola. The Nearly War. All this is a kind of reaction. ' She searched Nicola's face. 'The old ways of doing things – the nation-states that were really nothing but engines for waging war on each other's populations . . . It had to stop, and *this* is the result. Or one result . . . Which is why I totally believe what you say. Sorry. Malenfant will tell you I can get preachy.'

Malenfant grinned. 'Only over about half the explored manifold.'

She elbowed his ribs, not too gently.

'Well,' Lighthill said, 'speaking of the manifold – and I know it's rather premature of me to speak of leaving when I have barely arrived – but at some point we will have to talk about future plans. I'm well aware I need to get myself fit again, I'm sure the gentle gravity of Demeter will be just the ticket, and thank you to my hosts in advance. Similarly we need to get the dear old *Harmonia* shipshape again. Not to mention refuelled. Then we must move on.'

Emma mused. 'Where to, though, Geoff?'

He shook a too-heavy head. 'I've had time to think – too much time, alone. And I believe that we are entering a new phase of our – relationships. With each other, and the manifold itself.

'I believe it is high time that we moved from the exploration of the manifold to consolidating what we've found. We should establish regular transits between the realities, notably those Solar Systems containing Persephones I, II and III. We should replace Cook's *Discovery* with something like the White Star Line, what? But first, of course, I must visit scattered friends. Irina and Nadezhda and little Maria on Persephone II. The graves of those we left behind on Persephone I, and elsewhere. Joshua's grave.

And I must visit the friends and families of those we lost. Joshua's notebooks – his family must have them. And the academic institutions.

'And, Malenfant, Emma, I will if you wish take you home to your own Roads—'

'No,' Malenfant said suddenly. And he found he was surprised by his own interruption.

Surprised by the idea that had suddenly sprouted in his head, fully formed. Yet he knew, immediately, that it was right.

82

Michael.

Hello?

You've gone silent.

I won't let up.

You must know, since Bartholomew knows, that the reason I came with Malenfant on this quest in the first place was because of the Destroyer. The deflected planets, the incandescent wreck of two worlds that was, *is*, going to destroy my home world in a few centuries. *My* Earth, and Malenfant's . . .

And I know now, because we worked it out, my friends and I, that the Destroyer's deflection towards my Earth was deliberately caused – by you, right? Your meddling with the Persephone, Persephone I, in that system. Pushing around planets like it was a game, and dooming my world. Why?

Why, damn it?

You know why.

Do I? You speak of the manifold. All these possibilities of life, explored and studied. So why throw a world into the fire?

It was a side-effect. You calculated it yourselves. The damage done to the Earth by what you called the 'Destroyer event' would be incidental. The target of the deflection is Venus. Not Earth. It will be an impact of a magnitude not seen since the formation of the Solar System itself. Venus would be – reshaped.

What for? For what conceivable purpose would you sacrifice a world? . . . Oh. As you sacrificed Mercury. To get at its iron core. We guessed that.

Deirdra, the story of the Solar System is not over. The Sun is billions of years old; it will burn for billions more years yet. Heating up, pushing any surviving life ahead of it . . .

And you want to be around to watch it. So you need a new mine. Another world stripped. *Venus*, sacrificed. So you can build more fake moons to hold your manifold portals. *That's* what it's all been about?

So that I can build a new manifold sheaf. As with the Earth-Moon impact – now with the Venus-Destroyer collision. A rich flowering of new possibilities, as the Solar System ages . . .

All so you, or your masters, can watch, and observe, and tinker, and record . . .

Until the Sun dies, yes.

And my home world will be sacrificed in the process. As a, a side-effect.

There are many copies in the manifold, which will be spared—

None of them are mine, damn it. None of the copies of my mother will be *my* mother. Do you not understand? When my world is destroyed, everything that I will have cherished will be destroyed.

It can't be helped. In a sense, it has already happened.

Then what must I do?

Come with me.

*

. . . What?

Come with me.

Where to?

You need not die. You are with me now. As is Bartholomew.

I will not die.

We will not die.

Your world, in your memory, will not die.

Soon I will migrate to another sheaf. The Venus Sheaf, after the impact. A sheaf of new manifold possibilities. Think of it.

And then move on, to another world, another sheaf.

Until the Suns die out, the last of them, all of them.

And even then I – with or without you – I will go on.

You are talking about downstream. The very far future.

I will see the age of the black hole farmers. And beyond.

Where those who made me wait for me, and they will listen to my accounts of my achievements, and enfold me in their love.

Love. You speak of love.

I'm trying to get a grip on all this. So humans found themselves alone, in an empty universe. But they filled that universe with life. And they created suites of parallel universes too, and seeded *them*. It's magnificent. I can't deny that.

I think the Russians would have understood. Anna, Vasily. Fedorov, the Cosmists. Their 'common task', the transformation of mankind and the cosmos. Your downstreamers have done it all. No wonder it drew me in.

But there was a cost. Worlds thrown to the fire – worlds like mine. And the destruction of living things – the Runners, reduced by the very presence of the Russians.

Come with me.

I . . .

I.

I am lonely.

Come with me.

Maybe if I come with you we can do things better. Right some wrongs.

Let me speak to my friends.

83

Lighthill studied Malenfant doubtfully. 'You all right, old man? Need to borrow the chair?'

Emma looked at him more worriedly.

'No, no,' Malenfant said. 'Sorry. I'm thinking it through. Or rather I have thought it through, by accident.'

'I can believe that,' Emma murmured.

Impulsively he grabbed her hand. '*Let's stay*. You and I, Emma. Let's stay here. Oh, we can always take trips to the rest of the manifold once Lighthill gets his multidimensional *Titanic* afloat. But – let's make this our home. Demeter, I mean.' He looked at Nicola, who unsurprisingly seemed as startled as the rest at his impulsive outburst. 'I mean it, Nicola,' he said. 'What you're doing here – building a new place, a new world, without the old barriers between peoples – not even between biospheres . . . I didn't come out here looking for this, but I sure feel like I've found it.

'Like I found you, Emma,' and he squeezed her hands harder. There were tears in her eyes – or maybe in his.

But she pulled her hands away. 'You are an idiot, Malenfant. I mean, you're not *my* Malenfant. Just as I'm not *your* Emma Stoney.'

'I know, I know. But we talked about this. You're the Emma

I've got. The one I came to save. Isn't that enough?'

Nicola coughed. 'Well, I hate to intrude . . . Look, we would have a place for you, if you choose to stay. Well, *I* think so, though there are various governance bodies we would have to consult. But in the spirit that welcomes people here from across our world, our Earth – as I've said before, why not from across the manifold too? But speaking of journeys into the manifold—' She turned hesitantly to Lighthill, who was listening to all this stoically. 'This move would leave you rather bereft of a crew, once again, Wing Commander.'

Lighthill forced a grin, to Malenfant's huge admiration. 'The *Harmonia* is a good ship. Coped alone before, will cope again.'

'Well, you may not have to. Commander, we are a nation of explorers, on Demeter. We wouldn't be here otherwise. And when we heard your talk of the manifold, many of us were – intrigued. It might take some training up, but I suspect that if you were prepared to take on a crew of New Paris personnel, you would not be short of volunteers.' She hesitated. 'For one, me. I . . . would like to learn more of this other Nicola Mott with whom you travelled. I'm sure I could never fill her shoes but – it would be an honour for me to try.'

Lighthill smiled tightly. 'Then the honour would be mine.'

That was when one of Nicola's assistants came running up, flushed, agitated, with a note for her.

'News about Zeus,' Nicola said, staring at the note. 'That damn moon.

'It's gone.'

84

My name is Reid Malenfant.

You know me.

Yeah, that new guy. Thanks for letting me talk to you all.

All of you here in New Paris. Those of you down on Persephone. Those of you coming home from Zeus, or where Zeus used to be, before . . .

Well, I guess that's what I need to talk to you about.

Where Zeus went.

Not that I understand it. But at least I, and Emma Stoney, my partner here, misunderstand it in a different way from you. If only because one of our closest friends disappeared with it. Two, if you count a mouthy medical robot.

Yeah, to you I'm just that new guy. Back where I came from, far across the manifold from here, I was known as the guy who crashed an American space transport system we called the space shuttle. Not that I knew about that, as for centuries I lay as close to death as it's possible to be without actually *being* dead.

It's still a mystery to me who I am *here*, by the way. In this strand of the manifold. I mean, there has to be a version of me, who grew up on the East Coast, and dreamed of flying like his father and grandfather in the wars they fought – the same wars as happened here, as far as I can tell. I would have been twenty-five years old when the Soviet tanks rolled into West Germany in 1985.

And I don't know what the hell I, that 'I', was doing. Maybe I had joined the space programme. Maybe I was in the military – once I myself flew aerial tankers in war zones. Maybe I got myself killed in a tanker over Hamburg or Munich, as part of the Air Bridge that saved Europe.

Or maybe it's none of the above. For sure, any local copy of 'me' or his family hasn't shown himself, even though my and Emma's faces have been plastered all over the news, what with our mysterious arrival here and such . . . Maybe I don't blame them. But if you are out there – respect. Peace and love, as John Lennon would say.

Which leaves me, and Emma, standing here. You couldn't get much further from home, right? And what I want to talk about is what it was that has drawn me so far from home. For, you know, I was only in the left-hand seat of that space shuttle booster stage in the first place, I only went through the crash that all but killed me, because I was always an incorrigible space cadet.

But, as to why I became a space cadet – it all started with a simple question.

Where is everybody?

As a kid I used to lie at night out on the lawn, soaking up dew and looking at the stars, trying to feel the Earth turning under me. It felt wonderful to be alive – hell, to be ten years old, anyhow.

But even then I knew that the Earth was just a ball of rock, on the fringe of a nondescript galaxy.

As I lay there staring at the stars, I just couldn't believe, even then, that there was nobody out *there* looking back at me down *here*. Was it really possible that this was the *only* place where life had taken hold – that only *here* were there minds and eyes capable of looking out and wondering?

But if not, *where were they*? Why wasn't there evidence of extraterrestrial civilisation all around us?

As a kid on that lawn, I didn't see them. I seemed to be surrounded by emptiness and silence.

And that question was what drew me on. In a whole number of different iterations – different *lives* – across the manifold, as I would discover.

And it was what drew Greggson Deirdra to me, and, ultimately, to her own strange destiny.

Well, we found an answer of sorts. The most brutal possible answer to that question – *where are they?* – was always that *they* didn't exist at all. That intelligence, maybe even life itself, was a kind of unlikely accident that happened only once, *right here*.

But that turned out to be the truth, didn't it? Strange and scary as it seems.

But we fixed it. In the future, humans spread out and seeded worlds and filled the universe.

We did that. Us.

Well, Deirdra is still following the story. She has travelled on, further than I can ever go. She called one last time to tell me so.

Which is what I have to talk to you about today.

Because that's why your moon, Zeus, has vanished.

Well, I think so. *We* think so. There are no experts here, not about the manifold. Maybe in a thousand years . . .

Here's the first thing you must understand. Zeus is not a

moon. It never was. It was not even a . . . simple object. It was embedded in the manifold, somehow, so that it existed in multiple realities. All at the same time. If you want to know how an object can exist in more than one place at the same time, ask an expert. Or wait uncountable *billions* of years, and ask the downstreamers who, dissatisfied with the universe they had evolved in, ripped it all up and built the manifold instead.

And accept too that the place you saw Zeus, orbiting this version of Persephone, wasn't its *prime* location. If you want to think of your Zeus as a kind of projection of a master copy elsewhere, you won't be correct, but be my guest.

But we think that 'master copy' exists in another strand of the manifold we explored, and called the Vanilla System. Where Zeus is orbiting Saturn, not Persephone.

A Saturn that had no rings, by the way. We could see it was an anomaly, even from Venus, where we arrived in this manifold strand. We went to study it.

So, you know that Greggson Deirdra contacted . . . something in the heart of Zeus. An ancient entity, watching, waiting. Part of it, at least, calls itself 'Michael'. Possibly one of a whole suite of such entities, living and otherwise, that we ended up calling the 'World Engineers'.

Because that's what they seem to do. Working across the manifold, they tweak the evolution of systems like ours, in order to achieve some desired outcome – or sometimes, we think, just to see what happens. Michael is not a god. But – *Creator*. That comes closest to what he does. He quickens dead worlds, after all.

But also, above all – we think – he watches, and records, and remembers. Because his ultimate purpose is, some day, to take all he learns back to the very far future.

And that is a journey Deirdra is beginning now, even as Zeus, having vanished from this system, leaves the Vanilla System too.

Well, we think that's what's happening. Thanks to partial observations by Geoff Lighthill, who risked his own health to pilot *Harmonia* through the Zeus manifold portal, back to the Vanilla System, to go see . . .

Zeus, as you know, has a belt of Towers. Chimneys, built around its equator. You had it up in the sky to study as long as you've been here; you know this better than I do. An unresolved mystery, right? Well, we now know they are essentially the exhausts of rocket engines.

And in one reality we visited we saw such rocket engines light up. They were on a copy of Persephone, which had been pushed out of its orbit. So we saw fusion engines, working on that planet. We expected the same technology here, I think. But that wasn't what we saw.

Yes, we saw the engines of Zeus light up. Those shafts are rocket nozzles, all right. But the technology is much simpler than fusion.

It's steam, that's all. Zeus is rising out of its Solar System – and apparently taking all its manifold manifestations with it – driven, like some nineteenth-century locomotive, by nothing but steam.

In a way it's a very elegant solution. The core of Zeus is what seems to be an AI – huge, very ancient, very powerful. And we know that intelligence, the physical processing of information, takes a lot of energy and releases a lot of waste heat. The Zeus AI is a product of a super-advanced technology, but still bound by the laws of thermodynamics. Stuck in that moon, we *know* that it glows as hot as the surface of the Sun. Produces so much heat that much of Zeus, the moon itself, is a cavity filled with superheated steam.

And that, ladies and gentlemen, is how the ice moon is pushing its way out of Saturn's orbit. With steam rockets, a belt of them around the moon's equator, firing in sequence so you get a steady thrust in one direction. Steam! Driven by the heat emitted by the AI itself.

An elegant solution.

But it's kind of slow. We think the steam is expelled at about three thousand degrees, and that most of the energy output of the moon is directed into hosing it out. You can estimate velocities and mass usages from those numbers . . .

You can get to the stars that way, in short. It's a slow progress, and it will use up most of the mass of the moon in the process, and you would never be travelling at more than a few tens of kilometres per second. *But*, if you are patient – and Michael is nothing if not that – you can get to the nearest star in a few tens of thousands of years. Hundreds of thousands, tops.

That seems like a hell of a trek to us, right? But we are mayflies. We *know* that Michael works on longer timescales – monstrously long. How do we know? Because he told Deirdra so.

And when they get to their target star, presumably, the AI, exposed, glowing like a star itself – glowing from the destruction of antimatter fed to it by a wormhole link to the Big Bang itself – the AI will settle into the core of another innocent ice moon, and start all over. In an entirely different planetary system, where Earth life will be smeared across more worlds. And even stranger evolutions might follow.

All of which Deirdra is going to witness. She told me so.

How she is going to be – saved – I don't know. Maybe the technologies that will preserve her are as unimaginable to me as the cryosleep pods that preserved me for centuries on the Moon would have been inconceivable to Ham. Who was a Neanderthal I knew. Long story.

Anyhow, in a few billion more years, I guess, they will move on again.

Effective immortality.

But all that's for the future.

What's happening right now – look, picture it in your minds. You have Zeus whizzing around and around that copy of Saturn, leaking out that watery rocket exhaust, superheated steam that quickly cools and congeals to ice. Around and around it goes, those trails of ice getting longer and longer . . .

Picture it.

You're picturing the rings of Saturn, aren't you? Which add up to a few per cent of the mass of an ice moon like Zeus.

When we arrived in the Vanilla System, one of the first things we noticed was that Saturn, there, had no rings. What we should have concluded was that it had no rings *yet*.

So there's a tip for future explorers of the manifold. If you find a Saturn with rings, you're seeing the exhaust trail of a departed starship.

Been and gone.

So anyhow that's my story, and Emma's and Deirdra's, and – yours, I guess. All of *ours*.

You might ask me if I'd like to be travelling with Deirdra. Hell, yes, once I would have envied her. But not now. Not now that I have found this place. Which I already call home. Because I found Emma. And where Emma is, I am home.

I hope that little kid who used to lie at night out on the lawn, looking at the stars, would understand.

So.

Questions?

My name is Greggson Deirdra.

Aged seventeen, I left home. I left Earth. I promised my mother I would come back.

I guess I was seeking a kind of revenge. Revenge for the looming destruction of my world.

What I found, though, is magnificent. Magnificent and terrible.

Humans are alone in this universe.

But, alone, we filled the universe with life and mind. Terrible mistakes were made. But we did that. We did.

So that's why I'm going on. To see what we did. And maybe to challenge some of those mistakes.

Address some of the cruelty.

Please tell my mother I'm sorry.

I'm not coming home.

Afterword

As noted in *Destroyer*, the first volume of this duology, Reid Malenfant and Emma Stoney were recurring characters in my *Manifold* series of novels (1999–2001), in which the title 'World Engines' was first used. On the physics of the manifold, Lee Smolin in *Life of the Cosmos* (Oxford University Press, 1997) set out the hypothesis that universes might propagate through the creation of black holes.

Recent useful references on exoplanets include *One of Ten Billion Earths* by Karel Schrijver (Oxford University Press, 2018), and *Catching Stardust* by Natalie Starkey (Bloomsbury, 2018). The so-called 'five-planet Nice model', which explains the current nature of the Solar System by having the four giant planets of the present system migrating alongside a fifth which was later ejected from the system, was given by D. Nesvorny in 'Young Solar System's Fifth Giant Planet?', *Astrophysical Journal Letters* vol. 742(2), L22, 2011. Recent, and startling, speculation that Venus may have been habitable for most of its existence is given by M. J. Way et al., 'Was Venus the First Habitable World of Our Solar System?', *Geophys. Res. Lett.* vol. 43, pp. 9376 ff., 2016. My own depiction of the events of the formation of the Solar System, while drawing on such studies, is fictional.

Similarly any depiction of conditions on a super Earth is

speculative. For example the likelihood of Earthlike plate tectonics on worlds larger (or smaller) than Earth is not well understood; see the paper by J. Korenaga (*Astrophysical Journal Letters* vol. 725, pp. L43–L46, 2010). However the idea that a super Earth, orbiting at a suitable location around a suitable star, might be *more* hospitable for life than the Earth was put forward by R. Heller et al. ('Superhabitable worlds', *Astrobiology* vol. 14, pp. 50–66, 2014).

A recent and thoughtful speculation on the nature of life and complexity in the universe is Paul Davies's *The Demon in the Machine* (Allen Lane, 2019). Theoretical physicist Sir Fred Hoyle argued strongly for theories of panspermia (see *The Intelligent Universe*, Michael Joseph, 1983). Hoyle's collaborator Professor Chandra Wickramasinghe (see his *Our Cosmic Ancestry in the Stars*, Inner Traditions, 2019) has argued that there may have been a single origin of life in the universe (not necessarily our Earth), so that the whole Galaxy is a single biosphere. This is scientifically controversial, but remains one interpretation of the facts as we have them at the time of writing.

A recent survey of mass extinctions is Peter Brannen's *The Ends of the World* (HarperCollins, 2017). Steve Brusatte's *The Rise and Fall of the Dinosaurs* (William Morrow, 2018) is a fine new survey of the eponymous beasts, and Mark P. Witton's *Pterosaurs* (Princeton, 2013) is similarly useful.

David Reich's *Who We Are and How We Got Here* (Oxford University Press, 2018) is a survey of the recent revolution in our understanding of human evolution thanks to genetics research. Speculation that modern humans may be 'self-domesticated' goes back to Darwin in 1888; modern genetic analysis seems to confirm the hypothesis (see B. Hare et al., 'The Self-Domestication Hypothesis', *Animal Behaviour* vol. 83, pp. 573–85, 2012).

A comprehensive survey of turning points in the birth and development of the USSR is *Was Revolution Inevitable?* by Tony Brenton, Oxford University Press, 2017. A recent survey of Cosmism is *The Russian Cosmists* by George M. Young (Oxford University Press, 2012). Some details of the *Electrod CMIX* reference a spacecraft depicted in *Vne Zemli* (*Outside the Earth*), a novel by Konstantin Tsiolkovsky (first appeared in 1916 but subsequently reworked; for a translation see *The Science Fiction of Konstantin Tsiolkovsky*, University Press of the Pacific, 1979).

Contemporary military studies of the kind on which my depiction of a 1985 'Nearly War' was based were fictionalised more extensively in General Sir John Hackett's *The Third World War* (Sidgwick and Jackson, 1978).

All errors and misapprehensions are of course my sole responsibility.

Stephen Baxter
Northumberland
September 2019